The Cyrus Syndrome

A Novel
By

Arley Owens, Jr.

SHORTY MAE PRODUCTIONS

Movin' On Up
Composed by Ja'net Dubois & Jeff Barry

1999
Composed by Prince

Bible quotations from the
Authorized King James Version

Cover Art: The Author
Editor: Pitman Sanders

First Printing Jan 2013
Printed in the U.S.A.

Soft Cover Edition
ISBN: 978-0-9848195-3-9

SHORTY MAE PRODUCTIONS
P.O. Box 81102
Midland, Texas 79708

Dedicated to that
rarest of breeds, the precious
few honest Defense Attorneys

Special Thanks to Dylan J Morgan
& Sue Smith

Thus saith the Lord to his anointed, to Cyrus, whose right hand I have held, to subdue nations before him; and I will loose the loins of kings, to open before him the two-leaved gates; and the gates shall not be shut; I will go before thee, and make the crooked places straight; I will break in pieces the gates of bronze, and cut in sunder the bars of iron; And I will give thee the treasures of darkness, and hidden riches of secret places, that thou mayest know that I, the Lord, who call thee by thy name, am the God of Israel . . . I have surnamed thee, though thou hast not known me.

-Isaiah 45:1-4

PART ONE

ONE

According to his mother, Darius Darkfire descended directly from Cyrus the Great, ruler of Persia, the most powerful kingdom in the ancient world until it was conquered by Alexander some years after the monarch died in five-twenty-nine BC. She named him after Darius the Great. Though not a blood heir to the throne, his namesake had defeated Gaumata, who tried to usurp it after Cambyses II, the son of the king, died.

Darius's paternal lineage could be traced to the Chiricahua Apaches. His surname was a derivation of an Apache Chief named Dark Fires, whose descendants eventually abridged it. The most famous Chiricahua, Geronimo, died at Fort Sill, Oklahoma, where Darius came into the world six weeks before his father's army hitch ended. After being honorably discharged he moved the family to Dallas where Darius grew up and happened to be at the moment, nervously fidgeting in his seat as the ceremony commenced.

Supposedly this marked the thirty-fifth time such a ritual would take place—a small number, considering the first one happened almost five hundred years before the birth of Christ. Every seventy years after its inaugural a gold signet ring alleged to have belonged to Cyrus himself was given to the eldest child of whoever possessed it at the time. The last ceremony took place the first of June nineteen twenty-nine when Darius's grandmother acquired it. His mother inherited it when she died.

Legend contended that a Jewish prophet had been commanded by God to seek out a certain craftsman who would give him the band of gold. Constructed by the artisan at God's behest, the ring had been delivered to Cyrus the Great with the admonishment that it be passed down from generation to generation with the sacred ceremony of presentation until Shiloh came down from the heavens at the end of the age.

When the ring was being transferred to a female the proceedings had to begin at midnight. Males received it at noon. Ten friends of the beneficiary were required to attend. If the heir didn't have such a number willing to, or lacked enough acquaintances to reach that tally, then only the presenter and recipient could be present.

The ceremony itself was a simple matter: the donor had to recite the receiver's name, a salutation to Cyrus, and pray aloud for Shiloh to descend from heaven and establish the kingdom of God. Then the ring would be presented and all present would take a small sip from a single cruse of wine. The dregs had to be emptied on the container the recipient chose to house the ring, for it was never to be worn except by Shiloh—even Cyrus had been forbidden to wear it. The vessel would then be broken by the new ring bearer after reciting a vow to keep the golden band as a most prized possession until parted from it by death or presentation. Once the presenter was bereft of the ring, the container used to store it had to be destroyed.

Though his mother resolutely believed it to be true and had entrenched the legacy of the ring in his mind since early childhood, he didn't know what to make of its veracity. With his ten friends in attendance, Darius tried not to show the embarrassment he felt as she opened a small ceramic box and raised it in the air, cupping it with both hands.

"Stand before me, son, and we shall begin."

Humoring the woman who bore him, he awkwardly rose to his feet.

"Darius, in the name of Cyrus, the great king of Persia, who graciously permitted God's children to return to their most holy city Jerusalem, I present you this ring given to Cyrus by a prophet of The Most High. Under God's watchful eye it is entrusted to you until either death, the passing of seventy years, or the coming of Shiloh compels you to part with it."

She withdrew the ring and closed her eyes. "I pray to you, Holy God, send Shiloh to this wicked earth so that truth, justice, and mercy shall reign at last."

His chosen container in hand—a glass cube with a scarlet cushion incised to hold the circle of gold—he pulled the hinged lid open and she inserted the legendary signet. Darius closed the box and placed it on a small table draped with a waterproof tarp as his mother took the first sip of wine from a vessel of clay she'd had inscribed with the same insignia as the ring. She raised the goblet to his lips and he took a nip. After doing likewise for each of his friends, she held it out for him to take.

Accepting the cup, he looked at the ancient Persian hieroglyph etched on its side and cleared his throat. "I vow to keep the ring of Cyrus until death, or the passing of seventy years, or the coming of Shiloh compels me to part with it."

He poured the remaining grape liquor over the crystalline enclosure protecting the loop of precious metal his mother held in such high esteem, dropped the chalice to the tarp-covered floor, and shattered it with a stomp of his foot. His mother then threw her container into the fireplace where it splintered on impact, completing the ceremony.

She turned and embraced him.

Rusty Wurly, one of his ten friends, chuckled. "Do we applaud now or what, Amia?"

Warily, Darius examined the expression on his mother's face. Her scrutinizing dark eyes looked threatening for a moment, but then softened with a smile.

"Why not . . .?" she started clapping.

Darius joined her and everyone did likewise, rising to their feet in the process. When he lowered his hands so did they. He glanced at his friends. Rusty Wurly—tall and gangly with a buzz haircut atop a well-tanned face that always seemed to be smiling—stood beside the black Derby twins. Jock and John were slightly taller than Rusty, very muscular, wore their long coarse hair in dreadlocks, and were impossible to tell apart.

The Rothschild cousins hovered beside Sash Temple, a pretty brunette. Bernice Rothschild was quite a looker but Bernadette had a nose that made Barbra Streisand's look petite. Short and stocky Eval Santa Anna and his brother Caruso shadowed the three girls. They claimed to be related to the Mexican dictator that conquered the Alamo. Darius's ex-girlfriend Avery Buntzinghammer—an extremely well favored blue-eyed blonde—looked cozy next to Marcus Laxx, the SMU quarterback who'd stolen her away from him a year ago.

He'd considered the jock his archenemy until they ran into each other at a frat party one night and got into a fistfight. After he kicked the quarterback's ass, Marcus promised to leave Avery alone. Avery tried to throw herself into Darius's arms after he won the duel but he'd pushed her away, helped Marcus to his feet, and told him, "You want her? You got her."

After that night she'd repeatedly begged him to give their relationship a second chance, but he'd refused. His feelings for her had somehow cooled from fiery passion to brotherly affection. She'd finally given up when he told her as much, and had gone back to Marcus.

His ex squinted at him quizzically. "Would you mind telling me who Cyrus was? I've never heard of him before today."

"Ask Mom, she's the resident expert." Darius grinned at the pleased expression on his mother's face upon hearing the words. She loved talking about her pedigree and proceeded without hesitation.

"Cyrus was the king of ancient Persia, Avery. He defeated the Median and Babylonian empires, and turned Persia into a world power which stood for two hundred years until Greece took over through the skill and cunning of a Macedonian general whose name I'm sure you've heard of."

"What was his name?"

"Alexander the Great."

"Oh sure, I've heard of Alexander the Great." A skeptical smile appeared as Avery spoke. "You don't really believe that ring goes all the way back to Cyrus do you, Dare? I mean, if it really does, it must be worth a fortune."

He'd picked up the nickname in grade school, and though it didn't bother him, his mother hated it because his name was pronounced DUH-RYE-US rather than DARE-EE-US. Giving his mom a wink, he turned back to Avery. "I can't say it does and I can't say it doesn't, because I just don't know."

A sigh of irritation billowed from his mother. "It does. The ring has been passed down through the generations, and will continue to be passed down until Shiloh comes."

Avery squinted again. "Who's Shiloh?"

"Shiloh is the messiah," Darius answered with embarrassment.

Jaw sagging, Avery giggled out, "Shiloh is Jesus?"

"Shiloh is Jesus," said his mother. "When Jacob blessed his sons, he said 'The scepter shall not depart from Judah till Shiloh comes, whose right it is.' Jesus Christ is descended from the tribe of Judah."

One of the Derby's started twisting the end of a long dreadlock around his right hand and grinned. "I thought you guys believed in Allah."

Face ablaze with indignance his mother zeroed in on the twin. "Muslim's call the God of Abraham, Isaac, and Jacob, *Allah*. We are not Muslim, and refer to him as God. We believe Jesus is the son of God and they do not."

"Well, to the Muslims wouldn't Shiloh be Mohammad?"

"No, he would not," snapped his mother. "Mohammad was a man not the messiah."

"Well wasn't Jesus a man too?"

Rusty donned a nervous smile. "Come on, man, lighten up.

Remember the two things you don't argue about—politics and religion? Which one are you anyway?"

"Jock . . ." he raised his brows in acknowledgment of the reprimand and quit toying with his hair. "Sorry, Amia, no disrespect intended. I'm an atheist myself."

"Me too," said John, a huge grin conveying he was only cutting up like his brother.

Eval Santa Anna snickered and pointed at the twins. "Man, you're liable to go to hell for saying that, pachucos."

Jock smirked at him. "I agree with The Doors. Hell appears so much more fascinating than heaven."

"Ha! You're definitely gonna go to hell for that one, vato. You better say some Hail Mary's pronto."

Everybody laughed except his mother. Darius knew it was time for him to gather his friends and leave before his mother turned into an angry defender of her faith. "Okay, guys, chow time. Let's go get some barbecue."

* * * *

They reconvened at a restaurant called The Barbecue Barn. The Rothschild cousins were vegetarians and tried to persuade everybody to accompany them to a place that specialized in soy burgers, but everyone else wanted real meat so Bernice and Bernadette opted not to tag along. They were sitting at a long table, enjoying the house special along with several pitchers of beer. Marcus proposed a toast to him, and everyone raised a mug in salute which embarrassed Darius.

He sat his beer on the table and cleared his throat. "Thank you all for coming to the ceremony. It's probably just a bunch of bullshit, but it's real important to Mom since she totally believes it's not just a legend."

Avery ran a French-manicured finger around the frosty rim of her root beer, having to forgo the real thing in public since she, like Sash, hadn't turned twenty-one yet. "What does your dad think about it?"

Darius eyed the long fingernail, wondering how she could function with such protuberances. "That it's a bunch of bullshit."

Everyone laughed.

"Of course he takes his own pedigree very seriously."

"Which is . . .?" she stopped tracing her drink and took a sip.

"There was an Apache Chief named Dark Fires and that's where the name Darkfire originated."

One of the Derby's flipped a stray dreadlock from his face. "No foolin'?"

"No foolin'. Who am I talking to, Jock or John?"

"Jock. Can't dig it. How'd you pop out of yo mama's twat with fair skin, brown hair, and blue eyes if you're a half mix of Camel Jockey and Native American, Homes?"

"Some mix huh," said Darius with a chuckle. "A quarter Apache and half Persian, or I guess it would be more politically correct to say Iranian or Arabian since Persia no longer exists."

The twin's remark embarrassed Sash Temple, who'd silently rebuffed him with a harsh glare, but Avery had chuckled and was now eyeing him with a half grin. "Why do you say quarter Apache?"

"My grandfather was full blood Apache but my grandmother was Irish, so that makes my dad half, and me only a quarter Apache."

"So you took after your mick grandma," snickered Jock.

This time Avery also shot the brother a dirty look—apparently finding the quip as insulting as Sash—before turning her attention back to him. "What about your mom, is she half and half too?"

"Oh no," he laughed out, picturing the offended scowl on his mother's face if she'd heard the question. "She's totally Arabian, or Persian as she prefers to call herself."

"I have no idea what I am."

Marcus grinned at her. "You're probably just a mongrel like me. I'm a mix of Swedish, Dutch, and German or so I am told."

Jock patted his brother on the back. "Well there can be no doubt about me and John."

"Oh you might have a whitey back in the woodpile somewhere for all you know," said Rusty over the rim of his mug before taking a swig.

"No way, but that's every white man's fear, isn't it—that somewhere in his ancestry there's a nigger in the woodpile."

Rusty cackled but Sash leered at Jock. "I can't believe you said that word!"

Jock gave her a puzzled look. "What, you mean nigger?"

"Yes."

"Why?"

"Because it's so demeaning."

"Hell, girl, only to someone who's ashamed of their heritage. John and me, we be real proud to be niggers. Huh, bro . . ." he held up a closed fist for his brother to tap with his own.

John complied and grinned at Sash. "Yeah, since we escaped from the plantation, we be real proud."

Laughing so hard he had a coughing fit, Rusty hawked into a napkin and used another one to blow his nose. "You niggers kill me."

"Now wait a minute!" shouted Jock, face ablaze with mock indignance. "Don't none of yo white boys be calling us niggers, especially a skinny-butt honky like you, or we'll whup up on your bony white ass."

Rusty rolled but Sash just shook her head. "Whatever."

Eval picked up an ear of corn. "Speaking of heritage, I'd like to say something."

Heaving an exaggerated sigh, Jock rolled his eyes. "Now what the hell you got to say, chili choker?"

Darius tried not to laugh but couldn't hold it in. Neither

could anyone else.

When the laughter died down, Eval continued. "I heard that some people believe Mexicans are a pure Native American tribe like the Cherokees and Apaches instead of a Spanish and Indian mix."

Rusty nodded. "I've heard that too."

"Wonder if it's true."

A devilish grin crossed Jock's face. "True or not, you still just a chili choker to me, my brotha. I don't give a flying fuck who or what yo brown ass evolved from. Probably some jalapeño-snortin' warthog and a taco-chewin' goat got together one night and spawned yo kind. Wouldn't surprise me none."

Rusty slapped the table, roaring with hysterical laughter. "Stop it, dammit . . . I can't breathe! I can't breathe!"

Scowling at Rusty, Jock whacked the table in return. "Look at you, fool. *I can't breathe! I can't breathe!* Why a white boy gotta breathe? Hell you gonna die anyway?"

That got to Darius and he couldn't stop guffawing. "Come on, Homes, settle down, you're killing us all."

Even Sash wound up gasping for breath she was giggling so hard. Eval gave Jock the finger and munched away at his corn, involuntarily snickering between bites.

Jock eventually did settle down, everyone managed to finish their barbecue, and the group parted . . . .

He spent the rest of the afternoon in his parent's swimming pool, then got ready for a night on the town with Rusty, Eval, and the Derby twins. The five of them had decided to take courses that summer so they could graduate from Southern Methodist University in December instead of having to wait until May like Avery, Sash, and the Rothschild cousins. Marcus, who came close to winning the Heisman Trophy last season, had one more year of college football glory left before going to the NFL.

It surprised him Marcus had decided not to make himself eligible for the draft as a junior since he'd have been drafted high and could have snared a multi-million dollar contract. The quarterback maintained that his football career would likely be a short one, and even if not, he couldn't play forever. He planned to get his bachelor's degree before entering professional football, then go to law school after he took off his helmet and pads for the last time.

Darius played football in high school and as an All State running back, had professional football aspirations of his own. But a vicious head-to-head collision with a linebacker had knocked him out cold, sending his mother into such a panic she'd keeled over in the stands with a mild heart attack. He'd suffered a minor concussion but it had a major affect on her, and she'd made him promise not to play college ball. She was so high strung, he knew she might not survive the stress if he got injured. So instead of taking law courses after a career in football as Marcus planned to do, he'd be enrolled in the school of law at SMU a few weeks after receiving his bachelor's degree.

Rusty picked him up at eight and by nine the party was in full swing at their favorite hangout. He, Rusty, and Eval were sitting at a table near the dance floor, watching the Derby twins dancing with two white girls to the tune of Prince's *1999,* being played by a popular local cover band. Darius grabbed a tortilla chip from a large platter, dipped it in salsa and popped the whole thing in his mouth. While washing it down with cold beer he thought about this being nineteen ninety-nine and the exhilarating fact that when two thousand rolled around in six months he'd be entering law school.

TWO

The intercom interrupted his perusal of a deposition.

"Darius, there's a man named Jock Derby asking to see you."

A smile jumped on his face when his secretary said the name. Though they'd spoken a few times by phone he'd only seen the old class clown once since the Derby twins moved to Houston after graduation. "Send him in."

When the muscular black man walked into his office, Darius rounded his desk to give him a hug.

"Great to see you, Jock—man it's been years."

"Seven of them to be exact. You were in your last year of law school at the time." Jock wore his customary large grin and looked like the prominent businessman he'd become. Gone were the dreadlocks, and the close-cropped hair wasn't the only change, he also sported a neatly trimmed moustache.

"So how's life in Houston been?"

The grin vanished. "Life in Houston has been great . . . until now."

His old friend's last two words and the way the big guy's face dropped when he voiced them alarmed him. It took a great deal to dampen the spirit of a Derby twin. "What's wrong?"

"John's been arrested . . ." he looked to the ceiling and clinched his eyes closed as tears began oozing from them. "For murder."

Darius went numb all over. He'd last seen the Derby's while in his third and final year of law school. After graduating from Southern Methodist three years prior the brothers had worked as roughnecks on a drilling rig for six months, saving every penny while living with their parents. They sank their savings into an upstart oil company in Houston and sold their shares after the stock split six times. From there they continued their joint venture as entrepreneurs and had gone on to become immensely successful by making several high-risk investments that had yielded handsome rewards. His stomach soured at the thought of John's happy, almost fairy tale life coming to ruin.

His secretary appeared outside the door which Jock hadn't bothered closing. "Is everything all right?"

Sucking in a deep breath, Darius turned to her. "Excuse us, please."

She immediately stepped back and closed the door behind her. Ricca Stonewall had been his secretary since he'd started practicing law. The pretty dark-eyed blonde was a sharp woman and knew how to read his looks. The one he'd just given her conveyed *This matter is private so don't eavesdrop.*

Still recovering from the shock of hearing his homey had been accused of murder, he pointed to an armchair and returned to his desk. "Sit down and tell me about it. Would you like some coffee?"

Jock shook his head and wiped his nose with a handkerchief. After stuffing the soiled cloth into the breast pocket of a suit he must have paid at least a grand for, he sat down and leaned forward, elbows resting on his knees. "Three days ago John went to San Antonio on a business trip. He flew there in the morning and flew back to Houston that night. When he got home he found his girlfriend stabbed to death on the living room floor. He called me right off—it was all he knew to do—man he was hysterical. I told him to call the police but he was bawling so hard he asked me if I'd do it, so I called them. I got to his house just after the police did. John told them all he knew, and they acted like they believed him, but this morning they . . . they charged him for the murder."

He lowered his head and broke down again.

"Jock . . . I'm so sorry, man."

"I know, Dare," he moaned into his palms. A moment later

he sat up and roughly wiped tears from his face with both hands. "This is like a fucking nightmare. Man, they wouldn't even let me bail him out."

"He was remanded to custody?"

"Yeah."

Darius eyed the twin with sympathy, wondering why he'd want to retain him for his brother's counsel which could be the only reason he'd come all the way to Dallas to see him. He should have already hired a Houston attorney with a lot more experience. It couldn't be because he hoped to save money since the Derby brothers had become millionaires.

"I take it you want me to represent him. I'm confused as to why. You'd be much better off with a lawyer who specializes in homicides, Jock. I've only handled one in my short career."

Jock looked offended, as if he'd just been lied to. "But you won it, and that's why I'm here. Money's no object, man—we'll pay the going rate—I didn't come here hoping for a discount. That case may have been your only homicide, but it was a blockbuster."

It *had* been a sensational case, a real boost to his career, but so dissimilar to the one before him he couldn't imagine that experience being of any help. In that situation a farmer had been accused of vehicular homicide, but all that really happened was the man happened to spill hot coffee on his lap when a lidless take-out cup slipped from his hand while going thirty miles an hour in a Fort Worth suburb. He slammed his foot on the brake but it slid off and hit the accelerator. That happened simultaneously with him leaning down towards the passenger floorboard, attempting to grab the large container before it emptied the rest of its contents on a bag of groceries. A little boy ran out on the road to retrieve his football. By then inadvertently going fifty miles an hour, the farmer looked up, saw the kid, cut the wheel to the right to miss him, and succeeded. Unfortunately he veered onto the sidewalk and hit a female jogger who died before the ambulance arrived.

It wouldn't have been so newsworthy except the casualty happened to be the judge who'd ruled in favor of the driver's ex wife when he'd fought to get custody of his kids a few weeks before the tragic incident. The prosecution set out to prove a case of revenge purposely disguised as an accident, the press had eaten it up, and the case made local headlines.

His client was one of those men that smacked of honesty, and Darius never doubted his innocence. The child—an articulate six year old—had testified that after he picked up his ball, he saw the pickup coming and thought no one was driving until he saw the man rise up sideways. "He got a scared look when he saw me," the little boy had said. "And he started turning the steering wheel real, real fast so he could miss me. I didn't know what to do so I just stood there. When it was over and he got out of his pickup, his pants were real wet like he peed in them."

The paramedics and police officers on the scene also testified that his client had wet pants, which corroborated the coffee spill. The State painted a picture of a seized opportunity for vengeance, but in his closing argument Darius pointed out that unless the boy had conspired with his client and committed perjury, the child's testimony proved it had to be an accident since the defendant couldn't have arranged the circumstances. Jury deliberation lasted less than an hour, and twelve honorable citizens of Tarrant County had returned to the courtroom with a verdict of not guilty.

Folding his hands together on a desk he'd bought from a consignment store, Darius leaned forward. "You know I believe John's innocent, but my advice is for you to find another lawyer. The one homicide I handled was open and shut. It was clearly an accident and I lucked into it, to tell you the truth. It's given me somewhat of a reputation which enabled me to raise my rates but it was the kid's testimony that won the day, nothing I did through my legal skills. You need a real expert—a Johnnie Cochran type—not a lucky lawyer."

Two pain-filled eyes blazing with rebuke zeroed in on him. "Have you ever lost a case, Homes?"

Hearing the moniker made him smile. He hadn't been called *Homes* since he'd last seen Jock and John. "No, but you have to remember I've only been practicing law for six years, and like I said before, I've only handled that one homicide."

Jock straightened in the chair, sniffed a big gulp of air, and slapped his knees. "You and Rusty have been our homeys since high school, and I've never seen you lose at anything. My brother's butt is on the line. Now, we still homeys or not?"

"Of course we are but—"

"But nothing . . .!" Jock rose and leaned across the desk, balancing himself on brawny knuckles, his piercing gaze both accusing and pleading. "You know he's innocent, that gives you the edge right off. Any other lawyer is liable to think he's defending some ol' guilty rich nigger that somehow managed to hustle his way out of the ghetto, so all he'll really be worried about is collecting a fat fee instead of giving his all to defend my brother. Can't you see that?"

He hadn't thought of that and told him so.

"So we on, or what?"

Darius shrugged his shoulders. "I guess if you're going to shame me into it, I really don't have much of a choice do I?"

Without breaking eye contact, Jock did a four-beat drum roll and stood erect. "Then you'll do it?"

"Yeah, I'll do it . . . even though I think you'd be better off seeking other counsel—someone with an impressive track record, a full staff, and an investigative team. You've already seen my whole staff, my secretary Ricca."

Jock adjusted his tie and smoothed his lapels. "We'll hire you all the help you need. You want to get some slicked-up lawyer to assist you, that's fine. But you da main man. You da one what gots to run da show, Dare. We cool?"

"We cool under one condition."

A wide grin spread across the brother's face. "Name it."

"I'm not going to make you pay for some *slicked-up lawyer* to help me, but I am liable to need an investigator and that won't be cheap. I can't afford to do this pro bono or I would—you know that—but I can't charge my homeys the full rate. So I'm radically reducing my fee to fifty dollars an hour plus living expenses because I'll have to stay in Houston throughout the trial, and I doubt accommodations are cheap there."

"Good accommodations won't be. But hell you can stay with me if you want. What is your fee anyway?"

"Two hundred an hour."

"An hour . . .?" he raised his brows, obviously finding the amount excessive.

"Yes."

"We can afford you at full rate, don't worry about it."

Whether or not he was telling the truth, Darius could tell by his expression Jock thought the price too high, even though he seemed hell-bent on paying it. "Fifty or nothing."

"Tell you what, Homes, we'll pay you one-seventy-five."

"No way, Homes."

"Okay, one hundred plus expenses, but not one cent less."

Darius thought that over. It was half rate, twice the hourly fee he'd charged before getting lucky with the farmer. Maybe his conscience would let him live with that. "Okay. I'll do it for half rate."

Ricca's voice rang out on the intercom. *"Darius, the clerk just called. The jury has reached a verdict on the Lunson suit. You're due in court."*

He pressed the response button. "See if you can find a decent hotel in Houston that isn't too pricey. When is the Branch hearing?"

"Ten o'clock next Monday."

"There's nobody else up to bat after that is there?"

"No."

"Call Robert and tell him I've agreed to represent a close friend in a homicide case in Houston, and ask if he minds handling Branch for me." Robert Edison was a colleague with an office in the same building as his, and they sometimes helped each other out as well as refer clients to one another when either had a full caseload.

"Do I need to make a flight reservation?" said Ricca.

"No, I don't want to have to rent a car once I'm there, so I'll just drive down. If Robert's willing to handle Branch for me then find a hotel and tell them I'll be arriving some time tonight and will need the room for an indeterminate period of time. If Robert's tied up then hold off on the reservation."

"Am I going with you?"

"No, we're trying to hold the expenses down on this one."

"Okay, I'm on it."

"What's the Lunson hearing?" asked Jock.

He grinned. "Lunson is a client who's being sued over a dog bite."

An almost worry-free expression came over Jock as he let out a short laugh. "A dog bite?"

"Yeah. Chew on this a minute. His girlfriend's ex-boyfriend was stalking her, followed her to Lunson's house, and was trying to peep through a window so he could see what she was up to. He didn't realize Lunson had a mean-ass bulldog. He spotted the dog and took off running, and before Lunson could call off fido he'd chewed his leg up pretty good. Now the dude wants Lunson to cough up ten thousand dollars for the incident, claiming there was no *Beware of Dog* sign, and if there had been he wouldn't have trespassed."

"Oh I've heard it all now. That dude has some set, huh."

"Yeah, but I hope they're about to be cut off. This won't take long, but I have another court date Monday. That's what I just asked Ricca to check on. If my buddy Robert's willing to take the Branch case for me, I'll head home and pack for

Houston right after I finish up the Lunson case this afternoon."

The intercom buzzed and Ricca said, *"Robert said he'll do it but you have to buy him dinner when you get back from Houston."*

"Okay, tell him I'll treat him to a Big Mac when I get back." Darius chuckled when he said it, but a moment later all levity evaporated as his thoughts centered on the grave responsibility he'd just taken on.

THREE

Darius sat in a Houston café situated across the street from the hotel Ricca had reserved for him. The place had a warm mom-and-pop atmosphere and the pretty waitress pouring coffee made him wish he had time to socialize. Her name tag read Holly. He'd just complimented the establishment and asked if she'd worked there long.

"Yeah, it's got a real nostalgic air doesn't it. Hasn't changed much since my mom brought me here when I was in kindergarten. I started working here part time when I was in high school. Now I work full time during the day to put myself through college at night. So what do you do for a living?"

"I'm a lawyer."

Her lightly freckled cheeks, framed by short brown hair with blonde highlights, swelled with a smile as a gleam of excitement twinkled in her pale-blue eyes. "Attorney at law, huh?"

"Yeah."

"Small world."

Blowing steam away, he took a small sip. "Why's that?"

"That's what I plan to be."

He winked at her and lowered the old fashioned mug. "Just what the world needs, another one of us loathsome shysters."

She giggled. "Know what you call five thousand lawyers on the bottom of the ocean?"

"Yeah," he said with a grin. "A good start."

"Oh you've heard that one."

"I think I've probably heard them all."

"I heard it on the movie *The War of the Roses*."

"Is that right . . ." he added a touch more cream and stirred the tasty brew. "I heard it from a comedienne on TV years before that movie came out, but as I recall his number was three thousand rather than five."

"Touché, score one for you. So what kind of law do you practice?"

"Mostly criminal, some civil but not divorces."

"I take it you're a defense attorney then."

A few tables away a man held up his cup, signaling for a refill. She took care of him and returned. "I want to be a prosecutor. So what do they call you, if you don't mind me being so nosy?"

"Darius."

"Darius what?"

"Darkfire."

"Unique and quite lyrical—a three-two beat, syllables I mean. I like it. Mine's a two-two but both start with the same letter as well. I'm Holly Hepburn. And before you ask, yes I am aware that Audrey Hepburn played Holly-go-lightly in *Breakfast at Tiffany's.*"

Her hasty enumeration about her name both amused and confused him. "Since I've never seen that one, I doubt I would have asked, but thanks for the insight."

She looked dumbfounded. "You've never seen *Breakfast at Tiffany's?* Surely you know who Audrey Hepburn is!"

"Yeah. I've seen My Fair Lady."

A couple walked in and took a table which she had to tend to. After she left he opened his briefcase and pulled out his notes. He'd arrived yesterday and had called Jock first thing after getting settled in his room. The twin picked him up and they'd gone to the county jail to see John. The incarcerated Derby had also grown a moustache and shortened his hair, so the two still looked identical. John's deceased girlfriend was a twenty-five year old black woman named Joanna Wacker who sold real estate for a living. They met at a nightclub called Baker's Dozen and had been dating for the last six months. She'd moved in with him a few weeks before someone stabbed her five times with a knife that had been found beside a dumpster the day after the murder.

John had no idea who did it. Darius reasoned it had to be someone she'd felt safe letting in the house since there were no signs of a break in. Unfortunately the knife belonged to John. It had been taken from a drawer in his kitchen where he kept it with four others of a set, each designed for a specific purpose. It happened to be one he used a lot because he liked to cook and frequently chopped fresh vegetables with it.

When the detectives asked if anything was missing from the house, John—unaware the knife wasn't there—had told them it didn't look like it. A lady taking out her trash spotted the bloody utensil and called the police. Finding his prints on it and discovering the empty slot in his cutlery set, the detectives assumed he'd lied, thinking the weapon would never surface. The blood type on the blade matched Joanna Wacker's.

After seeing John he'd gone to the district attorney's office and met his adversary, Nathan Longstreet, an aloof middle-aged intellectual with an imposing disposition. The witnesses the assistant DA intended to call were the investigating detectives Hallmark and Sage, the coroner, a fingerprint expert, the man John had the business meeting with in San Antonio, and Mary Davis, who found the murder weapon.

Darius had yet to compile his witness list but that didn't matter at the moment. The preliminary hearing, scheduled for nine-thirty tomorrow morning where a judge would determine if sufficient evidence existed to bring the case to trial, would be academic and he knew it.

* * * *

As he figured, the judge bound the case over for trial to commence in three weeks. After going to the coroner's office and gathering what information could be found there, he visited Mary Davis—a very friendly community-minded individual. She showed him the spot where she'd found the knife, he thanked her for her time, and went to see a private investigator named Dirk Amos.

Darius had hoped to do his own investigating so as not to run the bill up anymore than necessary. He'd planned to meet with the victim's family and friends to get some insight into her lifestyle before she met John, hoping that would steer him in the direction he needed to go. But the woman was a complete mystery. She apparently had no family or friends because no one had claimed the body. Not one of the many real estate agencies in the area knew a Joanna Wacker, and the address on her business card turned out to be an apartment complex.

She'd been sitting alone at a table the night John had introduced himself, and though they became intimate soon afterwards, he'd never met any of her relatives or acquaintances during their six month relationship. Other than mentioning she'd lived in Houston all her life, the mysterious woman had refused to talk about her past.

Located in a strip mall, snuggled between a dry cleaners and a pizza parlor, the office of Dirk Amos Investigations, fronted by a glass wall, appeared to be only one long narrow room which obviously hadn't been cleaned in weeks. Worn blue carpeting had several pathways of dirt embedded in the weave, and a desk in front—frosted with a thick layer of ash-colored dust—apparently hadn't been occupied for quite some time. A slender young Mexican rose from a more pristine one in back and ambled towards him.

An eye-catching ad in the yellow pages promised quick results at a low price which had prompted him to choose the agency over the many listed. He hoped the scruffy surroundings weren't a reflection of Dirk Amos's detective skills.

"Can I help you?"

"Are you Dirk Amos?"

"No, I'm Juan Enez, his associate."

Darius identified himself as he shook his hand.

"What can I do for you, Mister Darkfire?"

"I'm an attorney and I need a good investigator."

His dark eyes lit up. "Hey, you came to the right place. My associate is tied up at the moment but I'm available."

The slim man looked younger than him which meant he couldn't have that many years of experience, and he seemed too eager to land his business. "When will Mister Amos be free?"

"He's out of town, won't be back for a good while, but like I said, I'm available. What is it, a messy divorce case? Man, that's our specialty. We'll find out who the cheater's been seeing on the sly, believe me. We'll get you pictures, motel receipts, taped phone conversations, all the evidence you need."

Darius heaved a sigh to emphasize his impatience. "This is a homicide."

"Oh . . ." the thin man's enthusiasm evaporated.

"Don't get too many of those I take it."

"Try nada."

"I see. Can you recommend someone?"

Enez crossed his skinny arms over a bony chest. "For the sake of curiosity, what exactly do you need investigated?"

"My client has been accused of killing his girlfriend, and I can't find out anything about her. The police haven't been able to find any family, and no one has claimed the body."

"What's her name for the sake of curiosity?"

"Joanna Wacker."

"White woman?"

"Black."

"Hmm. Got a picture?"

Darius sat his briefcase down on the edge of the dusty desk, opened it and produced a glossy color eight by ten.

Enez studied the photograph. "Good looking. Did she have a driver's license?"

Once again he dug into his briefcase and pulled out a copy of Joanna Wacker's driving permit the police department had provided him.

"Hmm . . . Houston address."

"It's the same as her work address."

"What did she do?" Enez continued eying the photocopy as he spoke.

"She said she was a real estate agent, but I called all the agencies listed and none of them have ever heard of her." He reached for the license and returned it and the picture to his briefcase. "Can you recommend someone?"

The bantamweight Latino pursed his lips with a thoughtful frown. "All you need is information on her—nothing more dangerous than that, right?"

"Right."

"I'll do it."

He was reluctant to use him but decided to check his rates. "What do you charge?"

"Two fifty a day plus expenses."

Issuing a disdainful laugh, he glanced around the shoddy office. That price was outrageous. "If you could just recommend someone. No offense, but I can tell by looking you guys must not get much business with rates that high."

A smile of embarrassment spread across Enez's brown face. "Yeah, this place is a dump all right."

"So can you recommend someone or not?"

"One hundred dollars a day plus expenses. I can do just as good a job on this type of investigating as anyone else, trust me."

Wearing a half grin, he studied the Mexican. Juan Enez was pretty tenacious. Maybe he *could* do as good a job as anyone else. "Tell you what, let's make it an even five hundred dollars if you get me the information I need, and nada if you don't."

"Hmm . . ." he rubbed his chin, visibly mulling over the offer. "How soon you need the information?"

"As soon as possible. The trial's in three weeks."

Enez stuck out his hand. "Gotta deal, but it's got to be under the table. Gentleman's agreement, no paper trail."

After the binding handshake Darius dug out a card and gave it to him. "I'm from Dallas so ignore my office number, just call me on my cell or the number I scribbled on the bottom, that's my hotel phone."

"I'll need the picture, and let me copy down her license info."

He handed over the requested items. "I'd appreciate it if you could get on this pronto."

Sliding a drawer open, the young P.I. placed Joanna Wacker's picture inside and closed it. Then he grabbed a note pad coated with silver micro particles, waved it in the air several times to clear off the debris, and plopped it back on the desk, causing a small dust cloud to form. Pulling a pen from his shirt pocket, he jotted down the information and handed the photocopied driver's license back.

"I'm on it as of right now. Tell me everything your client knows about her—especially where they met and the place she was last seen alive . . . ."

* * * *

"What'll you have?" Holly Hepburn asked.

"Hamburger and coffee please."

She took his order to the cook and returned with the coffee. "So how's it going?"

Darius admired her for a moment and smiled. "Hectic, I have to say. How about yourself?"

"Hectic covers it. Lived in Houston long?"

"No, I'm from Dallas. I'm here on a case. In fact I'm staying in the hotel across the street."

"Oh . . ." she appeared disappointed to hear he wasn't a resident. "What sort of case, or am I allowed to ask?"

"My friend is being accused of murder."

Her eyes flew wide. "Wow, a homicide."

Watching Holly almost licking her chops, and recalling she wanted to be a prosecutor, he could tell she relished the idea of one day bringing a murderer to justice.

"And whether your friend did it or not, you've taken an oath to defend him. That's why I want to be a prosecutor. I'd never want to defend a guilty person. My conscience wouldn't let me sleep at night."

He laughed, savoring the cute sour-face she'd made while giving her explanation. "Well my friend's innocent, so if I get him off—which I hope to do—my conscience will be clear."

"But what if he told you he did it? Wouldn't that just be so horrible?"

Now taking note of her lovely pouting lips, he shook his head. "If he told me he did it, I wouldn't represent him."

"A defense lawyer with character," she sighed through a thoughtful smile. "So are you doing it pro bono since he's your friend?"

"Nope."

"So much for character, huh . . .?" she strolled away to take care of a customer needing his cup replenished. The cafe got busy and she didn't make it back to his table until delivering his hamburger.

"So how's the trial going?"

"Hasn't started yet."

"When does it start?"

"In three weeks." His cell phone rang and he brought it to his ear. "If you'll excuse me."

"Oh . . . ."

Darius hoped he hadn't offended her, but the look on her face and rapidity of her exit indicated he had.

"Hello?"

"Mister Darkfire, this is Juan Enez." The private eye sounded much different on the phone than he had in person.

It had only been three hours since he'd left Dirk Amos's office, so it surprised him to get a report this quickly. "Got something for me?"

"I'm afraid I'm gonna have to back out of our deal. Got another case."

"That's not very professional of you." The phone went dead before Enez heard the whole sentence. The bastard had hung up on him. Reaching for his burger, he made a mental note to have several duplicates of the photograph made after he got it back from the irresponsible punk in case he got burned by the next investigator as well. He planned to retrieve it in the morning since he'd have to spend the rest of the afternoon searching for another private eye.

Thinking about it as he ate, he grew angrier and decided not to wait until tomorrow to get it back. Maybe he'd find Enez in the office since it was only two o'clock. He checked his cell, comparing the number of the call he'd just received with the one he'd scribbled down for Dirk Amos Investigations. They were the same which meant the sham of a detective had called from there. A busy signal insulted his ears after punching the numbers and he snapped his cell closed with resentment.

Though an officer of the court Darius never hesitated resorting to fisticuffs to settle matters when occasion dictated or justice demanded it, but he made a promise to himself not to touch the skinny Mexican for fear of breaking his scrawny neck with one punch. It wouldn't do for John Derby's defense attorney to get arrested for the same charge as his client.

Holly never came back to his table so he left her tip with the cashier. "Please see that Holly Hepburn gets this."

* * * *

Darius found the door locked when he got to Dirk Amos

Investigations. It didn't much surprise him since the bottom-feeder obviously lacked any real concept of professionalism and probably closed for the day whenever the mood suited him. Then again the scruff might have been pounding the pavement on behalf of the new client he'd blown him off for. Gazing through the glass wall, at first he attributed the brilliant illumination within the narrow confines as a result of sunlight streaming into it from a cloudless sky before noticing the lights had been left on.

A cold knot of tension coiled in his gut as he peered through the glare, past the front desk, towards the back where the hack investigator had been sitting that morning. Horrifying shock snapped his face from the transparent veneer—forcing him to step backwards, the instinctive reaction almost causing him to lose his balance. A section of the worn blue carpet had been stained crimson with blood. Juan Enez lay sprawled on the floor—his eyes, frozen in fear, staring lifelessly at the ceiling.

FOUR

He'd waited for the police after calling nine-one-one and Darius had just explained to two detectives—Dunhill and Morris—why he was there. A couple of paramedics carried the body of Juan Enez out the door that had been forced open by the officers who'd first arrived.

"So you came back just to get the photograph?" said Dunhill.

"That's right."

"How did Enez sound when he called? Did you get the impression he was under duress, anything like that?"

"No, but he sounded markedly different over the phone than he did when I talked to him here earlier today. And in light of what happened I'm not sure it was really Juan Enez that made that call."

Dunhill looked at his notebook. "Okay, let me make sure I've got this right. You're Darius Darkfire of Dallas, the attorney of record for one John Derby who's in custody being charged with capital murder. The victim was a black woman named Joanna Wacker. You came here earlier today to hire Enez to investigate Wacker's background, and you never saw him or talked to him before today. Enez called you shortly before two p.m. some three hours later, and said he was backing out because he'd gotten another case. You know the call was made from here because the ID on your cell phone is the same number as the phone in this office. You came back here to get the photograph of Wacker. When you got here you found the door locked, saw Enez had been assaulted, and called nine-one-one. Can you think of anything I haven't asked you about that might be important?"

Darius shrugged. "Only that the photograph isn't here and Enez sounded different on the phone."

The detective handed him a card. "If you think of anything else give me a call. Good luck with your case, Mister Darkfire, you're free to go. By the way, my brother-in-law is a crackerjack private investigator if you're interested."

"I sure am. What's his number?" He took out his pen and prepared to record it on the back of Detective Dunhill's business card.

Dunhill recited the name and number, concluding with, "Tell him Mack Dunhill referred you."

"Thanks . . . ."

He called from his car while driving away from Dirk Amos's office. A lady answered on the third ring.

"Thank you for calling Coolidge Research and Investigations. How may we be of service . . . ?"

* * * *

Darius left Coolidge Research and Investigations at eight-thirty and got lost on the way back to his hotel. Shortly before ten he finally got to his room, dropped a MacDonald's bag containing supper on the table, and stripped out of his suit.

Detective Dunhill's brother-in-law was a retired commander who'd spent twenty years in naval intelligence before opening his agency. The dignified scholarly gentleman went by the name of Preston Coolidge.

As soon as Darius had told him what he needed, the former member of ONI set his mind at ease when he said, "If the driver's license is valid, the number will enable me to learn all there is to know about Joanna Wacker's public records, and through that I'll be able to trace her family. I'll have a report for you by noon tomorrow."

The man had a subdued confidence, a refined voice, and a cerebral gleam in eyes shielded by wire-framed spectacles that never wavered from his when he spoke. Darius suspected he couldn't have chosen a better investigator if he'd gone through every name in the phone book.

"And if the license isn't valid?" he'd asked his new acquaintance, whose demeanor made him think of the fabled wise old owl.

"Then we'll have to take a different approach, but rest assured you'll receive the information you seek or there'll be no charge."

He ate the Big Mac and fries in his underwear, looking at the crime scene photographs as he dined. Joanna Wacker had several bruises and contusions on her face along with the five stab wounds on the front of her upper torso. Poking a fry in his mouth, he concentrated on the body shot—her corpse a rude infringement upon the lavish white carpet of John's living room. Something didn't seem right about the scene but he couldn't put his finger on precisely what. Knowing fatigue might be blurring his judgment, he let the matter drop.

The prosecution would have no difficulty proving John had the time to travel by car from San Antonio to Houston and back. His flight arrived at San Antonio at ten a.m. and the return flight landed in Houston at nine-fifteen p.m. He'd made the trip to meet with a man named Howard Gold who was looking for investors to help him expand his tool company. That meeting took place at eleven a.m. and Gold verified John's statement that it lasted through lunch and ended around one p.m.

Having planned to visit the Alamo, River Walk, and Sea World while in town, he'd asked Gold to accompany him but the industrialist couldn't spare the time. John had been alone from that point on, which meant his alibi ended when Gold last saw him, leaving a seven hour window of opportunity for him to sneak back to Houston, kill Joanna Wacker, and make it back to San Antonio in time for his return flight. The coroner had set the time of death between two and six p.m. which made the burden on the prosecution all the easier. Driving to and from the crime scene would have taken no more than six hours—and that was without speeding—leaving sixty minutes to commit the deed.

To make matters worse, John had driven around San Antonio to kill the time before his flight home instead of visiting the three sites he'd invited Gold to, which had put enough mileage on the odometer of his rental car to cover the distance of a round trip to Houston.

He'd made several stops at various convenience stores for snacks and soft drinks, ate dinner at a pizza joint, but paid cash and hadn't kept a single receipt. If he'd retained at least one—which would have the time of the sale and the location of the merchant printed thereon—it potentially could have verified his presence in San Antonio when the murder took place in Houston.

Darius anticipated Longstreet would point out to the jury that most businessmen kept careful records of expenditures on business trips so they could deduct the expenses on their income tax, making John appear all the more suspicious by his failure to do so. The only rebuttal the defense could offer was the fact that John didn't like charging incidentals on credit cards, and since all his monetary outlays while cruising the streets of San Antone had been meager, it hadn't occurred to him to keep the receipts.

He had no chance of finding an eye witness to place John in San Antonio during the critical time frame. Since his client didn't know the city, he couldn't recount precisely which convenience stores or pizza parlor he'd patronized. He'd driven aimlessly all over the area—listening to the radio, taking in the views—eventually finding his way back to the airport via a city roadmap.

This wasn't going to be easy. Darius washed down the last bite of his burger with a gulp of cola and went to bed, feeling very much like David about to take on Goliath.

FIVE

The alarm went off at seven. Forty minutes later Darius went across the street for breakfast. Once inside the door, mouth-watering aromas of bacon, sausage, ham, and hash browns titillated his nose, altering a previous plan to order oatmeal and toast.

An older woman with Sherry inscribed on her name tag waited on him. He asked about Holly and was disappointed to hear she'd been sent on an errand. Not long after she dealt out his fried, high cholesterol breakfast the cell rang. It was Preston Coolidge . . . .

* * * *

John looked worn down and routed. Spending the last few days in jail had taken a serious toll on the previously carefree bachelor. Nonetheless the twin managed a weak smile as an officer seated him. "Please tell me you've got some good news, Dare."

Trying his best to look optimistic for the incarcerated Derby's sake, he sat down across from him at the narrow table of the conference room. "Not good, necessarily, but helpful. Your girlfriend wasn't Joanna Wacker. Her real name was Jacqueline Springfield."

John gawked at him with wild surprise. "No foolin'?"

"No foolin'. She's not from Houston like she told you. Seems she grew up in Dallas just like us, and chew on this a minute—she majored in criminology and graduated from SMU the year after we did."

"You shittin' me, Homes?"

"No."

"Damn . . ." he rolled his weary eyes with disbelief.

"Her family is being notified of her demise as we speak."

A trace of relief swathed his weary façade. "So she does have family then. How'd you find all this out?"

"I hired an investigator yesterday. He's digging a little deeper into her past because he's got a hunch she was working undercover for the FBI or the DEA. I'd previously hired a different investigator yesterday morning and later in the day he called me and said he couldn't do it because he had another case. I'd given him the picture of her and went to his office to get it back, and by the time I got there someone had shot him."

John's black face turned almost pale. "You saying someone killed him?"

He answered with a grim nod. "Anyway one of the detectives at the crime scene gave me the name of another private investigator. His name is Preston Coolidge and he's top notch, used to be with the Office of Naval Intelligence. He thinks whoever killed Joanna Wacker slash Jacqueline Springfield also killed Juan Enez, the investigator I hired before Coolidge."

The emotionally exhausted inmate craned his head back and stared at the ceiling. After several moments passed, he heaved a sigh of frustration and leaned forward, enveloped by an aura of helplessness. "So what do we do now?"

"The circumstantial evidence against you is so strong, I don't see any way out of this except to solve the murder ourselves, and we're going to need the assistance of Preston Coolidge to do it. That's why I'm here, to get your permission to extend his services."

A look of feral incredulity leapt on John's face. "Hell, you got it, Homes! Why'd you even bother asking me? You the one in charge of this fucking runaway train."

"Because Coolidge doesn't come cheap, that's why."

"Shit, tell the dude to write his own check, just get my black ass out of here . . . ."

* * * *

Darius met Jacqueline Springfield's mother at the coroner's office moments before she tearfully identified the body of Joanna Wacker as that of her daughter.

* * * *

They were supping at a nice restaurant located near the Texas Commerce Tower. The smell of steak and fish hung in the air around their table. Darius had finished briefing Jock and they were discussing Jacqueline Springfield. The free twin wondered aloud whether she really liked his brother or had been investigating him, thinking John might be connected to whatever she'd gone undercover for.

"Preston Coolidge only suspects she was an undercover agent, he doesn't know for sure yet. But if she was, I don't know why she'd think John was a part of whatever she was investigating."

Slicing off a wedge from a flame-broiled T-bone, Jock brought it to his mouth and held it there a moment. "Does he have any other reasons to suspect that besides her using an assumed name?"

Eyeing the juicy chunk of beef as it passed between his old friend's lips, Darius halfway wished he hadn't ordered seafood. "Yeah. She majored in criminology and there's no work history under the name of Jacqueline Springfield after she earned her degree. He thinks she was recruited some time during her senior year at SMU. Remember he was with Naval Intelligence so he knows a lot about the way these things go down. Jacqueline Springfield graduated in Dallas the same year Joanna Wacker got her real estate license in Houston. Springfield graduated in May and Wacker became a real estate agent in September. Preston thinks she spent that summer in special training."

Jock frowned attentively as he chewed.

"Her mother wouldn't confirm or deny it when I asked if Jacqueline worked for any form of government agency, but swore she didn't know her daughter was going by the name of Joanna Wacker so it seems reasonable to assume if Springfield was working undercover her mother didn't know it."

The twin swallowed and took a long pull of beer from his frosty mug. "Does Coolidge think whoever killed Enez was trying to frame you for that murder, the way John got framed for Wacker's?"

A fearful chill shot through him, he hadn't thought of that. But it quickly dissipated when he realized whoever killed Enez couldn't have known he'd try to retrieve the picture of his client's girlfriend. "He hasn't said so if he does, but I wouldn't think so. Wacker was killed with John's knife. It wasn't my gun that shot Enez."

"Ah—" Jock raised his brows while cutting off another bite of dripping steak "—I see your point."

Darius stabbed a catfish nugget and raked it across a pool of ketchup. "We've got less than three weeks before trial, twenty days to be exact, and like I told John, the only way I see to win this is to solve the murder. If this thing courses all the way to jury deliberation, the circumstantial evidence is going to bury him."

"That's why we wanted you, Homes. Another lawyer might want it to go that far so he could collect a fatter fee . . . ."

After they finished eating, Darius tucked a twenty dollar tip beneath his plate and scooted his chair back. "Thanks for supper. Guess I'll head back to my room."

Rising to his feet Jock glowered with disapproval. "Why you staying in some ol' funky hotel anyway? Why don't you stay with me?"

He laughed. "Because I need peace and quiet so I can concentrate, and that's the last thing I'd get hanging at your place. And before you suggest I stay at John's, he's already tried to talk me into it. But I'd be too distracted—too worried about spilling something on that fancy carpet of his. All I need is a bed, a table to work on, a bathroom, and four walls to keep the elements at bay. But if you're worried about the hotel bill we can always go back to my first offer of fifty an hour instead of a hundred."

"Not on your life, Homes . . . ."

* * * *

Darius met with Nathan Longstreet at ten that next morning, telling him what he'd learned about Joanna Wacker, hoping he'd investigate the possibility that John had been framed, but he wasn't interested.

"I'm confident we have the right man in custody," he said with an arrogant smile. "The murder took place in his house, his prints were on the murder weapon, he had the means and the opportunity even though he cleverly tried to make it look like he had neither by that trip to San Antonio."

"But you left out one thing. What was his motive?"

Longstreet winced as if he found the question insulting. "Why do lovers usually murder one another? Infidelity, jealousy, a lover's quarrel gone over the edge—she might have threatened to leave him—the possibilities are practically endless. I knew you were young but I didn't think you were stupid."

Anger welling, Darius steeled his jaw while glaring at the insufferable prosecutor. "Oh I'm far from stupid, sir."

"Are you?" Donning a self-satisfied smirk, Longstreet adjusted his tie. "How long have you been practicing law?"

"Six years."

"Six whole years. And in that time you've handled only one homicide case."

His adversary had certainly done his homework—a fact which impressed him, but he didn't let it show. "That's right, only one until now. And since you know that, you must also be aware of the fact that I've never lost a case."

"All I can say is you must be one lucky son-of-a-bitch."

Despite a surge of fury over having his mother so insulted, Darius calmly folded his arms across his chest. Feeling every muscle tighten with anticipation of battle, he steadied his eyes on the assistant district attorney. "Mister Longstreet, if you ever call me that again I'll be where my client is because you'll be worm food. Do I make myself clear? And think carefully before you fire off some glib retort or try to threaten me, because I never make idle caveats and I never exaggerate. I bench three hundred pounds and can knock a pussy like you out cold with one punch. And court battles aren't the only skirmishes I've never lost. Not once in my life have I ever been on the losing end of a fistfight either, and believe me when I say I've been in more than a few.

"I'll accept your apology now or stomp your ass, the choice is yours. If it comes down to the latter and you press charges, I'll sue you for defaming my mother's good name. Which will it be?"

Visibly shaken—eyes gaping, soft chin quivering— Longstreet gasped, "I-I'm sorry! I didn't realize you'd take it so personally or I would never have used the term. I didn't mean it literally by any means, and I do apologize."

Almost disappointed the mouthy bighead hadn't retaliated, Darius shot the rattled lawyer a cynical smile. "I'm glad we got the air cleared, Mister Longstreet. If you'll excuse me, think I'll go to lunch now . . . ."

* * * *

Seating himself at a table he spotted Holly carrying a platter of savory-looking chicken fried steak across the diner. She hadn't noticed him yet and he hoped to see a positive reaction when she did. Strolling back across the room empty handed she glanced his direction. A cute smile sprang to her face and she darted towards him.

"Hello there."

"Hi, Holly."

Her smile broadened. "Hey, you remembered my name."

"Naw, just read your name tag."

She glanced down at her breast and laughed. "You jerk!"

He grinned. She'd forgotten to wear the tag. "How's college life treating you?"

"Good. How's the pretrial prep going? I bet it's so interesting."

Sighing, he adjusted his position on the chair. "A little more interesting than I'd like."

"My shift ends in half an hour, I'd love to hear all about it."

"I have an appointment but you can tag along with me if you'd like. It probably won't take long but I can't promise it won't."

"Great!" Countenance beaming like a floodlight, she fished a pad and pen from a pocket on her apron. "What can we get you today?"

"That chicken fried steak you were carrying looked pretty good. Believe I'll have that and coffee."

"Baked potato or fries?"

"Fries."

"It comes with a salad and you have your choice of dressing."

"Italian."

As she bustled off, he eyed her alluring derriere, moving rhythmically with her steps . . . .

After he finished lunch Holly accompanied him to Preston Coolidge's office—the furnishings of which were polar opposites of Dirk Amos's. During the trip from the café he'd told her all about the case. She'd hung on his every word, listening intently, the excitement on her face reflecting keen anticipation of her upcoming law career. Preston favored her with a cerebral smile after being introduced and beckoned her to have a seat in a sumptuous leather armchair.

Darius settled into a similar one. "Okay, Preston, what have you got?"

The investigator sat down at his desk and opened a manila folder. "My suspicions were correct. Jacqueline Springfield also-known-as Joanna Wacker was employed by the Drug Enforcement Administration and was working undercover with another DEA agent and two FBI agents. My contact didn't know, or pretended he didn't know anything about the two agents with the FBI—not even their gender—but he did tell me the DEA agent is a black male whose undercover name is John Derby."

"What . . .?" he reared back with shock. "It can't be my John Derby, I've known him since high school, and in college he majored in business administration rather than criminology."

Preston adjusted his glasses. "It's not your client. Remember John Derby is the man's undercover name, not his real name. Here's what I think happened. I believe the bar where your client met the victim was a contact point, and she'd been instructed to go there and wait to be approached by a black man going by the name of John Derby. When your client hit on her and introduced himself, she naturally assumed he was her contact. Your client was in the wrong place with the wrong name. But there's one thing that troubles me."

He leaned forward, eyeing the frowning commander. "What's that?"

"Although I can see why she would think he was her contact initially, why would she continue seeing him when it must have become obvious soon after meeting him that he wasn't the DEA John Derby, just coincidentally happened to have the same name?"

"Maybe she just liked him, and fell in love with him by the time she realized he wasn't," offered Holly with a grin.

"That's not possible . . ." Preston leaned back and merged his fingertips, forming a steeple in front of his chest. "She'd have known he wasn't the John Derby she was looking for within minutes of their first conversation. I need to know if your client saw another black man approach her that night. If he did, he may have been the real contact, and if that's the case, she knew it was coincidence straight away. And that would pose another question. If she knew he wasn't the contact, why did she engage him in conversation?"

Holly let out a giggle. "Like I said, maybe she just liked him."

"Maybe so," agreed Darius.

His serene expression clearly indicating he found that possibility unlikely, Preston lowered his hands. "I also need to know if he frequently patronized that nightclub. Coincidences rarely occur in the covert world. If he was a regular, there's a possibility she was simply following instructions to fraternize with him, and if that's the case it's of the utmost importance for us to learn why."

The statement alarmed him. "Are you suggesting John was deliberately set up?"

"It's a possibility, especially if he frequented that particular nightclub. Of course at this point all this is merely conjecture on my part. There's one last thing I need to know. Ask your client why he chose to go there the night he met Joanna Wacker."

On the way back to the café Holly gave him a perplexed look and said, "Why doesn't he just go see your friend instead of having you ask him those questions?"

"Because the more leg work I can do, the less money Preston Coolidge will cost my client . . . ."

He dropped Holly off at her car, went to see John, and called Preston with the answers to his questions.

John visited the Baker's Dozen nightclub on a semi regular basis. The night he met Joanna Wacker she was already there, sitting by herself when he walked in, and he had no particular reason for going there the night in question. He and a friend named Thomas had gone out for drinks at another club but Thomas developed a headache so he took him home. After leaving Thomas's place he'd planned to call it a night himself but when he passed Baker's Dozen decided on the spur of the moment to have a nightcap. John remembered the night clearly because if Thomas hadn't gotten that headache, he wouldn't have met Joanna.

When he'd heard the last, Darius couldn't help grimacing inside at the irony of what a headache this Thomas had inadvertently created for his client.

SIX

Darius ordered the daily special for lunch. Though the meatloaf and mashed potatoes tasted good, he feared a case of indigestion might be forthcoming due to gathering tension in the pit of his gut. The trial would start in nineteen days but the way things looked it might as well have been only nineteen minutes. Without some sort of break the outcome would be the same, John was sure to be found guilty. He'd spent the entire morning brainstorming with Preston and they had developed a theory but that wasn't going to do any good without some sort of proof. Holly's shift started shortly before he finished eating. After servicing a few customers she dropped by his table.

"I had such a great time yesterday, thanks again for letting me tag along."

He daubed the corners of his mouth with a napkin, welcoming the pleasant diversion from his racing mind. "Glad you enjoyed it. When this is all over I'd like to take you out on a real date."

She blushed with excitement. "Why wait? I can skip class tonight and we can go dancing or something."

"Can't do it till this is over."

A cute pout formed. "Okay, but I'm gonna hold you to it."

"I'm counting on it." He dropped his napkin on a thin smear of residual gravy on an otherwise empty plate and rose from the table, hating he had to leave her pleasurable company . . . .

John looked worse each time he saw him. Puffy bags beneath eyes saturated with anxiety revealed a serious lack of recuperative sleep. His lean face that had always reflected a cavalier attitude, now seemed permanently stamped with anxiety and exhaustion. The county coveralls he wore contrasted sharply with his brother's tweed suit, further enhancing a washed-out appearance. Darius reminded himself he was the twin's legal counsel and couldn't allow pity for his imprisoned homey to sidetrack him.

He'd asked Jock to accompany him on this visit so the brothers could simultaneously hear the hypothesis Preston and he had come up with.

"We think Joanna was murdered by the agent who was working with her undercover. After hashing it out dozens of times we've come to the conclusion that she already knew the other John Derby before she met you at Baker's Dozen, therefore her only motivation in seeing you afterwards was because she liked you.

"Preston was told by a high government source that a rumor is floating around intelligence circles in Washington that an agent in Texas has turned rogue. Preston's connection doesn't know if the agent is with the CIA, FBI, ATF, or DEA. We're speculating it's John Derby and Joanna somehow discovered that fact or Derby feared she did to the point she had to be silenced.

"We know John Derby is the man's undercover name but we don't know his real identity, and we can't locate him. Preston has been trying to get the information since he first learned about him but keeps getting stonewalled. He thinks the corruption goes higher up than a crooked agent because his source also told him one of his contacts may have been placed in jeopardy because of his inquiry. We desperately need a break, John. Is there anything Joanna ever said to you that might give us a clue to finding her undercover partner?"

John sadly shook his head.

"Preston and I combed through all her personal effects and couldn't find a rolodex or any sort of address book. Did she ever mention keeping a journal or diary, anything that might possibly have his address on it?"

He shook his head again, his dog-tired face looking as

though he'd already acquiesced to defeat.

Jock put a hand on his brother's shoulder. "We won't let you down, John. Cheer up. One way or another we'll find that motherfucker."

John managed the semblance of a smile. "I know Dare's doing all he can, bro."

A surprised look came over Jock, followed by a deep frown.

"What is it?" asked Darius.

"Just remembered something Joanna told me the last time I saw her."

"Which was?"

"She told me . . . shit, how did she put it? She was making a joke about leaving all her fortune to my medicine cabinet but I can't remember how she said it. It made sense at the time because we were cutting up, but I can't remember the details now. I had her and John over for dinner. John had to use the bathroom and popped a comic as he excused himself, that's what got us on a joking jag, but damn if I can remember. Anyway, what if she was trying to tell me something?"

"When was this?"

"Just a few days before she died."

Darius furrowed his brow. "She said she was going to leave her fortune to your medicine cabinet?"

"Yeah, something like that."

"Well, Homes, I make a motion we adjourn to your house and check it out."

John's countenance brightened a smidgen as a glint of hope appeared in his weary eyes.

* * * *

They took everything out of Jock's mirrored medicine cabinet, carefully examining each item, hoping to find a note, a piece of microfilm, a key to a safety deposit box, anything. Then they scoured the bathroom cabinets beneath but found nothing in them either.

Jock put his hands on his waist and vented an angry hiss. "Shit, not one fucking thing. I guess she *was* only joking."

Darius wasn't so ready to say die. "You have more than one bathroom, let's check them all before we give up."

"But she knew this was my bathroom. We won't find anything in the other two."

Sadly, the prediction proved correct—they found nothing in the other medicine cabinets either. When they walked out of the last bathroom a thought swam up. Not only were the Derbys identical twins, their voices sounded remarkably alike as well, so it was a possibility. "Can you remember what you and John wore the night you last saw Joanna Wacker?"

"No, Homes, I sure can't. Why?"

"Don't laugh, but I'm wondering if Joanna thought she was talking to John instead of you when she mentioned the medicine cabinet. If you guys were wearing similar clothes, then maybe she thought it was you that went to the bathroom. Let's try to recreate the evening . . . ."

Jock's dining table was a large square of varnished hardwood with two chairs adorning each of the four sides.

"Where did you sit?"

Darius pulled out the chair Jock pointed to and sat down. "Okay, I'm you on that night. Where did John and Joanna sit?"

"Seems like Joanna sat there to your right, and John sat across from her."

"Once you all sat down, did you ever get up before John had to use the bathroom?"

"Yeah, I might have."

"More than once?"

"Maybe."

"Can you remember if she ever got up during dinner?"

Stroking his chin, Jock frowned with thought for several moments. His face relaxed and he lowered his hand. "Just not sure, Dare."

"We're probably spittin' in the wind, but let's go to John's house and check his medicine cabinets on the off chance she may have thought she was talking to him instead of you."

* * * *

Apparently Joanna's statement *had* only been spoken in jest. John's medicine cabinets contained nothing unusual either. Now in the living room, Darius gazed at the spot where her body had lain. Recalling how the photograph bugged him, he looked towards Jock, standing a few feet away, hands in his pockets, an expression of helplessness on his face.

"Odd how nothing got knocked over, isn't it? Don't know why it didn't dawn on me before now."

"What do you mean?"

Darius pointed at the floor. "She wasn't shot from a distance, she was stabbed up close, so she wouldn't have just stood there and let her assailant repeatedly stab her. Yet in the crime photographs the blood on the floor is the only thing in this living room that's not pristine. That vase over there, all those knickknacks against that wall, those magazines on the coffee table—you'd think something would have at least got knocked over if not broken in the struggle. Any woman would've tried to defend herself, but we're talking about a trained DEA agent who'd have at least a rudimentary knowledge of hand-to-hand combat. And there were bruises on her face, so she was hit several times. You'd think she'd hit back."

Jock puckered his lips while thinking that over. "Maybe the killer knocked her out with the first blow."

"Not likely. Since his intent was obviously to kill her, I doubt he'd waste time punching an unconscious target. He'd start in with the knife straightaway. Chew on this a minute. The coroner said none of the five stab wounds or bruises to her face were postmortem which means she lived long enough to put up some sort of struggle." He stabbed at the air with an imaginary knife. "One Mississippi, two Mississippi, three Mississippi, four Mississippi, five Mississippi."

Gaping at him like he'd lost his mind, Jock chuckled out, "What the hell you doing, man?"

"Murdering Joanna Wacker. It took me almost a whole second to administer each knife wound, so that's five seconds there, and that's without any resistance from her or having to pull the blade out of the body each time. And she was certainly alive long enough to receive several blows to the face before she bled to death. I'm guessing it took the killer half a minute at the very least before she was totally incapacitated."

The perplexed brother shrugged his shoulders. "Maybe she did put up a fight and some stuff got knocked over but the killer put everything back in its place before he left."

"Why do that . . .?" he again looked at the spot where the victim was found. "Signs of a scuffle would only make it look more like John was angry enough to kill her. Something's been bothering me about the pictures of the body. I didn't know what it was until just now. It either got past everybody that examined the crime scene as well or the prosecutor thinks he has a reasonable explanation for it. There should have been more blood on the floor. Homes, I've got a feeling we've just stumbled across Defense Exhibit A."

"What's Defense Exhibit A?"

Darius grinned at his homey. "The photograph of Joanna Wacker lying on this floor. Not enough blood around the body coupled with no evidence of a struggle can only mean one thing—Joanna wasn't killed here. She was stabbed somewhere else and the killer brought her here to die. It'll only take one juror to believe what I'm arguing here to hang the jury.

"Here's my theory. Joanna finds out the DEA John Derby is corrupt and confronts him. He pulls out a knife and stabs her but she fights back, maybe knocks the knife out of his hand

and they battle each other. During the scuffle she loses too much blood and passes out. Being her partner he would know she'd moved in with our John Derby. Whether he knew about John's trip to San Antonio or not, he would assume he'd be at work and not at home at mid afternoon on a week day so he decides to bring her here to make it look like our John did it.

"He bandages her wounds so she won't bleed to death, strips, washes all her blood off, puts on clean clothes, and obtains a package of rubber gloves. Careful not to leave any prints on her car, he puts her in the trunk, wrapped in plastic left loose enough around the face to keep her from suffocating. He drives here, using Joanna's recently acquired remote garage opener to raise the overhead door. Once inside he closes it, moves her body to the living room, unwraps it, rips off her bandages, and changes gloves.

"Then he goes to the kitchen, finds a knife similar in size to the one he used initially, and stabs her some more to make it look like the only murder weapon. While waiting for her to bleed to death he stashes the bloody plastic, bandages, previously worn gloves, and the knife into a garbage bag.

"Wearing a clean pair of gloves now, he slips out the back door, walks down the alley carrying what any observer would assume is just a bag full of trash. When he passes the dumpster of Mary Davis, he pulls the knife from the bag and drops it to the ground, making sure it'll be discovered. He walks a good ways, at least several blocks, before finally tossing the trash bag into a dumpster. A few dumpsters down from there, he takes off the gloves and tosses them, continues on to some public place like a gas station and hails a cab to take him home."

A dubious laugh rang out. Jock cocked his head with a disbelieving grin. "That's pretty farfetched, Homes."

He pulled out his cell. "Not really. Like I said, all I need is one juror to buy into it. I want to call Preston and run it by him and see if he's as skeptical as you."

* * * *

Unlike Jock, Preston didn't find his theory farfetched at all, and with a fine-tooth comb examined Joanna Wacker's car as well as John's house looking for evidence to support it. Though he didn't find any, he did discover something stashed under the spare tire, stored in a compartment at the bottom of the trunk.

An address book.

Darius, who'd assisted in the search, stood beside Preston, peering over the investigator's shoulder. "Pretty clever place to hide an address book."

Without interrupting his perusal of the small pages Preston said, "And since it *was* hidden it's bound to contain sensitive information."

"Let's just hope it has John Derby's address."

Preston looked up from the book with a knowing smile. "It does. He resides in Pasadena."

* * * *

The house was veneered with white clapboard that badly needed a coat of paint. An empty drive indicated John Derby wasn't home. They drove through the alley behind the house to get a view of the rear but a six foot cedar fence prevented any scrutiny of the back yard from the car.

Returning to the innocent John Derby's house where Preston had left his vehicle, he dropped off the investigator and drove straight to the district attorney's office. Darius told Nathan Longstreet the hypothesis he'd come up with, gave him Derby's address, and asked him to get a warrant so the detectives assigned to the case could search the place.

Longstreet refused but did so in a polite and very respectful manner, cautiously explaining he still felt he had the right man in custody.

He'd never broken the law before but after speaking with the assistant DA he toyed with the idea of breaking into the agent's abode. He needed to find some sort of evidence that would reveal the motive for the murder of Jacqueline Springfield, and talking to the corrupt DEA agent would only serve to alert him.

* * * *

Only seventeen days until trial, his mind warned as he shut off the alarm clock.

Skipping breakfast, Darius drove to Pasadena and once again found the driveway vacant. He pulled into the alley, killed the engine, and got out of his car. On the off chance someone might be inside the house watching, he walked boldly through the gate, up to the back door, and knocked. No one answered.

He tried the door but it wouldn't budge, so he glanced around for something to break a window with. A circle of rocks the size of softballs surrounding the base of a mimosa sapling appeared to be his only option. Bending over to pick one up he reached for the stone but froze the moment his hand made contact. Despite the fact his intentions were noble, he couldn't make himself go through with it. The old saying *the end justifies the means* echoed in his mind, but to no avail. Heaving a harsh sigh of resignation he stood erect and prepared to leave.

The door swung open and an angry black man appeared. "What are you doing knocking on my back door?"

Swallowing a lump of shocking surprise Darius stepped towards the guy he assumed was the DEA agent and donned a polite smile while extending his hand. "Are you John Derby?"

"Never mind who I am. Who are you, and what are you doing in my back yard?"

The guy was wearing gray sweats, and an upside down

triangle of sweat on his muscular chest suggested he'd been working out. He was about his height—just shy of six feet— looked to be a few years older, and had a gold tooth Darius found hard not to stare at. Disguising his exasperation over this unfortunate turn of events, he firmed his jaw and looked the man square in the eyes. "I'm Darius Darkfire, an attorney. I represent the man accused of killing your partner Joanna Wacker. And before you say you don't know what I'm talking about and try to insult my intelligence by pretending you never heard of her, let me tell you that I know she was an undercover agent for the DEA and her real name was Jacqueline Springfield. Let me further add that I know that you and two agents with the FBI are working on some sort of undercover operation that included her before she died."

The black man glanced past him, seemingly to satisfy himself they were alone. "Let's see some identification."

Darius produced his credentials.

Wiping a necklace of sweat beads from his forehead, the agent took a step back. "Come in."

He followed John Derby into a small dining room through which the kitchen could be seen.

"Take a seat."

As he sat down his irritated host strolled into the kitchen.

"I take my coffee black. How do you take yours? Or are you one of those wimps that won't partake of caffeine or nicotine or dentine or anything that ends with een?"

The *een* sound in each of the words had been emphasized, and Darius couldn't hold back a laugh. "I'm no wimp but I do like a little sugar and cream in my coffee if you don't mind."

That extracted a chuckle from the agent. A moment later he walked in with a steaming mug in each hand, one of which held a spoon. He handed him that one and sat down. "So you're the one representing my alter ego."

Darius stirred the coffee, colored a light tan from a splash of milk. "In a manner of speaking since you both go by John

Derby, which of course is not your real name."

"Why did you knock on the back door instead of the front?"

He looked Derby over before answering. The gold tooth gleamed from a face displaying no form of nervousness, and his eyes exhibited curiosity rather than fear. His humorous remark about the coffee had sounded completely spontaneous rather than an effort to camouflage panic. A strong aura of integrity enveloped him, and Darius no longer thought this man killed Joanna Wacker. He wanted to tell him the truth—that he'd planned to break into his house to search for clues—but caution dictated otherwise, so he lied.

"I know you're an undercover agent which I figure means you're constantly watching your back, concerned about who you're seen with. I thought you might appreciate the lawyer representing the man accused of killing your partner not being seen at your front door on the off chance whoever you're investigating lives across the street or next door."

Derby took a sip of coffee and lowered his cup. "Where's your car?"

"In the alley."

"Good. I like a man who thinks ahead. Now then, what exactly do you want from me?"

Raising the steaming mug, Darius blew across the surface and partook of the creamy brew, finding it a tad strong for his taste but palatable. He set the cup on the table and circled it with both hands. "My client is a personal friend. We've known each other since high school. I know he didn't kill Joanna Wacker which means someone else did. The way this case stands at the moment, my only hope of clearing him is to find out who really killed her. So I'm eager to learn anything you can tell me about Joanna Wacker, especially the name of anyone that had it in for her."

Blatantly eyeing him for several seconds he finally said, "You're not going to like what you're about to hear, but up until now I thought your friend was the one who killed her. I really did."

"But you don't think so now?"

"No."

"Why?"

"Because I can see you're a cat that wouldn't represent a man you thought was guilty even if he was a friend. Since you were able to get your hands on secret government information I can see you're not a slow thinker either, which means your friend has either got you totally fooled or he's innocent. But being that I can also see you're not a chump that gets fooled for long, your friend must be innocent."

Darius frowned. "Why would you think all that, you just met me?"

"It's a knack I have . . ." he took a quick nip from his mug. "I read people quick. *Real* quick."

Although lacking that enviable ability, when instinct kicked in it was seldom wrong, and the one goading him now strongly insisted this John Derby hadn't committed the murder. "Well if you believe he didn't do it, can you think of anyone who had a motive?"

"The only thing I can tell you for certain is that I had nothing to do with it. I can't discuss anything to do with my job, you understand, but I will tell you this—she wasn't killed by any of the people we're investigating."

"How can you be so sure?"

"Because if that was the case, I'd be dead too."

That made sense to a large degree but Darius didn't see it as a certainty. However, he didn't say so. "What about the two FBI agents?"

"Couldn't say."

"Do you trust the FBI agents involved in the operation?"

Derby let out a hearty laugh.

"I take it that's a no?"

"N-O, definitely."

He thought about Preston's fear that the corruption went

higher up than John Derby. It appeared the dirty agent wasn't with the DEA but the FBI. At least if the man across from him was telling the truth like he thought. "Do you know anything about Joanna's relationship with my client? Did she ever talk about it?"

"Oh yeah, she talked a lot. We had a big laugh about what a coincidence it was, her falling for a guy with the same name as my cover moniker. She was crazy about him but he had a real jealous bone. That's the only negative thing she ever said about him, and I figured it for a crime of passion."

Hearing John had a jealous streak totally surprised him. But since neither of the Derby twins had steady girlfriends back in school, he'd never seen his old friend in a situation which would have revealed it. "Not to sound accusatory but where were you the day she was murdered?"

"Couldn't say."

"Couldn't say because you can't remember, or because you can't talk about it."

"Couldn't say."

"I understand. Hope you understand I'm not accusing you."

"Not a problem." His expression and tone conveyed he believed him.

"Can you tell me where and when you last saw her alive."

"The where I couldn't say, but the when was the day before she died. I saw her early in the day and talked to her on the phone that night."

"Can you tell me where and when she last saw the FBI agents?"

Derby's expression turned somber and he leered at him, carefully studying his face. Darius sensed the agent was wrestling with how far he could trust him.

"The where I honestly don't know but I can tell you the when because it's the last words I'll ever hear her say. I remember them word for word. We were on the phone. I was here and she was at your friend's house. We were discussing the next day's itinerary and she said, 'I have to meet with the assholes in the morning. Oh, John just walked in, Mary, let's talk about the house tomorrow.' *The assholes* was our mutual term of endearment for the two FBI agents. The bit about calling me Mary was to keep your friend from knowing who she was really talking to."

"Would either or both of the agents have a reason to want her dead?"

Mouth slightly ajar with a half grin, gold tooth glistening, he appeared to be analyzing him again. "You don't know who they are, do you. And you don't know my real name either."

Darius chuckled. "When you said you had a knack for reading people I didn't know you were referring to mind reading. You pegged it, I don't know. How did you know I didn't know?"

Derby took a pull from his mug. "Because you never called them by their undercover names just like you never said my real name."

"And I don't suppose you'll tell me either."

"You suppose right."

"Just tell me their gender then?"

"What difference does that make?"

"I'm just curious."

"They're both female."

He shot the agent a knowing grin.

"Why are you smiling?"

"Because you're lying to me now. They're really both male, at least one of them is."

The undercover sleuth smiled back, the golden tooth drawing Darius's eyes to it like a magnet.

"You're right, how did you know?"

"Your term of endearment for the two of them." He sampled some more of Derby's stout coffee. "If they were both female the term would have been something along the lines of bitches rather than assholes."

"I'm impressed."

"So which is it? A guy and a girl, or two guys."

"I really couldn't say. You'll have to leave now, I'm expecting company shortly and I need a shower. But I've got a question before you do. How did you find out we were DEA agents?"

He donned a friendly smirk. "Couldn't say . . . ."

Back in his car, pulling out of the alley, Darius changed his theory, substituting one or both of the FBI agents for Agent Derby. He still felt the victim had been initially assaulted somewhere besides John's living room. The same scenario could have happened, the theory didn't hinge on Derby being the culprit. In the midst of his hypothesizing something else jumped to the front of his mind. *What if the killer thought he was framing John Derby the DEA agent rather than John Derby the businessman?*

Several scenarios presented themselves with that likelihood. In one, the assassin knew the agent but not where he lived. He must have followed Joanna Wacker to John's house at some point before murdering her or he wouldn't have known the address since there were several John Derbys listed in the Houston phone book.

Another possibility was the perpetrator not knowing either of them. Contracted to kill Joanna Wacker in order to frame the agent, he inadvertently picked the wrong John Derby. Then again the killer might have only known the name and not the face of the agent, and had no idea there were two John Derby's in Joanna Wacker's life.

Face knotting with a frown, he heaved a bitter sigh—there were endless possibilities. Blowing out a second harried breath, he mulled over what little he could be sure of. The killer obviously hadn't acted in self defense, and unless something had been stolen from the victim no one knew about, the motive couldn't have been robbery since John's possessions weren't touched other than the knife. No evidence of sexual assault eliminated the prospect of a rapist silencing his victim.

If his supposition that a corrupt agent slew Jacqueline Springfield to silence her wasn't correct, then the conclusion DEA John Derby had previously drawn and Nathan Longstreet still clung to seemed highly likely—it *had* been a crime of passion.

"A crime of passion." He said the words aloud several times as he pulled onto the Loop Freeway encircling Houston.

When he got to his room he once again studied the crime scene photographs. Holding a close up of the agent's face, he studied the swollen abrasions on her otherwise smooth black skin. Still looking at it, he grabbed his cell and speed-dialed Ricca's office phone.

"You've reached the offices of Darius Darkfire, attorney at law. This is Ricca speaking, how may I help you?"

"Next time check the ID and you won't have to go through the preamble," he snickered. "Ricca, I need you to book me a round trip flight from Houston to Dallas and find a lady named Shanequa Springfield in Oak Cliff. That first name is spelled S-H-A-N-E-Q-U-A. When you get hold of Mrs. Springfield set up an appointment for us to meet at my office, and book the flights around that schedule. Allow a few hours for the meeting then get me back to Houston as soon as possible afterwards. Tell her I need to talk to her about her daughter, and that it will greatly assist me in finding her real killer. Got that?"

"And if she refuses to meet with you?" It was Ricca's idea of a dry joke.

"Make her an offer she can't refuse."

"Okay, Godfather. I was wondering if you were going to check in today."

He'd been giving her a call after breakfast each morning. "I had planned a breaking and entering caper that went afoul, so that's why I'm calling late. Sorry."

She laughed. *"Well as long as you've got a good excuse."*

"Call me when you get everything set."

"Okay, talk to you then."

He hung up the phone, dropped the photograph on top of the others, and headed for the door. It was past noon and he still hadn't eaten breakfast.

SEVEN

With only sixteen days until trial this one would be consumed by a mid morning flight to Dallas, a meeting with Jacqueline Springfield's mother, and an evening jet ride back to Houston, so he hoped the conference would prove fruitful. Ricca picked him up at the airport and they had lunch before going to the office.

At one o'clock his faithful secretary escorted Shanequa Springfield through the door. The lean black woman had short graying hair and rigid features that formed a natural frown. He thanked her for coming and offered her a seat.

"I'll get right to the point, Mrs. Springfield. As I see it your daughter was killed for one of two reasons. I asked you to meet with me so we can eliminate or confirm one of them. As I told you at the coroner's office in Houston, the man accused of her murder is a personal friend of mine. I've known John Derby for years, and he's a good man who loved your daughter and deeply mourns her death. He didn't commit this crime and wants to see whoever did brought to justice as much as you do.

"I believe she was either killed by someone connected to the case she was working on or by a jilted lover or ex husband, and that brings me to what I want to talk to you about—her love life. I hope I don't seem insensitive, but I need to know. All I'm trying to do is uncover the truth here. Everything you say will be kept in strictest confidence, and though my secretary will be taking notes, I assure you they are merely to help me remember. This is not a deposition, and everything you say is completely off the record. Will you help me, Mrs. Springfield?"

Her tough expression softened with a smile. "You have honest eyes, Mister Darkfire, and I adhere to the old saying that the eyes are the windows to the soul. I'll help you if you swear to me before God that you really believe your client is innocent and aren't just pulling some lawyer's trick to help get a guilty man acquitted."

He placed a hand over his heart. "I swear to you before God, John Derby did not kill your daughter, and I believe that with every fiber of my being."

The smile waned and she gave her head a single nod. "Good enough. What do you want to know?"

"Was she ever married?"

"No."

"Who was the last man she was involved with before my client?"

She thought about it for a minute. "I can't be sure about the last one because I don't know hardly anything about her personal life after she joined the Drug Enforcement Administration. She had to be very careful about what she said to me over the phone, and the last time I saw her alive was when she paid me a short visit almost a year ago. I wasn't allowed to go see her. The only time I ever saw her in Houston was the day I met you."

Tears had gathered in her eyes so he gave her a moment to collect herself. The memory obviously tormented her. "So you did know she was undercover?"

"Yes."

"Do you recall telling me you didn't know she was going by the name Joanna Wacker?"

"Yes, and it's true. I knew she was undercover but I didn't know she wasn't using her real name. You see, she told me we wouldn't be able to write each other, that it was too dangerous, and she couldn't even tell me where she lived or even give me her phone number. She told me she could call me on occasion but that we had to be very careful, and had to assume everything we said was being monitored. My caller ID always said anonymous when she called."

Cutting his eyes to Ricca, he watched until her pen stopped moving, then continued. "Did she ever mention having a boyfriend after she moved to Houston?"

"No. But like I said, that doesn't mean she didn't. The district attorney told me that according to his statement, John Derby had been seeing her for the last six months, but she never said word one to me about it."

He took a sip of water and it dawned on him he hadn't offered her anything to drink. "Where are my manners? Would you like some water or coffee, Mrs. Springfield?"

"No thank you, I'm fine."

Ricca had a giggle frozen in her throat induced by his foul up, he could tell by her expression. She'd have offered Shanequa Springfield refreshment right away but had been warned never to speak unless spoken to while in his office with a client present. "Okay, tell me about the last guy she was interested in that you did know about."

"His name was Gershon Pate. They dated on and off through college."

His brows shot up. "The basketball player?"

"That's right. You said that like you know him."

"I knew *of* him. He was a year ahead of me at SMU. I graduated a year before your daughter, by the way."

That dug a second smile out of her. "Is that right?"

"Yes, ma'am. I thought Gershon would play pro ball for sure."

Her face resettled into its normal glower. "So did Jackie and I."

"I assume you mean Jacqueline."

"Yes. I always called her Jackie."

"Do you know why they stopped dating?"

"Mm hmm. Jackie quit having anything to do with Gershon after he started messing with drugs."

"Is that why he didn't pursue a career in the pros?"

"Couldn't say for sure but I would imagine so. I don't know

what happened to him."

He recalled the shock that reverberated around the campus at Southern Methodist when Gershon Pate dropped out of college just before that year's basketball season began. He'd forgotten all about it until now, but the scuttlebutt at the time was that he'd gotten hooked on drugs. Could it be Gershon took to dealing them to support a growing habit? That seemed a very likely scenario. If the former basketball star happened to be part of whatever Jacqueline Springfield was investigating, it wasn't a reach to assume he'd suspect she might be an undercover agent since he knew her real identity, and that certainly provided a strong motive for murdering her. This could be the break he so desperately needed. He'd have Preston find the whereabouts of Gershon Pate, and if he lived in the Houston area, things might be starting to fall into place.

"Did she have other boyfriends during her college days besides Gershon?"

She shook her head. "None she felt serious about that I know of."

* * * *

Preston located Gershon Pate in Texas City. Darius was standing in Pate's entryway looking down at him, waiting for the police who he'd just called. The old star of the court from SMU had been stoned but conscious when Darius arrived. When he identified himself as the lawyer representing the man accused of killing Joanna Wacker who he knew to be Jacqueline Springfield, Pate had panicked and swung at him. After easily dodging the telescoped punch, Darius had slammed his left fist into the big man's abdomen, took a step back as instinctive reaction forced Pate to bend forward, and sent the six-foot-niner into dreamland with a right uppercut.

Two officers arrived. He told them what happened and one

of them roused Pate. Looking up from the floor, rubbing his bruised chin he shouted, "I'm glad you're here! This man just assaulted me."

Darius shot him a humorless grin. "I was only defending myself."

The lawmen helped the wayward athlete to his feet. He stood head and shoulders taller than both of them.

Reaching inside his coat, Darius pulled out a document for the officers to see. "I have a subpoena for Mister Pate."

Pate bolted through the door. Darius ran after him and tackled him on the sidewalk.

* * * *

Nathan Longstreet finally relented when Darius presented the evidence Preston Coolidge had gathered. The investigator had collected fingerprints from several places around John's house and Jacqueline Springfield's car, and Darius had asked the assistant DA to check them against those of Gershon Pate, whose prints were on file because he'd been arrested once for possession of a controlled substance. That case hadn't gone to trial because Pate had plea-bargained and received eighteen months probation. The prints matched, Pate was arrested, and after intense interrogation by detectives Hallmark and Sage, he confessed to being an accessory to the murder of his ex girlfriend Jacqueline Springfield, and once again sought to plea his way out rather than go to trial.

Darius had theorized correctly that she hadn't been initially assaulted at John's house, but wrong about the killer acting alone and covering his tracks by using several pairs of rubber or plastic gloves. There had been another man with Gershon Pate named Joe Hunter, one of the people Jacqueline Springfield had been investigating.

She'd gone to Hunter's house because he'd invited her over for lunch. While they were outside having a pleasant meal on the patio, Pate—a member of Hunter's drug ring—dropped by. When Hunter introduced her as Joanna Wacker, Pate told him she was really Jacqueline Springfield, his old girlfriend from Dallas, and rumor had it she'd gone to work for the DEA.

Hunter flew into a wild rage and started slapping her around. She kicked him in the groin and ran into the house. He cornered her in the kitchen, grabbed a knife and stabbed her, and she passed out from shock. After wrapping her in garbage bags and encircling her body with duct tape, he had Pate open the trunk of his car whereupon he placed her inside.

Knowing where she lived Hunter drove his car and had Pate follow him to John's house in hers. When they got there Pate used her remote door opener to access the garage. Hunter drove his car inside and Pate, leaving the victim's parked in the drive, closed the overhead door after walking in. With Pate opening doors for him Hunter carried her to the living room. When he unwrapped her she began to regain consciousness so he punched her face until she once again passed out.

Tearing a pristine section from one of the garbage bags, Hunter used it as a glove, took John's knife from the drawer, and finished her off. Gathering up the plastic, he had Pate— whose hands were blood free—open the trunk of his car and close it once Hunter stashed it and the knife within. Lastly, Pate drove the victim's car into the garage and hit the close button before hurrying outside.

Hunter knew she'd moved in with her boyfriend and assured Pate he'd be blamed for the murder, so the defamed basketball star thought he was home free when the police arrested John after finding the knife Hunter planted in Mary Davis's alley.

But the wheels of justice had turned righteously. Gershon Pate and Joe Hunter would stand trial for the murder of Jacqueline Springfield.

The Juan Enez homicide got shifted to the jurisdiction of

the Federal Government. After it had been established that one of their own had not been killed by an angry lover but by the man she'd been investigating, the FBI and DEA swarmed the case. In his deposition Darius testified about what happened the day Enez had been murdered, and the investigators were convinced it was related to the secret investigation of Joe Hunter and his cohorts. The press got wind of it and though his second homicide case never went to trial, it didn't just make the local news like the first one had.

This one went national.

They were at Jock's house and the celebration liquor flowed freely. The Derby twins were half drunk and kept repeatedly thanking and hugging him and giving him high fives. Also in attendance besides himself and Ricca were Holly, decked out in a dazzling black dress, Preston, Rusty Wurly, and none other than DEA Agent John Derby, whose real name Darius still didn't know.

"Shit, Homes, you did it just like we knew you would!" John slapped him on the back for the umpteenth time. "But I got to admit, I was pretty worried there for awhile."

"There was never a doubt," said Rusty, wearing his usual grin. "Man, you don't beat the keeper of the ring."

Jock squinted at Rusty. "What you talking about, white boy?"

"The ring, nigger. The one passed down from Cyrus the Great."

Jock's face brightened with recognition. "Oh yeah, I'd forgotten about that. Hey everybody, I want to propose a toast!" He held his glass high. "Here's to Darius Darkfire Esquire, the keeper of the ring!"

After everyone except Darius downed a sip of booze in response, Holly—champagne glass in hand—gave him a quizzical look. "What is he talking about?"

He wanted to kill Rusty for bringing it up. Holly didn't need to hear about that stupid legend. "It's nothing, really."

Ricca, knowing every detail because his mother had embarrassed the hell out of him by telling his then new secretary all about it, proudly said, "I'll tell you, dear. Darius was given a ring that was passed down from Cyrus the Great, the ancient ruler of Persia who allowed the Jews to return to their homeland and rebuild Jerusalem. The ring must stay in Darius's family until Shiloh comes down from the sky and puts it on."

Holly giggled and took a sip of champagne.

Fiercely irritated, Darius hissed a scornful sigh. "Thanks a lot, Ricca."

His secretary—who at the moment he'd like to see standing before a firing squad alongside Rusty—gave him a teasing smile. "Don't mention it, Boss."

Preston left the company of DEA John Derby and walked over to him. "I couldn't help overhearing. I've heard of this legend. So you're the keeper of the ring."

"You have?" Preston's statement absolutely flabbergasted him. He had no idea anyone outside his eccentric maternal family and his circle of friends knew about it.

"Yes. It was during my military days. An old Iranian who only spoke Farsi conveyed it to me. An aide translated for me."

"What's Farsi?" asked Holly.

"A language."

"Well I gathered that, Preston."

"It's modern Persian. My mother speaks it fluently," said Darius, still ticked and embarrassed but very impressed to learn someone outside his family knew about the legend.

Preston pulled off his glasses and rubbed the spot on the bridge of his nose where they'd been resting. "Which side of your family goes back to Cyrus?"

"My mother's allegedly."

"You sound skeptical . . ." he put the spectacles back on. "So you don't believe it really does?"

"I can't say one way or the other, but my mom believes it

does, and to appease her I accepted the ring. Did that old man tell you about the ceremony?"

The investigator nodded. "Every seventy years the ring must be given to the oldest child of whoever has it at the time. When did you receive it?"

"June first of ninety-nine."

"I'd love to see it. Would you describe it to me please?"

"Just a plain gold band with an engraved signet."

A knowing grin appeared. "You've never worn it of course."

"No."

Looking intrigued as much as confused Holly gasped, "Well why not?"

"Because only Shiloh can wear it," Preston answered for him.

"So they say . . ." he sipped his drink and glanced across the room towards the twins who were engaging John Derby in conversation.

Holly grimaced. "I couldn't stand having a ring I could never wear."

"Neither could I," said Ricca.

Preston favored Holly with one of his cerebral smiles. "According to the legend, even Cyrus never wore it."

Her eyes flared with incredulity. "So that ring has never been worn by anyone?"

Irritation at Rusty for bringing up the damn thing escalating, he heaved an exaggerated sigh to show it. "It's not supposed to have been."

"So whoever owns the ring can't lose at anything, right?"

"No, that's not part of the legend, Holly. Rusty was just popping off."

"It's certainly a part of the legend I heard," said Preston, brows raised above the silver rim of his lenses. "I was told the possessor of the ring couldn't be bested at anything."

Rusty coughed and emitted a nervous laugh. "Hey, how about that? Didn't know I knew more about the ring than you."

Intense curiosity danced in Holly's pale-blue orbs. Afraid she was starting to buy into it, Darius winked at her to signify he didn't. "He's only joking."

An odd look came over Rusty—he almost appeared fearful. "Yeah, I was just mouthing because I don't remember you ever losing at anything, Dare."

Holly lit up with a smile. "Dare? How cute, he calls you Dare."

"It's my nickname . . ." he turned towards Rusty, wondering why his old friend seemed so nervous.

Wearing a grin that appeared forced, Rusty pulled a quarter from his pocket. "Let's test it, shall we? Call it."

He flipped the coin in the air.

"Hey, you didn't call it!" barked Holly. She picked up the quarter and tossed it. "Call it this time."

Darius shook his head. "You guys are retards. Think I'll freshen my drink . . . ."

The DEA John Derby was mixing a highball when Darius got to the bar. "When are you heading back to Dallas?"

"Tomorrow."

Mouth slightly ajar, exposing his gold tooth, the agent eyed him thoughtfully. "I like you, Darkfire. You're a man after my own heart."

He grinned. "Does that mean I can finally talk you into answering my question?"

"What question is that?"

"The one about the FBI agents."

"You mean their gender?"

"Yeah."

"The assholes are two dudes."

"Thought so . . ." he stiffened his drink with a shot of bourbon. "And your real name?"

"Don't press, Darkfire. I don't like you that much."

Darius chuckled and held his drink up to him. "Here's to

truth, justice, and the American way."

Derby clicked the glass with his own. "And to Lois Lane."

"You were wrong you know, about it not being anyone you and Jacqueline were investigating."

He nodded with a frown of concern. "I know. I'm lucky my cover wasn't blown. There's a lot I know now that I didn't then. I can't divulge it, you understand, but I will tell you the murder of Juan Enez is connected to it. You were slated for assassination if the trial seemed headed for an acquittal. Good thing it never got that far. That's all I can say on the matter."

A frightful chill raced through him. Darius wanted to dig further but knowing the agent wouldn't divulge anything, he held his peace.

John the civilian walked up with his twin and draped an arm around him. "Whatever the bill winds up coming to, I want you to double it, Dare."

"Double it? Hell, I'd triple it," the agent John laughed out.

Jock grinned at his brother. "Why stop there? Let's quadruple it."

Darius forced a laugh, hoping it concealed the disconcerting emotion of learning he'd been marked for death and had apparently avoided the grim reaper only because the case never went to trial. "Why stop there? I'll just quintuple it."

John smacked him between the shoulder blades. "You'd damn sure be worth it, Homes."

Rusty and Preston ambled to the bar. The investigator helped himself to some scotch. "I'm going to allow myself one more cocktail."

A grateful smile rose on John's face. "Dare told me he couldn't have done it without you, Preston. Just want to thank you again. Thank you so much."

Darius grinned at his liberated homey. It felt so good to see him looking like his old cocky self again. "His bill will be thanks enough, I'm sure."

Preston tipped his glass towards John, took a pull from it,

and focused on Darius. Peering through the shiny lenses, he narrowed his eyes as his face became gravely serious. "I have a proposition for you, Darius. With the growing publicity this case has generated, you're bound to be inundated with wealthy clients who find themselves in situations similar to John's. If you'll promise to use me exclusively for all your investigative needs, I'll forgo my fee on this case, but only if you'll do me one small favor."

He was elated for John's sake, and flattered the commander thought such a lucrative future lay ahead for him. Not bothering to explain he'd already planned to use him any time he encountered a situation requiring a superior investigator, he put a hand on Preston's shoulder and said, "Name it."

"I want to see that ring . . . ."

* * * *

They had breakfast at the café and now it was time for them to drive back to Dallas. Ricca and Rusty, who'd flown down for John's celebration party, waited in his car while he said goodbye to Holly on the sidewalk.

"I'm going to miss you, Darius."

"Let's keep in touch, okay . . .?" he pulled her to him in a warm embrace.

"Sure." She squeezed him tight before looking up at him with glistening eyes that pled for a kiss.

Last night hadn't been a real date because they'd never managed to get off by themselves like he'd planned before learning she had to be at work by five to handle the early breakfast run. Unable to leave the party without offending the Derby's, he'd given her fifty dollars for cab fare and sent her home. She'd tried to talk him out of it, saying she could go a night without sleep, but he'd insisted. Her face had been a weepy portrait of extreme disappointment when he'd walked her to the taxi. "I wish I hadn't told you I had to be at work so early!" she'd angrily asserted. "Please don't make me go home!"

Fearing she'd never relent if he were to give her a goodnight kiss, he'd refrained. Now things were different. He lowered his face to hers and the moment he tasted her sweet lips she thrust her tongue against his, moaning in the process. It took all his resolve to keep both hands on her back instead of latching onto one of her full breasts. Soon the urge became overwhelming so he yanked his mouth from hers and sucked in a deep breath. "Holly, I didn't mean for our first kiss to take place on the sidewalk in broad daylight. The next time we kiss it'll be in a much more romantic setting, I promise."

Tears forming, her lower lip started quivering. "Just make sure there is a next time, will ya?"

"I promise." Unable to resist, he kissed her once more.

EIGHT

He knew Robert Edison had only been teasing about being owed dinner for handling Branch for him but Darius wanted to show his appreciation anyway. Suzette—a stunning blonde with a razor-sharp wit—sat beside her husband across from Ricca and him in a pricey Dallas restaurant. Also an attorney, she'd finally agreed to marry Robert three months ago after repeatedly turning him down during a two year courtship. He'd wanted her to practice with him and call their office Edison and Edison, but she wouldn't leave her job at the district attorney's office where she had her cap set on becoming Chief Assistant DA. The man currently holding the position would be retiring soon and the way things stood, she'd be chosen to fill his slot.

She'd just told a risqué joke and when the laughter ebbed, Robert smiled at him. "You'll be needing a swankier office now that you're famous. Guess I won't be getting any more of your leftovers."

"I like it fine where I'm at."

Suzette took a sip of wine and sat the glass beside a plate of Brasato Al Barolo. "Ricca might like a nicer place though, huh, Ricca."

"I sure would, and a raise as well." Ricca turned to him and winked.

"Hey, I buy you dinner on occasion don't I . . ." he patted her on the back. "Don't be so greedy."

"How sharper than a serpent's tooth is an ungrateful secretary," said Robert, twirling spaghetti around his fork.

"I used to like you," Ricca chided.

Robert laughed and motioned at him with the pasta-laden utensil. "You really did an amazing job, Darius. Maybe you should specialize in homicides."

"He never had to go to court," spouted Suzette, eyeing him though speaking to Robert. "If he ever gets a homicide that I'm prosecuting, I'll own his butt."

Darius winked at her. "I don't doubt that for a minute. Anyway, Robert, thanks again for handling Branch for me."

Suzette brought a forkful of braised beef to her mouth, cut her eyes to her husband, and said while chewing, "Refresh my memory on the Branch case, hon."

"Cal Branch is a bank security guard who was accused of rigging the monitoring equipment so it wouldn't work properly which made it look like he was planning to rob the place. He was merely trying to fix a malfunction and his effort to do so resulted in a bigger glitch which affected all the security monitors. Darius had already done the work. Branch had managed to fix such errors in the past, a fact which several credible witnesses attested to. This particular attempt just somehow went awry. The man was innocent, though a malcontent fellow worker had convinced Branch's superiors otherwise. All I did was follow the game plan Darius had outlined. I don't know if I've ever told you, but he's never lost a court battle. He's batting a perfect thousand."

Sparks seem to fly out of Suzette's sexy green eyes. "He better hope we're never in the same courtroom or that record will be shattered."

She seemed serious which made him wonder if she was jealous for her husband's sake. Though a good lawyer, Robert had lost his share of cases as had most defense attorneys. He didn't like what the expression on her face conveyed when she mentioned shattering his record, and the tone in her voice sounded like she'd thrown down a gauntlet which stirred the fighter in him—he never backed down from a fight of any kind. But for Robert's sake he faked an air of being impressed. "I take it you've never lost a case either."

A menacing look of steely confidence saturated her striking visage. "Nor will I. Ever."

Not sure what to say—or if anything should be said—Darius gulped a mouthful of beer and went back to work on his steak.

* * * *

"Suzette's pretty competitive isn't she," said Ricca as he drove her home from the restaurant.

"That's putting it mildly." Darius glanced at his secretary. He could tell she was also wondering what motivated the prosecutor. "I hope I don't wind up in the same courtroom with her someday."

"Me too."

"You think she resents me?"

"Not losing? Suzette can be a bitch at times, but I can't believe she resents your track record. I could understand it if you'd achieved one of your victories at her expense, but since that's not the case—"

"No, I mean because of Robert."

"Oh . . . maybe. Since she's never lost she may have a modicum of disrespect for Robert because he has. If she does have a lack of respect for him, maybe it makes her resent your success."

He nodded, that seemed plausible. "She's certainly confident she'll never lose, isn't she."

From the corner of his eye he saw Ricca don a teasing grin. "Maybe she has a ring of her own passed down through the ages from Cleopatra or something."

"Maybe so," he chuckled.

"Preston Coolidge is such an interesting man. Isn't it weird that he's the only person you've ever met who's heard the story of that ring? And of all the investigators you could have chosen, you picked him."

"It *was* quite a coincidence. Add to that the fact I wouldn't have ran across him if I hadn't tried Juan Enez first. If Enez doesn't get murdered, and if Preston's brother-in-law doesn't get sent to the scene, then we don't meet."

"That really is quite a legend."

He squinted at her. "Don't tell me you're starting to believe it?"

All he got for an answer was a closed-mouth smile.

"You haven't mentioned it to Suzette have you?"

"Believe or not, your highness, we have better things to talk about than you. Though she did ask me once if we were secretly lovers."

"So what did you say?"

"I told her 'Hell yeah we are!' what else? Seriously, I told her I wasn't into incest—that you and I were more like brother and sister than any real pair of siblings on earth."

A short laugh escaped him. Truer words had never been spoken. Ricca had never married and during the six years he'd known her she'd dated sporadically but never had a steady boyfriend because, according to her, "I've yet to meet the man who measures up to my standards." She turned thirty-two on her last birthday and he knew she was beginning to fear Mister Right might never cross her path.

They met the day she applied for her current job. Several applicants preceded her and he was about to make a choice between two that were equally qualified and had exemplary employment histories. After agonizing over the two choices he finally decided to flip a coin. He'd stuck his hand in his pocket to fetch one when a pretty dark-eyed blonde walked in, asking if the position had been filled. He started to tell her it had, but something came over him—something he still couldn't define to this day—and he asked to see her resume instead. After she handed it to him, he told her there were two applicants he was already considering, but he'd look hers over and make a decision within a few days. He knew before she walked out of his office that if her qualifications were commensurate with the other two, he'd choose her. They were, so he did, and in practically no time they became the best of friends.

His own love life had been about as void as Ricca's. He hadn't had a girlfriend since Avery Buntzinghammer dumped him for Marcus Laxx back in college. Not counting escorting Holly to John's celebration party at Jock's house, it had been almost a year since he'd taken a girl out.

The last date had been a disaster. Her name was Britt and she'd mindlessly jabbered non-stop throughout the dinner, the movie, and the drive home. The evening had come to a merciful end when he refused an offer to come inside for a nightcap after walking her to her door.

Britt was a friend of Ricca's and she'd dropped by the office one day to say hi to her. He'd felt a twinge of lust when Ricca introduced the leggy brunette. After she left he quizzed Ricca about her and wound up asking her out despite a stern warning from his secretary they had nothing in common. Apparently interested in only herself, she'd seemed incapable of participating in conversation about any other subject.

The girl before Britt had been interesting and engaging as well as attractive. During their dinner conversation he'd been in the process of plotting a scheme to manipulate his way into her bedroom, but the plot fizzled when she'd let it slip that her ex husband had given her genital herpes.

After dropping Ricca off at her apartment he thought about Holly, wondering what the aspiring prosecutor was doing at the moment. He decided to give her a call when he got home.

* * * *

"Oh my god, you actually called me!" Holly squealed excitedly when he identified himself.

"I was hoping you wouldn't be at class."

"I just got home as a matter of fact. I just can't believe you called. How are you?"

"Fine. How about yourself?"

"Missing you horribly, that's how I am."

That brought a smile to his face. "Me too. I know we haven't known each other very long, and haven't even gone out on a proper date yet, but I was wondering—if I pay your airfare would you like to spend the weekend with me? I have a nice comfortable bed in my guest room." He spoke the last with nervous haste.

"Oh I'd love to, Darius!"

"Great. I'll have Ricca make the arrangements first thing tomorrow morning and she'll give you a call."

"You have my work number, right?"

"Yeah, but I forgot to get your cell number."

"I don't have one. Have her call me there if I'm not at home . . . ."

* * * *

Ricca arranged Holly's flight and had just passed on the information to him through the intercom.

"Good. Give her a call and fill her in."

"I will not." Ricca sounded indignant.

"Why not?"

"You really don't know women, do you."

He frowned. "I don't recall ever claiming I did."

"Well trust me. You need to call her."

"Why? I told her I'd have you call after you got her flight booked."

Expecting an immediate rebuttal, instead he heard someone enter the front office before a dead silence indicated Ricca had taken her finger off the button. A few seconds later the intercom buzzed and Ricca said, *"Rickshaw Rollins would like to speak to you."*

In spite of the fact he knew the man would hear him say it, Darius blurted out, *"The* Rickshaw Rollins?"

"Yes . . ." the word came out through a nervous laugh.

"Well send him in!"

Preston Coolidge had predicted he'd be approached by this type of clientele. Renowned oil tycoon Rickshaw Rollins was a legend in Texas. Born and raised in abject poverty in a small town in south Texas, he started working in the oil field when he was a sixteen-year-old greenhorn with nothing going for him but a strong back, a quick mind, and an insatiable hunger to succeed.

The Texas billionaire had a forty-year-old son who was also a legend but not for the same reasons as Rickshaw. Ernest Rollins, a mere figurehead as one of Rickshaw's vice presidents, had been married to five different movie stars, and his current wife Mona—wife number six—happened to be the sister of wife number five. Her maiden name was Clary which her sister Monique still went by.

Monique Clary had graced the pages of Playboy, won Playmate of the Year, and parlayed it into a successful movie career. Unlike many that had traveled to Hollywood via that route, Monique could act. Three years ago she'd been nominated for an Oscar around the same time that Ernest, the only man she had ever married, developed a yen for her younger sister and filed for divorce.

When Ricca brought the big Texan into his office, Darius gushed like a prepubescent cowboy back in the fifties getting to shake hands with Roy Rogers. "It's a real honor to meet you, sir!"

The vice-like grip of the seventy-year-old surprised him. Rickshaw withdrew his hand after a hearty shake and removed his cowboy hat. "Mister Darkfire, it's plain obvious to me you know who I am. Would you also like to know why I'm here?"

"Yes, sir . . ." he nervously pointed at two armchairs facing his desk. "Won't you please have a seat?"

"I assume you've heard the news," said the billionaire while settling into one.

Darius shrugged. "Guess I haven't."

"You must not have watched any TV or listened to any radio this morning then. My boy Ernest has been accused of killing Monique Clary. She used to be my daughter-in-law but Ernest has got one of those wandering dicks that does most of his thinking for him. He quit her and married her sister. Now he's about as useless as a man's nipple but this kind of thing just ain't in him. I know he didn't kill that woman. I heard tale you saved your friend's butt down in Houston for something similar, and I want you to get my boy off no matter how much it costs."

The bizarre coincidence momentarily stupefied him. Monique Clary had starred in the movie he'd taken Ricca's mouthy friend Britt to the last time he'd gone out on a date. He cleared his throat and looked at the big man. "Mister Rollins, I will only represent your son if I believe he's innocent, and I'll have to talk to him in person to determine that."

Rollins frowned, causing dozens of tiny wrinkles on his rugged face to deepen. "I guarantee you he didn't do it."

Darius steadied his eyes on the big Texan's. "I'm sorry, but I'm going to have to satisfy myself on that."

"So that's your last word on the matter?"

"Yes, sir."

He looked around the room, apparently evaluating the caliber of it and the furniture within. "Looks to me like you could use the money, this place don't look like no successful lawyer's office I've ever seen. How much you charge anyway?"

"Two hundred dollars an hour plus expenses."

A hoarse laugh bellowed from the tycoon. "Why shit, that's chicken feed. What if I was to offer you five hundred an hour, would you rethink your position then?"

"Mister Rollins, I won't alter my position even if you offer me a million dollars an hour."

Rollins cocked his head, eyeballing him closely. The

expression on his face lay somewhere between a frown and a grin. "A lawyer with a conscience. I didn't know they came in that flavor. All right. Let's go see my boy so you can make up your mind."

If he'd been asked to represent Rickshaw rather than his son, Darius wouldn't have hesitated taking the case, for he knew the rich Texan was a man of integrity. He briefed Ricca on what he'd just been told, reminded her to call Holly, and then followed the renowned Rickshaw Rollins through the door.

* * * *

Ernest Rollins was a slightly smaller version of his father, but his facial features were softer than Rickshaw's sculpted nose, jutting chin, and fearless eyes that appeared to be set on a facade of granite. Pete Halifax, Rickshaw's personal attorney, had successfully kept the billionaire's son out of jail but had to post a million-dollar bond to do it. In addition Ernest also had to surrender his passport. The press had been haunting his estate since the story broke so they met at Halifax's office. They'd just been introduced and Darius took a seat across from Ernest who sat on a sofa beside his father.

Pete Halifax was at his desk.

Rickshaw had told him what happened on the drive over. Some time during the night Monique Clary had been shot in the face with a shotgun, and this morning her body was found in a large water fountain adorning the front drive of Ernest Rollins' estate. A member of the maintenance crew discovered the corpse and called the police. Ernest, breakfasting at a private club, got a hysterical call from his wife notifying him of the tragedy. He drove straight home after hearing the news and by the time he got there the police had located a silver-and-gold plated shotgun wedged inside a hedgerow running alongside the drive that widened near the fountain before forming a large parking area in front of the mansion.

Mona had identified the weapon as one missing from a collection in a locked glass gun cabinet which hadn't been broken into, and Ernest had the only key. The police asked for permission to search the house and found a letter Monique had mailed to Ernest from Beverly Hills demanding twenty million dollars to keep her from telling Mona his *dirty little secret.* The letter went on to explain that she'd be in Dallas in three weeks to either receive the payment in cash or expose him to Mona. The postdate on the envelope was damning—it had been mailed three weeks ago yesterday.

Darius eyed the younger Rollins. "Your father has asked me to represent you, but I'll tell you the same thing I told him. I'll do so only if I believe you're innocent."

Ernest sneered at him and turned to his old man. "Get him out of here."

"Shut the fuck up, Ernest!" Rickshaw's tone of voice startled everyone, especially his son. "Excuse his lack of manners, Darkfire. Ernest, tell him what you told me, and do it in a civil tone."

The spoiled brat of a man gaped at Rickshaw like the older Rollins must have lost his mind. "Hell, Dad, this son-of-a-bitch is just a kid. Look how young he is."

Rising to his feet, Darius unbuttoned his jacket. "Would you like a piece of this kid, Mister Rollins?"

"Huh?"

"You heard me." He tossed the jacket over the chair and started loosening his tie.

Ernest frowned with confusion. "What the fuck?"

Unclasping his cufflinks, Darius put them in the right front pocket of his pants and rolled up his sleeves.

"What the fuck are you doing?" said Ernest from a face turned pale.

"Get up and take your best shot. We'll see who the kid is here."

"You can't talk to me like that, you son-of-a-bitch."

Darius donned a wry smile, put a hand on each hip, and looked down at him.

Ernest jerked his head towards his father who was grinning, obviously pleased that his son would have to put up or shut up. "Daddy, get him out of here. You heard him threaten me."

"I didn't hear a fucking thing. Did you, Pete?"

"I hear what you hear, Rickshaw," said Pete Halifax obsequiously.

Rickshaw's grin turned sly. "Of course if ol' Ernest was to apologize, maybe things could cool down a bit. How about it, Darkfire? Is that a possibility?"

"I'm a reasonable man." Darius kept eyeballing Ernest as he answered the elder Rollins.

"Well apologize to the man, Ernest, so we can get this show on the road . . . ."

* * * *

Ricca was painting her nails when he got back to the office. Her face animated into a sunbeam of anticipation when she saw him.

"Well, are we rich yet?"

"May well be on the way to it," he answered with a wink. "We're taking on the State of Texas on behalf of Ernest Rollins at six hundred dollars an hour. Rickshaw insisted on tripling my fee."

"Eeew . . .!" she jumped to hear feet, wearing the biggest smile he'd ever seen on her pretty face. "So you're already on a first name basis, huh."

"Yes."

"Wow, that must have been some meeting. What prompted him to want to pay you triple?"

"I whipped his son . . . ."

NINE

The trial lasted six weeks and Ernest Rollins was acquitted. Long time Chief Assistant District Attorney Tory Plack, the man whose position Suzette Edison coveted, had lost to a lawyer working only his second homicide in court. Mona Rollins had been taken into custody because Darius proved she killed her sister and tried to frame her husband.

With the help of Preston Coolidge he discovered that Mona was in Los Angeles at the time the blackmail letter had been posted. Two of her friends testified she had an amazing talent for copying other people's writing styles, especially her sister's whom she'd always envied. When a handwriting expert said under oath that most likely Mona rather than Monique had written the letter, Darius knew by the look on each juror's face the battle had been won.

Holly had caught the flu and couldn't make the trip to Dallas that weekend he'd invited her, and he'd been too busy preparing Ernest Rollins' defense to offer a rain check. Now on a jet bound for Houston, he planned to surprise her and hoped to spend the weekend with her.

As he stared leftwards out the window, admiring the top of a fluffy cloudbank floating some thirty thousand feet above sea level, he thought back on the day he'd agreed to represent Ernest Rollins.

Having been challenged in front of his father—who'd called him a pussy when he'd neither apologize nor fight—Ernest had flown off the couch and dove at Darius.

Darius sidestepped him which sent Ernest sprawling on the floor. When he got back on his feet, Ernest doubled up his fists and growled, "I'm gonna teach you a lesson you ain't never gonna forget, you son-of-a-bitch!"

He swung. Darius ducked, jabbed a rocket left into the

spoiled Rollins' gullet, and sent Ernest crumpling to the floor with a right cross to the face. Several minutes later he woke up with a new attitude, finally willing to cooperate and tell his side of the story.

Mona had always been extremely jealous of Monique, and her marriage was about to end because Ernest had found another actress he wanted. More than once Mona had warned that if she couldn't have him, no one could.

"Hell, she was planning on killing two birds with one stone," Ernest had contended, "get rid of the sister she hated and put my ass either on death row or behind bars for life where I'd never be able to touch another woman again."

When Ernest said he'd told Mona he wanted a divorce only days before the postdate on the blackmail letter, Darius hadn't needed any further convincing that he was telling the truth.

"Okay, Ernest, I'm your man," he'd said. "Sorry I had to kick your ass to get you to tell me all this."

"Hell, I'm not!" the elder Rollins had bellowed with joyful pride. "He may not have won the fight but did you see how he went after you, Darkfire?"

"I did indeed, sir."

"Ernest ain't a pussy after all, and that makes a daddy real proud. You're on my payroll as of now. You said two hundred an hour as I recollect."

"Yes, sir."

"Well make it six hundred plus whatever other tabs you have to run up . . . ."

Darius turned his head from the window and saw a brunette walking down the aisle, apparently heading for the restroom. Something stirred. Her eyes were hidden behind a pair of dark shades but she was fabulously built and dressed to advertise it. As she passed by the two empty seats to his right, the corners of her mouth turned up slightly in a perceptive smile. Resisting the urge to look back after she walked past, he eagerly waited for her to return, anxious to get a good look at her from behind when she retook her seat.

He'd planned to rent a car after he landed and surprise Holly, but now a pang of guilt swept over him. If the brunette was single and he could strike up a conversation, Holly might never know he'd made this trip unless Houston wasn't the beauty's destination or he failed to win her over.

Looking towards the front of the plane he spied an empty seat to the right of the aisle six rows ahead and hoped that's where she'd been sitting. A few minutes later he received two pleasures—a good look at her derriere as she walked past, and a wondrous profile view as she took the seat. Preparing to approach her, he tried to think of some clever introductory remark but she looked back at him, pointed at the empty seats, and silently mouthed, "May I?"

Hoping his face didn't betray his eagerness, he nodded. She got up and walked towards him, removing her sunglasses in the process. His throat went dry. On a scale of one to ten the woman was a twenty.

She seated herself on the aisle, leaving an empty seat between them, and turned towards him. "Hi, I'm Robyn Tuscany. That's Robyn with a Y."

Her dark eyes so extremely captivated him it took a moment before he realized he hadn't introduced himself. He offered his hand and started to proceed but she spoke instead while shaking it.

"I know who you are: you're Darius Darkfire. I've seen you on the news."

He released her hand and finally found his tongue. "Rollins or Derby?"

"Actually I first saw you when you defended that farmer who ran over the judge." She adjusted her seat back a bit and made herself comfortable.

"You must live in the Dallas area then."

"Yeah, Fort Worth."

Her perfume was sensuously titillating, and like her velvet

voice, perfectly accessorized her beauty which held him spellbound. The woman didn't appear to have a single flaw. He nervously cleared his throat and began his approach. "Are you getting off at Houston or heading somewhere else after we land?"

Still leaning against the headrest, she turned her face towards him. "I'm going to Houston to visit my cousin. And you?"

"Planned on surprising a friend."

"In Houston?"

"Yeah."

She put her sunglasses back on and faced forward. "If your friend's not expecting you, who's picking you up at the airport? Or are you just going to call them from there?"

"Planned to rent a car."

"My cousin will be waiting for me. I'm sure she wouldn't mind driving you to your friend's place if you want to blow off the rental."

He'd fixated on her sensuous mouth as she spoke. Everything about her tantalized him—he'd never felt so irresistibly drawn to a woman before. "Um, why don't I just take you and your cousin out for dinner instead? With your cousin chauffeuring of course."

Lips spreading into a sultry smile, she turned her head again. "In that case, why don't you go ahead and rent a car and I'll blow off my cousin?"

Whatever had stirred his insides initially, now made them whirl like a tornado. "Sounds like a plan to me. Hope your cousin won't be offended."

"She's a very understanding soul."

"I on the other hand don't have to worry since Holly doesn't know I'm coming." He cringed over the slip up of revealing his friend was a woman.

"No way! That's my cousin's name."

The shocked expression scrambling her features made the

goddess appear momentarily mortal which bolstered his confidence and elicited a grin. "What a coincidence."

"That *is* quite a coincidence."

"My Holly's last name is Hepburn."

Her jaw dropped. "No! That's my cousin—Holly Hepburn is my cousin!"

Covering his mouth to muzzle a nerve-induced cough, he kept his hand there while muttering, "Pretty, blondish brown hair, pale-blue eyes, studying to be a lawyer, works as a waitress?"

"That's her."

His heart sank. Once Holly knew he'd tried to hit on her cousin she'd no doubt write him off, and Robyn would have no choice but to do likewise out of family loyalty. Feeling like the greedy dog that lost his bone trying to steal its reflection in the water, he slumped in his seat. "Well, Robyn-with-a-Y Tuscany, it was fun while it lasted."

"What do you mean . . .?" she sat upright and jerked off her shades. "Holly's just a friend, right? You're not an item or anything are you?"

"You two must not be close."

"Why do you say that?"

"Because I think she would have told you about me. We met when I was in Houston working on the Derby case."

Her dark eyes squinted with a reproving frown. "Well she didn't, and for your information we are very close."

Realizing how arrogant he must have sounded, he vented a sigh, inwardly rebuffing himself for being so egotistical. "She and I were on the way to becoming close, but I had to get back to Dallas. That kind of threw a monkey wrench into the mix. I invited her up for a weekend but she caught the flu and couldn't make it, then I got wrapped up in the Rollins case."

She perused him warily, still frowning. "Well you must not feel very close to her now or you wouldn't have asked me out."

"Like I said, we were on the way to becoming close. There's

no commitment between us or anything. Since Holly's picking you up, why don't we go back to my original offer of me treating both of you to dinner? If Holly will still speak to me that is . . . ."

* * * *

Though Holly Hepburn had most of the physical attributes he'd described to Robyn, much to his relief the woman he met at the airport wasn't the Holly he knew. She was taller, not as pretty as the one he'd met at the café, had dark brown hair with blonde streaks that obviously weren't natural, and her eyes were gray rather than pale blue. Robyn tactfully explained to her that she wanted to get to know her new friend a little better. The two cousins said their goodbyes and he rented a car.

After her cousin left they had a good laugh about the mix up. He learned her Holly Hepburn worked as a waitress in a nightclub rather than a café, and though she aspired to be a lawyer like the one he knew, she planned to go into the tax field when the Esquire became attached to her name.

They toured Houston in a rented Lincoln until well past five o'clock. Darius wanted to find a place to eat. They'd been making small talk since leaving the airport, and he'd just asked her to tell him about herself.

"I grew up in Abilene. After I finished high school I moved to Fort Worth to attend college, and went to work for Lockheed after earning my degree."

"Where did you go to college?"

"TCU."

"Texas Christian Horned Frog, huh. I'm an SMU Mustang myself."

"Where did you go to law school?"

"Same place. Anyway, continue."

"Well, like I said, I went to work for Lockheed and have

been there ever since."

He guided the rental through a green light at a busy intersection. "So what do you do there?"

"Engineer."

"Sounds interesting."

"Oh yes, very much so. It's a great company."

"Yeah, great reputation. Got a friend who works there. It's been a long time since I've seen him. Can't remember what he does there."

"What's his name?"

"Eval Santa Anna."

"I know him!" she gushed with an ironic smile. "He works in finances. How long have you known him?"

"Since high school."

"He's a character," she said with a laugh.

"Well in that case he hasn't changed all that much since I knew him. He was a real character back then too. Did you ever meet his brother Caruso?"

"No."

"He decided on a career in the military and got killed in Iraq."

Her buoyant demeanor evaporated. A moody pout clouded her face as she meekly uttered, "How sad."

"Yeah . . ." he turned to her and smiled, not wanting the conversation to continue in that direction. "So you're an engineer. Electrical, mechanical, what?"

"Structural and electrical." She'd brightened a little, but seemed distracted, as if still reflecting on the death of a coworker's brother. "Enough about me, let's talk about you. What made you choose the law?"

Despite fearing she might find his answer hokey, he said it anyway. "Justice."

"And you're a defense lawyer?" she laughed out.

"Sounds like an oxymoron, doesn't it."

"In the times we live in it sure does, sad to say. Okay, justice got you interested in the law, then what?"

"What do you mean?"

"I mean, do you plan to go on into politics so you can fight for justice or what?"

Her explanation irritated him. "What makes you think I'm not fighting for justice now?"

She laughed again. "You're a defense lawyer, aren't you?"

"Yeah, but I don't take on clients unless I firmly believe them to be innocent."

"Hey look, there's the astrodome . . .!" she pointed towards the massive edifice.

He gave it a quick glance, then returned his attention to the road. "You've never seen the astrodome before?"

"Oh sure, but I didn't want you to miss it if you hadn't."

After they passed the domed stadium she turned to him with a grin. "You must have made a fortune off Ernest Rollins, huh?"

"No."

"You're kidding?"

"Nope."

"I can't believe you didn't make a lot of money off that case."

Darius pulled to a stop at a red light. "Now I didn't say that."

"Then I must have been right in the first place."

"No."

She grunted. "Oh quit talking in circles. Did you make a lot of money or not?"

"Yes, I did."

"Then you lied."

"Nope."

"Uuugggggghhh!"

A cute pout of frustration accompanied her groan and he couldn't help but laugh. "I made a lot of money but not from Ernest Rollins."

"Rickshaw Rollins paid the tab?"

He nodded and stepped on the gas as the light turned green.

"Why didn't you say so in the first place?"

Spotting a seafood restaurant that looked promising, he pulled into the parking lot. "You didn't ask . . . ."

They ate their fill of crab legs, oysters, shrimp, clams, hushpuppies, fries, and coleslaw, then got back on the road in search of a suitable nightclub.

When he saw Baker's Dozen he turned to her. "I've heard of this place. Ever been here?"

"No, but it looks fine to me . . . ."

Several hours, drinks, and dances later, he asked if she was ready for him to take her to her cousin's house. They were slow dancing and she had her arms around his neck.

She looked up at him with a smile. "And what are you going to do?"

"Find a motel and crash for the night."

"Mind if I join you?"

* * * *

Ricca gave him a big grin when he walked into the office Monday morning. "Boy, you sure look chipper. You and Holly must have had a ball."

Darius grinned back. "Ricca, I had a fantastic weekend, but not with Holly. Call a florist and have them send a dozen red roses to Lockheed, and instruct them to tell the powers that be they're for Robyn-with-a-Y Tuscany who works in engineering. Structural and electrical engineering if they need further instructions."

"Wow . . ." her brows flew up and her mouth gaped open.

"Ricca, I think I'm in love."

She snapped her lips closed and pursed them with a frown. "It's been a long time for you. Don't let a passionate weekend mean more than it's supposed to."

"I'm not stupid."

"When it comes to the opposite sex, all men are stupid."

Grinning again, he shot her the bird and walked into his office, leaving her laughing, but only after she'd given him the finger in return. Not bothering to close the door he plopped down at his desk, swirled around in his chair several times, then hit the intercom.

"After you call the florist start looking for a bigger office for us."

"You mean it, Boss?" Her voice soared with elation.

"I sure do." He leaned back, smiled at the ceiling, started singing The Jefferson's theme song *Movin' On Up*, and burst out laughing when Ricca joined in, doing a great impersonation of Ja'net Dubois.

* * * *

Throughout the rest of the day he'd been nervous and fidgety. There hadn't been a doubt in his mind Robyn would call about the flowers but she never did. Having different schedules for their return flights they hadn't flown back from Houston together, and he wished he'd gotten her number instead of just handing her his business card. He couldn't find her in the Fort Worth phone book and wouldn't be able to catch her at Lockheed because the work day had ended. If she didn't call, his only recourse would be to track her down at work tomorrow.

He called information, asking for all the listings for Holly Hepburn in the Houston area, hoping to get Robyn's phone number. The only one he didn't call was the number belonging to the Holly he knew. None of them were Robyn's cousin. He'd fully expected her to call even if he hadn't sent flowers, so the fact that he had, made her lack of contact all the more perplexing. Walking the floors of his lonely living room he let out a bitter sigh. It was going to be a long night.

* * * *

After he got to the office Tuesday morning he had Ricca track down Robyn at Lockheed, and she'd just buzzed him. He politely thanked her, and when she asked, told her no, he didn't want to talk about it.

Ricca's words echoed in his mind as he sat staring blankly into space. "Darius, I really hate to tell you this but there is no Robyn Tuscany working for Lockheed."

The woman he thought he'd fallen in love with was apparently some sort of loon. Why had she made up that crap? What possible purpose could it serve her? She'd come on to him, not the other way around, so it couldn't have been a protective tactic. Most women played some sort of funky head game during the initial stages of a courtship, but not to this extreme. If she didn't want to see him again, all she had to do was say so and she knew it—why the farce? The intercom pulled him away from his dark musing.

"Yes?"

"Thought you might be interested to know there's a Robyn Tuscany on the line."

He cut Ricca off and immediately grabbed the phone. "Hello?"

"Oh, Darius, the roses are beautiful! Thank you so much!"

Numbing disbelief gripped him like a vice. It took him a moment to collect himself as he wondered what the hell was going on. In the end he decided to play along for now. "Glad you like them. When did you get them?"

"Just now. Oh they're so beautiful!"

"So you're at work then?"

"Of course I am, silly. How else would I have gotten them?"

How else indeed, he thought. "Hmm . . . ."

"Is something the matter?"

"Well . . . I sent them yesterday."

Without missing a beat, sounding as innocent as a baby cooing she said, *"Well that may be, but I only got them just now. You are so thoughtful. How did you know red roses are my favorite flowers?"*

"I didn't."

"Just a lucky guess then, huh?"

"Afraid so. Glad you like them though."

"Oh I love them!"

"Good. Excuse me a minute." He covered the mouthpiece so she couldn't hear, and buzzed Ricca.

"Yeah, Boss?"

"Got that number in the ID?"

"Yeah."

"Don't delete it."

"Okay . . . ."

"Sorry about that, Robyn. Listen, I've got the morning free, why don't I drop by and see you at work? I'd love to nose around Lockheed."

"Did you say Lockheed as in L-O-C-K-H-E-E-D?"

"Yeah."

"Well nose around all you want but you won't find me there."

Dumbfounded, he jerked the receiver in front of his face, gapping at it incredulously. Slapping it back against his ear he said, "Why? That's where you told me you worked."

"No, silly."

"Robyn, what's going on here? You know damn well you said Lockheed."

"No. That may have been what you heard but I said Lochweed not Lockheed. That's L-O-C-H-W-E-E-D. Loch as in the Loch Ness Monster, Weed as in tumbleweed."

She was lying and he knew it, and the reason he did wasn't because he didn't think it possible he'd misunderstood Lockheed for Lochweed since they sounded similar. She'd said

Eval Santa Anna worked there, and he worked at Lockheed. He didn't say anything though. Strategy dictated he play along. "Okay . . . mind if I drop by and see you?"

Knowing she'd have to come up with a phony excuse as to why he couldn't, it came as a tremendous surprise to hear her say, *"Sure. How well do you know your way around Fort Worth . . .?"*

* * * *

Lochweed was a large plant located in the industrial section of Fort Worth with several buildings peppered around it, each having a large single letter identifying it. Robyn worked in building B. She was sitting at a large drafting table when he walked in, and hurriedly removed a pair of cat-eye glasses upon seeing him. Looking cute rather than sexy like she had over the weekend—hair pulled back in a pony tail and wearing an oversized long-sleeved shirt beneath baggy overalls—she had on very little makeup, no lipstick, and no jewelry.

Off to the right of the drafting table sat the roses amidst several open metal boxes containing colored inks, pens, and other types of drawing implements.

"See, I told you they were beautiful . . ." smiling brightly she pointed at the flowers. Then she got up and gave him a long kiss followed by a suffocating hug.

He broke free and held her at arms length. "Let's go see Eval Santa Anna."

Once again her lack of concern surprised him. He'd examined her eyes closely while saying the name, fully expecting to see at least a modicum of trepidation in them, but there was none.

With complete nonchalance she replied with a simple "Okay".

She led him from her building to one just like it labeled D.

Behind a glass wall sat a perky receptionist.

The young lady summoned a pleasant smile. "Hi, Robyn, what can I do for you?"

"Is Eval in his office?"

"Sure is."

"Is he busy?"

"Let me check." She pressed a button. "Mister Santa Anna, Robyn Tuscany's here to see you."

"Send her in."

Although it had been years since he'd heard it, there was no mistaking that voice, it belonged to his old buddy. Feeling very confused, he followed Robyn into the office and when Eval saw him he jumped up from his desk.

"Darius Darkfire! Of all the people in the world I least expected to see today, you'd be in the top ten!"

Before he could blink twice, Eval had him locked in a bear hug.

"How have you been, Eval?"

"Great, pachuco. I don't have to ask how the hell you've been, Mister Big Shot. Hell I see you on TV practically all the time these days."

Darius patted his old friend on the back. "It wasn't my idea, believe me. I didn't seek the publicity."

Eval stepped back and grabbed his shoulders. "Bet it ain't hurt your bank account none though, huh."

"This is true," he replied with a grin.

"So you actually met Mister Big Shot. Say, girl, how'd you hook up with this bum, anyway?"

Robyn smiled at him, then turned to Eval. "We met this weekend on a flight to Houston."

Though much relieved that Robyn hadn't lied to him about knowing Eval, he was still wrestling with confusion. "What are you doing here? The last I heard, you worked for Lockheed."

"I did for awhile, but then I came here."

"So that explains it."

Eval's face expanded into a frowning balloon. "What are you talking about?"

"He thought I said I worked for Lockheed rather than Lochweed," Robyn giggled to Eval before turning to him, eyes shining with gratification. "And he sent me flowers."

He shook his head with bewilderment. "Yeah, only I sent them to Lockheed yesterday. I wonder how the florist figured out to send them here?"

Slipping an arm around his waist, she looked up at him with a smile. "This type of thing probably happens all the time. I'm sure they'd much rather take the trouble to locate the right recipient rather than refund the money."

A warm feeling of joy rose up within him. His new love wasn't crazy after all, and *had* called when she got the flowers just as he thought she would. He didn't want to take a chance on any further mishaps. "Robyn, I need your phone number and home address. I don't want to have any more trouble locating you."

TEN

The day after he told Ricca to find a new office she located the perfect business suite for them. Three weeks passed before they got settled in.

Darius shelled out thousands of dollars to have it decorated and affluently furnished, including a new desk for Ricca. Being partial to his old one he didn't want to part with it, though he did allow himself the luxury of a posh leather chair. He'd also given her the money to update their computers, a task she'd recently completed. She wanted to use the system provided by their state of the art telephones for inner-office communication but he insisted on keeping the old intercom.

Three huge sprays of flowers covered Ricca's recently acquired desk, courtesy of his parents, Robert and Suzette, and Preston Coolidge. Each had arrived with cards of congratulations for their new accommodations. A silver paperweight adorned his old one. Shaped like a football it had the words *I said Lochweed not Lockheed, Dimwit!* engraved on it. Robyn had given it to him as an office warming gift, poking fun at his fear he'd fallen for a lunatic when Ricca had told him nobody named Robyn Tuscany worked at Lockheed.

A smile crossed his face, brought on by another item he'd spent some serious coin on which he hoped wouldn't have to be returned. Standing in front of Ricca's flower covered desk, he held out his hand. "What do you think? Will she like it?"

Ricca frowned. "That's not a very big rock."

"Hey, it's the thought that counts. Besides, it's very unique. Used to belong to none other than Cleopatra herself."

"Who told you that . . .?" she took it from his hand.

"The kid on the street corner I bought it from."

She threw it at him and laughed. "You got this from a box

of Cracker Jack."

"Would you like to see the real one?"

"Was Elvis sexy? Hell yeah I would!"

Reaching into his pocket he produced a diamond engagement ring and held it up for her inspection before handing it over.

Her lips puckered and a loud whistle shot through them. "Now that's more like it. Robyn is gonna turn inside out when she sees this . . . ."

* * * *

The setting was perfect. She'd invited him over for dinner and they were dining by candlelight. Sensuously attired in a form fitting lavender dress, Robyn looked ravishing. She was two different women he'd learned. As unconcerned about her appearance as the most casual tomboy while at work, she always dolled up after hours, transforming herself into a vision of beauty.

Tonight he'd ask her to be his for life, and if she accepted, he planned to introduce her to his parents. If she refused, he wouldn't have to hear his mother berate him over how stupidly he handled his love life, for she'd never know about it.

Robyn had prepared a delicious pot roast. He watched her enjoying it.

Noticing him staring, she squinted with concern. "Is something the matter?"

He gave her a silent smile.

"Don't do this to me, Darius. What is it?"

"You are so beautiful."

She scowled at him. "You know you make me nervous when you just stare at me without speaking."

"I can't help it. You make me speechless."

Her face softened into a blushing smile and she lowered

her eyes. "You're making me feel so self conscious. Please stop staring at me."

Hands folded beneath his chin, he continued taking in her beauty.

Fiddling with her napkin, studying it as though reading a book, she finally looked up. "Dammit, Darius, stop it!"

"Bought you a little something."

Though clearly still irritated with him, her eyes sparkled with inquisitiveness.

"Would you like to know what it is?"

She nodded.

"This type of thing requires a recitation of some sort, so here goes . . . ."

He wanted to wait until she was on the verge of throwing something at him for not finishing the statement. When she finally spoke he knew the moment had arrived.

"Darius, I'm going to stab you to death with my steak knife if you don't quit staring at me without saying anything."

Grinning, he sat upright, reached into his pocket, and showed her the ring. "I love you, Robyn. I think you're the most wonderful girl in the world. I hope you'll accept this as a token of my undying love, and become my bride, though I be totally unworthy of you."

Gently, he took her left hand and slid the ring on her finger.

Her eyes grew wide and she started crying. "Oh . . . how romantic is this? Oh, Darius . . . I love you too, of course I'll marry you . . .!"

When her tears passed, he shot her a sly smile. "Good. Then I'll get to stare at you all I want without ever having to utter a syllable."

Laughing, she scooped up some mashed potatoes with her fingers and slung the white mass at him. "The hell you will!"

"Oh yeah . . .?" he retrieved a handful of spuds from the potato bowl and smeared it on her cheek. She retaliated by dumping the gravy boat on his head, whereupon he grabbed the back of hers and yanked her facedown into the remaining pot roast. When he let her go, she came up growling like a dog with a huge chunk of it in her mouth and started chewing.

He let out a wolf howl. "Give me some of that meat!"

Chomping down on it himself, he snarled as she tried to tear it from his teeth with her own. Before long they were on top of the table making love.

* * * *

Robyn's jaw fell when he pulled into his parents' drive. "What a beautiful house. Did you grow up here?"

Darius killed the engine. "No. Each time my father got promoted we moved into a nicer place. He didn't buy this one till I was in high school."

She continued appraising the imposing structure. "What does he do?"

"He's an executive with Farbarger Advertising, just two rungs down the corporate ladder from the CEO himself."

"Wow!"

"So you've heard of it."

"Of course I have. It's only the most prestigious advertising agency in the state."

"So Dad wasn't lying to me then."

"About what?"

"He told me the same thing you said, but I thought he was just exaggerating, trying to make himself out to be more of a big shot than he really is. I've never had any interest in advertising and am basically ignorant about it. I knew Dad's company was considered upper echelon but figured it wasn't really the top of the heap like he always claimed."

"You said that like you resent your father. Do you?"

He let out a sigh. "No. It's just that he has a tendency to

brag on himself while putting others down. It's really annoying. Other than that and the fact he uses more than his share of clichés, me and the old man get along just fine."

"Oh."

They exited the car simultaneously. She'd mentioned being nervous about meeting his family and he could tell by her expression his last statement had made her even more so.

"Don't worry. He won't be a butt until he gets to know you. He'll be Prince Charming today, believe me."

His mother answered the door and greeted them with a big smile. "You must be Robyn Tuscany. I'm Amia, this character's mother."

"It's so nice to finally meet you, Mrs. Darkfire." She stuck out her hand but his mother hugged her instead, which made Robyn smile with relief.

"Come in and meet my better half. And the name is Amia, not Mrs. Darkfire."

She led them to the dining room and his father rose from the table when they walked in. Smiling like he'd just won the lottery, he extended his hand to Robyn.

"Good to meet you, Robyn. Whatever Darius has told you about me he's lying, I'm really a nice guy once you get to know me."

Robyn shook his hand. "So nice to meet you, sir."

"Sir? I'm your future father-in-law. Are you going to call me Sir from now on?"

She blushed.

Darius winked at her. "Dad's name is Douglas."

"Yeah, but call me Doug. Now have a seat right here." He pulled out a chair for her. "Amia made one of her luscious lasagnas. You'll love it, Robyn."

Darius sat down across from her as his mother removed the top from a huge rectangular pan of steaming pasta, laden with thick sauce and melted cheeses. By the time she dished out everyone's plate Robyn had relaxed and kept glancing at his dad.

"The resemblance between you and your father is amazing."

A tongue-in-cheek smirk appeared on his dad's face. "Only I'm better looking."

"Of course you are, dear," quipped his mother with a mocking expression before turning to Robyn. "I suppose Darius told you he's our only child."

"Yes, ma'am."

"Oh stop it—don't call me ma'am. But you can call me Mom if you want. You can be the daughter I never had."

His dad grinned wide. "Yeah. We wanted to have a dozen kids didn't we, dear."

"Yes we did."

The wistful expression appearing on his mother's face made Darius groan inwardly. Robyn was about to hear the details of the large brood she'd hoped to bring into the world.

"Doug and I had planned to have twelve little Darkfires. We were going to raise them with a rod of iron and send them out to conquer the world and make it a better place for all. We wanted to have six boys and six girls. One of the boys would go into law, one into medicine, one into the ministry, one into politics, one would be a brilliant teacher, and one would become a great military commander. The six girls would marry men from each of the six fields their brothers were destined to.

"But I had to have my uterus removed shortly after giving birth to Darius. We thought about adoption for awhile but I just couldn't shake the notion that I might be getting in God's way if we went that route, figuring if He wanted me to have more children He'd have spared my uterus. Darius turned out to be such a handful, I thought, 'Lord, you are wise in your ways—anymore like this little guy and I might head for the hills screaming and tearing my hair out'."

Robyn laughed.

"I now give him to you, Robyn. Let him drive you crazy, it's time for Mama to retire."

That one made him chuckle along with her. Then his mom turned serious and he cringed, knowing what was coming.

"Did you tell her of your lineage, Darius?"

"Oh, Mom, please don't start with that."

"Amia, Robyn doesn't want to hear about your ancestry," said his father, chiming in.

Face ignited with curiosity, Robyn leaned forward. "Oh, Mrs. Darkfire, I'd love to hear all about it. I'm really into genealogy."

"It's Amia, dear—or Mom. Anyway, Darius is a direct descendent of Cyrus the Great, the very one mentioned in the book of Isaiah in the Bible . . . ."

Darius focused on the cuisine as his mother told the tale. By the time he helped himself to seconds, she'd brought Robyn back into the twentieth century and the day she presented the ring to him.

"Now it belongs to Darius, and one day it will pass to his first born."

"How fascinating."

He glanced at Robyn, expecting to see an expression of polite patronization, but her face conveyed sincere acceptance instead. His dad spoke up and he grimaced.

"Aw that's nothing, Robyn. Let me tell you about Darius's paternal heritage . . . ."

His fiancé listened intently, seemingly enthralled as her future father-in-law spelled out every detail of his pedigree.

When his dad finally shut up, Robyn smiled and said, "Well I knew the moment I saw him he was someone special. So I'm really not all that surprised to learn he's a total thoroughbred from both sides of his family."

Lips stretched with gratitude, approval radiating from her piercing dark eyes, his mom reached over and gave Robyn a love pat on the shoulder. "How sweet of you to say. How did the two of you meet anyway?"

"We met on a plane."

"Is that right? Well God saw to it you were both on the same flight didn't He. So when are you two lovebirds going to make it legal?"

"That's up to your son. I want to get married as soon as possible."

"But you are going to have a wedding, right?"

Darius sighed. "We haven't discussed the details yet, Mom, but when we do you'll be the first to know. I'd just as soon get married at the courthouse and skip all the pomp and circumstance."

Robyn dropped her jaw. "Not me, buster!"

A loud guffaw erupted from his dad but his mother donned a reprimanding glare. "Every girl cherishes the memory of her wedding day, Darius. You can't just sign a document. I raised you better than that."

He arched his brows. "I don't recall you ever instructing me on how to get married, Mom."

"Well I'm instructing you now, aren't I, so there." She stuck out her tongue at him. Robyn giggled and did likewise, sending his father into hysterics . . . .

After they left his parent's house Robin said, "Your mom and dad are such sweethearts. I love them already. And by the way, as soon as we get to your place I want to see that ring."

"Why? It's just a legend."

"You don't know that."

"Not for certain, but common sense dictates it is."

"Well, I want to see it anyway. That's really something, you being descended from royalty on both sides. I haven't been able to trace my family tree much further back than my great-grandparents."

Frowning, he cut his eyes to her. "Where do you get royalty on both sides?"

"Cyrus was a king and Dark Fires was a chief."

"You consider an Indian Chief royalty?"

"Sure."

A humorless snicker vacated his throat. "I don't. And besides, there's no proof I descended from Cyrus."

"Sure there is."

"How do you figure that? What's the proof?"

"The ring."

Not believing his ears, he groaned with incredulity, wondering how an engineer could be so naive. "That ring could have been manufactured a few generations back by a madman with delusions of grandeur. Anybody can make up a tall tale. I wish Mom hadn't mentioned it. Of course I knew it was only a matter of time before she did."

Perturbed by his reaction, she briskly folded her arms but quickly dropped them when the seatbelt tightened between her large breasts, apparently making her uncomfortable. "Why don't you have it dated?"

"Huh?"

"Have it tested to see how old it is. See if it's old enough to have been made during the time of Cyrus the Great. If it is that old, the story's bound to be true."

That thought had never occurred to him. "Can they do that?"

"Sure they can."

"How? You can't use carbon dating to determine the age of a gold ring, can you? I think that only works on organic substances like bones and such if I'm not mistaken."

"I'm not sure, but I know thermoluminescence testing can be used on minerals to determine their age. I learned that back in college. They heat an object till it almost glows then they record the TL which is short for thermoluminescence. The TL can determine the age back as far as a hundred thousand years or so."

"That would be pretty expensive I'd imagine."

"Not necessarily. Not when you have a friend who's an

archeologist at TCU."

He grinned at her. "Which you no doubt do."

"No doubt," she said with a sheepish smile.

"Okay. If your friend can do it, I'm willing, so long as the ring won't be harmed in the process. Hell hath no fury like my mom would have if anything were to happen to that stupid ring. Gold is a metal, not a mineral, by the way. Are you sure that thermo lucite or whatever will work on metal?"

"Thermoluminescence. If it doesn't, something will, you can count on it. There's bound to be a way to date it. I don't suppose you know the date we're needing, do you?"

"You mean when Cyrus was king of Persia?"

"Yeah."

"Oh trust me," he laughed, "Mom has it permanently etched in my brain. Cyrus died in five-twenty-nine BC so the ring has to date prior to that if the legend's true."

Opening her purse, Robyn pulled out a pen, then reached back inside and fetched a wallet from which she extracted a business card. After scribbling the date on the back, she returned the items and closed it. "I believe it's true. I'll be so disappointed if it's not."

Darius heaved a weary sigh. "You'll never convince Mom it isn't true, even if your friend produces an undisputable certificate of authentication that proves the ring came from Tiffany's."

ELEVEN

Robyn's friend at TCU said the precise age of the ring couldn't be determined since it hadn't been uncovered in an archeological find with accompanying debris that could be easily dated. The signet, however, appeared to be a valid replica of ancient seals used during the time Cyrus reigned over Persia, so the ring couldn't be ruled a fake. The professor speculated that the quarter-inch wide gold band had indeed been formed several hundred years before the birth of Christ.

At the time Darius wished it could have been proven illegitimate so Robyn would have left the matter alone. She'd become convinced of its authenticity and obsessed with the legend surrounding it.

Their wedding plans had been put on hold but it had nothing to do with her new found passion. An old lover of hers had returned to Fort Worth. Though Robyn swore she had no feelings for her ex paramour, Darius didn't believe her. She'd started acting differently and seemed far more interested in the ring alleged to have belonged to Cyrus than the one he'd put on her finger.

Further complicating things, one evening she claimed to have a migraine and had to break their date. Later that night he called to check on her but no one answered. He drove by her apartment only to find her car gone. The next day, without mentioning that he'd gone to her place, he told her about the phone call. His heart broke when she said she'd been so sedated by her prescription medication a freight train running through her bedroom wouldn't have roused her. Instead of confronting her with the discrepancy, he merely told her they needed to cool it for a while, and she hadn't tried very hard to dissuade him. That took place a month ago and they hadn't spoken since.

The intercom buzzed. *"Darius, there's a very upset lady here who says she needs to speak to you right away."*

Irritated, he pressed the button, knowing it had to be Robyn since Ricca didn't say the lady's name. She used to barge in unannounced to surprise him, and his sentimental secretary had always permitted it despite not having his approval. "Send her in."

His brows shot up when the distraught woman rushed through the door. He knew why Ricca hadn't bothered with the name, knowing he'd want to see her immediately, having been told of their history. "Avery?"

"Dare, Marcus has been arrested!"

If she'd said his own mother had been taken into custody he couldn't have been more stunned. Marcus Laxx had become the darling of The Metroplex. "What for?"

"Rape and murder . . . ."

TWELVE

Marcus Laxx won the Heisman Trophy his senior year at SMU and followed that glory by being the overall number one pick of the draft, getting snatched up by his hometown Dallas Cowboys, who'd traded up for the slot. As the heir apparent to Tony Romo, Marcus had become a local hero. Though he'd yet to take over the reigns as quarterback he saw playing time as the holder on field goals and extra points and had scored a couple of touchdowns on fake three-point tries.

He and Avery had been living together for several years but hadn't married. Their relationship had thrust Avery into the limelight and she was well known by everyone who followed the Cowboys closely. Darius hadn't spoken to either of them since his last days at Southern Methodist but saw them often on the local news channels attending charity events and the like.

Though the evidence seemed to prove Marcus raped, then strangled a nineteen-year-old Cowboys Cheerleader named Sally Grant, he'd agreed to represent his one time rival against now Chief Assistant District Attorney Suzette Edison who, like him, had yet to lose a case.

Sally Grant's body had been discovered by a maintenance man who'd been the one that called the police. Besides him and the killer, only four people had seen the crime scene in its pristine state—two detectives, a criminalist, and the coroner.

The forensics overwhelmingly pointed to Marcus. A highball glass with the quarterback's fingerprints on it placed him at Grant's apartment, and a prophylactic containing his sperm and particles of Sally Grant's pubic hair had been found beneath the victim's bed. She'd been strangled with a monogrammed sash from an expensive bathrobe with the initials ML woven into it. The robe had been found hanging in the victim's closet. Darius didn't think his client capable of murder to begin with but even if he was, Marcus would never be stupid enough to leave a sash with his initials around the victim's neck. The state argued otherwise, maintaining he'd either been too drunk to think clearly or circumstances forced him to flee before cleaning up the crime scene.

Because of his client's local notoriety Darius sought a change of venue, but it had been denied on the grounds that Marcus would get as impartial a jury in Dallas as anywhere else since his celebrity had grown national because of the popularity of America's Team. Suzette had practically squealed with delight when the judge announced his decision. She'd gotten her hands on a big fish that would make her a household name throughout the country. Adding insult to injury, she'd also persuaded the judge at the preliminary hearing to hold Marcus without bail, reminding His Honor of the O. J. Simpson car chase when The Juice had been granted it.

An officer led him into a conference room. Marcus, much as John Derby had, looked as if he'd already been convicted. The quarterback had always carried himself with such confidence he appeared arrogant and unapproachable—broad shoulders perpetually squared, strong chin held high, taut athletic face brimming with ambition. Now, slumping at the table as if carrying the weight of the whole world on his back, the celebrated jock reeked of disparagement.

Stagnant air trapped within the barren confines gave off a musty stench, further enhancing the depressing moment.

"Man, I can't thank you enough for representing me."

Unbuttoning his jacket, Darius seated himself and leaned back in the chair. "This isn't pro bono, Marcus, and I don't come cheap. I appreciate your gratitude but the payment of the bill is all the thanks I need."

Marcus's eyes swam with desperation. "Darius, you know me. You don't think I did it, do you? I know it looks like I must have, but I swear I didn't."

He opened his briefcase and pulled out a legal pad. "I wouldn't be here if I thought you were guilty."

Sighing with relief, Marcus clasped his hands together. "Someone's trying to frame me."

"Sure looks that way. Now then, I need all the details about your relationship with Sally Grant, especially your sex life. It will have to be brought out in order to prove you didn't rape her."

The QB's muscular shoulders drooped further. "I'll get kicked off the team if it gets out Sally and I were having an affair. The players and cheerleaders aren't supposed to fraternize."

"Can't be avoided. I have to show you didn't have a motive to strangle her. The prosecution will do everything they can to prove rape because it's the only motive they have for the murder. I have to establish the sex was consensual, and once I've done that, it'll pull the teeth from the lion's mouth because they won't be able to come up with another motive. Or will they?"

Tears began dripping down his face. "That stupid bitch . . . she kept coming on to me and I finally gave in to the temptation. I never planned on anything but a one night stand but she wouldn't have it. Threatened to tell a reporter if I didn't continue seeing her."

"Even though it meant she'd get kicked off the cheerleading squad?"

"Yeah . . . the girl was psycho."

Darius winced. "Does Avery know?"

Marcus sniffed and ran an index finger under his nose. "Yeah. Sally made me come to her place at least once a week, and Avery was getting suspicious, so I finally told her everything, including the fact I had to keep seeing Sally because of the blackmail."

He scribbled that down, amazed Avery hadn't dumped the

football hero. "When did you tell her?"

"A good while before Sally got killed."

"Define 'good while'. Days, weeks, months?"

"A few months."

"Did you always use a rubber?"

Making a sour face, Marcus gawked at him as if responding to the stupidest question he'd ever heard. "Are you kidding? With that psycho I'd have been a fool not to. Man, she'd have loved nothing more than getting knocked up by me."

Recording the information, without bothering to look up he said, "Why did you toss it under the bed?"

"I didn't. One of us always flushed them down the toilet."

Whoever killed Sally Grant couldn't have gotten their hands on a rubber used in the physical union of Marcus and the victim if they were always disposed of in the manner he'd just been told. With a pang of doubt tugging at his insides over the explanation, Darius leveled his eyes on the celebrated athlete. "How do you account for it then?"

"I can't. I have no idea how it got there."

Eyes still locked on the quarterback's, he started tapping his pen on the table. "Well, my friend, it not only got there, but it got there with your sperm and some of Sally Grant's pubic hair on it."

"I know . . ." he seemed to shrink a size, as if emotional turmoil had somehow infiltrated his physical being. "You don't believe I'm innocent anymore do you?"

Darius cleared his throat. "I'm not sure what to believe at this point, but know this—if I come to the conclusion you did it, you'll have to get other counsel. Understand?"

Marcus clenched his eyes closed and slowly nodded.

* * * *

They were at the victim's apartment. Preston removed his glasses and cleaned them with a handkerchief.

"Initially, I thought the killer to be a male endeavoring to frame your client, who one would think to have more sense than leave such damning evidence on the scene. But now I submit, in light of what you've told me, that Avery might have framed her boyfriend in order to avenge his infidelity."

Darius stared at the fatal bed where the body had been found. "So you think Avery did it."

Preston reacquired his glasses. "It certainly seems possible."

"I've known Avery since high school, Preston. She's not capable of murder. Neither is Marcus . . . at least I don't think he is." The condom still bugged him but he hadn't told Preston of his small but nagging doubt about the quarterback's innocence because of it.

The investigator gave him a skeptical look. "Did you think Avery capable of allowing her paramour to continue an affair with another woman?"

"No. I'm surprised she didn't leave Marcus when he told her, but that's a far cry from being able to strangle someone."

"True, but Avery would have been very distraught upon learning of the affair. She'd be angry at the other woman, but even more so with her unfaithful partner. It's possible that after stewing on it for days on end she had a breakdown and decided to kill her competitor and get even with her unfaithful lover by framing him for it.

"And need I point out the difficulty of obtaining a condom containing Marcus's semen? Since he's never donated to a sperm bank, only a lover would have such access. A clever girl could carefully wash the outside to rid it of her bodily fluids after having sex with your client, and rub it vigorously on the victim's vagina to obtain the damning forensics after strangling her."

Darius sighed. Whatever doubts he had about her boyfriend, he knew Avery couldn't have done it. "It definitely looks like someone tried to frame Marcus, but we don't know that for certain. What have you got on Sally Grant?"

Preston pulled out a notebook and began reading. "She grew up in Cameron, Texas and moved to Dallas after winning a spot with the Dallas Cowboys Cheerleaders. She worked at a modeling agency but as a personal assistant rather than a model.

"No one at the agency knew anything about Miss Grant's personal life and the cheerleaders I spoke with only had cordial relationships with her as well. However, one of them told me the person I needed to talk to was Nina North who wasn't present. Miss North apparently knew the victim quite well from what she said."

"Is she a cheerleader too?"

"Yes."

"Did you get her address?"

"I was told she'd be at a meeting scheduled for eleven a.m. today—something to do with travel arrangements for a special appearance." Preston's lips spread into a closed-mouth smile of anticipation.

Darius grinned. "You sly dog. Well guess what, I get to see the cheerleaders this time . . . ."

* * * *

Relishing the opportunity of getting to exchange hellos with several of the cheerleaders, Darius finally located Nina North, a buxom redhead with long, gorgeous legs.

"Sure, I knew Sally real well. What do you need to know?"

Not wanting their conversation to be overheard by some of the other beautiful woman standing nearby, he lowered his voice. "Um, can we talk about this over lunch?"

"If you're buying we can," she said with a dazzling smile.

He smiled back. "Yeah, it's on me . . . ."

Nestled in the corner of a quiet café Darius began the interview after ordering their food—grilled salmon for the pretty lady, cheeseburger and fries for him.

"You say you knew Sally well. What sort of men did she usually date?"

An odd expression rose on her face, preceding a frown. "Why did you ask that?"

Her reaction to such an innocuous question puzzled him. "I'm wondering if she might have been the type that seeks out celebrities such as my client."

"Oh, so you didn't know then."

"Know what?"

"Sally was gay."

"She was . . .?" his stomach tied itself in knots as doubt of Marcus's innocence mounted.

"Yeah. I'm the only one on the squad that knows. I figured you did too because of your investigator—she'd told me it was no secret in her hometown. I had a dental appointment yesterday but heard he'd paid us a visit."

It took him a moment to regain his composure. "Could she have been bi?"

North shook her head. "Sally only liked girls."

"Are you sure?"

"Positive. Ask anyone that really knew her, they'll tell you the same . . . ."

On the way to see his client, Darius mulled everything over. Marcus had apparently lied to him about the affair, but he couldn't believe the golden boy who could have his pick of women had raped a lesbian. It didn't make any sense. Nina North being so adamant her dead friend only liked women made him wonder why none of the other cheerleaders knew about Grant's sexual preference. If any of them did they hadn't mentioned it to Preston.

The quarterback walked into the conference room looking totally dejected like before. He sat down at the table and ran his hands roughly over his face. "Anything new?"

Darius hiked his leg up on the chair, lean forward with an elbow on his thigh, and leered at the Heisman Trophy winner.

"I'm only going to say this once. Either quit lying to me or get another attorney."

THIRTEEN

The jury had been selected and the first day of trial arrived. Suzette looked sharp and imposing in a black pants suit with a blood-red blouse. Her face reeked with confidence when the judge—a gruff-looking senior citizen named Everett Steed— asked if the prosecution was ready to present its case.

"We are, Your Honor."

"Very well, you may proceed."

Suzette gave the opening statement everyone anticipated— that Marcus raped Sally Grant, then strangled her in a desperate act of self preservation, and the prosecution would clearly prove it beyond a reasonable doubt. Darius forwent his opening statement, and the judge told the ambitious prosecutor to call her first witness.

"The People call Detective Sergeant Jeff Robards."

Noticing Marcus fidgeting as the detective took the stand, Darius whispered, "Try not to show how nervous you are, the jurors have their eyes on you."

His client complied and Darius turned his attention to the witness stand. Suzette asked the detective to recount what he found when he arrived on the scene, and she presented the damning items as Prosecution Exhibits A, B, and C.

After Robards finished testifying, Suzette shot Darius a look that dared him to challenge the detective's testimony. "Your witness."

He stood. "No questions, Your Honor, but I'd like to reserve the right to re-call this witness at a later time."

Suzette then called Robards' partner to the stand and he gave identical testimony. Again Darius didn't question the witness but reserved the right to re-call him.

Judge Steed declared a recess for lunch and after court reconvened an hour later, the prosecution's third witness entered the courtroom—Albert Smith, the maintenance man who found Sally Grant's body and called the police. The radically self-assured blonde called him to the stand.

With Smith sworn in, Suzette clasped her hands behind the small of her back and approached the witness stand. "Mister Smith, please tell the jury why you entered the victim's apartment."

The chunky middle-aged man wore very thick glasses which suddenly slid to the end of his nose. He pushed them back up the bridge and began testifying. "I went there to fix the garbage disposal."

Suzette faced the jury for a moment before returning to her witness, hands now at her sides. "The victim told you it was broken, is that correct?"

"Yes, ma'am."

"How did she tell you?"

Albert Smith seemed ill at ease but most witnesses did. Darius examined his face carefully as he answered.

"Um, she called me."

"And told you it was broken?"

"Yes, ma'am."

"And when was this?"

Smith adjusted his position in the witness chair. "Around nine that morning."

"And what time did you enter Miss Grant's apartment?"

"That afternoon."

"What time that afternoon?"

"Um, around one-thirty."

This round of questions came as no surprise to Darius. He knew Suzette would press home to the jury that Sally Grant had been murdered between nine a.m. and one-thirty p.m. because Marcus had no alibi for that time frame, only his word that he'd been home alone.

"Did you talk to Miss Grant again after the initial phone call?"

"No, ma'am."

"Were you expecting her to be there when you arrived?"

Smith again shifted in his seat. "Um, no."

"Why not?"

"She said she'd be out for the day."

"Miss Grant, you mean."

"Yes, ma'am."

"How did you gain access to the victim's apartment?"

"With a master key."

Suzette folded her arms. "Please tell the jury what happened after you entered the apartment."

"I started for the kitchen but as I passed the hallway I saw Miss Grant through the open bedroom door. I knew something was wrong because she didn't have any clothes on and wasn't moving."

"What did you do then?"

"I called out to her, and when she didn't answer I went into the bedroom to make sure she was all right. When I saw her lying there with her eyes glazed over and that thing around her neck, I knew she was dead. After I got over the initial shock I called the police."

"From the victim's apartment?"

"Yes, ma'am."

With a smile of utter confidence she turned towards the defense table before seating herself. "Your witness."

Darius rose to his feet with a friendly grin. "Good afternoon, Mister Smith. My name is Darius Darkfire and I'm counsel for the defense."

A flicker of relief appeared in Smith's nervous eyes. The goggled maintenance man obviously dreaded being cross examined. The laidback smile had caused him to relax a little as intended.

"You say the victim called you and told you her garbage disposal was broken, is that right?"

"Yes, sir."

"Did she identify herself as Sally Grant?"

"Yes, sir."

"So if she hadn't identified herself, you wouldn't have known who had called you, is that right?"

"Objection!" barked Suzette. "Calls for speculation."

The judge nodded. "Rephrase, Mister Darkfire."

"Had the victim ever called you before?"

"No, sir."

"Did you ever speak with the victim in person?"

"No, sir."

"Had you ever seen the victim before?"

Smith's face widened with a smile. "Oh yes, on TV."

A small collection of laughter rose in the courtroom and quickly died down.

Darius turned towards the jury and grinned. "As a cheerleader for the Dallas Cowboys?"

"Yes, sir."

He faced the witness again. "The fact is, Mister Smith, you really don't know who called you for sure, do you?"

"Objection, Your Honor!"

"Withdraw the question," said Darius. "Had you ever been to Sally Grant's apartment before the day you went there to repair the disposal?"

"Not while Miss Grant lived there."

"But you had been there before she moved in?"

"Yes, sir."

"How long have you held your present job, Mister Smith?"

"Ten years."

"So you must be familiar with all the apartments at that complex."

"Objection, relevance!"

"Overruled. Witness may answer."

Smith had to push the heavy lenses up his nose again. "Um, yeah, I know them all pretty well."

"How old is the garbage disposal in the victim's apartment?"

"Not very. It was installed a short while before Miss Grant moved into the apartment."

"What turned out to be wrong with it, by the way?"

"A fork had dropped into it and jammed it."

"I see. Was it hard to fix?"

"Relevance, Your Honor!" Suzette protested.

"Overruled. Witness may answer the question."

"Once I got the fork dislodged it worked fine."

"So there wasn't anything mechanical to be repaired."

"No, sir."

"So someone other than Miss Grant could have dropped a fork in it on purpose and called you in order to make you find the victim's body in the hope of framing my client."

"Objection!"

The Honorable Everett Steed glared at him. "Sustain that, Mister Darkfire. The jury will disregard counsel's last statement."

Darius glanced at the jury, satisfied by their expressions that no matter how hard they tried, they wouldn't be able to disregard it. He turned back towards the witness. "Thank you, Mister Smith. No further questions."

Suzette jumped to her feet. "The People would like to redirect."

The judge nodded. "Proceed."

No longer looking quite so confident but wearing her professional smile nonetheless, Suzette strolled gracefully to the witness box. "Is it uncommon for a dining implement such as a fork to get stuck in a garbage disposal?"

Smith shook his head. "Not at all. Happens all the time."

"Thank you for your time, Mister Smith. Nothing further."

The judge dismissed Albert Smith and he waddled out of the courtroom, obviously relieved his civic duty had been fulfilled and he could now get on with his life. Suzette then called Avery to the stand.

Darius again cautioned Marcus to quit fidgeting which he'd

started doing when Avery, looking very nervous, took the oath.

". . . Miss Buntzinghammer, I hold in my hands a bathrobe sash marked Prosecution Exhibit C. Please tell me if you recognize it."

A pale-faced Avery nodded at Suzette.

Judge Steed turned towards her. "Speak out loud, please, for the court recorder."

"Y-Yes."

"How is that you recognize it?"

"It was given to my boyfriend as a gift."

Suzette glanced around. "Is he in the courtroom today?"

Tears welling in her eyes Avery looked down and nodded.

Steed furrowed his brow. "Miss Buntzinghammer, you have to speak your answers, and I don't want to have to remind you again."

"Yes . . . he's here."

"Would you point him out, please?"

She pointed at Marcus and started weeping.

"Let the record show the witness pointed to the defendant . . ." Suzette placed the sash with the other exhibits and returned to Avery. "Did you see the defendant the day of the murder?"

Trying to compose herself, she wiped her eyes and shook her head.

"Miss Buntzinghammer," snapped Judge Steed, "I'm going to hold you in contempt if I have to remind you to speak up again."

"No."

"So you did not see the defendant. Did you talk with him on the phone that day?"

The look on Avery's face made it clear she didn't want to answer, but she drew in a breath and said, "No."

"When was the next time you spoke to Mister Laxx?"

"A few days later when he called me after he'd been arrested."

"I'm a bit confused, Miss Buntzinghammer . . ." Suzette donned a sarcastic expression of puzzlement. "You live with the defendant, do you not? How is it you went several days without speaking with him?"

"I was out of town on business. I flew back when Marcus called and told me he'd been arrested."

"I see. Were you in town the day of the murder?"

"I left that morning."

"By plane?"

"Yes."

"But you testified you did not see the defendant that day."

"Marcus was gone when I woke up. He'd left a note saying he'd gone to Valley Ranch to lift weights."

"What time did you rise that morning?"

"At seven."

"And when did you leave for the airport?"

"A little before eight."

"Why is it he called you rather than his attorney after he was arrested?"

"He wanted me to speak to Darius and ask him to represent him."

Suzette did a slow pirouette, wearing a self-satisfied smirk. "You're referring to Mister Darkfire, are you not?"

"Yes."

"You two have known each other for quite some time haven't you?"

"Yes."

"So the defendant feared Mister Darkfire wouldn't represent him without you requesting he do so?"

"Objection, irrelevant," said Darius from his seat.

"Sustained."

"No further questions, Miss Buntzinghammer."

Full swagger regained, the sexy prosecutor turned and gave him a knowing look before sauntering to her table.

Darius unbuttoned his coat on the way to the witness stand,

forcing it open as he wedged his hands into the front pockets of his slacks. "It's not much fun being a witness is it."

That brought a nervous yet grateful smile to Avery and snickers from the spectators and jurors.

"No."

"Well I'll be brief as possible, I promise. Now then, did you know the victim?"

"Yes."

"To the best of your knowledge, did the defendant know her?"

"Yes."

"Again, to the best of your knowledge did my client ever have consensual sex with her?"

Avery's face reddened as she nodded.

Before Judge Steed had a chance to reprimand her, Darius humorously said, "The court recorder can't hear a nod, dear."

"Yes."

"How is it that you know that?"

"Because . . . I was there."

"You actually saw them have sex?"

She nodded again but quickly ejaculated "Yes" when he raised his brows as a warning for her to speak up before incurring Steed's wrath.

"You were there because you were also having sex, isn't that right?"

Tears gushed from her eyes. Head bobbing she cried, "Yes . . . oh my god, I'm so ashamed!"

The courtroom erupted with gasps and exclamations as the judge banged his gavel, demanding that order be restored. Darius pulled out his handkerchief and handed it to Avery. He glanced at Suzette. Her competitive demeanor couldn't quite hide concern over a possible first defeat. Though she appeared steadfast in every other aspect, he detected a trace of fear in her eyes.

With the courtroom quiet again, Darius turned his focus

back to the witness. "When did the three of you last have sex together?"

Avery buried her face in his hanky, blew her nose, and raised her head. "The night before the murder."

"Did the defendant use a condom?"

"Yes."

"I don't mean to sound crass, but do you know what became of it afterwards?"

She shook her head meekly. "No."

"What usually happened to them?"

"They got flushed down the toilet."

"But this one didn't. I wonder why?"

Her features soured as if she'd been insulted. "I never disposed of them so I don't know."

"Did the three of you have drinks the night before the murder?"

Avery started nodding but quickly said "Yes" when he once again prodded her to vocalize with an arch of his brows.

Pointing to the exhibits he said, "The prosecution has entered a highball glass into evidence as Exhibit B. It's sitting there next to the sash. Did my client drink from it or one like it the night before the murder?"

"Yes."

"There were only two glasses found, and one of them had the victim's prints. What happened to the glass you used?"

"I only had one wine cooler and took it with me when Marcus and I left."

He hated having to bring that out but felt it would be less harmful coming from the defense rather than the prosecution, which Suzette would have surely done on redirect after hearing Avery's testimony. If only she'd left the bottle at the victim's apartment it would have gone a long way to convincing the jury she'd been there that night. While Preston had found her prints on the handle of the refrigerator and other locations within Grant's abode—a fact Darius hadn't shared with Suzette—they could have been left there at any time prior to the night in question.

"Did my client keep a robe at the victim's apartment?"

"No."

"Was he wearing one the night the three of you were last together?"

"No."

"Did he ever wear a robe when the three of you were together?"

"Never."

"But you testified that Exhibit C does in fact belong to the defendant."

Avery cleared her throat. "Sally gave it to him the night we were last . . . together, but he never put it on and when we left I wouldn't let him take it."

"I see. So neither you nor my client had ever seen the robe or the sash before that night. Is that right?"

"Yes. Sally said she'd ordered it online and it had arrived that afternoon."

"If you know, why did she buy it?"

She grasped his handkerchief with both hands, nervously toying with it. "It's a robe like Hugh Hefner wears and she wanted Marcus to have it as a token of her love. His relationship with Sally was only physical—he'd made that clear to her from the beginning. That gift was too much of a romantic gesture, that's why I wouldn't let him take it with him when we went home."

"I see . . ." he looked around the courtroom before continuing. "Tell me, does it make sense to you that a man whose name is a household word would be stupid enough to leave a sash stitched with his initials on a woman he'd strangled?"

"Object!"

"Sustained."

"Did Miss Grant have other lovers?"

"Object, Your Honor!"

"Overruled." Steed turned to Avery. "Answer the question if you know."

Avery again cleared her throat. "I don't know."

The judge motioned for him to continue.

"Assuming she did, it's reasonable to assume that another lover would have been inflamed with jealousy upon seeing a monogrammed robe like Hugh Hefner wears with initials other than said lover's, would it not?"

"Objection, calls for a conclusion!"

"Sustained."

He'd expected Suzette would object and Judge Steed would sustain it, but he needed to plant the thought in the mind of each juror. Darius glanced at them. Twelve pairs of expectant eyes were glued to Avery.

"Did you and the victim ever have sex without my client participating?"

"Oh my god no! I wouldn't let her touch me and I certainly never touched her!" A sickened expression certified she found the idea beyond repugnant.

"Hmm . . ." he donned an exaggerated frown. "Did you enjoy sharing your boyfriend with another woman?"

"No. I only went along with the threesome because it rekindled Marcus's desire for me for whatever reason."

"Thank you, all done. Nothing further, Your Honor."

"Redirect," said Suzette, hurriedly pressing past him on her way to the witness stand.

"Miss Buntzinghammer, isn't it a fact that you're lying in order to protect your lover?"

Avery gasped with indignance. "No! I'm telling the truth. My god, I almost wish I *was* lying. Do you have any idea how humiliating this is to me?"

Suzette waved her off. "Pfft! Women have suffered much greater humiliation to protect their men. You say you only drank one wine cooler and took it with you when you left. My, my, how convenient. Can you prove you've ever even been inside the victim's apartment?"

She nodded eagerly. "Check for my fingerprints, they must be all over the place!"

That deflated the prosecutor and she couldn't disguise it. Perfect posture withering, she started for her seat. "Nothing further . . . ."

FOURTEEN

The last witness to testify for the prosecution was Nina North. Suzette's strategy called for the cheerleader to convince the jury the victim had been a lesbian, thereby casting serious doubt on the likelihood of her being willing to have intercourse with Marcus. After Darius forwent cross examination but reserved the right to re-call her the state rested and the judge had declared a recess until the next day.

Darius stood as the jury filed in and took their seats. Steed asked if the defense was prepared to begin.

"We are, Your Honor."

"Call your first witness."

"Defense calls Detective Jeff Robards."

Robards, a burly man with a calloused expression stemming from years of inspecting morbid crime scenes, retook the stand. As the judge reminded he was still under oath Darius glanced at Suzette. Her professional facade concealed whatever reaction she felt over the homicide cop being called as his first witness.

He made his way to the front of the courtroom. "Good morning, Detective."

Robards gave a single nod.

"Please describe your thoughts when you first saw the victim."

"My first thought was 'what a shame'."

"What did you think when you saw the sash?"

"Nothing."

"It didn't strike you as odd?"

"Odd?"

"Yeah, odd. Didn't you think it a bit strange that a monogrammed sash that belonged to my client had been left around the victim's throat?"

Angry insult erupted on his jaded facade. "What are you getting at?"

"Answer the question, please. Did you or did you not think it strange?"

Clearly aware his demeanor might affect the jury, he relaxed his face and shrugged. "No. I didn't know it belonged to the defendant at the time."

"I see. So what made you think—at the time—that my client did it?"

He turned his palms up. "Nothing."

"Oh . . .?" Darius twisted towards the jury and didn't face the witness again until certain his patronization of Robards hadn't gone unnoticed. "Then what prompted you to investigate my client and no one else?"

The detective settled back in his seat confidently. "The forensics."

"By forensics, you mean the fingerprints and the prophylactic, do you not?"

"That's right."

Darius leered at him. "You know, that was a superb job of forensic work. It's amazing how quickly the fingerprints and sperm were found to belong to the defendant."

Lips curling into a snarl he barked, "What are you getting at?"

He gave Robards a cheeky grin while speaking to the judge. "No further questions, Your Honor."

As Darius ambled to his seat, he noted confusion on Suzette's sexy face.

"Mrs. Edison?" said the judge.

"Um . . . no questions, Your Honor."

Steed turned to the stewing detective. "Witness is dismissed."

After calling Robards' partner and receiving the same answers to the same questions along with the same reactions, he offered the witness to Suzette who once again refrained from cross examination.

Told to call his next witness, Darius looked around the courtroom and couldn't spot him. "Your Honor, at this time the defense would like to call Albert Smith but he's apparently been detained. May we have a recess?"

The judge looked towards the prosecution's table. "Any objections, Mrs. Edison?"

"No, Your Honor."

"Very well, Mister Darkfire, I'll give you one hour to produce your witness."

* * * *

". . . I hold in one hand Prosecution Exhibit C, and in the other a sash from a robe I purchased yesterday. Mister Smith, please examine each closely. According to the testimony of two detectives, one of these was the murder weapon. Which one did you see around the victim's neck?" Darius extended his arms to give Smith a closer view of the sashes.

The maintenance man's face crumpled with such concentration his weighty spectacles slid to the end of his nose. He eased them back up with the tip of his thumb and pointed to Darius's right hand. "I believe it was that one."

"Let the record show the witness pointed to the sash I bought rather than Prosecution Exhibit C." He glanced at the jury box, pleased to see several bewildered expressions, then refocused on Smith. "As you can see, the sash you chose is not only a lighter shade of brown-and-gold than Exhibit C, it isn't monogrammed. How do you account for that?"

Smith raised his brows in puzzlement. "I didn't notice any letters on the one I saw."

The courtroom exploded in uproar.

Steed repeatedly banged his gavel while shouting for everyone to settle down. When he threatened to clear the court, order was finally restored and Darius continued.

"Mister Smith, you weren't in the courtroom when the sash

was admitted into evidence, were you."

"No."

"Are you sure you didn't notice any letters on the one you saw at the victim's apartment?"

Nodding, Smith repositioned his thick lenses. "I'm not saying there weren't any, only that I didn't notice them."

"You're positive?"

"Yes. I'll never forget how awful it was seeing that thing around that poor girl's neck . . . ."

Suzette tried to convince Albert Smith that he must have seen initials on the murder weapon but might have thought them to be some sort of stitching design, leaning heavily on his poor vision, but the maintenance man merely told her the same thing he'd said to him.

He checked the jurors but couldn't tell if the doubt about the veracity of the two detectives he'd hope to plant had taken root in their minds. If at least one of them thought the sash might have been planted he or she couldn't in all good conscious vote guilty.

Though he had no doubt the detectives were telling the truth, it was a fallback plan in case the next step failed. With Smith's coke bottle glasses betraying he had extremely poor vision, Darius knew he had a fifty-fifty chance the maintenance man might chose the wrong sash which he wound up doing. The only repercussion he'd risked if the ploy hadn't worked was looking like a foolish lawyer. No further damage would have been done.

Nina North took the stand next. Expecting an air of curiosity if not outright concern as to why he'd called her back to court instead of questioning her when she'd testified for the prosecution, Darius was surprised at the nonchalant way she made herself comfortable, nodded to the judge after being reminded she was still under oath, and turned towards him with a polite smile.

"Where were you the day of the murder, Miss North?"

"I was in town, if that's what you mean. Exactly where I was or what I may have been doing when Sally was killed, I couldn't say. I have a fulltime job besides being a Cowboys Cheerleader so I lead a busy life and most days are pretty hectic."

"May I approach the bench, Your Honor?" said Suzette, rising to her feet.

The judge frowned with curiosity but granted her request. Darius joined her in front of Steed.

"Your Honor, I'm not hearing anything from the defense indicating any reason for postponing cross examination at the time Miss North was called by The People. Like his re-call of the detectives, this is pointless and I respectfully submit that Mister Darkfire is wasting the court's time."

Finding it hard to believe she'd resorted to such a juvenile tactic Darius turned from her and faced the judge. "Since the state initially called Miss North, she's presumed hostile to the defense and I therefore have the right to question her as such, and I'll remind Your Honor, Mrs. Edison voiced no objection at the time I reserved the right to re-call."

Steed nodded. "He's right. You may continue, Mister Darkfire."

Suzette begrudgingly returned to her seat, and he resumed questioning Nina North.

"How about the morning of the murder, can you recall where you were then?"

"Um, I'm not sure. Like I said, my days are pretty hectic."

"Is that right . . ." he scanned the jury and turned back to the busty redhead, thrusting his hands into his pockets in the process. "Well then, let me refresh your memory. You and three other cheerleaders had breakfast with the victim at International House of Pancakes, popularly known as I-HOP. I can produce the other three, if need be, to testify that Sally Grant rode to the restaurant with them but you drove the victim home."

Her face paled slightly but she otherwise kept her composure. "Well yes that's right, but I don't recall what all I did the rest of the morning after dropping Sally off at her apartment."

Deliberately scratching beneath his chin, he summoned a slow-forming sardonic grin. "Tell me, Miss North, how long have you and Sally Grant been lovers?"

Verve disintegrating, she gaped at him with alarm, her upper body stiff as a board. "H-How did you know?"

"Know what, Miss North? That you and the victim were lovers, or that you strangled her to death . . .?"

* * * *

Judge Steed finally got order restored after pandemonium broke out in the courtroom when Nina North suddenly quit protesting her innocence and screamed out, "You're right, I did it, but that lying deceitful bitch had it coming!"

The judge cautioned her not to proceed until conferring with an attorney, advising the cheerleader of her Fifth Amendment rights, but she said, "No, I don't want a lawyer and I wave all my rights. This has been driving me mad. I want to get it off my chest—I want to tell it all, right here and now."

"Mrs. Edison?" said Steed.

Looking as thunderstruck as the jurors, Suzette awkwardly rose to her feet. "The People would like to hear what she has to say."

"Very well. You may speak, Miss North."

The redhead wiped her eyes and inhaled a deep breath. "We took off our clothes and made love as soon as we got to Sally's apartment after leaving I-HOP. Afterwards I had to pee. I looked in the bathroom mirror and saw my hair was a mess so I picked up Sally's brush but it slipped from my hand and fell by the toilet. When I reached down to pick it up something caught my eye. I saw a used condom lying behind the base of the bowl, and knew Sally had cheated on me with a man.

"Furious and hurt, I confronted her about the condom and asked why she'd done it. She said she'd fallen in love with Marcus Laxx. She'd lied to me about only having sexual desires for women the same as me, and she'd sworn I was the love of her life. I felt so betrayed and so used I was just devastated, but tried to keep my pride. I told her, 'Okay, so you're bi. I guess I'll have to learn to live with that.'

"She told me she was glad to get it out in the open and had something to show me that she'd bought for him. She pulled a robe from her chest of drawers and stood in front of her full length mirror, holding it against her as if it were her most prized possession, all the while telling me how much she loved him. I totally went berserk and the next thing I knew I was standing behind her, choking her with the sash, dragging her back towards the bed. I was much stronger than her anyway, but I was so besieged with rage the adrenaline made me at least twice as strong as normal. There was nothing she could do—I kept pulling the sash tighter and tighter until she stopped breathing.

"When I realized what I'd done I hung the robe in her closet, grabbed some tissue so I wouldn't get my fingerprints on the condom, and tossed it under the bed. As I was getting dressed it dawned on me the other girls knew I'd driven Sally home, so I thought for a minute and when I saw the number for the maintenance man on the refrigerator, I got the idea of jamming a fork in the disposal and calling him, pretending to be Sally. I told him I'd be out for the day and left right after hanging up the phone.

"I was so hurt and jealous at the time I was glad the police thought Marcus did it, but my real anger was towards Sally for betraying me. I think I knew all along I couldn't let an innocent man take the blame for what I did. I'm so sorry I put everybody through all this."

FIFTEEN

They were having drinks at his place. Darius stood at the bar sipping scotch, Robert and Suzette were sitting on a sofa with Ricca close by in an oversized armchair. Preston hadn't been able to attend the celebration.

Suzette seemed preoccupied while Ricca and Robert chatted with each other about their mutual love for televised sports. He looked at the sexy prosecutor and asked if she was okay.

"I suppose . . ." she raised her Manhattan in salute. "You're really something you know that, counselor? Hat's off to you, you handed me my first defeat. It didn't hurt nearly as bad as I feared it would."

"You weren't defeated, Suzette. Your asking the judge to dismiss all charges was a victory for justice."

Her sultry lips parted with a sigh. "I'm glad you see it that way, makes me feel a little better, though I've got to admit I still feel like you won and I lost."

Ricca swirled her drink, watching the ice cubes go round. "I'm so glad this is over and Marcus can concentrate on being a Dallas Cowboy again."

He winced with astonishment that his secretary, a Cowboys fan, could be so ignorant of the facts. "Ricca, his career with the Cowboys is over. He screwed a Cowboys Cheerleader. They're not even supposed to chat with them on the sidelines. Besides, Avery won't be able to show her face around here anymore she's so ashamed of their tryst becoming public. I invited them over tonight but neither wants to do anything but hide out right now. I'm sure Marcus will continue his career but it'll be with some other team. They'll want to move as far away from here as possible, believe me.

"I hated to expose their love life but there was no other way. Until Nina North broke down and confessed, I wasn't positive she'd killed Sally so I had to prove that Marcus hadn't raped her, because that was the only apparent motive he'd have for strangling her."

Suzette aimed a smile his way that he'd have taken to be flirtatious or even seductive if Robert hadn't been there. "When did you figure everything out?"

Appearing not to notice the odd way she was looking at him, he dampened his throat with a swallow of scotch and cleared it. "After I finally got the truth out of Marcus. He'd lied to me initially, trying to keep Avery out of it by telling me Grant was forcing him to be her lover through blackmail. When Nina North told me Grant was a lesbian, I knew Marcus hadn't shot straight with me.

"The truth was he and Avery had gotten into a rut but neither wanted to call it quits. Grant had a serious thing for him, and was calling him all the time, telling him she'd do anything for him. Marcus told Avery about it, and said maybe trying a threesome would spice up their love life. Avery said she was willing to try anything to save their relationship. Grant eagerly agreed to it.

"Nina North had been adamant that Grant only liked women, and that haunted me after Marcus told me the truth. I got to wondering if the reason North was so sure Grant preferred women instead of men was because she herself did. And if that were so, it wasn't a reach to assume she and Grant were lovers.

"Avery had reluctantly agreed to the threesome, and insisted on it only happening at Grant's place because she didn't want her in Marcus's house. She laid out two ground rules on top of that—she wouldn't have intercourse in front of Grant and wouldn't allow the cheerleader to touch her. The routine basically consisted of Marcus performing oral sex on Avery while having intercourse with Grant which is why there was no forensic evidence from Avery on the condom.

"I'd been racking my brains on how the killer obtained it,

and going on the assumption Marcus had finally come clean about everything, I drew a logical conclusion. He assumed Grant had disposed of it, and I believe Grant thought she had too. But she missed the bowl when she tossed it and didn't realize she'd flushed an empty toilet, probably because she hadn't bothered turning on the bathroom light.

"I suspected that Nina North spotted the condom after arriving at Sally's apartment that morning, confronted her lover, and the two of them got into a catfight that ended in murder. My theory was confirmed when North broke down and confessed."

Still wearing the strange smile, Suzette saluted him with her glass a second time. "So why did you reserve the right to re-call the detectives since you knew all this then?"

"Because at that point it was only a theory, I wasn't sure Nina North did it. I had to play it cautious in case anything went awry, so I couldn't do anything until I convinced the jury that Marcus hadn't raped Sally. I anticipated you'd have Avery verify the sash belonged to Marcus because that would have the greatest impact on the jury. But I had the truth on my side—the jury could easily tell Avery wasn't lying about the threesome. With the knowledge that the sex had been consensual fresh on their minds, I figured at least one of the jurors would be suspicious enough of the possibility the sash may have been planted to vote not guilty and hang the jury if I couldn't get the truth out of Nina North. If North hadn't come clean, things could easily have gone the other way if I hadn't lucked out with Albert Smith picking the wrong sash."

"It pays to be cautious," Robert said with a snicker while turning to his wife. "I'm so glad justice was served without you having to lose the case. My life would have been a living hell. May you die undefeated."

Suzette shot him a sarcastic grin. "You're a wise man aren't you, Robert."

Everyone laughed except Suzette, who looked at him. "So

what happened between you and Robyn?"

He inhaled a deep breath and sighed. "An old boyfriend entered the picture."

"Oh . . . sorry I brought it up then."

Ricca frowned at him and turned to Suzette. "Darius thinks Robyn still has a thing for her ex, but I don't."

Irritated, he downed a swallow of scotch and reminded her about Robyn lying to him over the broken date.

"But you never told her you'd driven by. She might be able to explain why her car wasn't there if you'd just ask her."

"There's only one explanation, Ricca. She drove it somewhere, most likely to her boyfriend's place."

"You don't know that for sure. You're making an assumption. You know what they say about the word assume. It's the ASS before U and ME."

Suzette rose, ambled to the bar, and sat her glass on the counter. "Ricca's right. You should ask her where her car was. What can it hurt?"

Replenishing her Manhattan he said, "Listen, it's over. When I told Robyn I thought it might be a good idea to give each other some space, she didn't protest very much."

Accepting the refill she gazed into his eyes with an alluring intensity. "Well if she's willing to let you go that easily, she's a fool, that's all I can say."

Guilt flared as arousal snaked through him. He turned away, wondering if Ricca and Robert had also taken note of the erotic glow on Suzette's face.

Ricca got up and started towards him. "Believe I'll have another, barkeep."

He glanced at his colleague, who didn't appear concerned about his wife's flirty expression. "How about you?"

"Thanks, don't mind if I do." Robert emptied his tumbler and made for the bar.

Suzette returned to the sofa and once again fixated on him. Darius felt awful but couldn't deny the strong attraction he felt towards her, knowing if she were single he'd set his cap for the hot blonde.

Downing his drink, it dawned on him he should call Holly Hepburn. If she hadn't become attached to some lucky college stud, maybe they could start fresh and see if their mutual attraction might blossom into something special, drowning out all feelings for the unfaithful Robyn and escalating desire for the unavailable Suzette.

SIXTEEN

The memory of last night's passion surge refused to relent—he couldn't get Suzette out of his mind. Darius leaned back in his fancy chair and screwed his eyelids together, trying to force that arousing look she'd given him from his brain. He couldn't call Holly feeling the way he did at present, he'd be using her and that would only serve to compound his ever growing sense of guilt.

Lurching forward, he rubbed his face as though washing it, then slapped both palms on his desk. "Dammit!"

The intercom quickened. *"What's the matter?"*

He pressed the button. "Sorry about that, Ricca, just thinking out loud."

"Oh . . . wanna talk about it?"

Staring at the intercom as if she could see him through it, he spouted out the problem.

His office door opened and Ricca leaned against the doorjamb, arms crossed beneath her breasts. "Stop feeling guilty, Darius, you haven't done anything wrong."

A sour groan forced its way out of his mouth. "I can't get her out of my mind. That crazy look she gave me last night went right through me and I've been lusting for her ever since. Why did she do it?"

"Because she's in love with you."

Dazed, he gawked at her for a pregnant moment, laughing as though she were joking, yet knowing she meant it. "That's crazy—absolutely absurd. She no more feels that way about me than I do her."

"Robert knows it too. We've been discussing it for some time." She studied him awhile, looking pensive as if in deep deliberation. At length she dropped into an armchair in front of his desk and let out a big sigh. "There's something else I need to tell you."

He arched his brows in response.

"Robert and I are having an affair."

"Come again?"

"We've been seeing each other since the Rollins case."

His arms fell lifelessly to the sides of his chair. "You can't be serious."

Ricca crossed her legs. "I'm not ashamed of it. I love Robert and he loves me. He and Suzette haven't slept in the same bed for months. He's been wanting to tell her about us but I made him wait until Marcus's trial was over. We just got off the phone a moment ago. He's going to ask her for a divorce tonight."

Still dumbfounded over her disclosure, he involuntarily pulled himself forward. The chair stopped rolling when his abdomen collided with his desk. "You've been having an affair since the Rollins case? How did it start?"

She leaned towards him, gripping her upper knee. "Remember that day Rickshaw Rollins insisted on treating you to lunch during his son's trial?"

Nodding, he was so numb he barely felt his head move.

"Robert called, wanting you to have lunch with him. I told him you couldn't and joked that I was available. He said he'd take me up on it. Over lunch I could tell something was really troubling him and asked if he'd like to talk about it. He didn't at first, but you know me, I kept prodding until he did. He told me that he and Suzette had somehow became mere friends and no longer shared the same bed, and confessed he'd had a thing for me for quite some time. I'd always had a special feeling for Robert but didn't know until that moment how special it was. I told him about it, and we've been seeing each other on the sly ever since. We're going to get married as soon as the divorce is final."

Shock glued him to his chair as he sat there trying to make sense of it all. Ricca had never shown any signs of feeling that way about Robert, and he'd never picked up any vibes for his secretary coming from the lawyer. If Robert had managed to conceal his desire for Ricca from Suzette as effectively, the sumptuous blonde was in for the surprise of her life.

When the initial blow finally ebbed he grabbed the arms of his chair and pushed himself to his feet. "Get up."

Alarm sprang to her face. "Why?"

"So I can give you a hug . . ." he stepped to her.

Her arms went around his neck and she broke into tears.

"I love you, Ricca, and I want you to be happy."

"Thank you, Boss. I've hated keeping this from you. It feels so good to get it out in the open."

He squeezed her tight. "I know."

She squeezed back. "So you're not going to fire me?"

"No, but I'm sure you'll be leaving me since you won't have to work anymore."

"Fat chance. I love my job. Wild horses couldn't drag me from it and Robert damn well knows it."

Breaking free of the embrace he gave her a warm smile. "Glad to hear it, but Robert's liable to want you to work for him."

"No way I'm leaving you. Besides, he has his own loyal secretary."

Relief poured over him. Unlike Robert, whose relationship with his secretary was purely professional, sans sex Darius depended on Ricca like a surrogate wife. Chuckling inside he thought about how lost he'd be without her. Before long his mind turned back to the sexy prosecutor.

"So what should I do about Suzette?"

Ricca snickered and gave him a knowing smile. "Tell her how you feel, silly."

Returning to his chair, he plopped down with a harsh sigh. "That's just it, Ricca. I don't know how I feel other than . . . you know."

"Horny for her?" she said, giggling again.

He nodded, feeling like a lowlife for admitting it. "Why do you and Robert think she's in love with me?"

"Remember that night when the four of us had dinner together and she vowed you'd never beat her if you guys ever got pitted against each other? Remember how adamant she was about it?"

"Oh yeah."

"Look at how mellow she accepted her defeat."

Frowning, he leaned forward, forearms crossed atop his desk. "But she wasn't defeated, I told her that."

"She thought she had been until you pointed out that justice was served instead."

"Well that's no reason to assume she's in love with me."

She gave him a reproving smirk. "You're not seeing the forest for the trees. Robert and I both agree her actions last night confirmed what we'd both suspected, especially that bedroom stare she kept giving you after asking about Robyn."

Hearing it expressed as a bedroom stare confirmed he hadn't misread Suzette's expression. That fact—coupled with knowing the hot blonde would soon be available—caused an erotic thrill to race through him. "Maybe I *should* talk to her."

Ricca turned deadly serious. "Are you sure it's truly over with Robyn?"

"I don't want it to be, but it is. Robyn can't help how she feels about her ex boyfriend."

"I still say you should give her a chance to explain why her car wasn't there."

The world had just turned so upside down, nothing would surprise him now. "Tell you what, why don't I do just that. Get her on the phone for me?"

A big smile spread across her pretty face which had been glowing since she'd confessed her feelings for Robert. "You got it, Boss."

SEVENTEEN

He told Robyn about driving by her house the night she'd complained of the migraine, and waited expectantly for her reply but heard only silence on the other end of the phone.

Pacing back and forth in front of his desk he said, "Robyn, are you still there?"

More silence.

"Robyn?"

"I . . . ."

"You what?"

"I lied to you about the headache but not for the reason you think."

Anger gripped him but he took a deep breath to calm himself. "Well then, tell me why you lied."

Silence.

"Robyn, tell me why you lied or I'm going to hang up this phone and never speak to you again."

"It has to do with who you are."

"Who I am?"

"You know . . ." her voice trailed. *"The ring and all."*

"What does that damn ring have to do with all this?"

She gasped. *"Oh no, you mustn't curse the ring, Darius— never!"*

Eyes cinched with mounting frustration he shouted, "Robyn, you've become fixated by that damn—"

"Please, you mustn't curse the ring!"

"Good grief . . ." he shook his head with bewilderment. Why did she find that ring so ridiculously important?

"Please let me fix dinner for you and we'll talk about this tonight."

Scratching his chin, he pondered whether to accept her invitation.

"Darius, are you there?"

"I'm here."

"Well? Will you come over for dinner?"

He raked his mouth with the back of his hand and stabbed it in the right front pocket of his trousers, making a fist in the process. "Okay. What time?"

"Is seven okay . . . ?"

* * * *

The mouthwatering savor of roasted chicken teased his nostrils alongside the light fragrance of Robyn's perfume. She looked lovely as ever but he refrained from admiring her through the meal like he used to enjoy doing. Instead he concentrated on the Cornish Hen and steamed vegetables, not uttering a word until he finished.

He rose from the table and folded his arms across his chest. "Okay, I'm ready to hear why you lied."

Nervously wringing her hands—the engagement ring sparkling on the left one, mocking him because he figured she'd only put it back on for this occasion to buttress the illusion she still loved him—she lowered them to her lap, clearing her throat in the process. "I know you'll find this hard to believe, but I was in a trance."

"Come again?" His voice replicated the utter disdain her idiotic explanation invoked.

"I know it sounds crazy, but it's true. I was told to tell you I had a headache, and then was instructed to meet with The Mede."

"The Mede . . .?" he creased his brow with a heated glare, wondering what kind of fool this bitch thought he was. "Who the hell is The Mede?"

A rose tint flooded her face. She drew an uneasy breath. "I'm getting to that."

Feeling his own features burn, but with anger rather than

apprehension, he leered at her. "Before you 'get to that', who told you to lie? Your boyfriend?"

"This doesn't have anything to do with my past with him."

"Quit dodging the question. You lied to me because you wanted to be with him."

"You're wrong . . ." tears dribbled from the corners of her eyes. She wiped them away with the tips of her index fingers. "Please let me explain."

"You've got exactly thirty seconds to tell me who told you to lie before I walk out of here convinced you're making the whole thing up." He looked at his watch. "Thirty . . . twenty-nine . . . twenty-eight . . . twenty-seven . . . ."

"Okay . . .!" she jumped to her feet. "Raul is no longer my boyfriend, but it *was* him who told me to lie to you and meet with The Mede. And before you accuse me of making that up, let me explain everything. Raul is like you, he's of Persian descent. He's an expert on ancient history so I called him to find out if he knew about Cyrus's Ring, and he flipped out, demanding to know how I'd learned of its history. When I told him about you he gave his two weeks notice where he worked in California and moved back to Fort Worth to investigate. I swear that's the only reason he came back. And as I've told you before, I broke up with him, not the other way around. There's nothing between us and there never really was to begin with.

"He's a magi mystic and has the power of hypnoses. He asked if he could hypnotize me to get the details of all I'd learned about the ring, including its description. I agreed and it worked—I went under. For reasons he still hasn't told me, he refuses to meet with you and actually see the ring for himself.

"He explained that while I was under his spell so to speak he implanted a phrase that would cause me to go back into a trance any time he used the command. That night I broke our date, I never intended to, but he called me and used the phrase. I went under . . . he told me to tell you I had a headache and couldn't keep our date. After that he told me to go see The Mede, and I did.

"I have very vague recall about what goes on when I'm in the trance, and have been in several since Raul first hypnotized me. When I started finding it hard to remember some of my work days I realized the command must have been inadvertently given at times by fellow employees. I told Raul to undo the phrase so I wouldn't go under anymore because it was liable to cost me my job.

"He apologized for not coming up with a more original key to put me under, not realizing that it would have the same affect if someone else said it to me. As incredible as you're going to find this, you called me today less than an hour after he removed it. He wouldn't tell me what the phrase was for fear it might become activated again."

Bellowing a short and bitter laugh, he sneered at her. "Are you really stupid enough to think I'd believe that?"

Tears again tracking down her cheeks, she raised her arms in a gesture of helplessness. "It's the truth, I swear it."

He stormed for the door.

"Darius, please . . .!"

EIGHTEEN

Feeling stiff and uncomfortable inside the rented tux, Darius stood nearby, smiling at the two of them as the preacher spoke. Serving as best man, he'd already handed the ring to Robert.

". . . And do you, Ricca, take Robert to be your lawful wedded husband?"

He'd never seen his secretary look so happy. Stars danced in her eyes as she said, "I do."

"Then by the power vested in me by the great state of Texas, I pronounce you man and wife." He turned to Robert with a smile. "You may kiss the bride . . . ."

After leaving the wedding reception they settled at a table in a nightclub. Suzette looked sensational in a low-cut dress with her shimmering blonde hair caressing her smooth white shoulders. Unlike the prosecutor who hadn't changed clothes after the wedding, Darius had traded the monkey suit for a turtleneck and blazer. Though not an official date, it was the first time they'd ever been alone together.

The waitress arrived with his scotch and Suzette's Manhattan.

She raised her glass for a toast. "Here's to Robert and Ricca, may they live happily ever after."

"Here, here . . ." he clicked his drink against hers.

"Thanks for asking me to have a drink with you." She downed a sip and smiled at him.

Admiring her sultry lips, he tasted his scotch and grinned. "Thanks for coming."

"You know—" she swirled her bourbon mix beneath her chin "—I really am happy for the two of them. I guess you find that hard to believe."

He shook his head. "Not at all."

"Robert and I should have just remained friends, as we are now and ever shall be. We just weren't meant to be lovers. Can you understand that?"

"Oh yeah. That's the way it is with Ricca and me, so I understand perfectly."

An erotic gleam rose in her eyes. "You and I on the other hand . . . ."

The look both excited and unnerved him. He wasn't sure of his feelings for her other than the certainty of lust. A relationship couldn't be built solely on that. "Suzette, let's take things slow. Okay?"

Her striking visage reflected offense had been taken by the remark, but she tried to cover it with a smile. "Of course."

"Let's get to know each other better and see where it takes us."

She sipped her Manhattan and set the glass on the table. "Whatever you say, counselor."

He'd never seen her look vulnerable before, and could tell she thought she'd concealed the hurt. "So tell me what I don't know about you."

Donning a responsive air he knew was contrived, she fluffed her hair. "Such as?"

"Tell me about your childhood . . ." he reached for her hand.

Pleasant surprise replaced her faked veneer as she placed a soft palm in his, looking down at the union. "Uh-uh, tell me about yours first. Did you always want to be a lawyer when you grew up?"

"Hah! No. As a matter of fact I had my heart set on pro ball."

She looked him over. "Hmm, I'd say you're not much over six feet tall so I don't figure you mean basketball."

"As a matter of fact I lack an eighth of an inch being six feet, and no, I meant football."

Raising the glass to her moist lips with her free hand, she paused before imbibing. "With your muscular physique, I'm going to guess you aspired to be either a running back or a linebacker."

The statement impressed him—she seemed to know her football. "I was an All State tailback in high school."

"Doesn't surprise me. So what happened, you weren't good enough for the pros or what?"

"I got knocked out from butting heads with a linebacker— left him unconscious too—and it caused my mother to have a panic heart attack, so I didn't play college ball. I like to think if I had, though, I'd have been drafted by the NFL."

A depiction of certainty draped her stunning features. "There's not a doubt in my mind you would have been since you're incapable of losing at anything."

He frowned. "Why did you say that?"

"What?"

"That I'm incapable of losing at anything."

"Ricca told me about your secret weapon, Darius. She said you're a direct descendant of Cyrus the Great and have a ring that passed down from him that makes you invulnerable to defeat of any kind."

Releasing her hand he straightened in his seat with a groan. "Oh man, don't start in with that shit. I can't believe Ricca told you that."

Her brows shot up and she broke into a giggle. "You cussed! I've never heard you do that before."

As happy as he'd been for Ricca a short while ago, at the moment he wanted to strangle her for mouthing off to Suzette about the stupid ring. He took a long drink and shook his head with a bitter sigh.

Suzette laughed again. "What's so terrible about it? I don't understand."

Studying her face for evidence of mockery, he found none. "You don't believe it do you?"

Comely lips spreading into a knowing smile, she shifted in her seat, the action reminiscent of a brooding hen gently adjusting herself over her eggs. "You beat me, didn't you?"

"I didn't beat you." He downed another swallow of scotch.

She grabbed his hand. "Darius, have you ever lost at anything?"

"Sure I have."

"Let's hear it then. What did you lose at? And don't say a football game or any other team sport. What have you ever failed at as an individual?"

It startled him to discover he couldn't think of anything at the moment.

Squeezing his fingers she said, "Well?"

"Nothing in particular comes to mind right now but I've lost at a lot of things."

Still eying him, she increased the pressure, forcing his knuckles closer together. "Ricca believes you're unbeatable and so do I."

He squeezed back affectionately, wondering why Ricca had never said those words to him. *Probably afraid I'd get the big head.* The thought made him chuckle inside. Straining to recall a loss, all jocularity vacated his mind when he couldn't.

"You're trying to remember losing at something, aren't you."

The insightful statement made him feel even more concerned. He'd lost at love with Avery but in the end wound up the winner so that didn't qualify as a loss. Robyn didn't count either because he'd dumped her. Was it possible he hadn't been defeated at anything? He never thought about it except when someone else brought it up, but he had to have lost or surely he'd have been aware he hadn't. That satisfied him. *If I'd really never lost at anything, I'd know it.*

"Penny for your thoughts, counselor."

He pulled his hand from hers and grabbed his drink. "I was just thinking about how much I enjoy your company."

"Not a very smooth segue," she said, narrowing her eyes.

"It's the truth."

She started drumming the fingers he'd just freed. "No it's not. I could tell by the look on your face you were racking your brain trying to remember losing, and couldn't."

Darius gulped more scotch, admiring and envying her powers of perception. Suzette was quite a woman.

"The truth is, counselor, you've never lost and never will. You ought to run for president someday."

"Nonsense." Robyn asking if he'd plan to go into politics to fight for justice flashed in the mirror of his mind. He immediately shook off the memory, wishing he'd never met the lying bitch. "Everybody loses sometimes."

She savored her Manhattan and set the glass on the table. "Except you."

Seeing he was getting nowhere, he gave up. "Let's change the subject . . . ."

NINETEEN

He followed up Marcus's case with four victories, none of them taking place in Dallas, and had gained worldwide notoriety in the process. The first trial had been in Los Angeles where he'd spent three months getting a celebrity acquitted for allegedly murdering a director who'd kicked her off a big time movie she'd been set to headline. The second took place in New York. The CEO of a renowned brokerage firm had been charged with embezzlement. After uncovering an elaborate conspiracy and proving his client hadn't stolen a nickel, he'd gotten the accused assassin of a congressman off the hook in Washington D.C. That trial had lasted six months. Before a week had gone by after returning to The Metroplex, he'd found himself once again on the east coast, defending a Boston millionaire accused of rape. Increasing his fee with each triumph, Darius had become a wealthy man.

He'd met Suzette for lunch and drinks a few times after their initial get together the day Ricca and Robert married, but being out of town so much had left him precious little time to pursue her. He hadn't even managed a first kiss, a depressing fact he planned to change.

Arriving at his office, he stopped at his secretary's desk. "Reserve two seats on a flight to Houston to leave as soon as possible after five this evening."

Still glowing with honeymoon fervor, Ricca looked up with a smile. "Taking Suzette away for the weekend?"

"Yep . . ." he gave her a wink and a grin. "I plan to hole up in a hotel till Sunday, and then we're going to a Texans game with the Derby twins. Book us a room at the ritziest hotel you can find and a late flight back Sunday night . . . ."

Sitting down at his desk Darius whistled a tune as he dialed the prosecutor's office to surprise Suzette with his weekend plans for the two of them, knowing she'd be thrilled.

"*. . . Dammit, Darius, I wish you'd told me sooner! My mother's flying in from Galveston to spend the weekend with me. I invited her yesterday.*"

Cursing silently, he bit his lip, disappointment gnawing at his gut. "So I guess it's too late to ask her to make it next weekend huh?"

"I'm afraid so. Listen, why don't you join us for dinner tomorrow night? I'd love for you to meet her."

"Can't. My friends are expecting us. They rented a luxury box for the Texans' game just for the occasion."

An annoyed sigh assaulted his ear. "The game's not till Sunday."

"Yeah, but I don't want to have to take a late flight tomorrow night. I'm fried. I want to get to Houston tonight so I can chill through the weekend."

She sighed again, this time with resignation. "I understand."

"Tell your mom hello for me. How about lunch on Monday?"

"You're on, counselor. I wish I'd known. You know I'd love to spend the weekend with you."

Hearing her say that—especially with the erotic tone she'd used—fiercely turned him on, compounding his frustration. "I know . . . ."

The plane landed at seven. By eight he'd settled in his room, still trying to resist a desire that had plagued him since touching down in Houston. Noticing the time pushing towards nine he couldn't withstand the temptation any longer. He picked up the phone.

"*. . . Hello?*"

Darius inhaled an excited breath. "Holly?"

"*Yes?*"

"Darius Darkfire here. Remember me?"

* * * *

They had a drink at Baker's Dozen and afterwards went to his hotel where Holly filled him in on her life since he'd gotten John Derby out of jail. Almost finished with her academics, she was excited about going to law school soon. She ranted about seeing him on television during the assassination trial and had just mentioned how privileged she felt knowing a celebrity lawyer.

"I'm no celebrity, just a lawyer."

She shot him a defiant grin. "Yes you are and you know it, mister modest."

He picked up the phone to call room service. "I'm going to order some scotch, what would you like?"

Holly glanced around at the sophisticated furnishings and turned to him with a worried pout. "Darius, this is one of the swankiest hotels in Houston. Do you have any idea how expensive room service must be here?"

That brought a smile to his face. "Do you have any idea how stiff my rates have become? Trust me, you won't break me. Now what'll you have?"

A blush rose up her cheeks. "I'm so embarrassed, I should have realized. Okay, how about a bottle of Chardonnay?"

"You got it . . . ."

He ordered some food as well and hung up the phone. "You didn't mention your love life when you got me caught up at the nightclub. Anything going on I should know about?"

To his surprise her eyes dropped to the floor and she turned so red he couldn't make out the few freckles on her face. "I . . . I'm engaged."

Feeling awkward and astounded, he sucked in a lungful of air and exhaled a groan. "When did you plan to tell me?"

Her pale-blue orbs rose slowly, covered by a misty glaze. "I wasn't going to. I don't know why I just did."

"I see."

"Please don't be angry with me."

He'd resisted the urge to call Holly at first for fear he would only be using her as Suzette's replacement. When it dawned on him that wasn't the case and he'd reminded himself that neither he nor Suzette had made any commitments to a relationship, the guilt over wanting to make love to the pretty waitress had dissipated. Over a year and a half had passed since he'd slept with Robyn, and he hadn't been intimate with anyone since, so his hormones were circulating with hurricane strength. Eyeing the lovely aspiring prosecutor, he wanted to go along with her plan to cheat on her fiancé but couldn't. She'd hate herself for it later.

Forcing a smile he said, "I'm not angry, just disappointed. I'd hoped to make love to you . . . and now I can't."

Anxiety drenched her face. "Why not?"

"Come on, Holly, you know why not."

"I'll break up with him! I'll call him right now and tell him we're through!"

"No you won't, because I won't let you."

Tears began. "Darius, I thought you'd forgotten all about me or I'd never have gotten engaged. You've got to believe that."

He believed her all right, but didn't say so. "Why aren't the two of you together on a Friday night anyway?"

"He's away on a business trip."

Their order arrived. The bellboy uncorked the wine and Darius tipped him on the way to the door. Closing it, he turned to Holly.

"You'd really break it off if I asked you to?"

Every feature reeking with sincerity, she nodded.

He poured her some wine, and whiskey for himself, quickly downing a big swallow. It went down his throat with a smooth burn that became a soothing balm in his stomach. Staring at Holly's full breasts as she took a sip from her glass, he undressed them with his eyes, imagining the shape of her nipples.

"I want to make love to you, Holly, but I don't want to leave you with a sense of guilt and mar your relationship with your intended."

Her cherry-lipped mouth went slack as blatant arousal ignited her face. She sat the wine down and started unbuttoning her blouse, the action of her lithe fingers holding him spellbound. "There isn't a relationship anymore. I'm in love with you, Darius . . . ."

* * * *

They slammed back one beer after another while watching the Texans battle the Indianapolis Colts. The Derbys had gone all out, not only renting the luxury suite but hiring a chauffeured limousine to escort them to and from Reliant Stadium as well.

The Texans had gotten a bum deal early in the game. A touchdown got called back because an official claimed the receiver had touched the boundary line while catching the scoring pass. Though the penalty had been challenged and video replay clearly showed the player's foot in bounds, the referee had inexplicably refused to overturn it. The drive stalled and ended with a punt. Towards the end of the fourth quarter the home team scored a rushing touchdown and made the extra point, leaving fifteen seconds on the game clock. After being behind all day, Houston now seemed assured a one point victory.

Like him, Jock and John—though lifelong Cowboy fans— also rooted for the Lone Star State's other professional football team. Holly on the other hand couldn't stand Dallas, and bled Texans red and blue. She was screaming at the top of her lungs, running in place inside the luxury box, drunkenly proclaiming victory.

Jock patted her on the back and grinned. "Careful now, darlin', the game ain't over yet."

With hair streaming down her inebriated face she screamed, "Oh yes it is, we won! We won! We beat the mighty Colts!"

Feeling pretty looped himself, Darius laughed and pointed his beer at her. "Holly, you'd best remember that's Peyton Manning's team they're kicking off to."

The Colts had to down the kickoff in the end zone so the ball was placed on the twenty yard line. On the first play Peyton Manning hit Dallas Clark for a thirty yard pass and he made his way out of bounds, stopping the clock at eight seconds. The center Jeff Saturday again snapped the ball and Manning threw a strike to Reggie Wayne who sidestepped a diving cornerback and sped downfield into the end zone, ending all hopes of a home victory.

Holly's face launched into a sweaty oval of horrified disbelief, and she grabbed him by the shoulders. "You never lose, Darius—say you want the Texans to win!"

He started to laugh but she clutched his collar with both hands, eyes threatening. "Say it out loud, say 'I want the Texans to win', say it!"

Realizing she was too drunk to be reasoned with, and more than a little afraid she'd have a conniption fit if he didn't, he humored her. With a shrug of his shoulders he said "Okay, I want the Texans to win" and turned up his beer.

Jock glared at him with wide eyes and a slack jaw. "There's a flag, Homes."

John did likewise. "I don't know how you did it, Dare, but you made that flag appear. We'd have seen it if it had been thrown, man."

He felt numb but not from the beer. John was right. A flag hadn't been thrown or they'd have seen it, yet the official picked up a yellow cloth as the referee announced a holding penalty against Indianapolis. Two plays later the clock expired with the Texans beating the Colts by a single point.

"Yaaawwwwweeeeeeeeee!!!!" Holly jumped in his arms. "You did it, Darius, you made the Texans win!"

* * * *

During the flight back to Dallas the mysterious flag consumed his thoughts. Besides Holly, Jock and John had also given him reprimands about his disbelief in being unbeatable. Though far from sober, Darius hadn't gotten as soused as the Derby twins, and attributed much of their zeal as booze inspired. Nonetheless, that didn't change the bizarre facts surrounding the holding penalty.

"Shit, Homes, that's what I told you when John got into trouble, don't you remember? That's why we wanted you. You can't lose."

Darius had stared blankly at Jock without answering. Meanwhile Holly tried to get him to call heads or tails as she clumsily tossed a quarter into the air in an effort to prove his invincibility. As he'd done at John's victory celebration, he refused to go along.

He'd been leaning back in his seat with eyes closed but opened them when he heard the landing gear being lowered. To his amazement the plane had already touched down and all the other passengers had disembarked. The jet sat motionless on the tarmac.

Must have dozed off.

"Marhaba."

Recognizing the word as 'welcome' in Arabic, Darius looked around for the source of the voice but saw no one.

"Marhaba, Darius Darkfire."

The voice came through the intercom, he realized. Confused, he unbuckled his seat belt and stepped into the aisle.

"Marhaba, we welcome you."

Darius made for the cockpit, figuring the pilot must be speaking to him. The door was locked. He banged on it.

"Who are you?"

"I'm known by many names, Darius Darkfire, but you may

call me The Mede."

Chills shot through him. Fearfully he inched back from the door, noticing the boarding hatch was closed. He pressed his face to the window, alarmed to learn the plane had landed some place besides DFW International Airport.

I must have been drugged—had to have been. But by who?.. . How? . . . Why?

"Please do not be alarmed, Darius Darkfire. As you can see, your destination has been altered."

His jaw fell when he spotted the name of the airport painted above the viewing windows of the boarding gates. Though he recognized the lettering because of his mother, he couldn't decipher the ancient Persian words.

Vertigo seized him as the floor disappeared, sending him hurtling through clouds.

A severe jolt accompanied the sound of plane wheels screeching against the unyielding cement of a landing strip. He jerked his eyes open to find he'd only been dreaming.

Relief swam over him as he saw the other passengers still in their seats, and recognized the friendly structure of DFW International.

TWENTY

The next morning Darius phoned Ricca and told her he'd be late. She asked if he'd managed to enjoy his weekend despite Suzette not being able to accompany him. He told her he'd fill her in when he got to the office . . . .

Robyn yanked off her glasses and sprang from her stool when he walked in. She'd been working on an elaborate drawing that he assumed to be the blueprints for a complicated electrical system. Despite her drab work garb and absence of makeup, she still looked beautiful, and *very* surprised.

"Good morning, Robyn."

Guilt tugged at his insides over sleeping with Holly. Though he'd been honest and up front after she confessed she'd fallen in love with him—telling her that a relationship with Suzette seemed likely to happen—the giddy college student had told him she wanted him even if that one night wound up being the only intimacy they would ever share. It wouldn't have been. They'd had such a wonderful time together that when he kissed her goodbye at the airport he'd already begun secretly laying plans for a romantic dinner the following weekend during which he'd ask her to marry him, knowing she'd soon replace Robyn in his heart. But last night had changed that—he now believed the voluptuous brunette nervously eyeing him had told the truth.

He could tell she wanted to hug him but was afraid to, obviously not wanting to weaken whatever motivation had brought him to her. Instead she crossed the room to refill her coffee, asking if he'd like some.

"Sounds good."

She handed him a steaming cup, still cautiously evaluating him. "I was afraid I might never see you again."

Giving no response, he sipped the coffee, relishing the rich flavor enhanced by a spoonful of sugar and a dash of cream.

"Um, what brings you here?" Her face reflected anxiety that she might have said the wrong thing with her previous statement.

"Relax, Robyn. I came here to tell you I believe you now, and I want to hear about The Mede."

Relief flooded her big dark eyes. "You do? I don't want to press my luck, but what changed your mind?"

"The weirdest thing happened . . ." he told her about the mysterious yellow flag at the end of yesterday's game.

"So now you finally believe you're unbeatable like the legacy contends?" she said excitedly.

"I didn't say that."

"Oh. Then you must have more to tell me, I guess."

Nodding, he told her about the dream he'd had on the flight.

Her pretty face knotted with a frown. "That's it? That dream made you believe me?"

"Not by itself . . ." he turned up the cup, again savoring the robust blend. "I had another one later last night."

Smiling with wonderment, she shoved her hands inside her baggy overalls, making it look like her stomach pooched out beneath her plentiful breasts. "I'm dying to hear how a dream convinced you I was telling the truth."

"Figured you might be." He raised the cup. "This is some mighty fine coffee."

"Well, don't keep me in suspense." The irritation in her voice revealed she now felt safe letting her guard down.

"I was in the throne room of a huge palace with a crowd of people, all of them dressed in ancient Arabian garb—turbans, shawls, shoes with curled up toes, the whole nine yards. A king sat on the throne—an imposing figure with jewels all over the place—his crown, his clothes, his scepter. You get the picture.

"He tapped his scepter on the floor and everybody moved to

one side or the other of the room, forming an aisle from the huge double doors at the entrance all the way to the elevated throne.

"I was confused and didn't know which side I should move to so I just stood in the aisle, staring at the king. Then I heard the doors open and in walked a man who looked like a beggar, wearing a hooded burlap robe. He had a shepherd's crook which he used to help him walk, and he limped all the way up to the king.

"It had been noisy up to that point, everybody chattering and stuff, but when the beggar went down to his knees the king raised his scepter and a hush fell over the room.

"Now don't laugh when I tell this part, but I remember the conversations verbatim so I'm just going to say it like they did, emphasis and all. The king looked down and said to the beggar, 'What brings The Mede into the presence of the king?' to which the beggar replied, 'Oh Mighty Cyrus, live forever. I have come to present you with the ring as instructed by The Most High.'

"The king—who I then knew to be Cyrus the Great—said, 'May the ring be presented to Shiloh, whose right the throne is.'

"The beggar handed a leather pouch to Cyrus and he pulled the ring out, holding it in the air so everybody could see it. Then he put it back into the pouch and said, 'It shall never be worn except by Shiloh when He comes at the end of the ages. Woe to any that strive against its keeper for they shall know defeat. The words of Cyrus on this matter have ended. And you—' he pointed his scepter at me, and everybody gasped except Cyrus and the beggar. I tried to ask him to finish the sentence but couldn't speak. Next thing I knew my alarm was ringing and I woke up. I've never had a dream like that. I believe God gave it to me to show the ring really did originate with Cyrus."

Robyn's face had paled during his discourse, and now her

brows were arched above two gaping dark orbs brimming with astonishment. "Darius, The Mede uses a cane."

He didn't know if he'd lost color as well but if his visage reflected the emotion her words evoked, Darius knew he must look like a ghost. An involuntary whistle blew through his lips.

"My sentiments exactly," said Robyn, slowly nodding her head.

"So tell me more about The Mede, and how soon can you arrange a meeting?"

A fearful gape leapt to her face. "He won't see you. Neither will Raul."

"How do you know?"

"Raul told me."

"Tell me where I can find him then."

Coffee dribbled over the edges of a suddenly quivering cup, clutched by her shaking hand. She looked terrified. "I can't."

"Robyn . . ." he inhaled a deep breath through his nose, trying to hold back rising anger. "You're seriously trying my patience."

Moisture packed her anxious eyes. "I don't want to upset you, Darius, but I can't tell you where he is because I don't know."

"Okay, tell me where you went to meet him the night you lied to me."

A solitary tear escaped, cutting a labyrinth down her cheek. "I don't know that either, because I was in a trance at the time and don't remember where Raul told me to go."

"Dammit! Okay, tell me where Raul is, I'll get him to rat out The Mede's whereabouts."

"It won't do any good. Raul won't tell you, and he'll only get super pissed at me for telling you his address."

He tightened his jaw. "I'm going to be super pissed at you if you don't . . . ."

* * * *

Robyn had been so distraught about giving him Raul's address that he finally settled for a phone call instead. It took some doing but Darius eventually convinced her to dial the number and make the call show up on Raul's ID as anonymous, then hand him the phone. That way she could honestly tell the dude, if asked, that she hadn't given away any information on him.

"Hello?"

"Is this Raul?"

A long moment of silence went by. *"Who gave you this number, Darkfire?"*

Stunned, Darius covered the phone and whispered to Robyn, "He knows it's me calling."

Blanching with trepidation, she whispered back, "I told you not to call him. Please don't tell him I had anything to do with this."

"Not to worry." He removed his hand from the mouthpiece. "How did you know it was me?"

"Never mind that, how did you get my phone number?"

He faked a laugh. "Give me a break, I'm a lawyer, it's easy for me to dig up information like that."

"What do you want?"

"To meet The Mede."

Ear-splitting laughter rang out, forcing him to pull the phone away from his face. When Raul's cynical snickering finally ebbed, he eased the receiver back to the side of his head. "Did I say something funny?"

"It's not yet time for the two of you to meet in person, Darkfire, but tell me—why do you want to see him?"

Not knowing what to say, he again covered the phone. Raul would only burst out laughing once more if he told him about the dream. He glanced at Robyn. "Does he know you told me about him and The Mede?"

She nodded and he removed his hand. "Robyn told me about him, and got my curiosity up."

To his surprise Raul became cooperative. *"You can't meet with The Mede, but I'll tell you anything you want to know about him . . . ."*

* * * *

After briefing Ricca on Holly Hepburn, the impossible flag, his two dreams, and his visit with Robyn, he sat down at his desk, thinking about what his estranged fiancé's ex boyfriend had told him.

Raul had said he didn't know where The Mede lived. *"He contacts me and arranges a meeting place when he wants to talk."*

According to the magi mystic, The Mede claimed he'd been alive since the Media-Persian Empire ruled the world, at which time he worked as a goldsmith. Though another artisan made the ring for the prophet to hand to Cyrus, it was The Mede that actually presented it to the king. Incredibly, Raul really seemed to believe The Mede was over two thousand years old.

He'd brought up the night Robyn broke their date, and asked why Raul had sent her to The Mede. His answer had chilled him. *"I sent her to him at The Mede's request. He wanted to meet the fiancé of the keeper of the ring."*

On the way to his office after leaving Robyn's workplace, he'd called Preston on his cell and asked him to see if he could find out anything about the mysterious person known only as The Mede.

TWENTY ONE

Suzette became very wroth when he told her the likelihood of their relationship advancing was nil due to the fact he seemed to be heading for a reconciliation with Robyn. Though he still lusted after the sexy prosecutor, he felt no real tenderness towards her. His feelings for Robyn had been strained for a long time but he'd never stopped loving her.

The weekend with Holly had been wonderful and he knew his strong affection for her would blossom into true love if given a chance, but he didn't want to approach her again unless it became clear things weren't going to work out with Robyn. He couldn't bear the thought of Holly being hurt.

He'd invited Robyn to his place to share in the discussion with Preston on what he'd learned about The Mede. The three of them were sitting around the dining table. Robyn, as always, had dolled up after work, and the gorgeous brunette was sipping a martini while he and Preston enjoyed a beer.

"Through my contacts at ONI I was able to learn a few things." Preston adjusted his gleaming spectacles. "The Mede's name is Arash Arshia. Arash means *a hero* in Persian folklore and Arshia means *throne*. He came under scrutiny after Nine-One-One but it's unlikely he knows about it. He's since been cleared of suspicion. My sources assured me there were no birth records to be found on Mister Arshia as they'd diligently dug up every scrap of information on him they could when it appeared he was part of the terrorist threat. They couldn't find any relatives, work or tax histories, and at the time they ceased investigating, had no idea how he earned his living. No one knows if Arash Arshia is his real name or a pseudonym."

Darius frowned. "Sounds suspicious as hell to me. Why'd they clear him?"

"They discovered he wasn't Muslim and concluded, though

quite an eccentric, he was merely a harmless religious fanatic."

Letting that sink in, Darius took a sip of beer, noting a look of deep concern on Robyn's face. "What's the matter?"

"Huh?" She seemed to have been snapped from a daze. "Oh, nothing."

"Well something's troubling you about what Preston just said."

"No. I was just wondering how he made his living. The Mede, I mean."

Preston gave her one of his intellectual smiles. "People like Mister Arshia usually have benefactors who view such as him a guru of sorts, and supply him with worldly necessities in return for his spiritual advice and guidance."

She acknowledged with a nod. "That's probably right. I know Raul thinks The Mede is almost The Second Coming."

"I'd like to investigate Raul as well," said Preston, no longer smiling. "What's his last name?"

Robyn looked agitated, almost as if Preston had insulted her. "Why do you want to investigate Raul?"

"To learn more about The Mede."

"Makes sense to me," agreed Darius. "Tell us his last name."

"Uh-uh."

"Why not?"

Fear sprang up in her dark eyes. "He's very radical and extremely impulsive as well as secretive. I know he wouldn't want me to tell you, so I won't."

Observing Robyn's frightened countenance, Darius wondered what kind of hold Raul held over her. "You look scared to death. Did he beat you? Are you afraid he'll harm you physically if he finds out you told us his last name?"

She quickly shook her head. "No, he never laid a hand on me, but you're right, I am scared of him. Like I told you, he's a magi mystic and he has certain . . . powers."

Intrigue glistened through Preston's glasses. "Such as?"

"I'd rather not say . . ." she looked away from both of them.

Now Darius was intrigued. "Dammit, Robyn, don't clam up like that. What kind of powers does he have besides being able to mesmerize people?"

The investigator perked up another degree. "He's a hypnotist?"

Still gazing off into space, she nodded.

"He hypnotized Robyn, allegedly to glean all the information she had stored in her memory about the ring."

Preston's brows rose above his wireframes. "How interesting that this all circles back to the ring."

He'd told Preston about the Texans-Colts game and his subsequent dreams when asked the reason for investigating The Mede, but hadn't mentioned Robyn's ex boyfriend hypnotizing her or his inordinate interest in the ring.

* * * *

They'd made love in Robyn's bedroom. A streetlight shining through the windows softly illuminated dark tresses spilling onto her pillow, framing a satiated angelic face deep in tranquil slumber. Darius eased himself out of the bed and groped his way through the blackness of her apartment.

Once in her study, he quietly closed the door and switched on the light. Examining the circle of cards in her rolodex he saw she listed the surnames first so he went through every one and found two possibilities—Robinson R and Wyncote R.

Grabbing a pen he scribbled down the phone number and address of each, ripped the page loose from Robyn's notepad, and turned off the light as he snuck back to her bedroom. He'd left his pants on a chair, and receiving just enough illumination from the streetlight to locate them, he stashed the slip of paper in a hip pocket.

Back under the covers he kissed Robyn on the cheek and whispered, "Sweet dreams . . . ."

TWENTY TWO

He'd been gone two months and looked forward to returning to America. Darius had taken on the task of defending an Australian billionaire accused of matricide.

Preston and Ricca had enjoyed their time down under. The investigator especially appreciated getting to visit the Sydney Opera House again after touring it during his military days. Robert, who'd flown down to spend a few days with Ricca midway through the trial, had been enthralled by the magnificent structure as well.

The case had been tried in the Supreme Court of New South Wales and unlike American jurisprudence, perspective jurors in Australia couldn't undergo voir dire so he'd been forced to rely mostly on gut instinct during jury selection.

With his mother dead, Dirk Johansson inherited complete control of an extremely lucrative telecommunications firm. The matriarch of the Johansson family, Matilda Virginia O'Brien Johansson, had fallen to her death through an elevator shaft under construction in an ambitious addition to the family compound. Two witnesses, members of the household staff, testified that Dirk and his mother had been arguing incessantly about which direction the family business should take. Dirk wanted to diversify while Matilda insisted things remain status quo. A proviso in her late husband's will stipulated she'd have final say on all business matters, and that power would transfer to the eldest son Dirk upon her passing. According to the witnesses, Dirk had threatened to kill his mother shortly before her demise.

Johansson's Chief Operating Officer had paid for his plane fare when he'd insisted on a face to face meeting with the accused before making a decision on becoming his attorney. Darius had initially been skeptical of Dirk Johansson's innocence, mainly because he saw no motive for the maid and cook to lie. But when the billionaire confessed to threatening his mother, it was the candor of his statement that made him take the case.

"Crikey, Mister Darkfire, if I had to face trial for every time I threatened to remove me mum from this earth, the courts would be jammed with endless dockets with me being the defendant in each. Yes, many times I threatened to kill her, and she me, that was our relationship—stormy. But I loved my mother very much and she loved me.

"We'd get into arguments over the most trivial things, like I'd say, 'Pass the marmalade, eh Mum?' and she'd glare at me and scream 'I'm not yer bloomin maid, fetch it yourself, ya bloody dill!'

"Next thing ya know we'd be at it and the row would be on, me threatening her, she threatening me. But not once—not one bloody time, Mister Darkfire, did either of us lay a finger on one another in anger. Ask me brother and sis, they'll tell ya the same. That's just the way it was with me and mum."

But the siblings did not tell the same. The fraternal twins, David and Dora, testified that they'd never heard their brother threaten their mother except for that one time the cook and maid attested to. After their testimony Dirk told him, "Poor bastards, they think they're helping me by lying when it's right way round, poor bloody bastards."

When Preston discovered the *poor bastards* would split the entire bulk of the Johansson estate if their older brother got convicted, and that Matilda Johansson had a double-indemnity clause in her obscenely exorbitant life insurance if fate dealt her any form of death other than natural causes, Darius smelled two twenty-year-old rats.

David had been completely unflappable on cross examination but Dora broke down when Darius managed to trip her up on her alibi, after which she told all.

Preston had returned to the states a few days earlier, and

now Darius was heading back to Dallas with the satisfaction of knowing Dirk had been acquitted and the twins had been arrested for pushing their mother down the elevator shaft.

Ricca sat next to him on the trans-Pacific flight. With their seats pushed back far as possible, both planned to sleep most of the trip.

Darius knew he was dreaming. He recognized Cyrus and the beggar known as The Mede. The king once again pointed his scepter at him, saying "And you—"

"Wake up, Darius, we've landed in Los Angeles."

"Huh . . .? Damn, Ricca, couldn't you have waited just a minute more before waking me up?"

His pretty secretary gave him a puzzled look.

* * * *

Though Darius discovered he'd hit pay dirt with the R Wyncote information he'd lifted from Robyn's rolodex, the Johansson case had prevented Preston from investigating her former paramour. Two days after he and Ricca got back to Dallas, the investigator called him.

"Whatever mysticism, philosophy, or religiosity he's into, Wyncote is a highly sought after motivational speaker in several major cities in California as well as Texas. On top of that he makes around a quarter million dollars annually as a financial consultant. He'd been working for a firm in Los Angeles but now lives in Fort Worth. He's never been married but I don't know if he lives alone or with a lover. So far I haven't found any information on his relationship with Arash Arshia. Wyncote dutifully pays his taxes and has no rap sheet. On paper he's a model citizen."

Darius exhaled a disappointed sigh. "Doesn't look like we're going to learn anything about The Mede at this rate."

"Do you want me to give up on it?"

"No, keep digging."

* * * *

Robyn lay wilting in his arms, the afterglow enhancing her incredible beauty. He brushed a lock of hair from her slightly damp forehead. "I found out Raul's last name."

Her eyes went wide. "You did? How?"

Shoving the hand under his head, he stared at the ceiling. "He's not the only one with *certain powers.*"

"What is it?"

"Humph . . . I can't divulge what my powers are."

A small giggle evacuated her pretty mouth. "Not your powers, silly, Raul's last name."

"Why tell you? You already know it."

She grinned and half sang, "Somebody's bluffing."

"Nope."

"Are too."

"Am not."

"Are so."

He laughed. "Okay, I'll tell you. It's Robinson."

Turning over on her stomach with a triumphant chuckle she said, "Nice try, but that's not it. I know you're trying to trick it out of me, and it won't work."

"Are you sure . . .?" he started rubbing the back of her shoulders.

With half her face buried in pillow a pleasant smile reflected she found his massage pleasurable as she nodded her head.

"Hmm, well I'll just have take a wild guess then and say it's Wyncote."

Her body went rigid. "How did you find out?"

"Is that really it? Man, I was only guessing."

Rising up she grabbed the pillow and smothered him with it. "You rat!"

He flipped her over, pulling her beneath him, took the pillow away, and began smothering her. Muffled laughter floated through the downy softness.

"Say uncle!"

The bulge in the center of the pillow shook a vigorous "No" as a dampened "Never!" emerged.

Darius lifted the pillow. "I win."

"Oh you do not, I didn't say uncle."

"Yes you did."

"Did not."

"Did so . . . ."

After their battle ended, Robyn again demanded to know how he'd learned Raul's last name.

"Simple, I snuck a peek at your rolodex while you were sleeping."

Her disheveled hair gave her frowning face a comical appearance. "Nice try but no cigar, I don't have him in my rolodex."

"Whatever," he snickered.

She slapped his shoulder. "Hey, I mean it—he's not in there. Now tell me how you really found out."

He rose from the bed and put his pants on.

"Where are you going?"

"To get your rolodex . . . ."

Scratching his head in confusion, he frowned at Robyn. While he'd been able to find the card with the name Robinson R, Wyncote R was no longer there. "You promise you didn't take it out?"

A sneer of frustration sprang to her face. "Darius, it was never in there."

Setting the rolodex on the night stand, he looked down at her nude form, half covered with a sheet. "Who's R Robinson anyway?"

"A friend of mine from college. Her name's Rebecca. Now quit teasing. How did you find out Raul's last name?"

Blubbering his lips like a horse to punctuate his bafflement, he turned up his palms. "I'm not teasing you. I found a card in your rolodex with the name, address, and phone number of R

Wyncote."

She wrapped the sheet around her upper body and sat up on the edge of the bed. "When was this?"

"Just before I left for Australia."

"Hmm . . . well if you're really not playing games with me then I say it's more proof that you can't lose. You wanted to find his number in there and it magically appeared for you."

"A more likely scenario is that you removed the card some time after I saw it," he said dryly.

"UUGGHHH . . .!" she groaned into her hands while bitterly shaking her head. A moment later she dropped them and shot him a defiant glare. "Have you forgotten the miracle of the Texans' victory over the Colts? If a phantom penalty flag can change the outcome of a pro football game for your sake, why is it so hard to believe a name can't magically appear in a rolodex?"

Mulling her words over, he thought about the two times he'd been challenged to prove his invincibility through the flip of a coin. Silly as it had seemed then, he decided it would be the one way to prove that his inability to lose was a myth even though he now believed the ring really had passed down through the ages from Cyrus. He dug some change from his pants pocket.

Robyn frowned. "What are you doing?"

He tossed her a quarter. "Flip it in the air."

"Why?"

"So I can call heads or tails. If I'm really unbeatable it'll land on whatever I call each time."

"Darius, that's silly. Of course you're going to lose a coin toss at some point but that's not the same as losing at something substantial. You've probably lost at cards or checkers or board games before, haven't you?"

Sniffing a large breath through his nostrils, he pointed at the silver disk resting in her palm. "Not that I can recall, no. Please. Just flip the quarter, and keep doing it until I lose."

She threw it at him. "That's silly, I won't do it."

"Fine, I'll do it myself. At least be good enough to verify how it lands. Here goes—" he flipped the quarter in the air "—tails."

It bounced on the carpet and came to rest.

Glancing down she said, "Tails it is."

He picked it up and tossed it again. "Heads."

After a large number of consecutive correct calls Robyn became enthralled and started counting the tosses. Growing bored with the routine, he stopped at fifty.

Excitement radiated from her. "You can't ever doubt it again—there's no way that could be coincidence."

"So it would seem." He grinned at her. "Do you know what this means?"

"What?"

"I'm going to raise my rates even higher."

Giggling, she started beating him with a pillow.

TWENTY THREE

Darius rang the doorbell of Raul Wyncote. The man who answered looked very much like he'd pictured. Unlike him, Raul's Persian extraction was very evident: black hair, dark piercing eyes, swarthy skin, and heavy lips.

"Hello, Raul, I'm—"

"I know who you are, Darkfire. I've seen you on television."

He gave him a friendly grin. "Sorry to drop by unannounced, but I wonder if we could have a little talk."

Raul didn't return the smile. "I'm not a rude man by nature, but I really don't want to talk to you face to face. I've already told you all I can over the phone, and I feel intimidated, you being the bearer of the ring."

"Well you shouldn't be. I'm just a regular guy like anybody else."

The irritated look on the man's face distorted into a resentful glare. "How dare you say that!"

"You don't seem too intimidated to me. Appears more like you just flat out don't like me."

"You're very perceptive, Darkfire. Now if you'll excuse me . . . ."

Darius stiff-armed the door before Raul could close it. "Look, all I want is for you to hook me up with The Mede, then I'll leave you alone."

An unnerving glower appeared. "What you ask is impossible. There's much you don't understand. Robyn should never have told you about him. If you're wise, Darkfire, you'll let sleeping dogs lie and get on with your life. Dig any further into this and I promise a rude awakening that you'll deeply regret."

Firming his lips, Darius grabbed Raul by the collar and jerked him to his face. "If you don't tell me how to find The Mede, I promise a rude awakening *you'll* deeply regret,

Wyncote."

Raul tried to break free but he forced him backwards into the apartment and kicked the door closed.

The heavy smell of incense assaulted his nostrils and he noted the only furniture in the dimly lit room consisted of large pillows and heavy cushions with decorative stitch-work of mysterious symbols and shapes somewhat resembling hieroglyphics on the inner walls of a pyramid.

"Let me go! You don't know what you're getting into. Let me go or you'll be sorry . . . I promise you, you'll be sorry."

Darius shoved him down on a cluster of purple cushions. "All right, I let you go. Now tell me how to find The Mede."

Scornful laughter ejaculated from the mystic's throat as he craned his head back and snapped it forward. "You don't find The Mede, Darkfire, he finds you."

His eyes took on a mystifying glaze and the dark pools compelled Darius to look into them. Remembering his powers Robyn had spoken of, it dawned on him Raul must be trying to hypnotize him, so he looked away.

More laughter erupted, cavernous and mocking. "What's the matter, Darkfire? Did I scare you?"

Refusing to look back, he took in the room. Everything about it seemed to belong to the distant past. Incense burners jutted out from Persian rugs tacked to the walls. Smoke swirled from them like angry genies threatening to materialize. Antique lamps flickered with solitary flames, their oily aromas contrasting with the burning resins of myrrh and frankincense, two fragrances he recognized because of his mother. The other scents were unknown to him but the combined odors were unsettling, almost nauseating.

At length he finally turned back towards Raul but immediately gasped for breath as Cyrus tapped his scepter and the throne room became divided in two, his subjects forming a long aisle. Jaw sagging with incredulity, he turned all the way around, dumbfounded at the sight. Wyncote's door had been replaced by the massive double portals of the king's palace and stood hundreds of feet away. They opened and in walked the beggar, the one known as The Mede. Shepherd's crook in hand, he limped past him, making his way to the throne.

Darius tried to speak but had no voice. Searching for Raul in the faceless crowd, he couldn't find him.

"What brings The Mede into the presence of the king?"

He spun on his heels to face Cyrus and the beggar.

"Oh Mighty Cyrus, live forever! I have come to present you with the ring as instructed by The Most High."

Cyrus stood. "May the ring be presented to Shiloh, whose right the throne is."

With all his might Darius tried to cry out but his vocal chords remained paralyzed. He heard Raul laughing as the floor disappeared, hurling him downwards like a bomb released from a highflying jet.

"I told you you'd be sorry, Darkfire."

* * * *

Birds were chirping and a swarm of colorful butterflies flittered past his head as he opened his eyes beneath a deep blue sky that seemed to be smiling down on him. It took a moment for him to ascertain the softness he lay on was a thick patch of green grass. Darius surveyed the surroundings. A beautiful pastoral setting stretched before him. He started to get up but fell back with alarm when he saw his business attire had been replaced by garb resembling a Roman soldier's without the armor.

Finally attaining his feet, a baaing sound made him turn around. A large ram galloped up to him and stopped.

"Welcome, Darius, I'm your guide."

He gaped at the talking sheep for a moment, then burst out laughing. "Oh man, what a dream."

Two massive horns moved back and forth with a shaking head. "This is no dream. The Mede sent you here."

Placing hands on hips, he looked around. "More likely something I ate brought me here."

Again the woolen beast shook his head. "Follow me."

The memory of being in Raul Wyncote's apartment returned. "Dammit, he must have hypnotized me after all!"

"Follow me." The verbalizing animal started towards a herd of pigs at the base of a grassy hill.

Darius followed, not knowing what else to do.

When they neared the swine a humongous pink boar barked and grunted though a pair of menacing tusks before snorting out, "Welcome, Darius."

"A talking sheep and a talking pig," he chuckled. "What's next, Mister Ed?"

"Mister Ed?" asked the ram.

"Yeah, the talking horse."

The hog turned his beady eyes towards him. "Haven't had the pleasure of his acquaintance."

Looking skyward he shouted, "Okay, Raul, you've had your fun, now snap me out of it!"

"Hmm . . . don't know him either."

The ram cocked his head. "Nor do I? Who is this Raul, Darius?"

"A guy that's going to get a severe ass whipping if he doesn't bring me out of this hypnotic state."

His curly-horned escort cackled and started onward. "Ass whipping . . . how quaint."

Darius followed up the hill. When they reached the summit the creature nodded towards a flock of snow-white ewes in an emerald valley below.

"That's my harem. Lovely, aren't they?"

Onward they went to the next hill and from the top Darius could see a castle in the distance.

"That's our destination."

He looked at the ovine. "Let me guess who the king is. Cyrus I'll wager."

The ram nodded. "There is no other."

Wondering why the pig and sheep didn't know Raul's name since the imaginary figments had been conjured up by him, he decided to ask about The Mede, hoping Wyncote might slip up and give a clue to his whereabouts through the puppet.

"You said The Mede sent me here. How did he do that?"

Leathery lips spread into a knowing smile. "The Mede can do a lot of things."

"Where's The Mede now?"

"Why in the palace of course." His slit pupils widened with apparent surprise at the question.

All the way there Darius tried to pry information from the conversing mutton but didn't learn a thing. When they arrived, the ram informed the guards that the keeper of the ring had come to call on Cyrus, and the soldiers moved aside while one called for the doors to be opened.

Darius stepped into the courtroom and found himself back in Raul's apartment.

"Had enough, Darkfire, or do you require further demonstration to convince you to back off?"

His eyelids fluttered as Raul's face came into focus. Darius had unknowingly been standing there the whole time. "Listen . . . I don't want any more crap from you. Just tell me where The Mede is and I'll leave you alone."

Raul howled with contemptuous laughter. "You're in no position to dictate terms, Darkfire."

With a swift right cross he sent Raul into a trance of his own and searched the apartment, looking for anything that might have The Mede's address on it. The search proved futile. Knowing the strange Arab wasn't going to tell him anything no matter how much physical pain he might have to endure, and fearing a return visit to the talking sheep, he left before the magi mystic regained consciousness.

TWENTY FOUR

When the doorbell rang he figured Robyn had paid him a surprise visit but much to his amazement he opened the door to find another good-looking brunette standing there instead—a girl he hadn't seen since college.

"Well I'll be, if it isn't Sash Temple."

Her face had matured in the good sense and she'd kept her figure. The last he'd heard she married some guy from out of town and moved away. He couldn't stifle a silly grin of astonishment upon seeing her, but she only managed a semblance of a smile which seemed to require a conscious effort to produce.

"Hi, Dare. I was shocked to find you in the phone book, figured you'd have an unlisted number. I know I should have called first but I wanted to talk to you in person. Hope you don't mind me dropping by unannounced."

"Of course not, come on in." He led her into the living room. "Make yourself comfortable. Can I get you something to drink?"

She chose a stool at the bar and took note of his glass. "I'll have whatever you're having."

He poured a scotch and stayed behind the counter to face her. "It's so good to see you. To what do I owe this honor?"

"I need a lawyer."

An inward groan reverberated through his brain at the thought of another school chum looking him up because of a legal hassle. Couldn't anybody from the past pay him a visit just for old time's sake? "Um, are you in some kind of trouble?"

"No, nothing like that . . ." she sipped her drink and swallowed with a grimace. "I want a divorce."

"I don't handle divorces, Sash."

Another attempt at a smile emerged. "Not even for an old friend?"

"Sorry, no exceptions. Besides, I doubt you could afford my fee." He pulled at his blended whiskey, hoping she hadn't taken it as an insult.

"That's what Raymond's counting on. My not being able to afford a good lawyer."

"Raymond. Is that your husband?"

"Mm hmm."

"So what happened? Why do you want to split the blanket?"

Sash's beautiful eyes—a very unique shade of sapphire—lowered to her drink and she began toying with it. "I found out he's not quite the honest, hard working man he purported to be. He owns an auto parts store but I recently found out he also sells drugs."

"Oh ..." he raised his brows. "How did you find out?"

"I was digging through our storeroom looking for art supplies. I go through these phases of wanting to paint, then loose the zeal, sometimes for months on end, and when that happens I can't stand seeing so much as a paint brush so I stash everything. Anyway, I spotted a cardboard box that I thought I might have crammed my acrylics in, and found it full of packets of white powder instead. I confronted Raymond and he confessed he'd been dealing cocaine for years, using his store to launder the money. Thank God we don't have kids—" she turned up the scotch and made another sour face as it went down her gullet. "Can you imagine? Anyway, he's got all his bases covered. His lawyer assured him that I'll walk out of this marriage with zilch if I leave him."

"I'm real sorry to hear that, Sash. Sounds like you need a good lawyer all right, but I'd be doing you a disservice. You need someone that specializes in divorce."

The trademark orbs turned misty with a glare of injustice. "Darius, I gave that bastard all my savings—thirty thousand dollars—to help him get his store through a tough time or so

I thought. I have no proof I gave it to him and he won't pay me back. He owned the house before I married him so there's virtually no community property. All I want is my savings back, that's all."

Anger at a man he'd never laid eyes on seized him. Sash had always been a sweet girl, she deserved much better than this, but he'd promised himself since law school that divorce was the one litigation he'd never undertake. Besides, if he charged current rates and the proceedings took any time at all she'd be in the red even with a victory.

"Can you prove he's dealing drugs?"

She looked to the ceiling with a harsh sigh. "Unfortunately, no. It'd only be my word against his."

"Where do you live?"

"Frisco."

"Texas?"

"Mm hmm."

"What's his lawyer's name?"

"R. Hubert Stubblefield."

He fished out a pen from beneath the bar and scribbled the name on a napkin. "Tell you what—I won't represent you, but I will give Stubblefield a call and see if I can work something out for you."

That cheered her up. For the first time a genuine smile appeared. "How much will that cost me?"

"Nary a thing. I'll try to connect with him in the morning."

Sash took a leisurely draw from the tumbler, barely squinting this time as she swallowed, and seemed to relax. He hoped her reaction wasn't due to a false sense of security because he wouldn't go any further than trying to reason with Stubblefield on the phone. If that didn't work out she'd have to seek legal help elsewhere.

The corners of her delicate lips turned down, but the action had nothing to do with liquor burn. "I couldn't believe what happened to Marcus. My god how embarrassing for him and

Avery, having that come out about a threesome with the cheerleader."

"Yeah . . . wish I could have kept that under wraps but there was just no other way. Have you heard from them?"

"Haven't talked to either of them since college." She emptied the glass. "I feel so sorry for them. And poor Marcus, having to leave the Cowboys."

"Another round?"

"Please."

Pulling the glass stopper from a crystal decanter, he winked and started pouring. "According to the sports news Marcus signed a multimillion dollar contract with another team so I wouldn't lose too much sleep over it."

"So I heard. Do you think he and Avery will ever get married?"

"I doubt it. Figure they'd have tied the knot by now if they were ever going to, but you never know. Anyway, enough about those two. What ever happened to the Rothschild cousins?"

She rose from the stool and leaned on the bar. "Bernice married an oil man and lives in a huge house outside Richardson, and the last I heard Bernadette was teaching high school English in Allen."

"So they still live in The Metroplex."

"Mm hmm. Do you and the Derby twins still keep in touch since John's trial?"

He grinned. "Oh yeah. Rusty Wurly too."

"Rusty was always such a cut-up. Did he ever marry?"

"Nah, still single like me."

"I heard you got engaged."

"Yeah, but we broke up for awhile, then got back together. Her name's Robyn Tuscany and there's a good possibility we might get hitched soon."

Cupping her drink with both hands, she took a sip and returned it to the counter with a sigh. "I'm never getting married again."

"Don't think you'll be able to trust another guy after this huh?"

"I'm afraid not."

They relived a large portion of their college days, then he began to feel drowsy. He glanced at his watch. "It's been great seeing you again after all these years. I hate to part with good company but I'm afraid it's getting near my bed time."

Hands flying to her mouth, she gasped with embarrassment. "Oh I'm so sorry, Dare! I've overstayed my welcome."

"Not at all, don't be silly. It's just, like I said, time for me to hit the sack. Come on, I'll walk you to your car."

She grabbed his shoulder. "If you mean that, I'd like to stay here. I don't want to be alone."

"Um . . ." he glanced around the room nervously. "Sash, I uh, like you and all but—"

"I didn't mean sleep with you, silly!" Her face was aghast with shock. "I'll take the couch if you don't have a spare bed."

* * * *

When he woke up the next morning he found his guestroom empty, Sash had already left. Planning to take her out for breakfast he'd set his alarm for six so he could shower and dress before she got up. He wondered why she'd risen so early, and though he hadn't told her of his plans, was surprised she hadn't left a note explaining her early departure.

When he got to his office he called R. Hubert Stubblefield.

"Thank you for calling Stubblefield, Bruin, and Mires. How may I direct your call?"

"This is Darius Darkfire and I'd like to speak to R. Hubert, please."

A click sounded and shortly thereafter a man spoke.

"Stubblefield here."

"Yeah, Mister Stubblefield, I'm calling on behalf of Sash

Temple. I understand you're representing her husband in their divorce."

"I'm afraid you've got the wrong attorney, I'm not currently representing anyone named Temple."

It dawned on him he'd used her maiden name, and hadn't thought to ask Sash what her married name was. "I'm sorry, Temple is her maiden name. Her husband owns an auto parts store if that's any help."

A rude scoff rang in his ear. *"This isn't really Darius Darkfire is it."*

"Yes, sir, it is."

"The *Darius Darkfire—the one who handled Ernest Rollins' murder trial?*"

"That's me."

"Well it's an honor, Mister Darkfire. I must say I never thought I'd have the pleasure of speaking to you in person."

Irritated at having his time wasted with the preamble, he gripped his forehead and roughly massaged it. "Thanks. Now then, about your client. Can you place him now?"

"Yes, you must be calling on behalf of Sash Masterson."

"I'm embarrassed to say I don't know her married name, but she lives in Frisco and her husband owns an auto parts store."

"That has to be her. What can I do for you?"

Trying to figure out exactly what he thought he could achieve since he'd so severely screwed up by not even knowing Sash's current surname, he downed a gulp of coffee.

"Are you still there, Mister Darkfire?"

"Yeah. Listen, I'm not representing Sash since I don't handle divorces but she's an old friend and I told her I'd give you a call and try to reason with you. All she wants is her savings back. Your client can have everything else."

Stubblefield chuckled. *"An old friend, huh? And yet you don't even know her married name. I don't know who you are but you're obviously not Darius Darkfire. I'm going to hang up now, and don't call here again."*

Darius stared blankly at the dead receiver for a second or two before slamming it down on the cradle.

A few moments later Ricca announced that R. Hubert Stubblefield was on the line.

"A thousand apologies, sir," said Stubblefield. *"After hanging up on you I buzzed my secretary to tell her not to accept any more calls from the man who'd just phoned. She checked her caller ID and informed me the call came from your office. I can't tell you how badly I feel about the misunderstanding. I honestly thought it was someone pretending to be you."*

"Apology accepted. Now then, as I said before, all Sash wants is her thirty thousand dollars back that she gave her husband to get his auto parts store through a lean time."

"Mister Darkfire, according to my client that's a pure fabrication. He maintains his wife has never given him any money at all much less her life savings. The fact is he's very concerned about her and fears she's suffering some sort of dementia because of the allegation."

He raked his fingers through his hair while mulling that over. "I see. Well obviously we have a standoff here—her word against his. I guess a judge will have to decide which one of them's lying."

"Uh, I thought you weren't representing her."

"I wasn't until now . . . ."

* * * *

Darius located Raymond Masterson's auto parts store and pulled into the parking lot. Sash still didn't know he'd become her lawyer and he didn't plan to tell her until after he talked to her husband.

The place smelled of brake fluid and rubber, the aisles were well stocked with merchandise, and the counters were tidy. He walked up to a young man beside a cash register and asked if the owner was in.

"Yeah, Raymond's in the office, but I can't let you go back there."

"Just tell him his wife's legal representative is here to see him, and hand him this." Darius gave him a friendly smile along with a business card.

A few moments later a man he'd never have figured for a drug dealer appeared, obviously quite taken aback that his wife was being represented by one of the world's most sought after attorneys. Tall and clean-cut with a boyish face, Raymond Masterson nervously uttered, "So it really is you."

"If by that you mean I'm Darius Darkfire you're correct, Mister Masterson. I went to college with Sash in case you're wondering how she managed to retain my services. We can talk here in front of the help if you like, or we can go somewhere more private, it's up to you."

Masterson cleared his throat. "Um . . . let's talk outside."

He followed Sash's soon-to-be ex to a wide sidewalk hugging the front of his store.

"I don't know what Sash told you, but she never gave me any money and I don't want a divorce. I love her." The auto parts dealer wore a frown of weary disbelief.

Darius locked eyes with him. "I'll be brief, Mister Masterson. I believe Sash when she tells me she gave you her entire life savings she'd earned before marrying you to help you during a tight business time. I also don't doubt her veracity when she tells me the reason she wants out of this marriage is because you deal in drugs as well as spark plugs, a fact you kept hidden from her when she said 'I do'. And I stand by her when she tells me you are bullying her into thinking she won't get out of this union with a dime if she leaves you.

"Here's the deal. We can do this the easy way or the hard way. The easy way, you give Sash her thirty thousand dollars back plus—oh let's say fifteen percent interest—and she leaves you to your affairs unscathed. The hard way, if she has to drag you to court I'll turn heaven and earth over until I find proof of your, shall we say extra curricular activities, and see to it you spend a good deal of time behind bars."

As expected, the wholesome Wally Clever-ish face turned fearful. "I . . . I think I should talk to my lawyer."

"Fine, let's go see him now. I'm sure he's going to rethink representing you when he learns there's more than just an upset wife claiming you sell cocaine."

Masterson threw up his hands in a gesture of helplessness. "Look man, I'm no drug dealer. I made the mistake of using it myself, I'll admit that, but I quit that shit, you gotta believe me."

Grinning, he propped his palms on the anxious man's shoulders. "Glad to hear it. And now to fully reconcile your mistake, you can cut a check to Sash for the amount I stated. I'll give it to her, arrange for the cheapest divorce possible with neither of you needing an attorney, and your worries will be over. Or shall we go see your lawyer and then a judge to set the court date?

"Just so you understand the proceedings, nine times out of ten the little missus wins these battles and hubby is left paying the court cost as well as the little woman's demands. Add to that the specter of doing hard time in the pen afterwards. It's your call, Mister Masterson. What'll it be, the easy way or the hard way?"

An hour later Darius rang Sash's doorbell and when she answered, handed her a check for thirty-four thousand five-hundred dollars. He received a face full of exuberant kisses and a spine-breaking hug of gratitude for his fee.

TWENTY FIVE

They were at his place, lazing in the sun by the pool, sipping hard lemonade on a Sunday afternoon. Robyn's skimpy bikini top covered little more than the nipples of her large perfectly-shaped breasts, and it had been difficult focusing on her face instead of them while relaying his visit with Raul.

"I wish you hadn't gone to see him, Darius. Please, just leave him alone, he's really scary."

He rose to a sitting position, crossing his legs on a beach towel. "How did the two of you meet anyway?"

"At a party."

"What kind of party?"

"Just a get together at a friend's place. She didn't know him. He showed up with a friend of a friend, one of those things. You have to leave him alone, he's very dangerous."

Straightening his legs, he leaned back on his hands. "The boy is spooky, I have to agree. I can't believe he managed to make me think I was talking to a sheep. Before that I dreamed of Cyrus again but Wyncote couldn't have engineered that. My subconscious must have filled in the void with that particular dream before he started directing a movie with me in it."

She leaned up on her elbow, still frowning with concern. "That's just the tip of the iceberg of what he can do. I wish you hadn't hit him. He's liable to want revenge."

"Think I should go see him again and apologize?"

Wide-eyed alarm replaced the frown. "Please don't ever go back there, Darius. If he wants revenge, he's going to get it, but there's no sense in you making it easy for him. Stay away from him, maybe he'll let it pass."

"Oh I'm afraid it's far too late for that, my friends."

Darius jumped to his feet, whirling around to locate the

speaker. Standing outside the sliding glass doors that led to his living room stood a bearded man with intimidating ebony eyes, leaning on a shiny black cane. A white turban atop his head contrasted sharply with the modern business suit he wore.

"Are you . . .?" Darius's voice faltered.

"Yes, Darius Darkfire, I am The Mede. We meet face to face at last."

The deep voice had a chilling edge. A profound sense of dread swam over him as intuition assured this moment marked a critical turning point in his life. Mustering what saliva he could, Darius swallowed, trying to moisten a throat turned bone-dry with shock. "I've been trying to find you."

"I'm aware of that."

Trepidation turned to indignation as it dawned on him the smug Arab had walked through his house uninvited. He grabbed his lemonade, downed a big swallow to further lubricate his oral faculties, sat the bottle down, and turned back to the intruder. "Do you usually go into people's houses without being asked in?"

"I didn't enter your house."

"You must have since I didn't hear the gate open. Those hinges are really squeaky."

He pointed his cane at him. "How I got here isn't important. Why I came is."

"Did Raul send you?"

Lowering the walking stick, he placed both hands on the crook. "Never mind Raul, he's inconsequential to this visitation. I've come for the ring."

Robyn gasped. "You know you can't do that! Only Shiloh can take the ring before seventy years passes."

"Of this I am very much aware . . ." The Mede curled his fingers around the handle, clutching it tightly, continuing to stare at him. "Now the ring if you please."

Crossing his arms over his chest, Darius widened his stance.

"That's not going to happen, but I tell you what is. You're going to tell me who the hell you are and what is going on."

The strange man's face ignited with insult. "You will not speak to me in such a manner, Darius Darkfire. I will demand of you, you will not demand of me. Shiloh is not coming, we will prevent it."

He thought of the many times he'd been embarrassed by his mother's strong belief in the legacy of the ring. Now as he took in the Arabian lunatic glaring at him with despotic black eyes, he felt guilty for being so faithless. Though he'd suspected the circle of gold really had been forged over two thousand years ago since dreaming of Cyrus, he hadn't believed in its importance until now. "You think my giving you the ring will thwart the return of Christ?"

The trespasser's fiery expression cooled. "There's much you don't know, Darius Darkfire, but I will enlighten you to this—the Shiloh coming for the ring is not the real Shiloh. We are not trying to prevent the return of Messiah. We hope to stop the rise of the antichrist."

Robyn rushed to his side and clutched his arm with a death grip. "Don't listen to him, Darius, he's lying!"

Stunned and confused by the man's words, he felt even more so when he saw Robyn's eyes blaze with a weird combination of what appeared to be intense lust coupled with animalistic selfishness as she made the accusation. Trying to shake off the mental image she'd burned in his brain, he looked at The Mede. "So you're telling me the ring has been passed down through the generations to be given to the antichrist?"

He nodded.

"Have all the generations believed it was for Christ like my mother does?"

"None of them knew the truth, not even Cyrus. Ask any theologian, Darius Darkfire, and they'll tell you there is no prophecy in scripture about a ring being given to Messiah to inaugurate the new order. That ring was made by an evil mystic and was given to Cyrus by a man who pretended to be a prophet of The Most High. The whole evil design is to make the world think Messiah has come. I have known of this wicked plan since the beginning. My mission is to stop the false Shiloh from receiving it. This is the final generation, Darius Darkfire. You are the last possessor of the ring. A ring that allows no defeat to the one who possesses it, and bestows unimaginable power upon the one who wears it."

Jaw sagging, heart pounding, mind reeling, Darius tried to make sense of what he'd just been told.

"He's lying, Darius, don't listen to him! Please don't give him the ring!"

Turning to Robyn, his insides twisted as the weird mixture of basal drives returned to her dark orbs, making her normally beautiful countenance appear vulgar, almost ugly. The lawyer in his brain warred against the lover in his heart. All at once it occurred to him something didn't add up about her, and he'd been a fool not realizing it before now.

First there was the odd coincidence of her cousin being named Holly Hepburn, a woman whose number he hadn't been able to find when trying to locate Robyn after they'd spent the weekend together in Houston. Then mysteriously, though he'd been certain she'd said Lockheed—the place where Eval Santa Anna worked—it turned out to be Lochweed and Eval had switched companies. The Lockheed/Lochweed ordeal might have been mere coincidence but the fact that she'd so radically changed since learning about the ring could not.

She'd been too obsessed with it to begin with, and her refusal to discuss Raul Wyncote beyond any superficial degree, along with his number disappearing from her rolodex, now struck him as ominous.

Robyn had been lying since Jump Street—about her cousin's name being Holly Hepburn, and about removing Wyncote's card from the rolodex. He began to wonder if he'd really won all those coin tosses since she'd been the one who verified them. Odds were she'd lied about that too, though he didn't know why.

The lawyer won out and cautioned the lover to proceed carefully. He eyed The Mede. "This is radical stuff you're telling me. I'm sure you can appreciate my need to sort this out. I need time to think this through—at least a week—and if I conclude you're telling me the truth, the ring is yours. If not, things will have to remain as they are."

The Mede stared at him for a long silent moment, his inky orbs unblinking and menacing. "Very well, Darius Darkfire, I'll return in one week."

From his peripheral vision he could see anxiety swimming all over Robyn's face. He started for the patio doors, motioning for the mysterious Arabian to follow. "I'll show you out, and don't ever come into my house uninvited again . . . ."

TWENTY SIX

After The Mede left, Darius told Robyn he needed to be alone. She'd driven to his place for the Sunday evening swim, and after kissing her goodbye at her car he called Preston, told him all that had happened, and that he wanted her investigated.

He no longer thought their meeting on that flight to Houston had been coincidence, and suspected she knew about the ring before then. She'd probably been stalking him a good while before somehow learning of his plans and deciding the time had come for them to *accidentally* get acquainted.

Thinking back on being introduced to her cousin he recalled something that hadn't seemed important then—a look of surprise on the woman's face when Robyn said, "Darius, this is my cousin Holly Hepburn." At the time he'd attributed the expression to the cousin being excited about meeting a semi-celebrity. He now felt it stemmed from Robyn calling her the wrong name, and the fact she somehow knew to play along troubled him. Robyn had told him the other information about her—that she worked at a nightclub rather than a restaurant, aspired to be a tax lawyer rather than a prosecutor—when the two of them were alone, driving around Houston. Preston would verify that part of the mystery one way or the other.

Mind racing, he poured a scotch and collapsed in his recliner. *The Mede can't just take the ring or he'd have already done it. But why can't he just take it . . .?*

Eval Santa Anna entered his musings. He sat his drink on the coffee table and made for the phone to call him. Half an hour later—pacing back and forth, drink in hand—he wondered what the hell was going on. He'd asked Eval if Robyn had anything to do with him leaving Lockheed for

Lochweed. *"Yeah, that's how I got the gig, vato. Robyn recommended me."*

When asked why he'd decided to change companies, Eval had replied, *"More money, man."*

"When did you meet Robyn, where did you meet Robyn, when did you leave Lockheed?" Darius had asked.

Two of the three answers had unnerved him.

"Sure I remember the day I met Robyn—it's easy for me to recall because it was the same day John Derby got out of jail. I went out to celebrate the occasion and saw you and John on TV at the bar I went to. I said, 'Hey everybody, those are my vatos, I know those guys!' This super foxy chick came up to me, asked if I really knew you, and introduced herself. That chick was Robyn. We closed down the joint talking about you. She just kept asking questions—where you grew up, how we met, what your interests were, wanted to know about your family, stuff like that."

"Why didn't you mention any of that when we were at your office?" Darius had asked.

"Aw man, I didn't want to embarrass her. She'd have killed me if I'd told you all that in front of her."

"Why didn't you tell me afterwards?"

"Shit, man, this is the first time I've talked to you since, and I wouldn't have even thought about telling you if you hadn't asked about it, been so long now . . . ."

The only part of Robyn's connection with Eval that appeared innocuous was her recommending him for his current position at Lochweed. According to his old pal, she and Eval had also discussed their jobs the night they met, and in comparing companies, Eval learned he could make more money at Lochweed doing what he did at Lockheed. Robyn said she'd put in a good word for him if a position ever came open and eventually one did.

Wishing he could press a fast-forward button to make time speed up so Preston could give him the real facts on her, he downed the rest of his whiskey and went to bed.

TWENTY SEVEN

"Bernadette Rothschild is here."

Darius hit the intercom. "Send her in, Ricca."

He rose from his desk to hug Bernadette and asked her to have a seat. Back in college she wasn't pretty like her cousin Bernice because of a prominent nose. She'd obviously gotten it worked on and the sex pot crossing her shapely legs after sitting down in one of his office armchairs looked nothing like the girl he'd gone to school with. The gorgeous woman now giving him a knowing smile looked brazen and utterly confident, radically contrasting with the shy mousy half of the Rothschild cousins he'd known at Southern Methodist.

She'd made an appointment to see him, hoping he'd represent her in a lawsuit. Darius hadn't talked to her but she'd told Ricca over the phone she'd been unjustly suspended by the school system she worked for. As instructed to do since he'd hired her, Ricca scheduled an appointment for a face to face meeting. He never talked to prospective clients on the phone before deciding to represent them, because body language revealed a lot more about a person's integrity than mere words.

As she made herself comfortable he returned to his desk. After discussing their college days and the old gang, he turned the subject back to the business at hand. "Okay, Bernadette, tell me what happened."

"One of my students propositioned me after class one day. I said no of course but he persisted. Every time the bell rang he'd wait until the other students left the room, then start rubbing his crotch, telling me how badly he wanted me and begging me to sleep with him. His name is Geoff Hodges and his father's the head of the school board. I finally warned him if he didn't stop I was going to tell his dad. He wouldn't stop, so I did what I warned him I would do. The next day I was suspended for sexually harassing Geoff."

He let the scenario play out in his mind a moment before speaking. "What do you want to happen?"

"I want my job and good name back along with financial restitution as punishment for them doing this to me. I think they should have to pay at least a million but I'll settle for the highest amount you think I can get."

Her expression made his stomach tighten. It didn't convey the look of someone seeking justice for being wrongfully accused but more like a desire to capitalize on an opportunity. "Did you ever touch him in any way that could be construed as sexual?"

Painted brows shooting upwards, she hissed with indignance. "I can't believe you'd even ask me that. Of course not!"

"Don't take this personal. I have to ask these things because Geoff Hodges' lawyer will. Does Hodges claim to have any proof of any misconduct from you?"

"Oh yes . . ." she rolled her eyes.

"Well, what is it?"

"Pictures."

"Of you sexually harassing him?"

"No, just naked pictures of me he claims I forced him to take if he wanted to pass my class. I was given copies of them when I got suspended."

Inhaling a deep breath, he frowned while emptying his lungs. "When you say 'forced him to take' do you mean forced him to snap the photos or forced him to take into his possession?"

"Both."

He cleared his throat. "I see . . . ."

Heavily made-up eyes angrily narrowing, she cast him an irate sneer. "I didn't pose for the damn things. Somehow he was able to photograph me in the nude without my knowing it."

Not only had Bernadette shortened her nose, she'd also bleached her hair platinum, and the makeup she wore made her look very much like a Gene Harlow or Marilyn Monroe in their sex symbol heydays. No jury in the world would see her as the victim of a sexual frame up.

"Did you bring the copies with you?"

She thrust a hand inside her purse, retrieved a mass of five-by-seven glossy photographs and threw them on his desk. "I can't believe you don't believe me."

"I didn't say that . . ." he gathered the pictures and stacked them neatly together like a deck of cards before examining each one.

Either Bernadette had been blessed with astounding mammary glands or she'd had more plastic surgery than merely the nose job. Her long and ample breasts seemed to defy gravity, jutting out from her chest in a straight line with no sag whatsoever. It embarrassed him to see her naked but apparently not her. When he looked up after inspecting the last one, she merely seemed perturbed that he might be questioning her honesty, which he did.

He leaned across the desk and handed the photos back. "All these were taken in a bathroom. Was it your bathroom?"

She nodded briskly.

"They're all very clear, obviously not taken through a window pane. Who took them?"

Sighing, she looked off into space. "I have no idea, but I assume it was Geoff."

"I see . . ." Darius rose from his chair and straightened his tie. "I'm afraid I can't help you, Bernadette."

Her scarlet-coated lips fell open with surprise. "Excuse me?"

Placing his hands on the desk, he leaned towards her. "Bernadette, it's very plain to see you posed for these shots. Now either you had some sort of remote control device or a timer on the camera and took them yourself or you know who did. Don't insult my intelligence by saying you don't know who took them."

She stuck her powdered nose in the air, rose from the chair, and started for the door. "You've changed, Darius."

He let out a weary sigh. "So have you, Bernadette."

As she slammed the door he wondered what had happened to the innocent girl he once knew, feeling sick to his stomach that she thought he'd be gullible enough to represent her. Then an even more nauseating thought filtered through his mind. Maybe she, like John and Jock, also thought he couldn't lose a case, even with a guilty plaintiff.

* * * *

Standing behind his bar facing Preston, sitting on the other side, Darius gulped whiskey and ran a shock-numbed hand across his mouth. "Man . . . I knew in my gut something was off with Robyn, but I never expected anything like this."

Preston removed his glasses and began massaging the upper bridge of his nose with thumb and forefinger. "It certainly surprised me too."

"And you're absolutely sure your contact couldn't be mistaken?"

"I'm afraid so. We have to accept the fact that there's a sizable conclave around The Metroplex area apparently trying to prepare the way for the antichrist. I'm sorry your Robyn happens to be one of them."

"She's not my Robyn any longer."

The investigator looked at him soberly, his unshielded eyes narrowed with concern. "You might consider going into hiding until we find out the extent of this. For all we know your life could be in danger."

Darius felt no fear for his life, only bewilderment and a deep sense of betrayal. "I'd like to hear the sordid details again if you don't mind."

Slipping the wireframes back on, Preston took a sip of

imported beer and glanced at his notes. "Robyn Tuscany belongs to a secret organization known as MWTB which is an acronym for Make Way for The Beast. According to my sources in the FBI this organization has never posed a real threat to national security because they're waiting for the rise of The Beast and False Prophet which the agency considers a mere fantasy. Nonetheless they continue to scrutinize them, though rather sporadically. They have a small branch in California but the majority of the members are here in Texas, although the exact number of adherents is unknown.

"Arash Arshia, also known as The Mede, may or may not be a member of the organization, but Raul Wyncote definitely is. Robyn has been involved at least since the FBI started investigating the cult five years ago.

"An undercover agent took some surreptitious photographs at several of their meetings, and my contact faxed that one to me. It was taken a week after John Derby was exonerated." Preston pointed to a sheet of paper resting on the bar with a color graphic printed on it. "As I said before, standing by the podium is Raul Wyncote, Robyn Tuscany, and a woman named Wilma Breese, apparently indoctrinating an unknown Hispanic male."

Darius picked up the page and looked at it again. Wilma Breese was the woman who'd purported to be Robyn's cousin Holly Hepburn, and the Hispanic male was Eval Santa Anna, a disheartening fact he'd yet to tell Preston.

"Are you going to confront Robyn, or string her along in the hope of gathering more information?"

He looked upwards and sighed. "I'm not sure I can hide my emotions well enough to fool her for long, but I'm going to try to string her along. The Mexican in the picture happens to be a friend I went to school with. His name's Eval Santa Anna and I'm blown away he'd ever get involved with something like this. That other woman may or may not be Robyn's cousin."

A single brow arched above the investigator's spectacles. "Why do you say that?"

"Robyn introduced her to me as her cousin Holly Hepburn when we landed in Houston after meeting on the flight."

"Holly Hepburn. Why does that name ring a bell?"

"She's the woman that accompanied me to your office when you told me Jacqueline Springfield was with the DEA. You saw her again at Jock Derby's when we had John's victory party."

"Oh yes, of course . . ." a smile arose. "She was quite interested in hearing about the ring as I recall."

"That's her."

Preston drummed his fingers on the counter a few beats, then reached for his beer. "Something puzzles me."

"What's that?"

"If they're after the ring, why didn't Robyn pretend she lost it or had it stolen from her when she took it to have it dated?"

Darius freshened his drink. "Maybe she was afraid I'd discover her involvement with the cult since she knew I'd do everything in my power to get it back because of its importance to my mother. What I don't understand is the contradiction between The Mede and Raul Wyncote when they appear to be allies. Wyncote apparently wants the antichrist to rise, and The Mede swears he's trying to prevent it. But I've got a real puzzlement for you. I'm convinced that badly as he wants it, The Mede can't take the ring without my permission for reasons unknown."

"Hmm . . ." Preston frowned with thought. "That would seem to be the case since you say he entered your house without your knowledge an indeterminable period of time before he stepped outside and alerted you to his presence. It stands to reason he'd have done so unless some superstition prohibited it, or he couldn't find it. Where do you keep it?"

"On the top shelf of my bedroom closet. It would be easy for any thief to find, that's why I think he can't just take it. Back to what you were saying earlier, I wonder why Robyn didn't just have a jeweler make a duplicate of the ring and hand me the phony one back when I gave it to her to have it dated."

"Perhaps she did just that."

"No, The Mede wouldn't be bothering me about a fake, and I'm certain he'd know if she pulled a swap."

"May I see it again? I'm no expert but I think I would know if it wasn't the one you showed me."

He went to his bedroom and returned with the ring. Opening the case, he set it on the bar. "Knock yourself out."

Preston examined it carefully and returned the troubling artifact to the container. "If it's not the same one I saw, it's an exact duplicate."

"It's genuine, rest assured."

Darius jerked his head towards the voice. In the middle of the living room—as if he'd just materialized from thin air—stood The Mede.

"How did you get in here?"

"Relax, Darius Darkfire, believe it or not I'm on your side. You must trust me when I say you need to give me the ring for safe keeping."

Preston's face lost all color as he gaped with astonishment at the turbaned trespasser, but Darius felt his own flush with anger.

"Man, you can't just barge into my house like this. I'm warning you—do it again and I'll have your butt thrown in jail."

The bizarre Arabian pointed his cane at him. "You'll do no such thing. You've had a taste of Raul's powers and I assure you, Darius Darkfire, his are nothing compared to mine."

Darius clenched his teeth and stormed towards the arrogant fanatic but only managed to whirl and fall to the floor from the momentum of throwing a hard right into empty space as The Mede vanished. "Dammit, did you see that . . .?" he turned to find the scholarly detective slithering off the barstool onto the carpet.

Preston had fainted.

The doorbell rang.

Darius regained his feet, roused Preston, and helped him to the couch. Several more chimes sounded in the meantime.

"You okay?"

The dumbfounded investigator managed a nod. "I wouldn't answer that."

"As you've just seen, if it's The Mede my not answering the door won't keep him from coming in here. I'll be right back . . . ."

Darius was shocked to find Bernadette Rothschild on the other side of the threshold. "Bernadette, you've really caught me at a bad time."

Tears swam into her eyes. "Please let me come in, I want to explain everything."

Though she seemed sincere, nothing could be gained by hashing it out. "Listen, a case like this isn't the type of law I practice anyway. I've never represented a plaintiff in a lawsuit and never planned to. The only reason I agreed to consider helping you was because of our friendship."

She started crying. "I'm not here because of that, although I do want to explain everything. I'm here because I want to tell you about a weird man named Raul Wyncote."

An alarm went off in his head. "How do you know him?"

"We met several years ago when he gave an assembly speech on motivational speaking."

"And he tried to persuade you to join Make Way for The Beast, didn't he?"

He whipped around with surprise. Preston, who'd just spoken, had followed him to the door.

Bernadette answered the investigator's question with a nod while still looking at him. "Not only me but everybody who attended the ceremony where your mom gave you that ring."

Her words hit him like a blow to the gut. Why had destiny

cursed him with Raul Wyncote and The Mede, and what was really going on with that goddamn ring? Dreading Bernadette's answer, he had to ask. "And did you join?"

She nodded again. "So did everybody else . . . ."

TWENTY EIGHT

He seated Bernadette at the bar and made her a stiff drink as she'd requested. Preston took the stool beside her, nervously drained his beer, and asked for a scotch. Darius was scarcely aware of accommodating them, his mind reeled so radically. His emotions swirled from angry betrayal to fear and helplessness. Nothing made sense anymore, and it was all because of that cursed ring. He thought of The Mede's words about the one who wore it having unimaginable power. How could a simple finger adornment accomplish such a feat?

Glaring at the golden band with the Persian hieroglyph, he wondered what the engraving represented. Even his mother didn't know. Could The Mede have spoken the truth—the ring had been made not for Jesus Christ but for the antichrist? Had the countless generations of his maternal line unwittingly guarded and passed down through the ages a piece of satanic jewelry?

A cold morbidity coursed through him. Why hadn't his mother been told the possessor of the ring couldn't lose at anything? And why hadn't she been unbeatable? She'd lost at canasta, bridge, checkers, and Monopoly countless times. Since she'd suffered defeat, it only stood to reason the other heirs had too. Why hadn't he? The thought of The Mede being right about him being the last in line to inherit a ring created for the antichrist terrified him beyond anything he'd ever experienced.

Then an even more disturbing implication manifested itself. Part of the legend had obviously gotten misconstrued long ago because the other ring bearers had tasted some form of defeat. That meant other misinterpretations might have been passed down the line as well. Darkness welled up from the center of his bowels at the gruesome possibility that the last ring bearer and the antichrist might be one and the same.

"Darius, you look as if you've just seen a ghost."

Preston's statement pulled him away from his ominous reverie. He slowly moved his eyes from the signet to the investigator. "I may well have seen something far worse. Me."

Bernadette emptied her glass and frowned. "Why do you say that?"

Darius leered at her. "I think you know why."

Startled, she got off the stool and took a step back. "No, I really don't."

"Yes you do. It all makes sense now. How long have you and the others who were at the ring ceremony thought I was Shiloh?"

Tears pooled between long lashes overloaded with mascara. "I lied to you before. I didn't meet Raul at any school assembly. I met him the day after your mother gave you the ring, and so did everybody else that was there."

"You were all told then that I couldn't lose—all ten of you—weren't you."

"Y-Yes."

"Well, Preston, that explains why my friend Rusty Wurly made the remark about the bearer of the ring being unbeatable at Jock's victory celebration. He wasn't just popping off like I thought and he claimed at the time. No wonder Jock wanted me to defend John so badly. Why did you all believe Raul though, Bernadette? That's what I don't understand."

She held out her glass. "May I have another? I'll tell you all you want to know, but please, I need another drink first."

He filled her glass with pure whiskey and she quickly gulped a third of it.

"Raul made us all see a vision of what lay ahead for you—fame, fortune, the whole world at your feet. Then he showed us what would happen to us if we ever told you about him. It's too horrible to put into words. Afterwards he promised each of us special rewards for keeping the secret. He asked Marcus what he wanted in the years to come. Marcus said he wanted to win the Heisman trophy. John and Jock said they wanted to have a successful business. Everyone else was too scared to ask for anything, but I finally mustered up the courage to say that I wanted a perfect nose and boobs that would never sag. He said that in the near future all our requests would be granted so long as we didn't tell you about him."

Her crimson lips turned up in a sad smile. "You thought I had my nose worked on, didn't you. Well I didn't. When I got my first teaching job I was as homely as you knew me to be back in college. During my first day of class I went to the ladies room and almost fainted when this beautiful woman stared back at me from the mirror. I don't have to tell you how successful John and Jock became, or that Marcus won the Heisman."

Preston, who'd been slack-jawed for the last few minutes, spoke up. "Did Wyncote tell you that Darius was Shiloh?"

Bernadette shook her head. "Only that he couldn't lose at anything as long as he was the keeper of the ring. I'm so ashamed that I tried to use you like that, Darius. I'm guilty as charged, only it wasn't sexual harassment. Geoff and I are in love. His father found the pictures Geoff took of me, and even though Geoff told his father he loved me and wanted to marry me, his father got me fired as I told you. I knew there was no way I could get my job back even if a jury believed that I hadn't sexually harassed Geoff. They'd think I took advantage of an impressionable minor. The only way I could win was having Darius Darkfire as my attorney. I wanted to seek a large financial settlement so Geoff and I could run away together and start a new life somewhere.

"I was so pissed at you when I left your office I never wanted to speak to you again, but when I cooled down, I couldn't believe what I'd done. I knew you deserved to hear the truth, and here I am."

Preston cleared his throat. "Aren't you afraid the threat Wyncote made will come to pass?"

She nodded vigorously. "I'm certain it will. If Darius had agreed to defend me, I'm ashamed to say I would have kept the secret, but now I have nothing to live for. My life is meaningless without Geoff, and I know he'll fall in love with someone else because two years is an eternity for a sixteen-year-old. My only option is to wait for him to turn eighteen and become an adult. I can't go near him or his father will press criminal charges against me. Though I know he'd try to wait it out for my sake, he's bound to get lonely and find someone else in that length of time."

Darius pulled at his scotch and swallowed hard. "Okay, you said Raul didn't tell you I was Shiloh. Did he tell you that Shiloh was the antichrist?"

A sickly expression came over her. "No, we didn't learn that until we joined the cult."

"Do you know about The Mede?" asked Preston.

"No. Who is he?"

"The one who is going to stop the rise of Shiloh."

The hairs on the back of Darius's neck stood on end, and he turned towards the man who'd just spoke. The Mede had reappeared.

He pointed his cane at Bernadette. "She's lying to you, Darius Darkfire. Behold—"

Darius gasped. A video appeared as if a large plasma television had been hung on invisible wires. It depicted Bernadette nude, standing in a bathroom posing in front of a camera with a light flashing at short intervals, indicating it was being controlled by a timer. The poses were identical to the photographs she'd thrown on his desk.

"As you can see, she took the pictures herself."

Feeling very unnerved by The Mede's ability to produce a home movie in midair, but equally baffled by Bernadette's actions on the magical screen, Darius turned to her. "What did you hope to gain by making it so evident you were posing?"

She buried her face in her hands and merely shook her head.

"Look, Darius Darkfire, here is the meeting she spoke of—the one that took place the day after you were presented the ring."

The paranormal telecast now portrayed Bernadette with her old large nose standing beside Eval Santa Anna, Rusty Wurly, Raul Wyncote, and Robyn. Wyncote was speaking but The Mede's production had no sound. His three college chums looked terrified.

"As you can see, there are only three of the ten friends who attended the ceremony. Only these were contacted by Raul."

A moment later the air cleared as the video slowly disintegrated.

"This woman—" he again pointed the cane at Bernadette "—is conspiring with the woman you just saw and your other two friends that attended the ceremony."

Darius reeled with such confusion and betrayal his stomach started cramping. Grimacing, he reached for the ring, planning to throw it at The Mede and demand he take it and leave him the hell alone. But the moment he touched the perplexing band a memory surfaced.

He closed the container.

The Mede thrust forth an open palm, anticipating Cyrus's circle of gold.

Folding his fingers over the glass box in a death grip, Darius leveled his eyes on the strange man with the shiny black walking stick. "The ring stays with me, end of story."

Angry shock overtook The Mede's swarthy features. "You must give me the ring—the future of mankind depends on it!"

Despite the turmoil raging in his mind, Darius spread his lips into a defiant grin. "If you don't get out of my house right now, I'm going to put the ring on and see just what sort of power it possesses, and I'll use you as my guinea pig to see what kind of misery it can inflict."

The Mede vanished.

"Figured as much." Threatening the mysterious Arab and temporarily outwitting him had released enough anxiety to allow Darius's mental gears to mesh normally. Logic prevailed and he forced the remaining negativity beneath the surface of his racing thoughts as a few pieces of the puzzle came together. Bernadette had to have known he wouldn't represent her once he saw the pictures since she'd so obviously posed for each one, and she'd shown little surprise at The Mede appearing from out of nowhere which could only mean she'd witnessed such events before. She was in this crap up to her pretty, new nose.

On his way to put the ring back in his bedroom closet, he winked at Preston, who'd been observing with shock-filled eyes, accentuating a face that had remained pallid since The Mede's first disappearance caused the commander to pass out from shock.

Back in the living room, he poured himself a fresh scotch, and pointed his glass towards Bernadette. "It's time for you to tell me the truth."

Her eyes widened in a manner he'd seen countless times in court when confronting a witness over false testimony. "But I already have."

He downed a quick gulp and shook his head. "Nope, but you're going to start right now. First off, when did you really meet Raul Wyncote? I know it wasn't the day after the ceremony. I'm going to wager it was the day John got released from jail."

Almost cartoon-like, her sexy visage contorted with surprise. "My god, that's right! But how did you know?"

"Later. Right now I want to hear the real reason you got suspended. I'm going to place another bet. You never did, did you."

She opened her mouth is if to protest, then closed it and

slowly shook her head.

"You knew I wouldn't represent you, so you felt safe thinking I'd never find out, didn't you."

A tinge of pink appeared through her makeup as she nodded.

"The whole thing was a farce to get me to look at those naked pictures of you, wasn't it."

The nod continued.

"Why?"

"He told me to."

"Raul Wyncote?"

"Yes."

A deep sigh emanated from Preston. "Darius, I dare say I have never been so confused as well as amazed in all my life. And would you please tell me how you knew she met Wyncote the day John Derby was released from custody?"

Still eyeing Bernadette he said, "Eval Santa Anna told me he met Robyn that day. Since Robyn and Wyncote are with him in the picture taken around that time, I had a hunch Bernadette and Rusty met him the same day as Eval because of that clip The Mede showed us of the three of them talking to Wyncote. Bernadette, start from the beginning. Tell me everything."

The blonde bombshell sucked in a nervous breath and blew it out slowly. "I lied about not knowing The Mede. I met him the same day I met Raul. And you're right, it was the day the murder charge was dropped against John. Raul really did threaten us, and he really did promise a reward for our silence. Obviously I also lied about Marcus and the Derby twins owing their success to Raul. They weren't even there when Eval, Rusty, and I met him. Jock and John had already become millionaires, and Marcus had won the Heisman trophy long before then. Raul wanted you to think he was responsible for their success, I can't imagine any other reason he'd demand I tell you that. But I'm only guessing of course since he didn't tell me his reasons.

"When I told Raul what I wanted—you know, perfect nose and that my boobs would never sag—he said he'd have someone come over and grant my request. That someone was The Mede. I had to lie about my transformation happening much later since you'd seen me numerous times the day after the ring ceremony and I still had a big nose. I'll never forget when John got cleared of the murder charge because it was my last day as a homely woman.

"Raul told me to go to the ladies room and wait. When I got there the room was empty. A few minutes later a man appeared and told me he was known as The Mede. With a wave of his hand he said 'Your requests are granted' then disappeared just as he did tonight. When I checked myself in the mirror nothing had changed, my nose was still gross, but I woke up the next morning with the one you see now.

"Anyway, I rejoined the others and Raul took us to a nightclub, but Rusty had some errands or something he had to tend to, leaving only me and Eval to accompany him. After we got to the nightclub a woman named Robyn Tuscany, the same one you later became engaged to, joined us after Eval shouted to everyone there that he knew the two people on the television—you and John.

"She told us about a group that wanted to save the earth, and that we should consider joining since we were privileged to know the keeper of the ring, meaning you. I asked if you were a member and Raul told me that you, as the ring bearer, couldn't even know the group existed until after Shiloh came to earth. Eval and I were very impressed with everything Raul and Robyn told us about the organization. They told us it was called MWTB. When we asked what the initials stood for we were told 'Make Way for The Best'. Eval and I joined and talked Rusty into coming in too. We soon learned it was really Make Way for The Beast but by that time it was too late to get out.

"Raul told me that I'd be given a mission in the future and until then I was free to do whatever I wanted so long as I kept attending the meetings which are held every new moon. A week ago he came to see me and gave me the camera set up. He told me to take a lot of nude pictures of myself which I wasn't to show to anyone except you. I asked him why but he wouldn't tell me. Several days ago he called and told me the time had come. I don't know how he knew about Geoff Hodges or that his father is on the school board but he instructed me to say I got suspended for the reasons I told you at your office, and to make sure you saw the pictures before I left there. All of that was a lie—Geoff Hodges is a sweet kid, he's never came on to me nor I to him. I don't know why Raul singled him out for the fabrication.

"I told him I knew you'd see right through me and would never agree to help me. He said he was counting on that and for me to convince you I was very angry when you refused to help me, and not to worry about what he was trying to accomplish. Everything I told you about being in love with Geoff—all lies. Raul made me come here tonight and tell you all that, along with the other lies, for reasons only he knows. I don't know what he'll do to me for telling you all this if he finds out I did." She stepped towards him, her stimulating perfume filling the air. "You won't tell him I told you . . . will you, Dare?"

Refusing to let his gaze explore the ample cleavage a low-cut sweater revealed, he took in her heavily adorned face, focusing on the accentuated mouth that years ago spoke nothing but truth. "No, I won't tell him."

"Thank God. Now then, how did you know I was lying about meeting him the day after the ceremony?"

Setting his drink on the counter, he backed away from the bar and shoved his hands in his pockets. "I was about to give the ring to The Mede awhile ago but just as I reached for it I remembered something. I don't know why I didn't recall it before when you said you'd all met Raul then, but the day after Mom gave me the ring, Eval and Rusty went with me and the Derby twins to Corpus Christi to go deep sea fishing. We were all together the whole time, so there's no way they could have met Raul then."

Eyes begging unashamedly as a dog's she whimpered, "Can you ever forgive me?"

He met her gaze, feeling sorry for the girl he once knew to be so honest and decent, wondering what had changed her. "You didn't do me any harm. If anyone needs to ask for forgiveness, it's me. You, Rusty, and Eval wouldn't be part of that awful group if it wasn't for me. I'm just glad Bernice and the others were spared all this. By the way, what did Eval and Rusty ask for as a reward?"

She shrugged her shoulders. "I don't know. If they asked for anything they didn't do it in front of me. I made my request in private because I was scared Rusty and Eval would make fun of me. I'm not sure they believed Raul could deliver his promise but I never doubted it since he had the power to show us the future and all. I was totally surprised that he sent The Mede to fix my nose and couldn't do it himself."

Preston cleared his throat. "I can't understand Wyncote's motivation in having you lie about being suspended and wanting Darius to see those pictures."

"Neither can I," said Darius.

Again Bernadette shrugged. "That makes three of us."

"Well, at least we now know The Mede's a liar," said Preston before taking a pull from his glass.

Darius nodded. "That we do."

Bernadette tilted her head, eyes questioning, provocative lips puckered with a frown. "What did he lie about, Dare? I'm confused."

"When he showed us that movie about the real meeting with Raul, he said it took place the day after I'd been given the ring which, as I said before, couldn't have happened."

"Oh."

"Think he was bluffing?" said Preston.

"He might have been . . ." he returned to the bar. "Maybe he knew who really met with Raul but not when, and made the mistake of taking Bernadette's word about the date of the meeting before she came clean. And if that's the case, he's not as all-knowing as he'd have us believe. I sure don't buy that he's been alive since the ring was given to Cyrus, if in fact it really ever was."

The look on the investigator's face troubled him. "Don't tell me you believe him about that, Preston."

"From what I've witnessed here tonight, I certainly think it's a viable possibility."

* * * *

After Bernadette left, he made a pot of coffee and joined Preston at the dining table. "How hard would it be to find Bernadette's plastic surgeon?"

"Pardon me?"

"Come on, Preston, she got a nose job. The Mede didn't zap it into shape."

"I don't know how you can be so calloused after all we've seen this evening—that mysterious movie, The Mede disappearing and reappearing."

"No, Preston, that's only what our minds told us we saw. Remember, Raul managed to charm me into thinking I was in another world conversing with animals, and he was able to do that with only a moment's eye contact. Assuming The Mede's right and his powers are greater than Raul's, he could put us under a hypnotic spell even quicker.

"If you can locate Bernadette's surgeon then we can convince her she only thinks The Mede did it through hocus pocus, and we'll be able to pull her out from under his and Raul's control. Once she sees them for the charlatan's they are, she can help us free Eval and Rusty from their dominance as well."

Preston stirred his coffee and sampled it. "How do you know your other friends are under their dominance?"

"Well I don't for sure, but they're part of that antichrist group so they can't exactly be in their right minds. Bernadette may be lying about Rusty being a part of it, but we know Eval is because of the picture you were given. She also may be lying about her nose. She may know full well a surgeon rather then The Mede fixed it. I'm not putting much stock in anything she says after all the lies she's told me."

Yawning, Preston rose from his chair. "I need to be going. Rothschild, right?"

"Right, Bernadette Rothschild."

"I'll see what I can find . . . ."

TWENTY NINE

Darius called Rusty and invited him to have lunch at their old haunt where they used to chow down during college. They were supposed to get together at twelve-thirty, and he spent the morning turning down two prospective clients.

The first one had been a no-brainer—a millionaire wanting a divorce from a money-hungry wife. After giving careful consideration to the second one, he decided to refer the lady to Robert. He believed her allegation about being given the wrong directions on a prescription which had led to near renal failure, forcing her to require dialysis twice a week—something she'd have to do the rest of her life unless she could get a kidney transplant—but he still didn't like the idea of representing the plaintiff, even one he felt deserved compensation. Robert had no such qualms and had an impressive track record with malpractice suits.

Arriving at The Barbecue Barn a few minutes early, he took the liberty of ordering for Rusty. The savory aroma of pit-roasted brisket and hickory-smoked ribs pleasured his nostrils as he recalled coming here after the ring ceremony.

Everyone had accompanied him that day except the vegetarian Rothschild cousins. A lot of water had flowed under the bridge since then. Like him, the Derby twins and Marcus Laxx—still living with Avery, he assumed—went on to achieve great financial success. Sash Temple had made a bad marital choice but the divorcee got her savings back and could now embark on a new life. Eval's brother Caruso gave his all for his country on an Iraqi battlefield. After a twenty-one gun salute by an Honor Guard his body had been lowered into the ground at Arlington Cemetery. Other than hearing from Sash that she'd married an oil man, Darius didn't know how Bernice Rothschild's life had turned out but hoped she'd fared better than Bernadette. Like the Derbys, Rusty became an entrepreneur after college and had holdings in several enterprises. Though none were cash cows, his share of their combined profits afforded a comfortable lifestyle.

He filled his buddy's mug with beer when he saw him turn the corner. "Hey, Wurly, sit your ass down."

Grinning from ear to ear, Rusty slid into the booth. "Thanks for the brewski, Darkfire."

"You're welcome. Grub's on the way."

"What's the occasion . . .?" he gave the place a looking over.

Darius shrugged. "Nothing. Just hadn't seen you in a while and got to missing your pretty face."

"Sure you did . . ." he downed a healthy swallow of cold beer. "You don't have time for casual lunches anymore, Dare. Not since you've become such a big shot lawyer."

"You know me too well." He filled his own glass and took a sip. "Talked to Bernadette Rothschild lately?"

A somber expression overtook Rusty's ever-smiling face. "Why do you ask?"

"She came to see me yesterday. She got a nose job. Did you know that?"

The customary grin returned. "Yeah, she's a real beauty now isn't she?"

Grinning back, he imbibed some more suds. "She sure is."

"Did I ever tell you I punked her cousin Bernice back in college."

That brought back a flood of memories. Rusty used to love bragging about his innumerable female conquests. "Only about a hundred times. Ever get a piece of Bernadette?"

"I wouldn't have touched her with a ten foot pole back in those days, Dare, you know that."

"True, she wasn't pretty back then but man was she built. Still is as a matter of fact."

"Yeah . . ." Rusty raised his mug again.

"She told me quite an interesting tale about a man named

Raul Wyncote."

Beer spewed from Rusty's mouth, preceding a coughing fit. Some of the spray landed on Darius's jacket. He daubed the wet spots with a paper napkin as the choking Casanova caught his breath. "She said you and the Derby twins knew him too."

Rusty jerked a handful of napkins from an old fashioned dispenser and hastily mopped up the mess he'd made. Then he peered at him from a face turned pasty white. "Dare, that guy is the weirdest dude I've ever met in my life. He scares the shit out of me."

"When did you meet him, the same day as Jock and John?"

He gave his head a quick shake. "I didn't know the Derbys knew him. I met Wyncote the day you got John off the hook."

His old pal passed the test. Unlike Eval Santa Anna, whom he could read like a book, Darius couldn't always tell when Rusty prevaricated.

"Tell me about meeting him."

Wadding the wet napkins into a ball, Rusty slid them to the edge of the counter and dried his hands on a fresh one. "I called Eval right after you called to tell me John got released. We got together for lunch and afterwards Eval wanted to pick up some batteries for his walkman. We ran into Bernadette at the store and told her the great news. The three of us went to a pool hall to have a beer and a game of nine ball to celebrate John being freed. You remember how much that boy loved to shoot pool when we were in college.

"Wyncote came over and introduced himself, and told us he knew you were the bearer of the ring. I didn't know what he was talking about until Bernadette said he must have been referring to the ring your mother gave you. He told us he knew we'd been at the ceremony. After giving us a history lesson on the ring he said he could do some special things for us, all we had to do was ask. The guy gave me the creeps and all I wanted was to get out of there. He offered to treat us to a night on the town but I told him I couldn't go because I had some things I had to get done."

Darius mulled that over. So far Rusty's account squared with Bernadette's. "She mentioned joining a group called Make Way for The Best, MWTB for short. Ever hear of it?"

He shook his head.

Rusty seemed sincere, but he wanted to test the waters. "Odd, she told me you joined too."

A scowl erupted. "Well she's lying."

"Hmm . . . she said Eval was a member as well."

"He may be for all I know, but I'm not. Like I told you, I've never heard of it before. I don't know what prompted Bernadette to tell you I was a member but that's a load of shit."

Studying his old pal's countenance for any signs of nervous tension that would indicate dishonesty, he took a languid pull from his beer and set the mug on the counter. "Remember popping off at John's victory party about nobody beating the keeper of the ring?"

"Yeah, Raul told us that."

"Why didn't you say so at the time?"

"Oh man . . ." fear and dread burned in Rusty's eyes as if he'd just been handed a death sentence. "He warned us a bunch of bad things would happen if we ever told you about him. I couldn't believe I'd let that slip out at the party so I played it down. He's got some kind of weird power, Dare. As crazy as this is going to sound he made us see into the future, and I don't know how to explain it but the three of us knew we were really seeing what was going to happen. Because of that we also knew he could do us harm like he threatened if we ever told you we knew him. If you ever cross paths with the dude, please don't tell him I mentioned any of this."

Rusty might have been playing him but he didn't think so, gut instinct told him otherwise, and he'd certainly take his word over the lying Bernadette's. "Did you ask him to do anything for you?"

ARLEY OWENS, JR.

"Like what?"

"Well, Bernadette told me she got her new nose by a miracle granted through Raul."

He didn't appear surprised. "I didn't ask him for a damn thing because I didn't want to owe a guy like that, you know?"

"Do you know if Eval did?"

"Not that I'm aware of. But then again, I didn't hear Bernadette ask him to fix her nose either."

The waiter brought their food and Darius picked up a thick rib with glazed pork barely clinging to the bone. "Yeah, she said she asked him in private because she thought you and Eval would razz her about it."

"We wouldn't have because there was nothing funny about meeting with that guy." Rusty selected an ear of corn, mowed off a section with bared teeth, and returned the cob to its saucer. "I'm surprised Bernadette told you about Wyncote. I'd have never told you about him voluntarily."

After voiding the scrumptious baby-back of meat, Darius bit off the bulb of a green onion and scooped some pinto beans into his mouth. "Ever hear of someone called The Mede?"

"Mm mm." Rusty sank his teeth into a rod of smoked sausage.

"Do you think Bernadette really got her nose fixed by Wyncote's hocus pocus?"

"I know he had the power to make us see the future, so I believe it's possible, but whether he fixed Bernadette's honker, I couldn't say. I wonder when Jock and John met Wyncote."

Darius cut off an inch of hot link and forked it in his mouth. "They don't know him. I was only bluffing to make sure you were shooting straight with me. That organization I told you about, Make Way for The Best? That's only a cover for their real name."

"Which is?"

"Make Way for The Beast."

"What beast?"

He eyed his old chum carefully. Every nuance of the boy's demeanor insisted he really didn't know about the group. "The antichrist."

Rusty's Adam's apple bobbled with a big gulp.

THIRTY

Preston couldn't find any records of Bernadette having surgery. *"Unless she used another name or got her nose fixed by someone without a license to practice medicine, she's telling the truth."*

Darius thanked the investigator for looking into it and hung up the phone with a sigh of frustration. If The Mede had miraculously shrank Bernadette's nose, there was no reason to assume his disappearing act hadn't been the real deal either, and that deeply unnerved him. The strange Arab might have been around since the time of Cyrus after all. That thought brought back the fear that he, the so-called keeper of the ring, might be the antichrist.

Though not a religious man, he believed in God and had no aspirations of usurping the throne of Jesus Christ. So a serious change in his very makeup lay ahead if Satan had in fact chosen him to fulfill the role of the most evil despot the world would ever know. That gave him a tiny degree of comfort, for if he spotted such alterations in his character, he could resist them with all his might and thereby thwart the devil's plan of using him as a tyrannical puppet. But as he mulled that over it morbidly occurred to him he might be powerless to resist the transformation even if aware his strings were being pulled by the prince of darkness.

He got up, donned his coat, and stepped through the door. "I'm going out for awhile. Be back in an hour or two."

Ricca glanced up from a magazine she'd been reading. "Where are you going?"

"To see Raul Wyncote . . . ."

* * * *

Darius hadn't told his mother anything about Raul or The Mede, intent on keeping her out of this sordid mess, so he was shocked to see her Volvo leaving the parking lot of Wyncote's apartment. She hadn't seen him and he thought about flagging her down to ask why she'd been there, but decided to confront the Arab instead.

Wyncote answered the door on the first ring and didn't seem at all surprised to see him. "Come inside, Darkfire."

"What was my mother doing here?"

A trace of a smile appeared. "I invited her for tea."

He took in the apartment's ancient Persian atmosphere, picturing his mother ooh-ing and ah-ing over the exquisite rugs, pillows, oil lamps, and incense burners. Then he glared at Raul. "Leave my mother alone, Wyncote."

"Not to worry." The Arab's countenance altered as if something had greatly inspired him. "I only wanted to meet the woman who bore Shiloh."

The statement raped his mind, hurling his very essence into absolute devastation. Reality seemed to peel away into madness, as if an oil painting of a pleasant landscape had been stripped to reveal the bowels of perdition beneath. Despair pummeled his gut as cold panic slithered around his heart, gripping it like an icy boa constrictor, hell-bent on freezing the life out of it. He *was* the antichrist—Wyncote had known it all along.

Feeling as if he'd just been thrown into a perpetual nightmare where nothing could be taken for granted, he darkly recalled some of his Sunday school learning which now taunted him. The antichrist was called The Beast and had a cohort known as the False Prophet, a role bound to be filled by either Raul or The Mede, he assumed.

The mystic's dark eyes took on a heady glow. "I can see the picture is coming together for you."

Darius's knees went wobbly as his stomach flipped-flopped with acidic nausea. Horrid waves of negative energy that seemed to emanate from every direction washed over him, the pressure as tangible as water at a great depth.

"Shall I show you what is to come, Darkfire?"

He felt weak, completely drained of mental or physical strength. Dread and foreboding pounded him with each beat of his trembling heart. "N-No."

A cruel grin widened Raul's evil, narrow face. "Oh come now, Darkfire, stop being so glum. The great visionaries throughout the ages—men such as Alexander and the greatest of the Caesars of Rome have tasted but a fraction of the power you are soon to possess. Even Cyrus the Great would envy you."

"I don't want the power."

"Nonsense. You're merely frightened of the prospect at present. Soon you'll embrace your heritage, I assure you."

Visions of people standing in long lines to receive the mark of the beast in their right hands or foreheads as forewarned in the book of Revelation tortured his already frantic mind. Trying to shake it off, he sucked in a deep breath. "What's The Mede got to do with all this? Is he the False Prophet or does that title belong to you?"

The swarthy face contorted with insult. "What a vulgar term to use, Darkfire. False Prophet indeed. There's nothing false about my powers as you have personally witnessed, and that was a mere pittance of what I can do."

"So if you're the False Prophet, what role does The Mede play in this?"

Raul clasped his hands behind his back and smiled. "Take a guess?"

A modicum of strength forced its way through his emaciated psyche. "I don't want to play guessing games, just tell me."

"Very well . . ." Raul brought his arms forward and crossed his chest, placing a palm on each opposing shoulder. Bowing his head, he muttered a few words that Darius couldn't understand, though he knew them to be ancient Persian. A moment later a cane appeared as Wyncote transformed into The Mede.

Confusion burned within Darius's head. If Raul Wyncote and The Mede were the same person it didn't make sense for The Mede to have demanded to be given the ring since his role was that of the False Prophet. "W-Why did you ask for the ring?"

The Mede turned back into Raul, who answered. "It was a necessary test. Had you given it to me—well, me as The Mede—your vow would have been broken and you'd no longer be invincible."

"And you'd have become Shiloh?" he gasped.

"No. The ring would also have become powerless and therefore useless."

A deep melancholia he'd never experienced in his entire life overwhelmed him. Bitter tears flooded his eyes. "You mean all I had to do was give you the ring and it would have stopped the coming of the antichrist?"

Ominous laughter rang out through Wyncote's lips. "No need to ponder such things since you didn't give up the ring."

Darius rammed his palms against his temples, violently shaking his head with frustration. "I don't understand any of this!"

Raul actually appeared sympathetic for a moment, looking as though he truly wanted to make him comprehend. "My course is unalterable. I am from the beginning of the ring, and am here to assist Shiloh. In this incarnation I am Raul Wyncote. Before that my name was Abdul Osa, countless generations back I was a goldsmith named Baba who pretended to be a prophet when I presented the ring to Cyrus."

Trembling with horror and shame, Darius slowly lowered his shaking hands and inhaled a chest-full of air he felt he had no right to breathe. "W-Why did I have to be tested?"

"A mere formality required by our leader."

Stunned even more, which he hadn't thought possible, Darius forced himself to say the word. "Satan?"

"Never call him that, it's blasphemy! His name is Day Star, or Lucifer if you prefer."

He groaned with excruciating confusion. "None of this makes sense. You, that is The Mede, said he was trying to stop the antichrist from coming."

A knowing grin appeared. "And so I am."

"Shit, man, stop talking in riddles!"

"Is it really so difficult for you to understand, Darkfire? A man of your intelligence should have grasped the obvious truth of all this immediately. Christ means *the anointed one* and the carpenter from Nazareth is but a pretender claiming to be the only begotten son. Day Star is the first begotten and the earth belongs only to him. We shall not allow the carpenter to rule over it. Since Day Star is the anointed one, ergo The True Christ, the carpenter is the antichrist. When our leader binds with your spirit you'll see all of this clearly."

Numbness permeated every nerve in his body as hot nausea flooded his gullet, forcing its way up his throat. "I-I'm going to throw up. Where's the bathroom . . .?"

PART
TWO

THIRTY ONE

She didn't know what had come over Darius. Since that day two weeks ago when he'd gone to see Raul Wyncote her boss hadn't been the same. Though she'd demanded to know what had gotten him so upset, he wouldn't discuss it.

Ricca glanced at his office door, wanting to barge in and try once again to find out what so drastically gnawed at him, but knowing it would be futile, she remained in her chair. He'd lost weight and tell-tale bags under his eyes denoted he wasn't getting much sleep. After Robert had failed to get him to open up, she'd confided her concerns to Robyn in the hopes that he might tell her what had happened, but Darius refused to speak to the woman he'd once been engaged to. Robyn, as distraught as she, didn't know why he'd broken up with her again. She'd even asked her husband's ex to talk to Darius but Suzette had met with the same results. Ricca knew better than to approach Amia about her son's condition. The woman was wound so tight where he was concerned she might have a nervous breakdown if Darius gave her the cold shoulder about it too. Even if she didn't he'd be so pissed at her for burdening his mother with it, he might actually fire her.

The phone rang. She checked the ID and saw the caller was Preston Coolidge.

"Hello, Ricca, Preston here. Is Darius in?"

"Well, what's left of him is."

"Is something wrong?"

A light bulb flashed in her head. Maybe Preston could dig the problem out of her morose boss. "Um, got a minute, Preston . . .?"

* * * *

When the home test showed positive, electric currents of excitement coursed through her body. The baby of the last keeper of the ring floated in the amniotic fluid of her womb. A physician would have to confirm it of course, but she'd felt certain of the pregnancy when her monthly cycle didn't occur for a second time.

Recently divorced she'd moved back to Dallas. She almost felt sorry for Raymond, the pitiful fool. He'd caved when Darius confronted him. Like the ring bearer, Raymond didn't know of her recent inheritance which allowed her the financial freedom to no longer depend on her husband's income. Now she could still pursue her artistic endeavors without wasting forty hours a week on a day job. Though presently renting an apartment, she'd soon be moving into the beautiful new residence she'd purchased in Plano.

Thirty thousand dollars amounted to little more than spare change to her, not that she'd ever been in jeopardy of losing that amount since she'd lied about loaning her ex husband the money. When Darius left after handing her a check for that amount plus fifteen percent she'd laughed so hard her sides ached. Never expecting him to represent her since she knew beforehand he didn't handle divorces, she felt mildly guilty for making up the story about giving Raymond her life savings since she'd only done it as a ruse to make the famous lawyer feel so sorry for her he'd find it hard to refuse her request to stay the night.

Darius offering to call Raymond's lawyer had totally surprised her. She figured he'd let the matter drop once he explained he didn't handle divorces, but she'd laid the ground work in case he'd been willing to make an exception and represent her. She'd planned to convince Raymond the best thing for both of them was to fly to Las Vegas, get a quickie divorce, and she'd forgive the money he owed her. But that had flown out the window when Darius decided to defend her.

The look on Raymond's face had been priceless when she'd

originally set the wheels in motion after obtaining her grandmother's entire estate, feigning tears and telling him she couldn't live with a drug dealer.

"What drug dealer?" he'd protested. "I buy most of the coke for us and sell some to my friends, and you know it!"

It was true of course. They'd had some memorable moments making love while riding a cocaine high. When she'd boldly lied to him about giving him her life savings, his jaw had dropped.

"What the fuck are you talking about? You've never given me a red cent!"

"See what the drugs have done, Raymond?" she'd cried through crocodile tears. "They've even made you forget that!"

Darius must have really frightened him. No amount of emotional browbeating could have convinced the penny-pinching auto dealer that he'd forgotten taking her life savings, yet he'd made out a check anyway.

Adjusting her position on the couch, Sash thought back on that night at Darius's house. An erotic thrill of anticipation had coursed through her while disrobing in his guestroom, laying her garments on the bed one by one with no intention of sleeping in it. During their reminiscing he'd excused himself to use the bathroom and she'd seized the opportunity to doctor his drink. She'd waited thirty minutes after he retired for the evening before sneaking into his room. Certain he wouldn't be able to wake up for several hours because of the sedative she'd pulled the covers down, rolled him over on his back, slid his briefs to the middle of his thighs, used her mouth to induce an erection, and lowered herself on his penis—silently beseeching Day Star for impregnation when the ring bearer ejaculated inside her. A little while afterwards she'd repeated the process, repositioned his underwear, then the covers, crept back down the hall, put her clothes back on, and left.

It was a shame she couldn't tell the notable attorney that his offspring would enter the world in about seven months. It might make what lay ahead for him a little less bitter. Tomorrow would be the new moon. She'd get the blood test and announce the good news to Raul at the assembly.

* * * *

After spewing his load, Rusty rolled off Bernadette Rothschild's fabulous body and stared at his bedroom ceiling while catching his breath. He'd wanted to punk her ever since he'd seen how pretty she looked with her new nose, and had finally accomplished the feat. But that wasn't why he'd invited her over. When his shaft dwindled, he removed the rubber and tossed it into a nearby wastebasket while still lying on his back.

Bernadette turned sideways and gently stroked his chest. "You said you wanted to talk to me about something. Did you mean that or was that just a ruse to seduce me?"

He cleared his throat. "No, it wasn't a ruse. Dare asked me to lunch a few weeks ago and told me you'd told him about Raul Wyncote."

"Oh."

Not bothering to look, he imagined Bernadette's eyes filling with alarm at hearing him mention the mysterious man. "What's this Make Way for The Beast thing you told him I joined, and why did you lie to him about it?"

A moment of awkward silence passed before she answered. "I'm sorry, Rusty. I was only doing what Raul told me to. I hated lying to Darius but I have to do what he says or face serious consequences."

Though he'd only seen Raul Wyncote one time, the weird Arabian had instilled a fear in him that still persisted which made Bernadette's actions seem perfectly logical. "Why did you start associating with him? I figured you'd know better than that."

Another short silence went by. "Did Darius tell you I'd asked Raul to fix my nose?"

"Yeah."

"I shouldn't have because it bound me to him, making me owe him for the rest of my life. Since you never saw him after we met him, I assume you didn't ask for anything when he made the offer."

"You assume right. Did Eval ask for anything?"

"I don't know."

"Man, I hope he didn't. Anyway, what's Make Way for The Beast about? Darius told me you guys are waiting for the antichrist."

He heard a deep sigh leave her lungs before she spoke. "It's a cult but I didn't know that when I joined. Robyn told me it was called Make Way for The Best and they were trying to save the earth. Eval and I were happy to join and both of us enjoyed the meetings while we were members of what they call the Initial Layer. We wanted to advance our membership and became part of what's called the Outer Layer, and that was our fatal mistake. That's when we learned what MWTB is really about."

"Robyn? You mean Darius's fiancé got you involved?"

"I'm afraid so."

"Does she know Wyncote?"

She let out a harsh moan. "Boy, does she ever."

Rusty felt sick to his stomach for Darius's sake. "Does Dare know?"

"That she knew Raul? Yes, but I think he'd just found out about MWTB shortly before I went to see him. Eval and I met her at the nightclub Raul took us to after the three of us met him."

He inhaled a deep breath. "Man am I glad I didn't go with you guys."

"I wish we hadn't gone either."

"Why did you? Couldn't you see Wyncote was nothing but

trouble?"

"I don't know why Eval did, but I was intrigued by him at the time. I was enthralled with his power and had secretly asked him for a perfect nose and . . . ."

"And what?"

"That my boobs would never sag."

A dour laugh forced its way out of his mouth. "Well I'd say you got your wish. So Wyncote really did it, you didn't get plastic surgery?"

"Yeah, only it was a friend of Raul's called The Mede that did it."

"Man . . . I wish you hadn't put yourself in his debt like that. You could have gotten a plastic surgeon to fix your nose, you know."

"No, my skin keloids horribly—I'd have looked worse than before with the scarring."

A grotesque image of her now beautiful face mottled with scars jumped to his mind, followed by a fearful thought. "Us being together like this isn't going to get me involved with Wyncote and that cult is it?"

She slid her hand down his stomach and gently caressed his genitals. "I hope not . . . ."

* * * *

Holly woke up screaming from a nightmare that had seemed so real it took her several minutes before she realized it had only been a dream. Slipping on her robe, she made for the kitchen of her tiny efficiency apartment and started some coffee. While waiting she recounted the awful scenario with an inward shudder.

A crowd of people were chanting something in a language she couldn't understand. Some were dressed casual, others wore formal attire, and there seemed to be an equal distribution of men and women. They were inside a large building with a stage, and beneath the spotlights hung a naked man on a cross, his limbs secured with heavy ropes. She pushed her way to the front and saw that the man on the cross was Darius.

Looking down at her with pleading eyes, he'd said in a hoarse whisper she could somehow make out above the chanting hordes, "Help me, Holly."

His entreaty angered the crowd and they began screaming the some eerie phrase over and over—"Praetendereot thanatos!"

Darius again whispered to her, "They'll kill me if you don't save me. Please . . . help me, Holly."

"What can I do?"

"Help me, Holly."

"Tell me how? How can I save you?"

He never told her how. She'd woken up with him still pleading for her help.

She checked the time and grimaced, knowing she couldn't call him at three-fifteen in the morning. Still horrified and desperately needing to hear Darius say the words, she kept telling herself it was only a bad dream.

THIRTY TWO

He'd pulled every string he could to learn more about Make Way for The Beast but came up empty. Ricca had asked him to find out what was wrong with Darius and he felt bad not telling her he didn't need to inquire, being painfully aware of the problem—Darius had become convinced he was the antichrist. He'd sworn him to secrecy and unless the troubled attorney had confided his fear to someone else, which Preston seriously doubted, no one else knew.

Relishing a sip of hot cappuccino, he lowered the cup, removed his glasses, wiped steam-induced fog from the lenses, put them back on, and began reading the morning paper.

His cell rang.

"Hello?"

"Preston?"

"Yes, Darius?"

"Holly Hepburn just called, panicked about a nightmare she had about me last night."

He marveled at the lengths some people went for an excuse to talk to his famous client. "The Holly I met?"

"Right. Are you in Houston or Dallas this morning?"

"Houston." He'd leased an apartment in Dallas shortly after becoming Darius's sole investigator, but when the renowned attorney didn't require his services he spent most of his time in Houston catering to other clientele.

"Good. I want her to come see you if you don't mind."

"I don't mind, but why are you making such a request?"

* * * *

Holly had been so relieved to hear Darius's voice she'd started crying. He'd asked what was wrong and she'd wasted no time telling him the nightmare and that she needed to hear him say everything was okay, which she'd fully expected him to do.

But he hadn't.

"No, Holly, I'm not okay but I can't tell you why, at least not right now," he'd said in a somber, helpless tone. *"That weird language you heard at the end of your dream might mean something. I want you to go see Preston Coolidge, he might be able to decipher it."*

"Why? I only remember the chant they kept repeating at the end, and it was just gibberish," she'd remonstrated.

"We don't know that for sure. Preston will be able to research it and find out what they were saying if it's an actual language. Believe me when I say that I don't think it's a coincidence you had such a dream at this time. I'm afraid it may very well be prophetic . . . ."

Sitting in the same luxurious armchair she'd chosen after accompanying Darius to Preston Coolidge's office when he'd been defending John Derby, she relayed the dream.

The private investigator sat behind a u-shaped mahogany desk, touching his lips with the tips of his long index fingers as he listened. He lowered his hands when she finished.

"Those are the only phrases you recall?"

She nodded.

"Hmm . . . well the first part's not a language I'm familiar with but the last word 'thanatos' sounds close to the Greek term for death, pronounced thay-na-tos."

"Not cut up like that," she protested. "One word—thanatos."

"I know, merely making a point. Let me write it down phonetically." He scribbled on a legal pad and looked up. "Now the first one, please."

"Praetendereot."

He jotted it down and studied the yellow paper. "Say them to me again, please, and keep repeating them until I tell you to stop."

Watching him write, she chanted the phrase again and again like the angry crowd had done in the dream. An odd frown crinkled his face and he looked up.

"You can stop now . . ." he turned the pad around and shoved it to the edge of his desk. "Ignore my hen scratch above the last part. This is what I think the people were saying."

Holly gasped when she saw what the investigator had written. Beneath a list of syllables scribbled in longhand he'd printed in large letters, *DEATH TO PRETENDER.*

"I could be mistaken, but I believe that's what it is. It's a combination of Latin, Greek, and English. Take away the *ot* sound at the end of preatendereot and you have praetendere which is Latin for pretender. Ot spelled backwards is the English *to,* and as I said before, thanatos sounds like the Greek *death.* A lot of English phrases get swapped around when spoken in another language, the subject sometimes coming after the verb instead of before it, etcetera. I find this very intriguing. I'm going to ask you to step outside while I call Darius."

Holly went to the reception area. Preston's secretary asked if she'd like some coffee. She shook her head and nervously waited. Twenty minutes later he buzzed and asked her back into his office.

Preston was standing and looked rather ill at ease. "I'm about to tell you something Darius has confided to me and no one else, and he insists that you keep it to yourself. Understand?"

She nodded and said, "Why doesn't he tell me himself?"

"He wants to talk to you afterwards but asked me to break the ice so to speak. It concerns us both that you saw Darius tied to a cross before a formal gathering, and I'll explain why momentarily. I'm going to start at the beginning and it's rather unnerving so I advise you to sit down . . . ."

* * * *

"You must have made some sort of mistake, this just can't be right!"

"I'm sorry, Mrs. Masterson, but I'm afraid it's no error. You're not pregnant."

Being referred to as Mrs. Masterson only added insult to the injury of learning she didn't have a fetus in her womb after all. She'd planned to go back to her maiden name at some point, but hearing the physician call her Masterson in conjunction with such horrid news sent it to the top of her priority list.

"Then why did I miss two periods, and how come the home pregnancy test turned up positive?"

"These things sometimes happen, I'm afraid . . . ."

Sash was so despondent she didn't attend the assembly of the new moon. Her high rank permitted such latitude. Now she'd have to devise a new scheme to get Darius's semen inside her.

* * * *

Her swollen clitoris ached as it always did during this part of assembly, and it would be at least another hour before relief would come. She watched Bernadette Rothschild closely, wondering if the Marilyn Monroe wannabe suspected the truth. *Probably not*, she reasoned. *Raul has her so befuddled by now, the poor girl's bound to be confused about everything.*

The thought of how dumbfounded Darius must be, made her sad. As expected, he'd dumped her a second time. All was going according to plan.

It had been surprisingly easy getting him to fall in love with her. The day Raul called and told her he'd made reservations for a flight to Houston because the time had come for them to meet, she'd really been apprehensive that the savvy attorney would see right through her ploy.

"Tell Darkfire you're paying your cousin a visit," Raul had

instructed. "Wilma Breese will be waiting for you at the airport when you arrive, and will play the role. I've arranged for Darkfire to be sitting by himself. When you're airborne strike up a conversation with him, coax him into letting you sit next to him, and turn on the charm. If you can't convince him to forget about the woman he's planning to see by the time you land, tell him you insist on having your cousin drive him there. Wilma will then plead with him to come to her house for dinner, refusing to take no for an answer. That will give you more time to manipulate him. If you still can't win him over by the end of the meal, Wilma will take him where he wants to go and we'll have to come up with another plan."

The name stunt had been totally her idea. She'd done it on the spur of the moment to gauge the depth of his feelings for the girl he'd planned to surprise. Expecting to go by her real name, Wilma had almost blown it initially when being introduced as Holly Hepburn. But she'd quickly caught on, thinking the pseudonym must have been a last minute change in Raul's plan.

Robyn found it hard not to fall in love with Darius and wasn't quite sure she hadn't, but emotions had to be set aside to achieve her goal. She already deeply regretted her role in what lay ahead.

* * * *

Rusty had never been one to take charge of a complicated situation. *Live and let live* had always been his credo. No more. Two of his friends had gotten themselves into some deep shit and he couldn't stand idly by and do nothing. If Darius hadn't told him, he figured he'd never have learned about the strange organization to begin with, much less that Raul Wyncote had duped Bernadette and Eval into it. He hoped to God Dare never came face to face with that weird Arab, but knew the ol' scrapper inevitably would if he couldn't convince Bernadette and Eval to leave MWTB soon. There was no way Darius Darkfire could look the other way while two of his friends were being forced to worship the devil. Rusty feared for his dear pal's safety because of Raul's inordinate interest in that ring his mother gave him, so he couldn't risk telling him what he was up to.

Having formed no strategy as yet, he hoped Eval hadn't also become indebted to Wyncote so he could simply quit MWTB and help him find a way to free Bernadette. He wanted to call Jock Derby and tell him everything she'd told him about Make Way for The Beast, but feared he wouldn't believe him.

* * * *

Eval's dick felt like it would rip open if it got any stiffer. That's what that bastard Raul counted on. He hated having to come to these assemblies but couldn't control the lust that rose up during the part where they all had to watch the mass orgy—a porno produced by that son-of-a-bitch Wyncote.

The naked figures didn't appear on a silver screen, Raul created the actors in three dimensions on the stage and they looked like real people getting it on. The men were all hung and the awesomely beautiful women had cock-ripping hot, perfectly proportioned bodies.

Shame filled him as he stared at Wyncote's production of writhing flesh at the head of the auditorium, each fictitious man and woman rapidly approaching orgasm. He should have had the foresight not to ask that Arabian weirdo for anything. Now he was bound to the magi mystic for life. Turning away, he spotted Bernadette. Though her panting lips revealed she too was on fire with passion, he knew she felt the same contradictory emotions as he did—hating everything about this evil organization, yet powerless to resist the arousal.

One by one the figurines cried out with orgasmic release before disappearing. When the last one vanished, Raul took center stage. After offering a benediction and prayer to Day Star, he said anyone seeking to advance their membership should come forward and wait at the stage. He then dismissed the Outer Layer members of the convocation not presently interested in advancement.

Eval quickly made for the exit along with Bernadette and other members of the tier. He had no idea what went on after the first group left and though tempted at each meeting to advance, hoped he'd never find out. Robyn Tuscany acknowledged him with a nod of her gorgeous head as he walked past. As always, she stayed for the next part.

THIRTY THREE

Holly applied her makeup and hastily dressed. She had less than hour to get to the airport and clear security before her flight to Dallas was scheduled to take off. Darius would pick her up at DFW International. Ordinarily she'd relish the chance to see him, but under the circumstances a part of her dreaded it.

How a man with his intelligence and such a high degree of integrity could believe he was the antichrist baffled her. If anything, because of his inability to lose, she'd buy into the idea of him being the second coming of Christ rather than The Beast.

Catching a bus to the airport, she hurried through the terminal, got her baggage checked, and made it through the security gate with only minutes to spare.

Seated near the wing, fighting the urge to bite her nails, she nervously eyed the other passengers. None of the people looked like they belonged in a coffin and that appeased her fear of flying somewhat.

A woman sitting next to her introduced herself. "Hi there, my name is Wilma Breese . . . ."

* * * *

He pushed a button to silence the ringing and brought the plastic rectangle to his ear. Darius was on the other end and sounded panicked. *"I can't find Holly, Preston. She boarded the plane in Houston according to the flight manifest so I know she made the trip. I got rear-ended on the way to the airport and the lady who hit me was absolutely hysterical, I liked to have never got her to calm down. By the time I got to Holly's gate all the passengers had left the area. She doesn't have a cell phone but I figured she'd call mine from a payphone and tell me her location, but it's been over an hour and she still hasn't called. I'm worried something must have happened to her . . . ."*

* * * *

She gazed ahead down a stretch of interstate highway as Wilma Breese drove. Her chauffeur had said she'd known Darius since childhood, and Holly couldn't help feeling a little jealous that she hadn't gotten to grow up knowing him.

He'd sounded so paranoid over the phone she'd felt little surprise when Wilma told her he'd called and asked his long time friend to chaperone her from Houston. When he hadn't shown up at the airport to pick her up, Wilma said some important legal business must have detained him, and insisted on driving her to his house.

Though eager to see the man she loved, Holly didn't look forward to hearing further details about why he'd become convinced he was the antichrist. She almost wished she hadn't told him about her nightmare, even though she feared he and Preston might be right in believing it to be prophetic.

Before they made love for the first time that Friday he'd flown to Houston to see the Texans and Colts play, he'd warned her they might not ever be intimate again after that weekend because of a female prosecutor in Dallas of all things. The irony had greatly intensified the heartbreak she'd managed to hide. Every kiss, caress, and sensual thrill had been a two-edged sword of physical pleasure and emotional pain. When he kissed her goodbye at the airport late that Sunday night, she'd bawled all the way back to her apartment. Once there she'd called her fiancé, tearfully explained she couldn't marry him because her heart would always belong to another man, and cried herself to sleep over Darius. Now—though romance would be the farthest thing from the lawyer's mind—fate had given her another crack at him.

"How much further?"

Darius's old friend turned towards her, an odd smile rising on her face. "We're almost there."

THIRTY FOUR

Raul's huge and grossly purplish penis had finally begun to deflate. The animal had screwed her three times in the last ninety minutes, taking a break between ejaculations only long enough to allow his libido to reset. She felt blood oozing from both her vagina—which had been stretched far beyond its normal boundaries to accommodate the massive shaft of rigid flesh—and anus. Her throat hurt as well from having him ram his inordinately thick eighteen inches all the way down it. At least he hadn't shot his wad in her mouth tonight like he usually did. That puzzled her somewhat, but since his semen tasted worse than anything she'd ever had the displeasure of experiencing, she wasn't about to ask why for fear he might decide to remedy the situation and gag her with a dose of it after all.

Lying across the mystic's Persian cushions receiving her dripping life fluid, she couldn't help thinking of how wonderful Darius's normal-sized manhood felt inside her. She'd never felt any pain with him, only immense pleasure. Aware she couldn't entertain such memories and keep her sanity for long because of what had to be done, Robyn forced her thoughts away from the attorney and rose to get dressed.

Raul grabbed her arm. "What do you think you're doing? I'm just getting warmed up."

She wanted to scream when his colossal sausage began lengthening and thickening like a snake-shaped balloon being pumped full of air. He'd never screwed her more than twice in one night before, much less four times.

After another nightmarish sexual bout, again ejaculating in her overtaxed vaginal canal rather than forcing her to receive it on her tongue, he asked if the problem had been taken care of.

Robyn tearfully eyed the Persian's limp purple rod and nodded, fearing even the sound of her voice might arouse the awful serpent. To her immense relief he got up and began to put his clothes on. She quickly followed suit.

"You're sure you put Wilma on top of the right girl—the one you saw him with in Houston."

Nodding again, she fastened her bra and reached for her blouse. Darius hadn't a clue of the many times she'd been ordered to follow him. She'd been tortured by jealousy when the lawyer took Holly Hepburn back to his hotel after leaving Baker's Dozen, the very nightclub he'd taken her to the day they met.

"Good . . ." Raul pulled up his trousers. "The stage is almost set, and at long last our destiny shall be fulfilled."

Robyn didn't understand why Holly Hepburn had to be kidnapped and held as bait to lure Darius to his fate, and Raul had refused to explain. She could only surmise that just as the ring couldn't be taken without its owner willingly handing it over, the bearer of it had to come to the presentation assembly of his own free will.

Though her old archeology professor's efforts hadn't provided the proof she'd hoped for, she'd known the ring was valid even before Amia had presented it to her son back in ninety-nine. But she couldn't tell Darius that he had to be convinced of its validity when he finally gave it to The Mede or its power wouldn't be transferred. When the professor's examination failed to make her then-fiancé a believer, Raul instructed her to tell Darius they used to be lovers and he'd returned to Fort Worth. That action was supposed to prompt Darius to seek out Raul through jealousy and upon seeing how important the mystic found the ring, and witnessing his supernatural power, make the counselor finally believe the gold band really had been passed down from Cyrus. That too had failed, and in the end only served to make Darius break up with her.

She'd received a severe reprimand from The Mede over it, and in trying to defend herself, asked why he just didn't go see Darius and give a demonstration of his power. "After all," she'd said at the time, "that's how you convinced me." The Mede had gotten furious and warned that if she ever disrespected him like that again, her future position would go to another more worthy.

The only other time the mysterious goldsmith had gotten angry with her was when she'd asked why he and Raul were never together, pointing out she'd never seen the two of them at the same time. After The Mede chastised her for asking, he told her to inquire of Raul, that he'd tell her. Raul said they couldn't be in the same proximity until Day Star personally inhabited The Mede. That had made no sense whatsoever to her, but she knew better than to confess the fact to either of them.

Knowing Darius had fallen in love with her, she'd assured both The Mede and Raul that it was only a matter of time before the bearer of the ring would want her back after he broke off their engagement the first time. She hadn't lied to Darius about being told to break their date, and still didn't know the reason for that odd command.

So many of their tactics seemed contradictory to her but she didn't doubt their powers and believed with all her heart that soon the three of them would prevent the Nazarene from usurping Day Star as the rightful ruler of the world. So, though many times she didn't understand the reasoning behind their directives, she always obeyed.

A pang of remorse knifed through her as the memory of The Mede demanding Cyrus's ring from Darius played in her mind. She'd made certain her ex fiancé took full note of her feigned anxiety, knowing it would create a deep suspicion in his mind and lead him to once again terminate their relationship. Little did the lawyer know how close he'd come to actually being the one—after all these centuries since the prophet handed the ring to Cyrus—to personally witness the second coming of Jesus of Nazareth.

Like the abduction of Holly Hepburn, she hadn't been told the reason she'd been ordered to play out the scene that insured Darius would eventually dump her, but she did know that once they accomplished their ultimate goal, the second advent of Jesus Christ would be thwarted for at least a thousand years. In return for her role in the mission, she'd been promised an extremely powerful position in the new world order, the third highest in the chain of command, second only to Raul who's only mortal superior would be The Mede. Through the universal power of Day Star which would be bestowed upon The Mede not long after the ring got placed on his finger by Darius, the three of them would become a triumvirate surpassing that desired by the carpenter and his so-called Father and Holy Spirit.

Realizing she'd once again allowed a memory to whip up her feelings for Darius, Robyn squeezed him from her thoughts as she stepped into her shoes. She bade Raul a goodnight and walked out the door very slowly, each movement reviving the pain between her legs.

* * * *

Rusty Wurly had told him the biggest cock-and-bull story he'd ever heard in his life, the joker. Shaking his head with a grin Jock turned to his new girlfriend he'd met only a few days ago—a good looking piece of white meat named Wilma Breese. "That was one of my homeys on the phone, and you won't believe what that fool tried to pull on me . . . ."

* * * *

Rusty's instincts had been right, Jock hadn't believed him. John wouldn't either, even if the twin did tell his brother like he'd asked. Because of their long history of razzing one another, the more he protested he was telling the truth the more Jock thought he'd been joking. The Derby's probably couldn't have done much to help with the situation anyway. Darius would know how to handle this but he didn't dare get him involved—Raul would sniff out the plot to free Bernadette and Eval from the cult. The scary Arab wasn't interested in him at all but Darius probably couldn't take a leak without that mysterious weirdo knowing about it.

Still void of any sort of plan, he crossed the front porch and rang his buddy's doorbell.

Eval's chubby cheeks flared with a big grin when he opened the door. "Hey, Essie!"

"How you doing, Eval?"

"Fine, come on in."

He followed the chunky Latino into his living room.

"Take a squat, I'll get you a brewski."

Rusty sat down on a comfortable sofa and looked the room over. Not much had changed since he'd last been here. The furnishings reflected a bachelor's taste much as his own did. There were few pictures on the walls and no knick-knacks. Every stick of sensible furniture was aimed towards a huge plasma TV and an elaborate stereo system.

Eval handed him a bottle and plopped into a recliner where he aimed a remote at his television, silencing two commentators on ESPN. "So what's up?"

Gulping a mouthful of cold suds, Rusty wished he could empty a six pack before bringing up the subject, maybe then he wouldn't feel so nervous. He didn't like to even think about the bizarre man, much less have to talk about him. Unfortunately he had no choice. "I'm here about Raul Wyncote."

The Mexican's eyes flashed so wide his irises seemed to shrink in the center of two glistening white marbles. "Why the fuck you bringing that bastard up for—shit, next subject."

"Eval, I'm going to be honest with you. I talked to Bernadette and I know you and her have joined Wyncote's cult. I want to know . . . no, I *have* to know: did you ask him for anything that day we met him?"

A blush came over his brown face. "Did you?"

"Uh-uh."

"Good, vato . . ." his lower lip trembled for a few seconds, then he started crying. "Oh fuck, man, I wish to hell I hadn't."

Rusty's heart fell, but for his old friend's sake he tried not to show it. "What did you ask for?"

"Too damned ashamed to say."

"I assume he gave you whatever you requested."

Eval nodded, tears dribbling down round jowls from eyes cinched shut. "You know, man . . . you wish for something and get it, you never figure it's gonna ruin your life. Wyncote is one evil bastard. I wish the motherfucker was dead."

"So you don't like being a member of his cult?"

He rubbed his eyes dry and sat up. "Hell no, man. But like Bernadette, I'm fucking stuck in it for life."

"Darius knows about it. Did you know that?"

"You tell him?"

"He told me. That's the first I heard about it. Bernadette had lied to him and said I was a member too."

"Why the fuck did she do that?"

"Wyncote."

"Shit . . . that son-of-a-bitch. Thank God me and her are only part of what's called the Outer Layer which is creepy enough. Got no idea what goes on with the higher memberships. I guess you know they're waiting for the antichrist to rise."

"Yeah. Why is Wyncote so interested in Dare?"

"The ring his mama gave him, vato."

"Are you sure that's all?"

"Far as I know. Like I said, me and Bernadette aren't high enough in MWTB to be in the know."

He took a long pull from the bottle and wiped his mouth. "I

want you and Bernadette to quit, Eval. I don't care what that creepy Arab did for you, it's not worth ruining your life over. I'm afraid Darius might get himself killed trying to get the two of you out."

A contemptuous sneer tore across Eval's face. "Don't you think we want that too? But we can't. He's got us, and there's nothing anybody can do about it."

Chills raced up his spine at the finality in Eval's tone. "Man . . . will he kill you if you leave, or what?"

"Worse. Remember when he gave us that awful vision of what would happen to us if we told Dare about him?"

Remembering all too well, he answered with a sad nod.

"That's what will happen to us if we quit. Man, we ain't even allowed to miss a meeting much less give it up. Thank God they only take place once a month at every new moon. It's nobody's fault but ours. He didn't force us to join, just like he didn't force me to ask for a twelve inch—" Eval slapped a hand over his mouth.

Despite the morbid topic, he had to laugh. "Why you son-of-gun, you asked him for a twelve inch dick, didn't you."

Blood rushed to his face as he nodded.

"Oh man . . . ."

"I really fucked up on that too, and not just because of getting tied to Raul Wyncote. Shit, you'd be surprised how many chicks don't like big dicks, at least not that big. The damn thing gets harder than steel when it's on the juice, just like I asked for, and it hurts them too much. It wasn't like I had a pencil dick or anything before—I was a decent size and should have been satisfied with what God gave me."

Resisting the urge to ask if it stayed that long when not erect, he headed in another direction. "I called Jock and told him about you guys getting tricked into joining MWTB, but I don't think he believed me."

"Did you know Sash Temple is a member too?"

He winced at hearing it. "No. Wonder if Bernadette told

Darius she was."

"Don't know. But man she's a true believer, really high up in it."

The thought of that sweet girl being part of the cult made him sick to his stomach. "Wyncote must have tricked her too."

Eval shook his head. "No, I don't think so. Like I said, she's really, really into it. I wouldn't be surprised if she isn't at the highest level."

THIRTY FIVE

Sash stared through the window, watching a driving rain pound the redwood patio deck of her new home, snickering inside at Robyn Tuscany's gullibility. The fool believed every lie Raul told her. She hated the truth had to be kept secret because she'd always been jealous of the dark-haired pretty and would love nothing more than to tell her she was only a pawn in Raul's plan.

Robyn had been promised she'd be number three in the pecking order. Little did the dupe realize she wouldn't even be alive when Day Star finally revealed himself to the world. The impregnation had taken place only last night but Robyn wouldn't know Raul's baby had been conceived inside her foolish womb for at least a month or so since she was unaware Raul had switched her birth control pills for fakes. Robyn's child would be sacrificed, while her own—the spawn of the last ring bearer—would rule the world. She still hadn't devised another plan for obtaining Darius's sperm and knew she had to act soon because the lawyer's days were numbered.

Raul had Darius convinced he was The Beast, but the poor dear didn't realize he'd only been called upon to sire the last sovereign of the world, not rule it himself. She'd always been very found of Darius and wished he could go on living after being persuaded to put the ring on Raul's finger. Alas, the holy command from Day Star held no ambiguity and didn't allow any interpretation other than the renowned attorney's death.

Little did Robyn know her life would also be sacrificed after she gave birth to her first and only child.

* * * *

"Once you go black, you'll never go back," she'd always heard. Whoever said that was full of shit. Allowing that nigger to kiss her had been bad enough, but to actually have his black dick inside her had been nauseating. Of course he'd never know her squeals of pleasure had been as fake as her orgasm.

Raul's suspicion had proved correct. The ring bearer's friend *did* contact Jock Derby about MWTB. She'd called the mystic the first chance she got after Derby laughingly told her about it, not believing a word. Wilma had begged Raul to let her bail from the faked relationship now that it seemed neither Jock nor his brother would pose any sort of threat, but he'd refused.

It hadn't been difficult getting the big black man to give her a tumble. Parking near his house, she'd let the air out of a tire, rang his doorbell, and pleaded for his help, making sure he got an eyeful of cleavage and upper thigh. He'd asked for a date before he even got her car jacked up.

After Bernice's two assistants pulled the terrified Hepburn girl from the vehicle MWTB had provided for her in Dallas, she'd called Raul to tell him the delivery had been successful. Instead of receiving a thank you for her trouble, he'd given her the description and address of Jock Derby and told her to finagle her way into a relationship with him when she got back to Houston. Her mission was twofold: monitor Jock Derby closely because Raul anticipated a guy named Rusty Wurly might tell the wealthy nigger about MWTB, and coax him and his brother into coming with her to the last assembly.

* * * *

"More . . . need more . . . please fuck me again." She felt as though her body might burst into flames if Raul didn't quickly stab his marvelous dong inside her once more and extinguish the firestorm raging in her cunt.

"I swear you're insatiable, Bernadette."

She looked up at him from the floor of his living room, aching to be ravaged once more. "I can't help it. I'm addicted to your wonderful dick. Like I told you the first time you fucked me after The Mede made me pretty, I'm totally hooked for life."

He smiled down at her. She knew he was admiring her jutting tits which turned her on all the more. She'd do anything for him—anything. Evil though he was, she had to have him inside her on a regular basis as badly as a strung-out junkie desperately needed a fix. It always started out so painful, but after a few minutes of torture, waves of pleasure overrode the agony, escalating into an erotic bliss that flung her to heights of ecstasy she could never experience by any other man or any other means. Raul owned her and he knew it—mind, soul, and especially body.

She groaned with anticipation as he lowered his purple shaft to her lips.

"Will you suck it for me, Bernadette, even though it's fresh with residue from your ass?"

Grabbing his butt she forced him hungrily down her throat for an answer.

* * * *

Rusty felt helpless. Eval and Bernadette wanted to be free of Wyncote and that dreadful cult but neither would even consider trying to leave for fear of what he'd do to them. Though severely tempted to call Darius for tactical advice, he dared not involve him.

Tremendous sadness had clung to him since hearing Sash Temple was mixed up in it too. He'd been told the shocking news several days ago but still found it difficult to absorb. Of all the girls he'd gone after during his college days, only Sash had refused him. Perhaps that's why she'd always haunted him as well.

He'd found her address through the White Pages on the internet but hadn't called. Staring through the stormy darkness, he estimated if he ran full blast he'd reach the safety of her illuminated covered porch with only a few seconds' drenching. Hoping she was home, and wishing he had an umbrella, Rusty bailed from his car and sprinted through the cold rain.

The door opened almost immediately after he rang the bell. Sash looked beautiful. It had been years since they'd seen each other, and her face had changed slightly. She appeared remarkably serene and confident, as if her already exquisite features were being enhanced by some extraordinary inner strength.

"Rusty Wurly, is that really you?"

Relieved she seemed glad to see him, he grinned wide. "Honest and for true."

She held out a welcoming arm. "Well don't just stand there dripping, come in."

He stepped inside and halted on a tiled entryway, not wanting to get her carpeted floor wet.

"Let me get you a towel . . ." she closed the door and crossed the room, disappearing down a hallway.

The gracious fixtures adorning her living room, like the house itself, made it obvious she didn't hurt for money. She returned with a neatly folded square of pink terrycloth and handed it to him. He dried his face and crew-cut head before daubing his casual attire.

"This is such a cool surprise. I was thinking of you just the other day."

Flattered, he smiled at her. "You know, I'm not sure a single day goes by without me thinking about you."

A coy grin crossed her face. "Oh really?"

"Really."

"That's sweet."

Her last statement sounded patronizing. He reminded

himself he hadn't come to romance her anyway, so her continued disinterest in anything more than a friendship didn't hurt like it had back in college. "Sash, the reason I came to see you is because Eval Santa Anna told me you were a member of MWTB."

Alarm sprang up in her sapphire eyes. "Did he now?"

He nodded.

She motioned nervously towards a couch covered with pink felt. "Sit down and tell me about it. What can I get you to drink?"

"Nothing, I'm fine."

"Well I think I'll have a cold toddy. Excuse me a minute, be right back."

It seemed an inordinate amount of time to make a drink. At least fifteen minutes had gone by and she still hadn't come back. Unable to see past the entrance to the hall, he decided to look for her, hoping she wasn't staying away on purpose so he'd take the hint and leave. When he rose to his feet she returned to the living room holding a drink in one hand and a condom in the other, wearing nothing but a sexy smile . . . .

* * * *

Stretched out behind her on the couch, relishing the feel of breasts he'd so long been denied, he whispered in her ear, "That was wonderful."

Eyes closed, face aglow with sensual gratification, she smiled. "It certainly was."

"Don't you wish you hadn't turned me down way back when now?"

Sash answered with a lazy nod. "Oh I wanted to, believe me, but I was saving myself for my husband. I was a virgin until I married my ex."

So that's why she refused me! Rusty felt his chest swell with pride. "You know, if you had given in, we might have gotten married."

The smile broadened but her lids remained sealed. "Wonder what that would have been like?"

"We'll never know, will we?"

"Mm mm . . . there's no changing the past."

The thrill of rectifying his lone college failure to conquer prim-and-proper Sash Temple had made him temporarily forget the purpose of this visit. He hated to ruin the moment but had no choice. "How did you get involved with Make Way for The Beast?"

This time she showed no response to the topic—didn't even open her eyes which he'd expected to bolt wide with apprehension.

"Do you believe in God, Rusty?"

"Mm hmm."

"The Christian God?"

"Yeah."

"Well, I believe *that* God is evil, and I worship the first being created by Him. Christians, Jews, and Muslims call him Satan but his name is Lucifer which means Day Star. He's the most misunderstood individual in existence, totally maligned, and I love him more than anyone I've ever known. He first appeared to me when I was only a child. He's beautiful beyond imagination."

Astonishment hammered at his brain. Sash Temple, who'd been the most straight-laced member of the old college gang, had just told him she'd seen the devil. Not bothering to disguise how ridiculous he found it, he stated rather than asked, "You saw the devil."

Her stunning eyes—an extraordinary shade of blue—finally appeared as she turned over to face him. "You don't believe me?"

He laughed. "Come on, Sash, of course not."

A slow smile crawled across her face as an odd gleam twinkled in two cerulean orbs that suddenly appeared intimidating. "Want me to prove it?"

His stomach twisted into a fearful knot. She meant it.

Sash rose from the couch, her gorgeous body sheened with a gossamer film of passion-induced sweat generated by his sexual prowess. Hands raised, she twirled like a ballerina while uttering a language he'd never heard. It sounded guttural yet strangely poetic. She cried out while gracefully lowering herself to the floor, and crossed her legs.

Lights flashed, almost blinding him before a starburst sphere about a yard in diameter appeared, rotating in the air a few feet above Sash like a miniature planet. Mesmerized by the globe, he gasped when it exploded to reveal a being standing behind her, so tall its head almost touched the ceiling. Too unbearably wondrous to behold at first, he slammed his lids closed, but only for a second because he had to look again. What gazed down upon him was so agonizingly glorious, so excruciatingly beautiful, an ecstatic joy he'd never known flooded him from head to toe—intoxicating, enchanting, thrilling, and utterly captivating him. Tears of gut-wrenching sorrow gushed from his eyes when the angelic presence disappeared. His life would never be the same. No matter what it took, he had to see that thing again so he could bask in its mind-boggling breathtaking glory.

"I know . . ." Sash rose from the floor with a sympathetic smile. "It hurts so badly to see him go. But you'll see him again, Rusty. I promise."

THIRTY SIX

There were no windows or doors, and the only opening led to a bathroom. Evidently the room could only be accessed by a movable section of wall like a revolving bookcase in an old time movie. Unfortunately whatever switch or lever controlled it appeared to be located on the other side since she hadn't been able to find it from within the enclosure.

Holly didn't have the foggiest notion of where she was. Wilma Breese had driven her to a regal house she claimed belonged to Darius, and two thugs had pulled her from the car. That's the last she recalled before waking up in a comfortable bed occupying a corner of her rectangular prison.

Whoever her abductors were, they obviously didn't plan on starving her to death because a portable pantry and large refrigerator had been packed with food and drink. The appliance, along with an electric stove situated by cabinets containing a sink, cooking utensils, and dishes, looked oddly out of place with the other furniture, as if a kitchen had been jammed into a bedroom. They'd put her suitcase and purse on a small table situated a few feet from the stove. Nothing had been taken from either.

Though it had been weeks since her abduction and she hadn't eaten a proper meal since leaving Houston, Holly had no appetite. She ate only when her stomach ached from emptiness to such extremes pain rather than hunger forced her to put something into it. Even then she nibbled only enough food to quell the misery.

She'd been unconscious when brought here, so she might have initially slept around the clock for all she knew. Since then, each time she dozed off in a fitful non-recuperative sleep, she checked her wristwatch first thing after waking up. Her captors hadn't furnished a radio or TV, and the room had no clocks, so it was her only means of determining night from day. Her digital time piece didn't show the date, but it did label the hours as a.m. or p.m.

Though she hadn't seen them do it, they'd obviously knocked her out with some sort of drug before taking her here. She'd woken up with an acrid tang in the back of her throat, and a sore buttock indicated she'd been stabbed by a hypodermic. Locating the bathroom, she'd rinsed out her mouth and the face in the mirror had reflected the horror gripping her. The panic in her eyes had looked identical to that of a young girl's she'd seen in a photograph taken at Auschwitz during the Nazi reign.

After frantically searching for a way out and finding none, she'd beaten on the heavily plastered walls, demanding to be released. When that too had proved futile she'd broken down and cried, praying for God to send Darius to the rescue. Eventually the tears stopped and she'd faced the horrid fact that neither he nor anyone else that cared had a clue of her whereabouts.

Holly knew she'd been taken hostage because of Darius but didn't know what the kidnappers were after. It seemed ludicrous for them to think he'd pay a large sum of money in exchange for the release of someone he had no formal ties to.

Wilma Breese knowing her flight schedule and managing to get a seat next to hers had given her no reason to doubt the woman's veracity about being friends with Darius. But clearly Breese had lied—he hadn't given her that information—so how had she gotten it? Did she also know the reason Darius wanted her in Dallas, and of his fear of being the antichrist?

Thinking back she should have been suspicious from the start, but second guessing herself wouldn't help the situation. Deep concern over Darius's welfare compounded her anxiety. Something had kept him from meeting her at the airport like he'd planned. He hadn't been abducted too, she was sure of that since her kidnappers were using her as bait to coax whatever they were after from him. Breese had to have known he wouldn't make it to the airport, so an accomplice must have detained him. But how? She worried he'd been physically prevented from picking her up and might have gotten injured in the process.

At least she had the comfort of knowing he was still alive. The fact she still drew breath meant her jailers hoped to obtain a ransom, something they couldn't get from a dead man.

It didn't matter whether the woman who introduced herself on the plane as Wilma Breese had used her real name or made that one up. Breese knew full well she could give a sketch artist a very detailed description of her abductor. That, coupled with the fact the two henchmen hadn't bothered covering their faces, could only mean they weren't planning on her getting out alive. At some point they were bound to have her speak to Darius on the phone or force her to record a message to be sent to him. Once they no longer needed her it would only be a matter of time before they'd insure she'd never be able to testify against them.

She sat at the table, riveted with raw fear and hopelessness. Hands folded in front of her face she prayed aloud for a miracle—that Darius would somehow find her before it was too late.

* * * *

Bernice Hoff couldn't help laughing at the monitor. Judging by the look on the poor girl's face, she really thought she was done for. She turned to one of her assistants. "Is Bernadette ready?"

"Yes."

"Good. You know what to do. She always wanted to be an actress. Now it's time for my cousin to make her Broadway debut."

PART
THREE

THIRTY SEVEN

Darius played the DVD again. Holly looked so frail and helpless, bound to a wooden chair with her mouth gagged, eyes frozen with fear. But she was alive!

Two months had passed since her disappearance from DFW International. When the police couldn't find her, he feared she'd somehow been abducted by a rapist at the airport, who'd successfully disposed of her body after abusing it. That had sent him into a funk even darker than the one he'd been trapped in for weeks. The crushing emotions plunging him into abject despair over Holly's apparent death had driven him to once again contemplate something he'd seriously considered after Wyncote's awful confirmation—suicide.

Hearing her voice that day she'd called to tell him about the nightmare had been the only bright spot in the darkness enveloping him at the time. He knew then he'd fallen in love with her. Thinking he'd unwittingly caused her demise by asking her to come to Dallas had so compounded his misery he'd almost lost his mind.

As the days went by, sorrow and bitterness eventually coalesced into numbness, and he'd become an impassive automaton, bleakly grinding out his existence moment to dreary moment. But the disk that arrived in the mail that morning changed all that. Despite the circumstances, seeing the woman he loved still remained among the living had revitalized him with electrified joy.

The disk contained another jarring surprise. Bernadette Rothschild had been kidnapped as well. Strapped to a chair next to Holly, she looked every bit as terrified. The nostrils of Bernadette's miraculous nose were flared because of a ball stretching her painted lips out of proportion. The lower features of both women appeared almost apelike because of the gags shoved into their mouths.

A printed ransom demand scrolled across the bottom of the screen as the camera stayed focused on Holly's and Bernadette's petrified faces.

It read:

Greetings, Mister Darkfire. As you can see, we are holding your friends captive. Notify anyone about this and we'll obtain two more people you care about. We waited this long to contact you in order to impress upon you how futile it would be to have the police continue to search for Miss Hepburn. The place they are being held will never be discovered, and if you don't comply with our demands they'll be left here to die, slowly and painfully, of dehydration.

You'll soon be notified by phone of a location to which you will bring the ring presented to you on the first of June in 1999. A ceremony will be held, somewhat similar to that which took place when the ring was given to you. After you willfully place the ring on the finger of a person of our choosing, your friends will be released to you, and we will never trouble you again.

Because the kidnappers were after the ring, he knew Raul Wyncote, who was also The Mede, had to have engineered it, but it wouldn't do any good to tell the authorities. The Mede wasn't human, no jail cell could hold him. And since Wyncote could turn into Arash Arshia at will, he couldn't be kept behind bars either.

For several weeks after leaving the sinister Arab's apartment the day he'd been confirmed as The Beast, Darius had done nothing but mope around his office during the day and drink himself to sleep at night. Each passing moment he'd feared an insurgence of evil would overpower him and convert him into the monster he was destined to become.

But after one particularly grisly night of crying in his whiskey, he woke up the next morning angry at himself for meekly acquiescing to what appeared to be unalterable fate, and decided to research the horrid topic in the dim hope of finding some sort of proof that he wasn't the antichrist. After getting nowhere on his own, he conferred with several theologians. Each had a differing theory as to when the antichrist would become aware of his destiny. Their views ranged from The Beast being born with that knowledge, to him not knowing it until he became personally indwelt by Satan at the beginning of The Tribulation. Seeing he'd never solve anything going that route, Darius had purchased a roundtrip ticket to Iraq for his private investigator.

Preston's Middle East expedition had been for the sole purpose of digging up all he could on the history of the ring. The former commander had returned four days ago after striking pay dirt.

The legend *had* been misconstrued through the years. At the time Cyrus presided over Persia, the ancient wise men and mystics thought no one except the messiah would ever exercise more power on earth than their reigning king. A renowned prophet of those times really had presented the ring to Cyrus with instructions that it be passed down through his descendants every seventy years until Shiloh's arrival. However, the man of God never said it was to be given to Christ. That apocryphal myth got injected into the legend less than five hundred years ago.

After learning the truth about the legacy Darius concluded The Mede had somehow implanted the dreams about Cyrus since in each one the king had stated the ring would be worn by Shiloh. Not only that, he now knew the goldsmith hadn't really handed it to the monarch as had also been consistently portrayed. Until then, he'd thought them to be visions induced by the hand of God.

"The truth shall set you free," his mother often quoted from scripture. Darius would forever treasure those words because the truth had done just that. He wasn't the antichrist. Wyncote had only beguiled him into believing that so he wouldn't dare

THE CYRUS SYNDROME   279

put the ring on. The Mede had merely set the stage by demanding it those two times to buttress the illusion, knowing he would eventually confront his alter ego about it and be told Satan had tested him. The diabolical ploy had been devastatingly effective. The bastard had no doubt been responsible for making sure he recalled going to Corpus Christi the day after receiving the ring, thus proving the metaphysical video inaccurate which resulted in him refusing to hand it over just as The Mede counted on.

The gold band with the Persian hieroglyph had been passed down, unworn by anyone including Cyrus the Great, to finally reside on the finger of the last person to possess it before Jesus Christ returned from heaven to occupy the throne of David in Jerusalem. A certain sign had been promised which would alert the last ring bearer that he or she had the right to wear it: they'd never lose at anything so long as their cause stood on the side of truth and justice. The real mission of the last possessor of Cyrus's heirloom was simply to serve as a sign that the generation standing would witness the advent of its long awaited savior, and a warning that The Beast and False Prophet would rise beforehand. No one knew when that day would come but his unblemished legal record would serve as proof—at least to some—that the current generation wouldn't pass away before it did.

Though learning he wasn't The Beast had relieved him to the enth degree, a dark cloud of depression had continued hovering over him until seeing Holly was still alive. Now the possibility of a bright and happy future lay ahead if he could only liberate her from Wyncote.

Thinking about the other thing Preston had discovered about the ancient object, Darius opened his desk drawer and withdrew the container he'd placed there only a few days ago. Opening it, he gazed at the Persian signet he'd finally learned meant *God shall dwell with man.*

He couldn't put it on yet because The Mede would most

likely be instantly aware of it and no doubt order Holly's execution in retribution. And so, it wouldn't be worn until after he used it as bait to free her and Bernadette, who he figured must have really pissed off the evil duality for spilling her guts that night she'd come to his house.

When Ricca buzzed that he had a phone call, his heart lurched with the hope he was about to receive instructions from Holly's abductors. It turned out to be Sash Temple instead.

Closing the box with one hand, he picked up the phone with the other. A few minutes later he hung up, sorry he couldn't oblige his old college friend.

The intercom blared again. *"Darius, there's a man on the phone obviously disguising his voice. He wants to speak to you but won't give his name, and the call is anonymous. Should I tell him you're unavailable?"*

"No, I'll take the call." Pulse racing, he reached for the phone. "Hello?"

"Mister Darkfire, did you receive a certain DVD recently?" The kidnapper's voice was being electronically altered to sound like a hoarse Darth Vader.

"I did."

"And have you played it yet?"

"I have."

"Will you cooperate?"

"Yeah. When and where?"

"Eight o'clock tomorrow night."

"Why not tonight?"

"It has to be done the first night of the new moon."

"What's the address . . .?"

* * * *

Staring at the phone he'd cradled ten minutes ago, Darius continued deliberating on something that had crossed his mind since talking to the kidnapper. He finally gave in and buzzed Ricca.

"Yes?"

"Ricca, I need the number off the ID before the anonymous call."

"Who was that weirdo anyway?"

"Um . . . just an old friend pulling a prank."

"What an oddball sense of humor, huh?"

"Ricca!"

"Okay, sorry. I'd forgotten you'd completely lost yours. The number before the anonymous call is . . . ."

He phoned Sash to tell her he'd changed his mind about coming to her place for dinner. Not knowing when Holly's captors would make contact and demand his presence, he'd declined her invitation when she called earlier. Now, since his hands were tied until tomorrow night, he hoped the diversion would help keep his mind from frantically playing out endless possible scenarios and worrying about how it all would end.

Having little trouble locating her new residence in Plano, he pulled into her drive at six-thirty, the time she'd asked him to be there. Unlike her ex's house, there was nothing modest about the domicile she lived in now. Wondering how she'd been able to afford such a stylish home, he pushed the doorbell . . . .

After seating him at a dining table only a woman would own, Sash went to the kitchen and returned with a platter of delectable smelling steak fingers. She placed them on the heart-shaped countertop and sat down across from him with a smile. "Help yourself."

Though apprehensive about tomorrow night's outcome, the jubilation he felt at knowing Holly was alive had revived his long suppressed appetite. He heaped mashed potatoes onto a china plate, smothered the fluffy mound with cream gravy, and filled the remaining space with strips of battered round steak, fried to golden perfection. Gripping one with his fingers, he stabbed it into the savory white mountain he'd made, and brought it to his mouth. It tasted marvelous.

Sash made a sour face. "Darius, that's uncouth."

He grinned. "What's wrong with liking some taters as well as gravy on your steak fingers?"

With a reprimanding roll of her eyes, she got up, walked around the table, ladled some gravy into a small bowl sitting beside his plate, and put her hands on her hips. "Use this for dipping. Put some potatoes in there too if you must, but don't use your plate, that's gross. You weren't raised in a barn."

Scooping up a heaping spoonful of whipped spuds, he dumped them into the appointed bowl, stirred the mass together, and winked at her. "Tastes delicious, by the way."

"Thank you . . ." she returned to her seat.

"Really nice place you have here."

A peculiar, almost apologetic smile emerged. "Would you believe that after you got my savings back for me my grandmother died and left me a small fortune?"

"Is that right?" He pulled another stick of crispy coated beef from his pile. "Well, I'm just glad you're free of that dope dealer. You deserve so much better."

Topping a dainty portion of potatoes with a dollop of gravy, Sash returned the ladle and used a pair of tongs to move a single steak finger to her plate. She then picked up a fork and stabbed a cherry tomato sitting on the summit of a large salad, void of dressing. "I'm so grateful for what you did, Dare."

"Aw, it was my pleasure. So are you still swearing off marriage?" It didn't look like it. Judging by the overwhelming ratio of rabbit food over the good stuff, she planned on keeping her figure perfect for some lucky guy.

She took a sip of iced tea before answering. "At least for now, but you never know. I have my art and this lovely home. I'm quite satisfied, actually."

"Good for you . . ." he dutifully dipped a steak finger in the bowl instead of his plate and bit off a chunk.

There was a bite left of her solitary steak finger when she called it quits, while he'd gorged himself on seconds of everything before putting his fork down. Offering to eat it for her had prompted another lecture in proper dining etiquette, after which she led him to the living room and served coffee.

While savoring a cup an unusual fatigue set in. He started to apologize for having to cut the evening short, but Sash spoke first.

"Thanks for coming over tonight, Dare. Fixing dinner for you was the least I could do since you wouldn't let me pay you anything for helping me with you-know-who."

Darius tried once again to tell her he needed to get home, but nodded off without getting a word out. The last thing he recalled was an auditory hallucination of Rusty Wurly saying something about a star.

THIRTY EIGHT

Darius let out a deep yawn and lowered his feet to the floor. Slouching on the edge of his bed he wondered how he'd gotten home. The last thing he remembered was falling asleep on Sash's couch.

By the time first-waking fuzziness evaporated, he concluded that yesterday's adrenaline rush over Holly had been the last straw. After weeks on end of putting himself to sleep with booze and not eating properly, his abused liver and tortured mind had apparently decided enough was enough. Shortly after overstuffing his gullet he'd passed out, and Sash must have roused him or he'd woke up on his own later in the night. Either way he'd apparently driven home in such an exhausted daze his overtaxed brain couldn't recollect it.

The hot water of the shower stung his penis. He examined it and found raw spots along the shaft. Fearing it might be one of those incurable skin-devouring staff infections that had evolved in some hospitals, he hurriedly toweled himself dry and stepped out of the tub. Closing the toilet, he hiked his leg on the lid, bending close as he could to his midsection.

His jaw dropped. They weren't rashes: the skin had been irritated by friction. A sick feeling rose from the pit of his stomach and spread all over him like a fever. Sash had drugged him last night in order to have sex with him.

But why?

* * * *

Darius called Preston first thing after he got to his office. He didn't tell the investigator Holly had been kidnapped rather than murdered. The threat about abducting two more of his friends couldn't be ignored. They might even go after his mother next if he didn't play by their rules. He'd phoned because he wanted Sash Temple investigated.

Unusually striking and very intelligent, Sash was hardly a woman that needed to trick a man for sex, and he couldn't believe she had a fetish for making it with an unconscious partner. Besides, she hadn't screwed him for pleasure. He had no way of knowing how many times she'd raped him but the skinned hide of his penis proved she'd humped it with a dry vagina. She'd continued thrusting even though the natural lubricants induced by arousal had ceased coating her canal which must have been very uncomfortable if not outright painful for her.

He'd put two and two together during the drive to work, recalling the sudden drowsiness he'd experienced the night she came to see him about her divorce. She'd obviously drugged him then too, for the sole purpose of having intercourse. With the deed done there'd have been no need to linger, which explained why she hadn't been there when he woke up the next morning. For some reason once had apparently been enough on that night, since she hadn't humped herself dry.

Guys were always hitting on Sash back in college, even the extremely picky Rusty, but she'd repeatedly turned them all down. Her straight-laced personality didn't mesh with his, so he'd never asked her for a date in those days. Besides, he'd have been rejected like all the rest because she'd never given any indication she liked him more than a friend. Though some virginal types turned into total whores later in life, he knew that hadn't happened to Sash. She hadn't rendered him unconscious those two times in order to use him as a living sex toy.

She wanted to have his baby.

That was the only thing that made sense because he just couldn't buy into the idea of ultra-reticent politically correct Sash Temple being kinky. And he could think of only one reason for her having such a desire—she wanted to bear the offspring of Shiloh for reasons he didn't know. Sadly, she'd only succeeded in purloining the sperm of a mere human, and if she did wind up pregnant he'd never allow her to keep his baby even if he had to go all the way to the Supreme Court to gain custody.

Bernadette said everybody that attended the ring ceremony had met Raul Wyncote before later claiming she'd lied about that per Wyncote's instructions. She'd told him so many lies he couldn't help wondering if that confession itself hadn't been yet another untruth, at least concerning Sash. He feared the worse—that she'd gotten acquainted with Wyncote and had become a member of MWTB.

The afternoon dragged by slower than a snail's pace. He felt extremely anxious and continually had to force negative thoughts about the evening's outcome from his mind. Trying to cling to positive memories like the wonderful weekend he'd spent with Holly in Houston did little good. Images of Wyncote slashing her throat, or strangling her to death while he hung helplessly on a cross still managed to creep in. After battling away one particularly horrifying mental episode of Holly being crucified alongside him, he got an idea.

Cursing himself for not thinking of it sooner, he decided to ask Eval about Sash. Ricca put him through to Lochweed and he soon got hold of his old bud. After a bantering session, with Eval at first denying knowing anything about the cult, Darius finally got him to come clean. Without wasting a second afterwards, he asked if Sash was also a member.

Eval nervously cleared his throat before answering. *"Um no, not that I'm aware of . . . ."*

Swabbing his forehead, he gazed idly at the phone he'd just put to rest. Eval had to be one of the worse liars in the world. He'd always been able to tell when the thickset Mexican was fibbing. The fear in his old chum's voice, and his refusal to admit he knew Sash was part of the cult, could only mean

Eval had been warned not to tell him about her membership. That, juxtaposed with her lust for his seed, made him wonder just what role the azure-eyed brunette played in The Mede's evil scheme.

He checked his watch and grimaced. Three hours and forty minutes stood between him and his true love.

THIRTY NINE

Darius got out of his car and weaved through a crowded parking lot located on a farm to market road twenty miles off Interstate Thirty. Dressed casual, he carried the ring in the right front pocket of his jeans, having left the glass box at his house. Though the place had no sign advertising it, he knew the large building had to be where the members of Make Way for The Beast held their meetings. All the drivers and passengers belonging to the many sedans, station wagons, pickups, and SUVs were evidently already inside.

He stepped up to two metal doors, paused, and took a deep breath before entering a lobby full of people milling around. None of them looked like the type of folk that wanted the devil to rule the world. Yet every man and woman so casually conversing like a group of God-fearing Christians greeting each other before the beginning of a church service, somehow did.

As he'd been instructed to do over the phone, Darius entered the auditorium and walked down a long aisle that terminated at a stage. He hadn't seen the bastard since that day he'd barely made it to the bathroom in time to keep from emptying the contents of his stomach on the mystic's luxurious Persian carpet. Feeling much like that now, he walked up a short flight of stairs at the side of the stage and joined Raul Wyncote at a podium.

Wearing a confident smirk, Wyncote spoke into the microphone. "Would everyone please enter and be seated?"

The lobby doors of the two aisles separating rows of descending seats into thirds opened and people poured in, each individual apparently assigned a specific place to sit. His heart sank when he saw Robyn—all decked out like she'd been every time he'd seen her in the evening—taking a seat at the very front. He tried to make eye contact but she wouldn't, or couldn't, face him.

He scanned the room for Eval and didn't locate him. The slight reprieve he felt over his friend apparently not being required to attend the ceremony vanished and he almost swallowed his tongue when he saw Bernice Rothschild sit down beside Robyn. Then, all ambiguity over Sash Temple being a member dissipated. Her cobalt eyes were cold. Though she'd fearlessly met his gaze while walking down the aisle, her expression had been that of a stranger. She seated herself beside Bernice.

Holly's dream had been haunting him ever since he arrived, and he'd felt tremendously relieved at not seeing a cross anywhere. Once he put the ring on whoever's finger—which he figured had to be Wyncote or the Arab's other persona The Mede—Holly and Bernadette were supposed to be brought in and permitted to leave with him. Since Wyncote knew he was keenly aware of The Mede's power, there shouldn't be any suspicion that he wouldn't keep his two promises he'd been compelled to make over the phone: that he wouldn't say anything about the women being kidnapped, and would convince Holly to do likewise. However, he in no way expected the double personage to keep his word voluntarily.

Wyncote turned to him. "Will you bow your head with us for a prayer, Darkfire?"

Jaw tightening, Darius steadied his eyes on the evil Arabian. "Sure, when hell freezes over."

The dually incorporated entity laughed. "Very well, we'll pray without the addition of your heartfelt support."

A greasy feeling pitted his gut while Raul prayed, and he wanted to step off the stage and slap some sense into Robyn, so fervently paying homage to the devil they called Day Star. Like the woman he once loved, Bernice and Sash stood with arms held high, heads bowed, eyes closed in reverence as Wyncote petitioned Satan to bless the long awaited transfer of

Cyrus's ring, and asked to be anointed with the answer of who was worthy to receive it. When he finished, everyone retook their seats.

It struck him as ironic that Sash and Bernice had once stood beside Bernadette in his parents' living room to witness the ring being given to him. He wondered how long they'd been a part of the cult because they apparently had a very high standing. With the single exception of Robyn, no one else sat on the front row.

He edged towards Wyncote and whispered, "This goes no further until I see proof that Holly and Bernadette are okay."

Nonplused, Wyncote smiled at him. "Of course, Darkfire . . ." he stepped to the microphone. "Please bring in our honored guests."

The left lobby doors opened and in walked Holly and Bernadette, handcuffed to two huge muscle-bound men who looked like professional wrestlers.

Tears filled his eyes when he saw Holly's frightened face. Fighting an overwhelming urge to run to her, he ran a hand over his mouth and took a deep breath. It was time to get this damn business out of the way once and for all.

Darius faced the arrogant Arab and pulled the ring from his pocket, recalling the last words he'd said to Wyncote before leaving his apartment that fateful day. He'd threatened to melt the gold band with a blow torch, hammer it to pieces, and flush the particles down the commode if he ever saw him or The Mede again. Now he had to eat those words because of Holly and Bernadette. "As if I didn't know already, who gets the honor?"

The wicked tyrant looked down at the three women on the front row. "Trinity Leaders, stand and speak. Who shall receive the band of glory?"

Robyn spoke first. "The Mede."

Sash gave her a patronizing look which greatly surprised Darius. Something about it conveyed she knew much more than his former lover.

"And what say you . . .?" he pointed to Bernice.

"The ring goes to you, Raul."

"And what say you?"

Wearing a knowing smile Sash glanced at Robyn, obviously garnering some sort of satisfaction from the confusion on his ex-fiancé's face that sprang up the moment Bernice voted for Wyncote rather than The Mede. At length she turned her eyes back to Wyncote. "The ring shall be given to both you and The Mede."

Robyn's jaw dropped and a shocked Bernice raised a hand to her mouth as Raul turned into The Mede. Apparently only Sash knew they were one and the same because all the other spectators were gawking and gasping at the transformation. Darius found it hard to believe Robyn hadn't known, but there was no mistaking the astonished look on her face.

"Very well," said The Mede to the crowd before turning towards him. "I will accept it in my present incarnation if you please."

Darius calmly waited as The Mede's cane disappeared and he reintegrated into Raul Wyncote. A quick glance at Robyn revealed she seemed amazed the event hadn't frightened him as it apparently had her, and he once again wondered why Raul and The Mede had kept her in the dark about their unification.

Wyncote stuck out his left hand and spread his fingers. "You must vocalize that you believe the ring truly passed down through the ages from Cyrus the Great and that you are placing it on my finger of your own volition."

He nodded. "Indeed I do believe this ring was given to Cyrus to be preserved through his generations, and I present it to you of my own free will."

Grimacing inside at how upset his mother would be if she ever found out, he slid the band on the third finger of Wyncote's left hand. It fit loosely on the mystic's slender appendage, but Darius knew it wouldn't fall off.

Worry over his mom took a back seat to whatever was coming next. He'd have to improvise on the spur of the moment, and hoped whatever strategy sprang to mind would be the correct one. Bracing himself for battle he said, "I'll be taking the ladies and leaving now."

To his immense surprise, instead of the double cross he'd fully expected at this juncture, Wyncote actually ordered Holly and Bernadette to be released. A woman sat a suitcase and purse at Holly's feet as the muscleman removed her cuffs.

"Oh, Darius . . .!" she ran down the aisle.

Tears streamed downed his face as he jumped off the stage and scooped her in his arms. She looked so thin he tried to hug her gently but she squeezed him to her as they covered each others' faces with urgent kisses.

From the corner of his eye he noticed Bernadette looked awkward, as if she were intruding on them making love. Reluctantly he pulled away from Holly and embraced the platinum blonde. "Bernadette, you foolish girl you. I'm so glad you're okay too."

"Take them and be gone, Darkfire. We have private business to tend to."

Standing at the foot of the stage he looked up at Wyncote. "More than happy to oblige. Come on, girls, let's get the hell out of here."

Turning to leave, he saw Robyn staring at him with weeping eyes.

* * * *

Holly, who couldn't have weighed more than a hundred-twenty when they'd met at the café in Houston, had lost at least thirty pounds. Despite her insistence that the weight loss had been induced by lack of appetite brought on by emotions rather than illness, Darius called one of his early clients he'd defended in a medical malpractice suit, and asked him to come to his house. He had no intention of ratting out The Mede, knowing what a nightmare that would incur, so he couldn't risk taking her to a hospital because the police still had an all points bulletin out on her.

Having spent only two days in captivity, Bernadette had never been reported missing. But Holly had, and he feared her physical appearance would rouse suspicion when she claimed, as per their cover story, that she'd decided to take off on a whim and go sightseeing. People who did such things usually sported a robust demeanor and at least a modicum of color on their faces. Holly hadn't seen the sun in two months and her skin had paled accordingly.

Bernadette had been too afraid to be left alone, so he'd brought her home as well.

Garth Kirkindoll, a gynecologist who'd been sued for knowingly performing an unnecessary hysterectomy, had been Darius's third client and the case was his first foray into malpractice proceedings. His legal rates were cheap in those days, only thirty dollars an hour. The notable attorney representing the plaintiff had hoped to collect a third of the sought for ten million dollars for his fee.

The case hinged on a biopsy report of the patient's uterus which declared no signs of cancer and had been signed by his client. Darius proved the information had to have been altered. He accomplished that feat by having two experts examine the uterus itself which the plaintiff didn't know hadn't been incinerated along with other medical wastes at the hospital. It turned out Kirkindoll's patient had conspired with a male nurse who'd doctored the report in order to split the awarded money. The testicle-bearing Florence Nightingale had come up with the plan after mistakenly thinking the woman's cancerous womb had been destroyed.

Holly was lying in his bed wearing a pair of baggy pink pajamas she'd retrieved from her suitcase. Garth Kirkindoll checked her over, then motioned him outside, a look of deep concern etched on the physician's face.

Dread tugged at his gut as he walked Garth out the door. "What's wrong with her?"

The gynecologist looked at him suspiciously. "She'll be fine if she quits that fad diet she told me she's been on for weeks. All she needs is a steady dose of proteins and carbs."

"Then why do you look so worried?"

"I'm worried because I don't want to get into trouble. What's going on here, Darius? You're obviously very concerned about the young lady's health, so why did you call me instead of taking her to the emergency room? She's not wanted by the police is she?"

He drew a nervous breath and managed a smile. "Garth, I can't divulge anything because of attorney-client privilege but rest assured she's not on the lam and you haven't broken any laws. But you're right, I don't want anyone to know where she is right now, including the police. So will you keep this our little secret?"

Wiping the corners of his mouth with fingers and thumb, Garth exhaled an exasperated sigh. "Okay, but this is it. If she needs any further medical attention, you call somebody else. Deal?"

"Deal."

The doctor's face finally relaxed. "When you told me over the phone you were afraid she was suffering from malnutrition I prepared a vitamin serum. If she doesn't object I'll give her the injection, then I'm out of here."

His bedroom door opened and Holly stepped through it.

Darius turned to her. "Where do you think you're going?"

She shot him a teasing grin which almost filled out her hollow cheeks. "To your kitchen so I can fix me something to eat. I'm starved . . . ."

* * * *

Holly dug through his cookware, pantry, and refrigerator, selecting what she needed to make pancakes. Darius, who ate most of his meals out since he wasn't a very good cook, enjoyed watching her tend the stove, looking forward to witnessing many such domestic scenes in the future.

Bernadette made coffee and the three of them enjoyed a late night breakfast of buttermilk flapjacks, real butter, and maple syrup. Along with almost finishing four of the delicious hot cakes, Holly had drank two glasses of milk. She'd also accepted Garth Kirkindoll's vitamin shot before he left, much to Darius's relief.

He hoped Bernadette had seen the light and wouldn't be lured back to MWTB but knew if The Mede didn't want her to leave, she couldn't. The few times he'd had the opportunity to bring it up since leaving the auditorium he hadn't said anything, but learning what a liar Bernadette had become since their college days when to the best of his knowledge she'd never even exaggerated the truth, he hardly trusted her. As soon as they'd cleared the lobby and got to the parking lot Holly gushed out that Wilma Breese had somehow known she was flying to Dallas and even managed to get a seat next to hers on the plane. By the time they'd gotten to his car she'd hastily, and very animatedly, spouted all the details about her abduction. Yet Bernadette had remained oddly silent about her own. Already suspicious of her, not hearing anything about her ordeal had made him even more so.

"You know, it just occurred to me, Bernadette, you haven't said a word about what happened to you. Why did Wyncote have you kidnapped, and how did it go down?"

She stared at him for a long time, never blinking. Her platinum hair, radiated by incandescent light from the ceiling, had such brilliant highlights the follicles almost appeared electrically charged. Suddenly she lowered her head, eyes cast on the table, the action causing a new sheen to dance on her shimmering mane receiving illumination from a different angle. "Shit, I can't go through with it. Raul's gonna fucking kill me but I can't do it. I just can't fucking make myself do it!"

He'd never heard that kind of language pass through those lips before—his mind reeled at the radical change in his old college friend. Holly's eyes were two pale-blue pools of gaping shock, but he didn't know if it was the vulgarity or the way Bernadette had screamed the last statement that had startled her.

Though far from it, he tried to appear calm. "Can't do what, Bernadette . . .?"

She wept non stop. Rivulets of wet mascara trailed down her cheeks like thin black snakes, and smears of red lipstick streaked beyond the boundaries of her mouth, the result of wiping her face with a napkin before blowing her nose in it. At least five minutes had passed since he'd asked the question.

"D-Darius," she managed at last, then her voice faltered. She reached for a second napkin and blew her nose again. "There's goodness inside you . . . a wholesomeness that really gets to me and makes me wish I could be like you instead of the horrible slutty bitch I've become. I've only been dishonest with you because Raul made me do it. I've never wanted to lie to you. You've got to believe what I'm about to say because I swear it's the truth. You're in danger, Dare, very serious danger. When the next new moon comes, Make Way for The Beast will hold its final assembly. Raul plans to crucify you— literally—as a sacrifice to Satan, whom we in the cult call Day Star.

"I'm Raul's possession—his sex slave—and though I wish I could, I can't give him up. It galls me how weak I am, sickens me to admit it, but I just can't give up the sex. He makes me feel . . . shit, I don't know how to put it into words. I just have to be with him at least once a week.

"Nobody kidnapped me. Bernice is part of the leadership of MWTB, and Wilma Breese brought Holly to her house. There's a special room that can only be entered from the outside by making one of the walls turn around. That's where they put Holly, and later me. I had to pretend I'd gotten kidnapped too so you'd be willing to let me stay with you after the ransom exchange. Even though I'm only a member of what's called the Outer Layer, I know all about the inner workings of the whole cult because Raul tells me everything. No one else—not even Bernice, Sash, or your ex fiancé— knows that, even though they head the organization and only answer to Raul. In his own weird way, I think he's in love with me, at least physically.

"He told me that he had to have you give him the ring on the new moon preceding the final assembly, and that sacrificing you to Day Star was just as important as obtaining the ring itself. Listen carefully to what I'm about to say now because your life depends on it . . . ."

So Wyncote had planned to double cross him after all. He hoped Bernadette was lying about the mystic's plans to crucify him, but didn't think so. Her allegation seemed to confirm that Holly's nightmare about him being tied to a cross had indeed been prophetic. However, he knew not to bank on anything that came out of those lipstick-smudged lips.

FORTY

When Bernadette retired to the guestroom, he took Holly to his bedroom. Though he badly wanted to make love to her, he knew she needed sleep rather than sex. He kissed her goodnight, rolled over on his side facing away from her, and closed his eyes.

"Darius?"

"What?"

"Mind if I take off my pee-jays?"

Her tone of voice made his heart skip a beat. "Of course not."

Feeling the covers ruffle as she removed her pajamas, he hoped she was hinting and not just wanting to sleep in the raw. A moment later she pressed her naked breasts against his bare back and slid a hand inside his underwear.

His eyes sprang open. He feared she might be doing it for his sake. "Are you sure you're up to this?"

She put her lips to his ear. "I've never been so sure of anything in my life . . . ."

The way she wildly undulated her hips and cried out his name while climaxing verified she'd spoken the truth. Holding her in his arms afterwards, he realized what a fool he'd been allowing himself to get blindsided by Robyn. Holly fulfilled something deep within his heart that Robyn couldn't even approach. He'd never known such bliss.

"Been doing a lot of thinking since you got kidnapped and I thought you were dead . . ." he brushed a lock of hair from her forehead and kissed her parted lips. "I never told you this, but I was on my way to pay you a surprise visit when I met Robyn. If that hadn't happened, I would have known long ago what I've known since the day you disappeared. I'm in love with you, and my life is meaningless without you to share it with. Will you marry me, Holly?"

Eyes brimming with tears, she rapidly nodded, apparently too choked up to speak.

* * * *

"And you—" Cyrus pointed his scepter at him. Darius knew he was dreaming and fully expected to wake up when his voice wouldn't come as he tried to speak like the other times he'd dreamed of the Persian king. But he didn't. This dream had begun with Cyrus speaking. Glaring first at him and then The Mede, cloaked in sackcloth, shepherd's crook in hand, Cyrus continued: "Will remove the pretender."

The Mede humbly nodded. "That I will do, Oh Great One."

"Silence, fool! You *are* the pretender. I was addressing him."

Startled awake, he found himself thinking about the ring. Smiling, he gently caressed Holly's sleeping face, fluffed his pillow, and reconnected with it.

The Mede obviously hadn't transmitted the dream this time.

* * * *

They'd made love first thing after waking up, and he held her frail body against his. Her breasts had remained full in spite of her severe weight loss, and he was fondling her left one with his right hand.

"Remember that day we first met in the café?"

Her face blossomed with a sentimental smile. "I'll never forget it."

"Me either. You were the cutest little ol' thing."

"Cute? You don't think I'm pretty then?"

Laughing, he tweaked the perky nipple. "No, I didn't mean that, of course I think you're pretty. But there was just something so cute about you too."

She snaked an arm around his neck and snuggled closer. "I suppose your prosecutor is pretty with a capital P, no doubt."

"Suzette?" He looked up at the ceiling and sighed as Holly's hand found its way down his stomach and lightly teased his boys. "Yeah, she's pretty, but I'm in love with you, not her. I just couldn't get much past—"

He'd started to say *lust* but checked himself, realizing Holly literally held the upper hand if the word were to piss her off.

Her fingers tightened a little. "Couldn't get much past what?"

Reaching down, he took her hand in his for safety's sake. "You know, there just wasn't much between us other than a physical attraction, at least on my end."

Seeing that offended her, he quickly added, "Did I tell you we never even kissed?"

"Really?" Her expression mellowed.

"Mm hmm . . ." he rolled her onto her back and fused their lips together while gently easing her temporarily too-thin legs apart with his knee.

They made love again, then took a shower together.

When they finally exited the bedroom he discovered Bernadette had left a note saying she'd called for a cab to take her home. When he read it, Darius couldn't help wondering if by *home* she meant Wyncote's apartment.

Holly made biscuits from scratch and as they baked in the oven, she shredded some potatoes through a food processor and fried up a pile of hash-browns alongside ham and eggs while at the same time managing to whip up a pan of redeye gravy. Though he'd still want her even if she couldn't boil water, he felt blessed that his future wife really knew her way around a kitchen, at least concerning breakfast cuisine.

After they finished eating he reached for her hand. "That was wonderful. Not only are you beautiful but you're a fantastic cook as well. What more could a man ask for?"

She leaned across the table and gave him a quick kiss. "I love you so much. I have to be the happiest girl in the world right now."

He pecked her back. "Glad to hear it because you've made me the happiest guy, I guarantee you."

Grinning, she tousled his hair while rising from the table. She cleared it and started the dishwasher. "There, all done. So what's today's agenda, counselor?"

"Well, we need to figure out the logistics of our situation . . ." he took a sip of coffee and smiled. "I can't let you go back to Houston, I'd miss you too much. I hate to have to wait to get married but it'll have to be a carefully planned full-blown ceremony or I'll never hear the end of it from my mother. The kidnapping wiped out this semester anyway, so stay with me and finish college here, maybe at my old alma mater. Wouldn't that be great?"

Her countenance ignited with joy. "Oh, Darius, do you really mean it?"

"Of course I do. After you graduate you can go to law school at SMU too, just like I did. It's a great institution."

"Well I guess so," she laughed out. "You've certainly done okay."

A sobering thought dampened his mood. Robyn had been on the outs with her family—or so she'd claimed—but he'd have to ask Holly's father for her hand. The guy would most likely resent his daughter living with him before marriage.

Sensing the drop in his good spirits, she frowned. "What's wrong? You look glum all of a sudden."

"It just dawned on me your folks might get pissed at me when they find out we're living together, especially your father. I don't want to get started on the wrong foot with my future in-laws."

The frown turned grim. "I don't have any folks."

"You were an orphan?"

"My father abandoned me and my mother when I was only a baby, and she died a few years ago."

Seeing tears beginning to from, he got up from the table had hugged her. "I'm so sorry, Holly."

"There's something else you should know. The college I go to is just a city college. I doubt many, if any of my credit hours will be accepted by Southern Methodist University."

He reared his head back and gave her a reassuring smile. "Well, if SMU won't accept them we'll find a college around here that will, so you won't have to repeat any courses."

She perked up with a grin of relief. "You're right. There's bound to be several to choose from."

"After we check out SMU first of course."

"Oh, of course," she snickered.

Not wanting to spoil the moment, he didn't say anything when his thoughts advanced to the next new moon. The only chance they had for continued happiness depended on them getting past what Bernadette had ominously called the final assembly. If he survived that, he'd introduce her to his parents and she and his mom could plan the wedding.

FORTY ONE

An item in the morning news floored him. Darius almost choked on a doughnut he'd just bitten into when he ran across it. Bernadette Rothschild's body had been found strung up on a flag pool at an elementary school in Garland.

He called his house and heaved a huge sigh of relief when Holly answered. After warning her not to let anyone in the house or even answer the door, he hurried from his office, telling Ricca he had to get home.

His fiancé of four weeks was safe and sound but nervously pacing the floor when he got there. Her pretty face, which had regained the fullness it had when they first met, locked into a worried frown when she saw the look on his.

"Darius, what's wrong?"

"Bernadette's been murdered. The police found her hanging from a flag pool at a schoolyard last night."

Holly's jaw dropped and her restored complexion lost all color. "And y-you think they'll do that to me?"

Pulling her close he said, "I don't know what they're planning, but this is the morning of the new moon and their so-called final assembly is tonight. I'm afraid Bernadette might have been telling the truth when she said Wyncote wants to crucify me at the last meeting. I don't want you out of my sight because he may be planning to kidnap you again to lure me there. Evidently poor Bernadette was served up as a warning to everybody else in that damned cult of what'll happen to them if they disobey. She lied so much I don't know what to believe, but she's bound to have relayed something true that Wyncote didn't want her to. Something so important he killed her, or had her killed, for doing it. Having you here has been so wonderful I'm afraid I let my guard down. I should have never left the house this morning."

Shivering with fear, Holly meekly uttered, "We have to call the police, Darius."

"No, the police can't help us because we're dealing with the supernatural here. If I dared to tell the authorities what I know, The Mede might decide to convince them I did it, and he has the power to do so. Besides, they'd never believe Wyncote has the ability to turn into a devil, and would only think I was crazy."

She dropped her head on his shoulder. "I'm so frightened, Darius. I think we should leave town and hide out somewhere."

He kissed the top of her head. "I wish we could, but The Mede can find us no matter where we go."

The doorbell rang.

Through the peephole he spied Rusty Wurly standing on the other side and opened the door. His old buddy obviously hadn't heard about Bernadette or he wouldn't be smiling so cheerfully. Having checked his own emotions because of the situation, he didn't want to tell Rusty about it. There wasn't time for mourning and countless reminiscences which would surely follow the sad news. At some point Bernadette's death would hit him hard and he knew it, but right now he had to keep his wits about him or he might not live to see tomorrow.

"I dropped by your office and Ricca told me you'd gone home. Mind if I hang out for awhile?"

Though a visit from an old friend was the last thing he needed at the moment, he forced a smile. "Of course not. Come in . . . ."

"Holly, this is Rusty Wurly, you guys met at John Derby's victory celebration."

Holly donned a pleasant expression Darius could tell was as artificial as his own. "Yeah, I remember you, Rusty. How are you?"

Rusty grinned. "Fine, thanks for asking. It's good to see you again."

She motioned towards the hall entrance. "Would you like some coffee?"

"Sure, thanks."

They went to the dining room where Holly served the two of them and poured a cup for herself.

"Ran into Sash Temple the other day . . ." Rusty spooned sugar into a steaming cup. "She was worried about you. Said she'd had you over for dinner and you passed out on her couch."

Alarm bells rang out in his brain but Darius tried not to show it. *Worried about me huh? And yet she never bothered to check up on me.* "Yeah, still can't remember driving home I was so out of it."

"Too much to drink huh?"

The grin on Rusty's face when he spoke looked contrived, and it bugged him. But Holly appeared jealous so he tended to that. "Sash is an old friend of ours from college. That's all she is, just a friend."

"Relieved to hear it." She relaxed a degree but still seemed upset.

He turned to Rusty, hoping he wasn't somehow involved in all the sordidness of Sash's weird activities. "Actually I didn't have anything to drink."

Rusty frowned. "Then why'd you pass out? Sash said she couldn't wake you, so finally just tried to make you comfortable. She said you'd left by the time she woke up the next morning."

A memory stirred. Just before the last vestige of consciousness departed that night he'd passed out on Sash's couch, he'd heard Rusty's voice. At the time he thought he'd only been hearing things, but now knew he hadn't. The nauseating revelation turned his stomach sour. One of his dearest childhood friends had apparently conspired with Sash. He couldn't remember getting back to his house because he hadn't been conscious during the trip. Rusty must have driven him home. Now the traitor was apparently on a mission to see if he suspected what Sash had done. The fact that he'd picked this particular day to do it struck him as menacing.

Since Rusty was one of the few people familiar with him that could successfully pull the wool over his eyes, he decided not to play it subtle, and went for broke. "Why did Sash drug me, Rusty?"

"What?" The unmistakable glint of feared exposure flashed in his old pal's eyes.

"I didn't stutter."

"Hey man, I got no idea what you're talking about."

"Like hell you don't . . ." he rose from the table. "Start talking, Wurly, or get ready to go to fist city big time."

* * * *

They arrived at Lochweed at three o'clock. Holly stayed close by his side as they entered Robyn's building. The beautiful brunette chucked her glasses the moment she saw him and jumped to her feet, mouth slackening with rude surprise. "Darius?"

Not having a moment to lose, he didn't bother with pleasantries. "Drop whatever you're doing and come with me."

Fear radiated from her stunned visage—dark eyes gaping, lips trembling. "I can't and you know why."

"Forget about Wyncote, and do what I say. Look I've already called Jock and put him wise to Wilma Breese. She won't be bringing him and John to the assembly tonight like you thought."

A shrill gasp ejaculated from her lungs as Robyn's face contorted into a spasm of incredulity. "H-How did you know about that? Who told you?"

"Never mind. You're being played, Robyn. You're not going to be the third ruler of the new world like you were promised. You've been kept in the dark about a lot of things, just like you were about Wyncote and The Mede being the same person. Now listen to me—you're the third sacrifice, not the third governor. If you don't want to die a few months from now, I strongly suggest you come with me."

Her eyes glazed over with alarm and confusion. "Raul told you that?"

"No, someone else did, but it's the truth. I promise I can keep you safe, but only if you come with me. I have to leave now whether you come along or not. The choice is yours, Robyn. What's it going to be . . .?"

FORTY TWO

Darius's living room was crowded. Holly, his parents, Ricca, Robert, Suzette, the Derby twins, Eval, Rusty, Preston, and Robyn occupied the sofa, chairs, and barstools. Sash and Bernice—who he'd learned now went by Hoff instead of Rothschild—were tied up in the guest room. The last assembly had been scheduled to commence at eight. His watch read seven fifty-nine.

Convincing his mother of the truth about Cyrus's legacy had been one of the hardest things he'd ever had to do. It was the first time he'd seen her since the day Wyncote convinced him he was the antichrist. He'd told her about seeing her leave Wyncote's apartment and asked why she'd accepted an invitation from a stranger to have tea. It turned out she hadn't, the mystic had merely planted the illusion in his mind. She'd never laid eyes on Raul Wyncote or The Mede. Darius still wasn't sure she believed everything he'd carefully explained but at least she'd humored his plea for her and his dad to stay at his house until dawn. However, she rejected his appeal for her to wait out the night in his study or bedroom rather than the living room where she'd surely soon be frightened out of her mind.

As expected, not long after eight o'clock The Mede appeared, but not within the house. He was howling outside the sliding glass doors of the patio, demanding to be granted entrance. Darius had cautioned everyone to stay put no matter what they thought they might be seeing, hearing, or feeling. He hoped he'd be the only one to suffer Wyncote's wrath, but had warned the others just in case.

Again as expected, The Mede lashed out.

Darius tumbled downward through a vortex leading to what had to be the fires of hell. Ghastly demons with four hideous faces attached to one head spun around on red rocks covered with molten lava surrounded by cavernous walls of glowing coals. Each quarter turn of their scaly bodies presented a different horrifying facade. Blazing spiders with bodies the size of basketballs and legs at least eight feet long weaved electrical webs around him, biting into his flesh with fangs of hot iron as the energized silk of their webs electrocuted him. He felt the pain and screamed out in agony, yet at the same time kept reminding himself none of it was real.

"You will open your doors and let me in, Darius Darkfire, or suffer this torment for eternity!"

He knew he'd hear this threat many, many times before dawn forever freed him from the devil named Arash Arshia, who called himself The Mede. Darius had brought the people closest to him into his house to keep them from the entity's clutches, certain Wyncote would stop at nothing to lure him back to the auditorium to be sacrificed. Now, though he might be able to torment the minds of his future wife, parents, and friends until morning, he couldn't take them away and threaten to end their lives to force his compliance. They were safe . . . physically. He prayed to God his mother wouldn't suffer a fatal heart attack.

A giant skull appeared, black against the flames. The huge jaws parted and swallowed him, sending him deeper into the burning pit. Then, as had happened three times previously, he found himself standing in front of his patio doors with The Mede leering outside, demanding he open them. This time he actually managed to laugh at the bastard before being sent back to the burning torments.

Darius saw Holly being raped by a gang of devils and then witnessed his mother get ravaged by the electric spiders. Both of them cried out for him to let The Mede inside the house so their lives would be spared. If he hadn't known it was illusion he'd have lost his mind, but he held fast to the knowledge that everything would be okay if he could only hold out until the morning light.

Back at the door, The Mede cursed and howled when he still refused to grant him entrance.

Plunged back to perdition, a strange beast shaped like a giant beetle, covered with hideous unblinking eyes, peeled the skin from his body with razor sharp talons. Raising his arms in horror, Darius saw the bloody sinew, glistening white tendons, and pulsating veins of his own musculature. His exposed nerve endings burned with excruciation. He threw his head back and screamed at the top of his lungs as the agony continued.

To his horror, his face appeared before him—not a mere reflection—it had been ripped from his skull. The rubbery mask that was his own flesh howled with mocking laughter for an eternity before he saw The Mede standing on the other side of the glass.

"You fool, you can't possibly hold out! Save yourself from the torture, Darius Darkfire, open these goddamn doors!"

He sucked in air and hissed, "Fuck you!"

Again The Mede returned him to the torture chamber of his own mind.

Freezing winds whipped his naked body blue as he stood with his feet frozen to a floating chunk of ice being spun around in circles by violent sea currents.

"Welcome to Antarctica, Darkfire!" The voice belonged to Wyncote—The Mede had apparently transformed.

The biting blasts of sub-zero air gushing with hurricane speed inflicted as much misery as the flames of hell, forcing him to shriek with torturing pain.

A huge wave engulfed him, sending him into the icy depths of the Antarctic Ocean. Swarms of Jelly Fish thrashed at him with their tentacles, each penetration igniting fresh sparks of agony. Stingrays appeared, endlessly plunging their stingers into his frost-bitten hide as electric eels swam up to compound the torment. Freezing seawater surged into his mouth, filling his lungs to bursting when he couldn't help but once again cry out in anguish.

Gagging and unable to cough out the water, he seriously considered giving up. But seeing the mystic standing on the patio reenergized the fighter within and he gave Wyncote the finger instead.

Thank God the pseudo human hadn't realized how close he'd come to breaking him. Instead of sending him back to the South Pole, Wyncote devised a new set of horrors.

First he found himself flying through space and disintegrating as he neared the sun. After that his stretched out limbs were tied to something he couldn't see because darkness surrounded him. He heard an eerie noise that sounded somewhat like leaves rustling in the wind. Then a light came on and he saw he'd been tied to stakes driven in an earthen floor of a root cellar. The noise came from thousands of angry scorpions who soon covered his nude body with fiery stings.

He got cast into a vat of molten iron at a steel mill, felt his body get ground up into sausage as a giant Cyclops forced him through a meat grinder, a steam roller slowly moved over his feet and up his torso, crushing him inch by inch on the scorching asphalt of a desert highway—he got torn apart by ravenous sharks, a giant buzz saw cut him in half, he was buried alive, a river-full of starving piranhas tore every ounce of flesh from his angst-ridden body . . . .

* * * *

Sweat poured from his naked skin as he withstood the stifling humidity of a dense jungle. At first he thought Wyncote might have granted a momentary reprieve, until he heard an ungodly roar and a Tyrannosaurus Rex at least twenty feet tall and forty feet from head to tail appeared. The giant reptile stomped him to the ground with a three-toed foot, leaned over and began tearing him apart with hideously long teeth cemented in jaws much longer than a yardstick. Then, feeling the heat from the creatures' fowl smelling breath as it thrust what remained of him into its mouth, Darius vomited as the reptile's esophagus grossly undulated him into a pool of digestive acid in its stomach.

His tormentor illuminated the creature's belly. Darius roared with horror as he watched his lower extremities melt away into floating globs of quivering gelatin to be metabolized as nourishment for the beast. After the nightmare with the piranhas each subsequent torture had weakened his resolve a considerable degree, and he'd gone through a dozen or more before winding up here. No fight remained within—his spirit had been broken, his will to live utterly annihilated. Wyncote had won, and for the first time in his life he'd finally lost—he couldn't take anymore.

Darius tried to vocalize his surrender, but before the words could leave his lips he found himself lying on the floor of his living room with Holly cradling his head in her lap.

"It's over, my darling, look . . ." she pointed towards the patio.

The first rays of sunshine were careening through the sliding glass doors.

FORTY THREE

Only he had suffered at the hands of The Mede, now back in hell where the demon belonged. Everyone had witnessed him writhing on his living room floor, screaming in pain and addressing both Arabians throughout the night, but never saw him standing at the glass when he spoke to them. Apparently that too had only been in his mind, though had he opened them mentally, he knew the patio doors would have granted the dual being physical access. The only other horror his guests had been subject to was seeing the two ungodly Arabs repeatedly transform into one another before disintegrating at the crack of dawn.

Though his mother had fainted the first time he'd cried out, Preston—per his instructions—had continually reminded her, along with everyone else, that her son was merely experiencing a series of vivid nightmares induced by the demon screaming at the door, and kept reassuring her everything would be all right when the morning came.

Darius had learned all this through the many recounts of the long night given by everyone . . . except Robyn.

The memories of his terrifying ordeal seemed distant, like bad dreams that had taken place so long ago he could no longer recall them in detail. Feeling no more emotionally disturbed than if he'd just watched a horror movie, he uttered a silent prayer of thanks to his Maker for sparing his sanity. During the myriad tribulations he'd felt certain that even if he did manage to survive the night, he wouldn't come out of it with a sound mind.

Four hours had passed since The Mede's defeat at sunrise, and everyone's nerves had settled to a large degree. However his mother, who seldom imbibed anything stronger than a glass of sherry on holidays, demanded his father make her a strong drink at only ten in the morning. "I don't care what liquor you use, dear, just make sure it's a lot."

The Derbys, Eval, and Preston had left two hours ago. The investigator had a matter he had to tend to for another client, and the twins and Eval had gone to the mortuary to view Bernadette. Rusty, who couldn't bear the thought of seeing her dead, had stayed behind.

Ricca and Robert went to a bakery to get doughnuts and croissants for everyone and hadn't returned yet.

Robyn had been crying hysterically, spouting out endless apologies, even declaring that though she'd only pretended at first, she'd really fallen in love with him. He actually felt sorry enough for her that he resisted the temptation to rub his engagement to Holly in her face. Besides, she would soon be arrested along with Sash and Bernice as accomplices in the slaying of Bernadette. Wilma Breese would also be taken into custody before long for kidnapping. No telling how many others would wind up facing the same charge.

Since Bernadette's murder had taken place in Dallas County, Suzette—who still hadn't lost a case even though she still sometimes called their lone court battle a defeat—would almost certainly be chosen by the DA to prosecute since this was bound to be a high profile trial.

Thank God Rusty hadn't been involved in any of that. He *had* assisted Sash that night she'd drugged him, but thought he was doing a good deed at the time.

Yesterday, after he'd threatened to kick his ass, his old bud had told him, "Sash said she'd been picked by Day Star to bear your child, who was destined to save the world from corruption. I asked her why she just didn't seduce you instead of going about it the hard way, and she said she couldn't run the risk of you ever finding out the child was yours.

"I don't know what she used to knock you out but she said you'd be sound asleep not long after dinner. I'd been hiding in her bedroom but I got antsy. I snuck down the hall and peaked into the living room where I saw you sprawled out on Sash's couch. I asked if she was going to have Day Star appear but she shushed me and pointed at you. I knew she meant you'd just gone under and might be able to hear me so I clammed up.

"I waited until she whispered it was time, then heaved you over my shoulder and carried you to her bed. She told me to wait in the living room until she got through. Man, six long hours went by before she finally called it quits. By the way I'm sure you'd be interested to know that she bagged some of your sperm for artificial insemination in case she didn't get knocked up.

"I lifted you over my shoulder again and laid you in the backseat of your car. Sash followed me to your house and I used your keys to get in. She helped me put you to bed and we left.

"Eval had told me she was a member of the cult, but Dare—I swear—I had no idea about all that crap she was really into or I'd have never helped her.

"She called me this morning and asked me to check up on you to see if you suspected anything. She thought you'd call her the next day and demand to know what happened. She was going to tell you she woke you after you passed out and you asked if you could sleep on her couch and fell back asleep, and that you'd gone home by the time she woke up the next day. I told her since you hadn't called after all this time you must not be too worried about it and she shouldn't either, but she begged me to come see you today. For some reason I was supposed to hang with you all day and call her at five to let her know where you were."

Darius had known immediately upon hearing Rusty's statement that Sash—no doubt following Wyncote's instructions—had planned to send some hooligans to kidnap him and take him to the auditorium to be sacrificed. She hadn't been worried about him being suspicious of why he'd

316 ARLEY OWENS, JR.

passed out at her place, Sash had only used that to trick Rusty into staying with him and passing on his whereabouts with the five o'clock call. Bernadette had told him the truth—she *was* supposed to have stayed with him until the day of the final assembly so she could relay his location to the abductors at the crucial time. Though Wyncote had to have him come to the auditorium of his own free will to present the ring, no such restrictions applied to getting him to the final assembly. However, according to what Bernadette had told him, he couldn't be taken from his own house. Sash had obviously planned to use an unwitting Rusty to lure him away from home since Bernadette had abandoned her mission.

Bernadette hadn't known the reason he couldn't be physically forced from his residence but had warned him not to leave home for any reason on the next new moon. He'd forgotten about it until seeing the headline: *LOCAL SCHOOL TEACHER FOUND HANGING FROM FLAGPOLE.*

After enlightening Rusty, Darius had formulated a plan. Though he hadn't known the whole story of MWTB at the time, he knew who the leaders were because of the night he'd exchanged the ring for Holly and Bernadette. Enlisting his old pal's help they nabbed two of them—Sash and Bernice. They'd found Sash at home and forced her to guide them to Bernice's. The two massive goons that had brought Holly and Bernadette into the auditorium that night had shown up just as they were trying to leave Bernice's place.

Rusty, who'd never been in a fight before, had panicked when he'd leaned his head out of the car window and warned the two henchmen to let them pass. "Look at the size of those dudes, Dare! We have to let the girls go!"

"Relax, Wurly," he'd said. "Haven't you ever heard the old saying *the bigger they are, the harder they fall?"*

With Sash and Bernice bound in the back seat under Holly's watchful eye, he'd told Rusty to help her guard the girls, then got out of the car. The two men had arrived in a van and parked it sideways to prevent them from exiting Bernice's drive, the only opening in a tall rock fence that surrounded the grounds.

As he'd anticipated, the muscle-bound thugs—each pushing seven feet—got out of the vehicle and approached him. Before either of them could make an offensive move, he ran up and kicked one in the balls, forcing him to bend over in pain. The other dove at him but Darius fell to his stomach to make him miss. Quickly regaining his feet, he kicked the thug three times in the face before his attacker could get off the ground. Leaving the Hulk Hogan look-alike in a bloody stupor, he turned to light into the other behemoth but quickly found himself in a headlock.

The man had colossal strength and Darius couldn't break free, so he repeatedly stomped the punk's toes instead as Rusty flew out of the car and grabbed the guy's head from behind, pulling his chin back as hard as he could. The titan had no choice but to release him so he could fend off Rusty. When he did, Darius fired a right jab into the giant's larynx. As reflex forced the man's massive hands to his own throat, Darius gave him a fierce kick between the legs and backed up as the dude bent over in agony. Then, with all his might, he repeatedly punched the brute's face until the jumbo-sized bodybuilder finally managed to stand upright on legs visibly wobbling. Darius then lowered his head and plowed into the man's stomach, plunging him backwards onto the lawn.

"Quick, move the van!" he'd yelled to Rusty.

The Goliath had tried to rise but several rapid kicks to the face finally incapacitated him. His eyes rolled up in their sockets and the back of his skull struck the ground.

Rusty pulled the van out of the way, hurried back to the car, and they'd made their escape. Darius had then driven to his house, left Rusty to stand guard over the two abducted leaders after interrogating them, and took Holly with him to Lochweed where he'd gotten the third one to come along

318   ARLEY OWENS, JR.

voluntarily.

If Robyn hadn't done so, she might have gotten away since there were too many witnesses for him to take her by force. Darius had hoped Wyncote felt secure enough about Sash's ability to lure him into a trap via Rusty that he wasn't supernaturally monitoring him, and had begged God to blind the evil Arab to his actions if he was. However, he'd had no doubt the two muscular pawns would alert somebody at MWTB after they fled Bernice's house, so he hadn't been able to tarry at Lochweed.

He'd planned to tie her up when they got back to his place and put her in the guestroom with Sash and Bernice, but after filling her in on what she hadn't known about the cult, Robyn had become so obviously frightened of The Mede he'd felt certain she wouldn't leave the safety of his house, making it unnecessary. Now she didn't have to fear Wyncote, but was such an emotional wreck she'd made no effort to escape.

Sash had told him about Wilma Breese being instructed to bring Jock and John to the final assembly, while she was supposed to see to it Rusty and Eval came. The Mede had planned to permanently silence his four friends and afterwards arrange the death of his parents and anyone else outside MWTB who knew he was the bearer of the ring. While Robyn had known about that and had in fact been given the task of overseeing his parents' murder the day after his crucifixion, she'd never suspected her own execution had been carefully planned as well.

Avery and Marcus didn't know it but their lives had been spared. Bernice had been commissioned to ensure their deaths in the near future, and had The Mede succeeded, the NFL would have lost a star quarterback to that most serious of injuries, death. Without Wyncote's power backing her, and soon to be charged with capital murder, Bernice was no longer a threat to anyone.

Darius had gotten the real story of Make Way for The Beast

from the woman who'd raped him in his sleep. She had known The Mede since early childhood and assisted Wyncote in starting MWTB, inducting Bernice as the first member. Wyncote then brought Robyn into the organization and they started proselytizing. Bernadette had no idea her cousin was involved until she joined the cult. The femme fatale had told him the truth about when she'd met the Arabian devil. It *had* been the same night Rusty and Eval had taken her to a pool hall to celebrate John Derby's vindication. The poor girl hadn't gotten herself killed over something she'd said to him like he'd thought. The leadership of MWTB had ordered her execution solely because of what she'd said to Bernice—that she was quitting the cult and wouldn't be attending the last assembly.

The evil glare in Sash's sapphire eyes had been alarming. Spouting out every detail with complete confidence that her mission would still be accomplished, she'd seemed to relish telling him everything. "You're a fool to think you can escape Raul, Dare. He'll free Bernice and me any moment now and this time tomorrow you'll be dead and I'll be on my way to a glorious future."

Unlike her cohort, Bernice hadn't seemed quite so sure Wyncote would save the day, and had begged him and Rusty to release her.

Bernice had verified Bernadette's allegation that Holly had been held captive at her house. With Rusty more than willing to testify about Sash's actions, and Bernice's confession, Darius had no fear of legal repercussions from capturing the two women. But to cover all bases, he had officially placed them under citizen's arrest.

He'd called Suzette, told her what he'd done, and begged her not to have the police pick them up until he gave the okay, knowing Wyncote could free them from any jail and they'd never be found. The prosecutor had asked if he'd lost his mind, and he told her she'd just have to trust him for the time being and he'd explain everything the following day.

Darius glanced around his living room. Everyone looked exhausted yet greatly relieved with the single exception of Robyn who sat slumped in a chair, still weeping. He grinned at Rusty who—like his mom and Suzette—was imbibing alcohol instead of morning coffee. "So tell me, Wurly. Do you still want to see Day Star again?"

To his surprise his old pal nodded. "I can't explain it, Dare, but I've never felt so wonderful in my life as I did those few seconds I saw him. I'd give anything to see him again."

"Keep talking like that and you're liable to spend eternity looking at him, young man."

Rusty turned towards his mom who'd spoken. "I'm sorry, Amia. I know how offensive that must sound to you, but it's the truth."

Darius snickered. "What you saw was only an illusion manufactured by The Mede. It was his black magic rather than Lucifer's beauty that made you feel so euphoric, my friend."

"No, man, you don't understand, I really saw Day Star."

"No, Rusty. You don't believe me? Just ask Sash. Wyncote was at her house the night you dropped by unexpectedly. She told me he hid out in the bedroom just like you did that night she drugged me."

"When did she tell you that?"

"Yesterday after we brought her here."

"I didn't hear her say that."

"I know, you weren't in the room at the time."

Looking dreadfully disappointed as well as appalled, Rusty shook his head with disgust. "She must have been conferring with him about what to do with me when she left me alone in her living room that night. That explains why she took so long to make that drink."

Suzette strolled over, holding a Manhattan. "How did you put this bizarre puzzle together, Darius?"

He grinned. "Before I tell you that, I want to say thanks for humoring me and staying the night."

"Not at all . . ." she took a sip. "When Darius Darkfire tells me he believes my life might be in danger, I'm going to believe him even if I don't understand what in the hell he's talking about. Oh, and by the way, congratulations on your engagement to Holly."

She really seemed to mean it, and that made him happy for her. He winked at Holly and turned back to the prosecutor. "Thanks. Some lucky guy out there is going to bowl you over soon."

Her sexy lips curled into a big smile. "He already has. As a matter of fact I want to invite you and Holly, as well as Robert and Ricca over for dinner next weekend so you can meet him."

Smiling back he gripped her shoulders and gave them an affectionate squeeze. "Great, can't wait."

"Now then, before I have another drink for breakfast instead of orange juice, would you kindly tell me about all this weirdness you uncovered?"

Silence filled the room and everyone looked at him expectantly.

"It's very complicated so I'll have to start from the beginning . . ." he recited the legacy of the ring and how the legend had gotten twisted in a few places down through the years. Then he told her about Make Way for The Beast. Everybody else listened intently as well.

"Raul Wyncote wasn't a real man in the sense of being born, he was a physical manifestation of a demon that went by the name of Arash Arshia and called himself The Mede. He mistakenly thought that by getting the last bearer of the ring—yours truly—to put it on his finger, he'd become all powerful and rule the world as Satan's emissary. You see, unlike practically everybody else for generations back involved in the legacy, he knew the ring wasn't supposed to be given to Jesus Christ but was meant to be worn by the one who last possessed it before The Second Coming.

"A pentagram of events, if you will, had to take place before he could fully assert his power, and obtaining the ring on the night of the new moon before the final assembly was only the beginning. Four more things had to happen. The ring bearer had to be sacrificed to Day Star at the last official gathering of all the members of MWTB, and on the thirteenth new moon following, Wyncote's baby had to be slaughtered in homage to the devil, followed by the ritualistic dismemberment of the woman who bore it. Lastly, he had to be willingly given the first born of the last ring bearer that same night. The Mede would then inhabit that child's body and become the antichrist. On two occasions Sash Temple drugged me and tried to get pregnant with my sperm after I was rendered unconscious. She tried it the second time when the first rape didn't pan out. I can only hope the second attempt failed as well, but if not I'll make legal arrangements to find the baby a good home if the courts won't award me custody because if Sash isn't executed she'll hopefully be spending the rest of her life in jail, and if not she'll raise my child over my dead body."

He glanced at Robyn, still sobbing in the corner. "According to what I learned from Sash, you're carrying Raul Wyncote's child. Though I'm a staunch conservative, I believe I'd have that thing aborted, it's not human."

Robyn's bloodshot eyes flew wide. "Sash told you that?"

"Mm hmm, but I digress. Anyway, Suzette, to continue. The ring has no power per se, but it does have one peculiar ability. Excuse me a moment."

Grinning at his mother, he left the room and returned with the opaque glass case she'd put Cyrus's heirloom in when presenting it to him.

"Mother, if you please . . ." he held it out to her.

She set her drink on the bar and walked to him. "You want me to open it?"

"Mm hmm."

"Why, what good is the container? You gave the ring to that devil we all saw vanish at dawn."

He sighed. "Humor me, Mom."

Frowning, she took the case from him and opened it. A loud gasp preceded tears of joy. "Oh, Darius, you got it back! But how? I saw it on that demon's hand. How did you get it back?"

Removing the ring, he held it in the air so everyone could see. "I didn't. Remember when I said it has one peculiar ability?"

Everybody nodded.

"If anyone—or in Wyncote's case, any thing—dares to take the ring, even if the rightful owner gives it away, a curse from Cyrus himself will befall that person. At daybreak following the night of the second new moon said person obtains the ring, called by Cyrus *The Pretender*, said person will expire and the ring will return to its case of its own volition.

"The curse can't be undone. Once the ring gets on the finger of anyone other than the last ring bearer, that person can't take it off and no one else can pull it off. It stays on the illegitimate finger until that person's death fulfills the curse, then it instantly returns to its container. And the curse has another element, one that I gambled was true and not legend since it was the only hope I had of not being sacrificed to the devil. The person under the curse can't enter the residence of the ring's rightful owner uninvited, not even when said person isn't altogether human.

"You see, a prophet of God really did give this ring to Cyrus, and that prophet was aware of what would happen in the end times—that is, that a demonized man who practiced rituals every new moon would claim to be the messiah and get his hands on the gold band. He foresaw all of this happening just the way it did. That prophet told Cyrus that God wanted the king to place the curse on the ring and that's just what the old ruler did.

"Wyncote, knowing about the curse, thought he could

thwart it through Satan's power by sacrificing me as the quote-unquote pretender. God gave Holly a prophetic dream about it as a matter of fact."

Suzette shot him a puzzled squint. "I wonder why that creepy gook didn't have some of his converts break into your house and drag you away to be sacrificed."

He raised his brows in acknowledgement. "Good question, and one I can only answer with an educated guess. Bernadette Rothschild had warned me not to leave my house the day of the final assembly because it was the only place I'd be safe. I asked her why but she didn't know. She was supposed to have me take her home at five o'clock that day and she'd been instructed to jab a hypo into my arm once we got there to render me helpless so Wyncote's goons could take me to the meeting place to be crucified. At the time I thought there was a good possibility she was lying, and had forgotten about it until yesterday morning when I learned she'd been murdered. I can only assume the curse that prevented Wyncote from entering without my permission also applied to anyone associated with him.

"And there you have it. I, being the last bearer of Cyrus's ring, will now ask my dear mother to put it on my finger. Mom, will you do me the honor?"

Her dark eyes turned misty and wary. "Darius, are you sure that ring's not supposed to be given to Shiloh."

"Positive. The only reason I'm going to wear it is so I can be sure some other idiot with delusions of grandeur won't swipe it and wind up getting killed for his trouble. The Mede couldn't take it without me voluntarily placing it on his finger, but any mere human can steal it."

With a deep sigh she took the ring from him. "Shouldn't we have some sort of salutation?"

He shook his head. "I don't think so, Mom. If it troubles you that bad, I'll have Holly do it. I feel funny about putting it on myself, not that there'd be anything wrong with that."

She donned a reproving frown. "No, I'll do it—it's only fitting. By the way, I'm not going to let myself get attached to her until I'm sure she's not going to be another Robyn. That just broke my heart."

"Oh, Mom, please . . ." he turned towards Holly, sitting on the couch looking mortified, obviously hurt by his mother's declaration. He gave her a come hither motion with his right index finger. She nervously rose and came to him, whereupon he draped the same arm around her shoulders.

Before he could offer Holly some reassurance that his mom would soon grow to love her, his dad cleared his throat and said, "Too late for me, Amia, I'm already attached. You can call me Doug, Holly. Whatever Darius has told you about me, he's lying. I'm really a nice guy once you get to know me."

Holly gave him a shy, flattered smile. "Thank you, Mister Darkfire. You have no idea how much it means to me to hear you say that."

"No, no, dear—Doug, call me Doug."

Suzette walked over and hugged her. "Congratulations, that's quite a catch you've landed. My sincerest wishes that the two of you will have many, many years of happiness together."

His surprised fiancé thanked her and the embrace ended. The prosecutor then turned to him. "Darius, don't you think it's time I called the police?"

Pursing his lips, he grimly nodded.

Robyn, who'd been weepy throughout the morning, lunged forward, covering her face. Forearms atop her thighs, she began to wail, shoulders heaving from the intensity of her anguished sobs, dark tresses bouncing to the mournful rhythm. He couldn't help but compare his present feelings for the devastated brunette to the sisterly affection that had emerged when his desire for Avery had died after she'd left him for Marcus so long ago. The devil worshipper had made her bed and now she'd have to lie in it, but a part of him truly pitied her and wished she could be given a fresh start, something the heat-sinking missile Suzette would make sure never happened. She'd be lucky to wind up doing life in the state pen. The gruesome nature of Bernadette's murder guaranteed the district attorney would seek the death penalty for the three leaders of the cult along with whoever actually carried out Wyncote's command to end Bernadette's life.

Ricca and Robert showed up with several boxes of doughnuts but Darius decided he'd better have a scotch instead. Sash and Bernice had been taken to a squad car idling outside before he finished a second one, getting his secretary and colleague caught up on what they'd missed in the meantime.

"There's one more . . ." Suzette pointed at Robyn.

An officer handcuffed the beautiful woman who'd been corrupted by a lying demon from hell. A lump formed in Darius's throat. "Goodbye, Robyn."

The policeman read the devastated brunette her rights as she hysterically bawled all the way out the door.

Holly clung to him. "Thank God this is finally over."

"Such a waste," he uttered, squeezing her tight. "But you're right. It *is* over, and it's time to put it all behind us."

He turned to his mother. "Now then, Mom, I want you to understand that this is the woman I'm going to marry, and she's going to bear your grandchildren. You guys didn't meet under the most pleasant of circumstances but she's the only woman for me, and you'll soon learn that to be a natural fact.

"Holly, my mom's a great gal and I'm confident the two of you will soon become the best of friends. Dad on the other hand is a horse's ass like me." He shot his old man a wide grin.

Grinning back, his father quipped, "Like father like son."

His mom grabbed Holly's hand, pulled her forward, and embraced her. "I'm sorry if I hurt your feelings. It's just that I was devastated when Darius told me what sort of woman Robyn really was. She had me totally fooled, and I really thought she was the right one for my only son. You'll forgive me if I hold you at arm's length until I'm sure you're not going to break Darius's heart."

Holly sucked in an anxious breath. "Mrs. Darkfire, a team of plow mules couldn't drag me away from your son."

Releasing Holly, his mom took a step back. Her intimidating dark eyes sized up the woman he loved for several moments. "You really mean that don't you, dear."

"Yes . . . absolutely, resolutely, unequivocally I do. I love Darius more than my own life. I want to cook his meals, clean his house, wash and mend his clothes, listen to him bitch and moan when he's angry, cry with him when he's sad, laugh with him when he's happy, nurture him when he's sick, and bear his children. I'll take a bullet between the eyes for him if I have to, but I'm never going to leave him for as long as I live. He's my whole world."

"I see . . ." she folded her arms beneath her breasts. "How many children do you plan to have? Doug and I wanted to have twelve."

Darius groaned. "Oh, Mom, you can tell her all about that some other time. Are you going to put the ring on my finger or not?"

Ricca laughed from the bar. "Now this I have got to see."

"Me too," snickered Suzette.

His mother rolled her eyes and sighed. "Okay, Son, I will now place the ring of Cyrus on your finger. Even though it was never meant to be worn by Shiloh like I'd been taught, I thank the Lord God Almighty that Shiloh is still coming to rule this wicked world with justice, mercy, and truth."

"Hey, déjà vu all over again!" said Jock, who'd just stepped in the room with John and Eval. He could now tell the twins apart because John had shaved off his moustache. "Seems like the ceremony happened only yesterday. I see you got the ring back. So you're really gonna wear that thing huh, Homes?"

He nodded. "How'd she look?"

His homey's face dropped. "Man . . . she looked good, but so .

. . still. I just can't believe Bernadette's really been taken from us. Anyway—" Jock bowed towards his mother "—sorry to interrupt, Amia. Proceed on, girl."

The woman who'd made him memorize the legacy giggled at Jock, gave Holly a warm smile, and slid the golden band of Cyrus the Great onto the ring finger of his right hand. Rusty started clapping and soon everyone else joined in.

Totally amazed, Darius raised the adorned digit into the air for all to inspect. "Well what do you know? It's a perfect fit."

About the Author

Arley Owens, Jr. is a musician, composer, author, and rancher who resides in his native Texas with his lovely wife Cristi. He's a member of the musical group TORN PAGE.
http://www.tornpageband.com

Other books by Arley Owens, Jr.
A Tale of the Mojave
A Texas Ghost Story
I

Read Arley Owens, Jr. on your Kindle:
http://www.amazon.com/author/arleyowens

SHORTY MAE PRODUCTIONS
P.O. BOX 81102
MIDLAND, TEXAS 79708

www.ingramcontent.com/pod-product-compliance
Lightning Source LLC
Chambersburg PA
CBHW071204020726
47502CB00002B/537